DELTA GOLD

A Delta Jade Novel

Michael Cravatt

Michael Cravatt

—

ISBN: 1501080881
Cover design by CreateSpace

Printed in the United States of America

ISBN 13: 9781501080883
Library of Congress Control Number: 2014916115
CreateSpace Independent Publishing Platform
North Charleston, South Carolina

Delta Gold

A Novel from the Delta Jade Collection

Volume 2

Michael Cravatt

Other Books by Michael Cravatt

From CreateSpace
Delta Crossroads: A Novel from the Delta Jade Collection
Volume 1

To my wife whose ideas, patience, and inspiration made
The Delta Jade Collection a reality.

Delta Gold

Contents

"To many a man, and sometimes to a youth, there comes the opportunity to choose between honorable competence and tainted wealth. The young man who starts out to be poor and honorable holds in his hand one of the strongest elements of success."

—Orison Swett Marden

"It is to be regretted that the rich and powerful too often bend the acts of government to their own selfish purposes."

—Andrew Jackson, July 1832

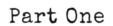

Part One

CHAPTER ONE

Aruba

1998
Hotel Riu Palace, Aruba

A week of peaceful bliss and relaxation had passed. The spectacular Caribbean sunsets had exceeded all expectations for Jade Colton and Jasen Prospero, and they both had accepted the extraordinary twists of fate that had cemented their souls and lives together intertwined through a romantic nightmare that had taken them to the very edge of death and back again. Reality had returned as they packed and prepared to return to Georgia and to dangers that neither could predict but silently feared.

They both suspected but tried to suppress thoughts that dodgy and vindictive elements of the KKK and its slippery leader Calvin Luther, nephew of the presumed dead Jake Luther, back in Greenwood, Mississippi, would probably never accept defeat by a very ordinary and unpretentious couple from Georgia. They knew that Calvin and his goons would never again be intimidated by an unassuming college professor and a director of technical operations at a telephone company.

Jasen had convinced Jade that they must go to the authorities when they returned and share their brushes with death and their secrets that had been hidden away in Jade's stuffed rooster for so many years. Narrow escapes from almost certain death had taken their toll. Jasen told Jade that he had begun to experience nightmares and bouts of depression. PTSD could happen to anybody. He told her that he battled with thoughts of seeking professional help.

The one hundred thousand dollars had dealt the couple yet another moral dilemma that must be faced. No one else knew of the money's existence except for Jade's mother Jean and her sinister nemesis from her tormented past. But Jean was dead, a victim of a mysterious car crash, and Jake Luther had presumably been vanquished to a well-deserved hell - the victim of little six year old Jade's courageous defense of her mother when attacked by the vile Jake Luther back in 1961.

But, why were they being pursued by the remnants of Jake's Klan? Not simple revenge, most certainly. It had to be because of the incriminating ledger pages that Jasen found hidden in the rooster. Not because of the money either, Jasen surmised. The money was Jake's secret, and he was dead by all accounts. The money was now Jasen and Jade's—the justly earned spoils of an undeserved war on their lives. They waffled with their decision. Tell or don't tell.

"I'm going to jump in the shower, Jade," Jasen said. "We still have three hours before we have to be at the airport. Would you mind ordering some room service while I'm cleaning up? Continental would be okay with me."

"No problem, Mr. Prospero," Jade said with her smile of witty politeness. "Hurry if you will. I still have to finish my hair and make-up."

"You don't need makeup. Natural beauty," Jasen quipped as he disrobed and turned on the refreshing, steaming water in the oversized shower.

"I wish!" she said, closing the bathroom door and walking back into the bedroom. Jade never focused on her gift of physical beauty, but it was undeniable. Her striking beauty ironically had always made her more vulnerable to any ill-intended suitor or gawker. Her radiant auburn hair, perfect figure, and unblemished skin made her a head turner. Around Jasen, she always seemed to wear a warm and infectious smile that complemented her mystical deep green eyes. Jasen always told her that her small pixie-like nose, her jade eyes, and her smile had won him over. She had told him that he was the only man who had ever liked her smile.

She phoned their breakfast order to room service and then continued packing their suitcases. Five minutes later she heard a knock at the door.

"Wow, that was fast," she said out loud to herself. She walked to the door and opened it, not feeling the need to glance through the peephole. In her subconscious mind, they had left danger far behind at Swan Lake, Mississippi.

A tall, bearded man dressed in a very bright, island-patterned shirt and white linen trousers stood in the hallway outside their door. He had an elongated bag with a strap looped over his shoulder. It resembled a large travelling bag for golf clubs. Jade was expecting room service and was momentarily confused to see an unexpected stranger in gaudy tourist garb and a golf bag instead.

"Oh, hi. May I help you?" she asked, a little nervously.

"Yes, ma'am," he responded. "I'm afraid that I locked myself out of my room. Would you be so kind as to let me use your telephone to call the front desk?"

Jade hesitated, thinking surely there must be house phones, and her nervousness and heart rate accelerated. "Well, this is really a bad time. We're getting ready to check out. Have you looked for a house phone down the hall?"

"No, sorry, I did not. My apologies for the interruption. Good day," he said as he appeared to be turning to leave. Jade smiled and started to close the door.

Suddenly, the stranger turned back toward her and forcefully stepped into the room, and Jade was propelled rapidly backward as he entered and then closed the door behind him.

"What are you doing!" she shouted. "Please get out of my room!" She heard the hair dryer roaring and echoing from the bathroom as she was about to scream for Jasen. But, in the next second the assailant had grabbed her arm, twisted it behind her back as he turned her, and pressed a strong-smelling handkerchief over her mouth. She struggled and made faint, muffled sounds for only a few seconds as the chloroform-soaked cloth quickly did its job. She fell limp and unconscious in the attacker's arms, and he gently let her body collapse to the floor.

He worked rapidly and efficiently as he unfolded the elongated bag that he had been carrying, unzipped it, and rolled Jade's flaccid body into it. Her petite and sleek frame fit snugly into the bag, which he zipped, then lifted and looped the strap back over his shoulder. The roar from the hair dryer in the bathroom had suddenly abated, and the stranger opened the door, exiting hastily into the hallway, and headed to the stairwell at the far end of the wide corridor, the large bag containing Jade in tow over his shoulder. The door to the guest room had not closed completely.

Jasen had thought he heard unfamiliar sounds or voices and had turned off the hair dryer. "Jade? Everything okay?" He heard no response. "Jade? Where are you? Everything okay?"

He stepped into the bedroom expecting to find Jade still packing or room service delivering breakfast. Instantly, he detected a strong chemical odor that permeated the room. He had smelled it before in the backseat of Calvin Luther's black sedan before he passed out and then woke up at Swan Lake—chloroform! Jade was nowhere to be seen, a folded white handkerchief lay on the floor near the door, which was ajar, and instinct told Jasen that a new nightmare was unfolding. He raced to the door in his t-shirt, trousers, and bare feet, and stepped out into the hallway just in time to see someone with a large, bulky bag with a strap hanging over his shoulder exiting into the stairwell at the far end of the hall.

He shouted at the fleeing figure. "Hey! Stop! Stop!" The stairwell door slammed closed and the man and his bag disappeared down the stairs. Jasen ran down to the end of the hall and jerked open the door that was labeled "Stairs." He frantically looked up, then down the stairs, then up again but saw or heard no one. The apparent abductor had vanished. Jade had vanished. It was déjà vu.

Jasen waffled for a few seconds between trying to follow the abductor and calling for help. What if the villain was armed? He ran back to his guest room and picked up the phone.

"Front desk? My friend has been kidnapped! Yes, kidnapped. Room number? 749. Her name is Jade Colton. My name is Jasen Prospero. Please call security immediately. I think the kidnapper has my friend in a large, duffle-like bag strapped over his shoulder. He's headed down the back stairwell, I think. Please, alert the valets and security to stop him if they see a man carrying a large bag. There's a woman in it! Please, hurry! I am on my way down to the lobby now." He dropped the receiver, grabbed his loafers, charged out of the room, and raced down the hall to the stairwell.

Jasen bolted into the lobby of the hotel, only slightly winded after running down seven flights of stairs. He surveyed the lobby for any signs of help but saw no one. Outside, under the front portico, Jasen saw two security guards dart past the entrance toward a white sedan with a raised trunk. A tall, bearded man dressed in white trousers was hoisting a large duffel-like bag into the open trunk. The bearded man turned and saw the two guards running toward him. He slammed the trunk lid closed, flung open the driver's door and slid into the seat. Just as the two security guards reached the sedan, it sped away, tires squealing and smoking, the car fishtailing briefly until the driver corrected its direction.

Jasen had closed the gap and caught up with the hotel's security guards, but they were all too late. The sedan and Jade were gone.

"He's kidnapped my friend!" Jasen shouted at the guards.

"Who? Who is he?" asked one guard.

"I have no idea. We have to do something." The security guards were huddling to discuss the situation. Jasen could not wait. He was on auto-pilot, and his mind was calculating his next move. He saw an old taxi parked nearby and ran over to it. The driver was napping, his head leaning against the window. He was startled awake when Jasen pounded on the window.

"I need you to follow that white sedan that just pulled out." Jasen was already climbing into the back seat. The driver looked a little confused and was not processing what was happening.

Jasen knew that time was critical. "For God's sake, man, get this thing started and follow that car! Now! I'll pay you well. Go!"

Pay well? The driver understood that language. He brought the old, light-green taxi to life and slammed his foot on the accelerator. The wheels screeched and burned rubber like their pursued sedan, and both he and his manic passenger began to study the road ahead for a view of the fleeing car.

They zipped past the Old Aruba Windmill and turned off of Irausquin onto L.G. Smith Boulevard, which would take them to the Queen Beatrix Airport just past downtown Oranjestad. Jasen was betting Jade's life that the kidnapper was headed to the airport for his escape. After about a mile and a half, Jasen spotted the car.

"There! There it is, just in front of that white pickup. Two cars ahead."

"Faster!" he directed the taxi driver. "Faster! You need to catch up with him."

The taxi driver was playing along but wondered what it was all about. He looked into the rearview mirror and glanced at the intensity on Jasen's face. In his broken English and Papiamento accent he asked, "You a cop? Spy? CIA? Like James Bond? Where's your gun?"

"No, no. I am not a cop or spy or anything close. I'm a teacher, a college professor. Just a simple tourist."

The driver looked again with curiosity at Jasen's face reflecting in the mirror. "No gun? What will you do, Mister Teacher, if we catch up with the car? Got a plan? I'm just a poor taxi driver. Don't want no trouble. Okay, mister? No trouble."

The traffic was thickening as they approached a busy traffic circle at the Belgie Straat intersection. The abductor was headed directly into the busiest part of L.G. Smith Boulevard. They had to get closer or lose him in the city traffic. The traffic light ahead was changing to red, but the white sedan accelerated instead of braking. The car's driver had correctly decided that he was being followed. No way was he going to stop and be overtaken. He sped forward into the traffic circle and cut off a double-decker sightseeing bus that had the right of way. The bus swerved and braked, throwing passengers flying into the aisles and somersaulting over seats. The sedan sideswiped a black BMW sedan as the abductor raced around the outer lanes of the circle and back onto Smith. He slammed the accelerator pedal to the floor as he zoomed down the busy four-lane boulevard. He weaved in and out of the slower traffic, causing a number of Aruban drivers to flash universal finger gestures back at him.

Jasen and his taxi driver had fallen behind as they were forced to slow when they entered the roundabout. They narrowly slipped by the braking tour bus and caught sight again of the fleeing sedan.

"Hurry. Don't lose him!" screamed Jasen at his driver. "Please, hurry!'

The taxi driver looked fleetingly in the rearview mirror at Jasen who was on the edge of his seat and holding tightly to the driver's headrest. "Doing my best, Mister Teacher."

They had pulled again within three car lengths of the fleeing sedan, and the taxi driver sensed danger ahead.

"If that guy does not slow down, he'll never make the turn at the Beatrix Circle. Much too tight. He is driving like crazy man."

Jasen saw the busy traffic circle dead ahead and could see the abductor still changing lanes frequently and whisking past car after car, barely missing bumpers and fenders.

As the car neared the circle, its driver had committed much too late. He had veered into the inside lane at a lethal speed. He had sped nearly out of control into a congested circle with no space between cars. Instinctively, rather than rear-ending the cars in front of him, he snapped the steering wheel violently to his right, attempting to slide to his right past the roadblock of cars. The correction was too late and too sharp. The white sedan began to tip to the right on two wheels. Within a fraction of a second, the momentum from his excessive speed and jerking of the steering wheel had flipped the bulky sedan over on its side and it continued to flip, rolling and rolling, four complete somersaults before smashing against a light post and immediately coming to a jolting stop upright on its four wheels. Miraculously it had not hit any other cars as it rolled over and over across the roundabout.

Jasen and his driver had witnessed the unfolding accident with disbelief and horror, as the taxi driver slowed and looked for a safe spot to stop off the right shoulder. As Jasen watched the sedan come to a reverberating stop, he did not want to imagine what may have happened to Jade locked away in the trunk of the crumpled and demolished sedan. Before the taxi had come to a complete stop, Jasen leaped from his back seat and stepped out of the moving car onto the pavement. His pulse raced as he vaulted ahead to the crashed sedan.

He reached the wrecked car and immediately tried to open the trunk. He rushed to the driver's side and saw the abductor slumped over the collapsed steering wheel, a large, jagged gash visible across his face. Blood was streaming down his forehead and cheeks. He reached across the stranger's body and felt for the keys in the ignition. The body blocked his view and he struggled to locate the key. Blindly, he finally felt the key ring and pulled the keys loose. He pushed the driver aside and hurried back to the rear of the sedan. There was no fire from the accident so far, but Jasen had not even thought of the possibility.

He fumbled to find the correct key to open the trunk, initially inserting the wrong one. His mind was in denial of finding an injured or even a dead Jade. The trunk popped open, and he saw the large bag, which he assumed contained Jade There was no sound or movement from the bag.

Jasen carefully pulled the bag to the center of the trunk and quickly unzipped it. There she was. Her eyes were closed and her body had assumed the fetal position. Jasen felt her neck for a pulse. She was alive. Her skin was warm, and Jasen could see no outward signs of injury. Nevertheless, he very gingerly lifted her from the bag with both of his arms under her torso and legs. He turned with her and very gently laid her on the pavement behind the car. He took off his t-shirt exposing his bare, bulked-up pecs and biceps and rolled it to make her a pillow.

By now, curious onlookers had surrounded the crash site and were hovering over Jasen and Jade. One woman spoke in English.

"Is she all right? What about the driver?"

Jasen's taxi driver had already hurried to the sedan driver's aid after Jasen had found the keys. He was walking back to the rear of the car where Jasen was checking Jade when he heard the bystander.

"The driver is dead," responded the taxi driver. "No seat belt. Probably snapped his neck. How's your friend, Mr. Teacher?"

Jasen looked up at him.

"She's alive. Unconscious but alive. I can't be sure, but I don't see any obvious injuries. Has someone called for an ambulance or paramedic?"

The taxi driver had. "I radioed dispatch and help is on the way. I think your friend is lucky to be alive, Mr. Teacher. Very lucky."

Jasen looked up at him again and then back at Jade. *If only he knew,* he thought to himself. *If only he knew.*

CHAPTER TWO

The FBI

After spending two extra days in Aruba, Jasen and Jade finally returned to Georgia. Sorting through the legal complexities of being kidnapped on a Caribbean island was almost as traumatic as the actual abduction, Jade had told Jasen. Jade had spent a day at the island's only hospital undergoing extensive testing for internal injuries and then being observed overnight. Both Jade and Jasen could only think of one word to describe the outcome—miraculous.

Except for some bruising and extensive muscle soreness, Jade had survived the catapulting car crash and was completely intact. It had been another in a seemingly endless string of nightmares that defined her recent life. She seemed to be defying all odds with her uncanny resiliency. It was almost as if something magical was protecting her, she thought. She compared herself to Steven Seagal's character Luther Storm in *Hard to Kill*. She told Jasen that she wished she had his physical prowess.

She couldn't imagine what would have happened to her if Jasen had not come into her life. In her mind, their lives had inexplicably collided—a fortuitous turn at a Georgia crossroad? Romance had blossomed spontaneously. Both had made independent choices at defining moments in their lives. Coincidence? Fate? Destiny? Dumb luck? Whatever it was, they were locked together, manipulated by an unknown force into unraveling perilous secrets, solving century-old mysteries, and surviving dangers and dilemmas. A genuine partnership had strengthened their relationship with each new twist. Their journey together was only beginning.

"Do you think that Calvin Luther sent that man to Aruba?" asked Jasen, as they drove back to Lawrenceville from the Atlanta Hartsfield airport.

"What do you think? It's a no-brainer," Jade said.

"He's supposed to be in jail, unless he made bail. But it doesn't mean he can't give orders to his henchmen. I think it's obvious that whatever the Klansmen know about us or think that they know what we know, they won't stop until they succeed. We're amateurs, Jasen. You're right. We need professional help. Our luck will run out soon if we don't get our lives under control. The only question that I have is which authority do we go to?"

"Good question," Jasen responded, as he looked away from her con-cealing his face. "And now the Aruban police are involved. Before we caught our flight, I got a call from an Aruban detective who told me that they had not yet identified your kidnapper but should know soon. He had rented a car and registered at the hotel under a fictitious name. I'm almost positive that they'll discover he's from Greenwood or that area of Mississippi. I also suspect that he was going to take you back to Greenwood somehow and squeeze you for information or even torture you, God forbid, like they did me. The detective suggested that we con-tact the FBI in Atlanta.

"Calvin and his gang are unrelenting. We obviously uncovered some very incriminating information. It can't be just the money. I keep getting this eerie feeling that your mom's boss Big Jake Luther has come back from the grave and is behind this. Someone wants you dead, Jade. I'm ready to share everything. Well, *almost* everything. We're going to the FBI tomor-row. Are you okay with that?"

"Yes. I'm okay with that. I'm tired of not knowing what or who's behind the next door or the next turn. But, I hope you're wrong about Jake. He *has* to be dead. I remember that day so clearly even though I was only six. He could *not* have survived. *No way.*"

Jade's face paled at the thought of another confrontation with Big Jake. Too many years had passed. "He *has* to be dead," she said again.

CHAPTER THREE

Resurrection

Eutaw, Alabama
1961

The gravely wounded stranger rolled slowly to his side and tried to focus his foggy vision in the dimly lit shed. His left eye was still swollen completely closed from his collision with his pursued target's car, and from his only useful eye his surroundings appeared double and blurry as he struggled to understand his circumstance. He lay in a large puddle of dark and sticky maroon-colored blood that had already attracted white flies, and with his right arm slowly he pushed his assaulted and much weakened body to a semi-sitting position. His left arm flopped at his side, and he stared at an arm that he could not feel, move, or even recognize as his own. He touched the left side of his neck and felt a gaping wound that was covered by a large, muddy clot of cold, congealed blood.

Three hours had passed since his last memory of the day's events. He tried to remember what had interrupted his well-plotted, vengeful attack on his former office assistant in the vacant alley's small storage shed. Struggling, he could not conjure any images of the one who had plunged something into his neck that suddenly exploded his world and sent him spiraling toward an eternal grave.

He correctly assessed his injury as critical and knew he needed help. With his still-working right arm, he pulled his semi-horizontal bulk across the dirty, wooden floor toward the door of the shed and managed to open it and peer outside. The alley was shaded from its bordering buildings, but he could tell that daylight was giving way to an early evening dusk. He saw no signs of activity or traffic in the street beyond.

He agonizingly army-crawled with one useable arm into the vacant alley and inched his way toward the front of the cafe that fronted the shed, now ghoulishly stained with what appeared to be more than a liter of his blood. After minutes and minutes of dragging himself down the alley, he finally reached the sidewalk that paralleled Main Street. He had not seen or heard any foot traffic or vehicles passing by.

The loss of precious blood volume was quickly sapping him of any remnants of strength, and he felt very cold, dizzy, and on the precipice of death. As he finally pulled himself onto the sidewalk, he heard the cafe door open, close, and then footsteps clomping on the wooden sidewalk, closer and closer. He could barely open his good eye as he struggled to focus.

The clomping suddenly stopped, and he heard a startled female voice say, "Oh, my God!" Then, his awareness of the last fading rays of dusk-dark light instantly changed to an inky blackness. He collapsed unconscious.

***

The beeping sounds of heart monitors and intravenous pumps needing attention were commixed with the to-and-fro, soft, whooshing blasts from life sustaining ventilators. The Intensive Care Unit at Druid City Hospital was at bed capacity with fifteen patients battling assorted maladies that required heroic and minute-to-minute care in order to buy each stricken soul a few more minutes, a few more days, or maybe a few more months of precious life. Heart failure patients, those with respiratory failure, septic patients infected with highly antibiotic-resistant bacteria, diabetics in tenuous states of ketoacidosis, major trauma victims, and renal failure patients requiring dialysis—all were dependent upon constant, superior care from their caregivers. The dedicated physicians, nurses, and assorted therapists buzzed around the unit working in a controlled orchestration performing complex procedures while conscientiously following life-sustaining checklists.

The patient in bed thirteen was connected to multiple intravenous lines, one infusing another unit of donor blood, as the ventilator clicked off and on rhythmically at a preselected rate and volume. The critical care nurse was hanging a second IV bag, readying it for the next scheduled dose of antibiotics. A young female physician walked into the glass-walled room and stood on the opposite side of the bed from the nurse.

The physician spoke first.

"So, how's our Mr. John Doe doing, Ms. Bounds? I was told that he apparently lost a lot of blood before he was found."

"Yes, doctor. That's the third unit of whole blood that we've given him plus albumin and fresh frozen plasma. I'm hanging the vancomycin now, also."

"I didn't get the full history on this guy. Fill me in on what you know." The physician had just come on duty to start her twelve-hour shift.

"Well, the history is pretty sketchy. He was apparently found crawling down an alley beside a little café south of here in Eutaw. Have you ever been to Eutaw? Not too much to do there. Anyway, the woman who found him said that he had blood all over him, and he collapsed just as she stumbled upon him. He had no ID on him, thus, the "John Doe" on his arm band and chart."

The physician had picked up the patient's medical record and was flipping through the copies of multiple registration forms, unsigned consent forms, lab and imaging reports, and emergency room notes. She finally turned to the dictated history and physical form and began reading. She then flipped forward a few pages to the operative note.

"The op note by the surgeon says he repaired a large stab wound to the left side of the neck—wow! This guy's lucky to be alive. If the carotid artery had been nicked, he wouldn't be here. It looks as if whatever he was stabbed with severed some cervical nerve roots. That explains his flaccid paralysis on the left. What's up with his right-sided weakness?"

Ms. Bounds, head ICU nurse, was well versed on her patients and responded. "After he arrived in the ER, he apparently had an occlusive stroke. Something thrombosed his left internal carotid. Poor guy's probably going to have major nervous system sequelae. He went directly to the OR before we got him. Major neck trauma, hypovolemic shock, a stroke, and no name. Just another day in ICU paradise!"

The physician shook her head and closed the chart. "I wonder who this guy tangled with in that alley. He's a pretty large man himself. Must have been a *really* big dude! Let me know if he arouses any after neurology sees him. I assume someone is trying to ID him and track down next-of-kin?"

"Yes," answered the nurse. "The ER told me that the state police were working on it. I guess for now, he's all alone in this world, barely."

***

The next day....

"Doctor Hawkins, a detective from the Alabama State Police is at the nurse's station asking to speak to the physician in charge of our John Doe in bed thirteen. Can you speak with him?" asked Nurse Bounds.

"Do I have a choice? Just give me a minute, Sandy, while I finish this progress note. Tell him I'll be there in a few."

Nurse Bounds delivered the message to the waiting detective who reacted with a little surprise that he was being put on hold. But, he quickly reminded himself, it *was* an intensive care unit. The staff had a job to do.

Carol Hawkins had already examined John Doe and headed to the nurses' station to check out what law enforcement had discovered. She found a rather tall, handsome, black-haired man in his mid-twenties standing by the desk. He was sharply dressed in a perfectly tailored navy-blue suit accented with a navy-maroon diagonal striped tie. His spit-polished black shoes reflected the overhead fluorescent lights.

"Hi, I'm Dr. Hawkins. I'm the physician treating the patient with the stab wound. How may I help you?"

He smiled politely at her and extended his right hand.

"Very nice to meet you, Dr. Hawkins. I'm Detective Marcus Bianco, Alabama State Police. I need to get a status update on your patient. I think we have located next-of-kin. We found an abandoned pick-up truck near the alley where he was apparently attacked and traced it to someone from Greenwood, Mississippi. Interestingly, we could not find his prints in the database. The registered owner of the truck seems to fit the profile of your patient.

"We located a nephew in Greenwood who confirmed that the truck belongs to his uncle. He also confirmed that no one in Greenwood has heard from his uncle in several days. I think your John Doe's real name is Jackson Luther. Not sure what he was doing over in Eutaw. Ever been there? Not really too much to do there. Anyway, bad decision, obviously, considering what happened to him. We need to give Mr. Luther's, if that's his name, nephew a report on his condition. And, I think the nephew is planning on coming over here to Tuscaloosa to positively verify that your John Doe is indeed his uncle."

"Sure, no problem, Detective Bianco," said Dr. Hawkins. *Goodness,* she thought silently. *Looks quite young to be a detective.* She couldn't help but notice his stare, as she coyly smiled and looked away from him. She glanced at the nearby smiling Ms. Bounds who was observing curiously as the two strangers struggled to hide their apparent attraction to each other. She refocused and continued.

"We can't change the name officially until next-of-kin gets here, so I'll leave him as Mr. Doe for now. As far as his condition, he is still listed as critical. He lost a lot of blood and has received multiple transfusions. He has no use of either arm—the stab in his neck damaged nerves to his left arm. He suffered a stroke upon arrival in the ER so has limited motion of his right arm. He has some right lower extremity weakness, but left leg motor function seems intact for now.

"As a result of his severe blood loss, he was in shock when he got here and has been unresponsive since. We put him on a ventilator to assist his breathing but I think he'll be weaned off later today. He's also on prophylactic antibiotics because of the stab wound. As far as other neurological deficits, it's too soon to tell. His stroke was not considered severe, however, I am not sure if it will affect his speech or not. Bottom line, he's lucky to be alive, and I have no idea if he'll be able to tell us what happened, if and when he wakes up. What else can I tell you?"

Detective Bianco had been quickly making notes of the physician's report.

"I think that's more than enough. Someone at headquarters will contact the nephew and fill him in. You may even see him before the day is over. Not sure about that. Thanks so much, Dr. Hawkins. We'll stay in touch."

He shook her hand again and noticed that she was not wearing a wedding ring. He could see that even dressed in her loose-fitting, green hospital scrubs, she was quite a looker. He smiled at her, momentarily shifting his eyes to Nurse Bounds as he turned and left through the automatic ICU glass doors.

Carol Hawkins followed the officer with a very interested gaze until he disappeared beyond the closing doors. She turned, looked down, and smiled to herself, her thoughts drifting for a fleeting moment to an imaginary, romantic rendezvous far removed from the chaos of the ICU.

Sandy was fanning her face with a note pad when Dr. Hawkins walked by.

"Wow! Too bad I'm a married woman. He looks like Mr. Wonderful!" quipped Ms. Bounds.

"Cool your jets, Sandy. He's probably married too. Back to work!" Dr. Hawkins grinned, walked away, and went back to her rounding on her fifteen very sick patients.

***

It was nearly 8:00 p.m. when the visitor walked into the glassed cubicle where John Doe rested in his state-of-the-art electronic ICU bed. The ventilator beside the head of the bed was idle, as the pulmonologist and respiratory therapists had successfully weaned him from the machine and removed his endotracheal breathing tube. He was breathing comfortably on his own but was not awake.

Monitor wiring and multiple intravenous tubes created an aura of a large, adult puppet being manipulated by a twisted collection of strings and wires. The male visitor walked over and stared at the patient's face, which was severely swollen and distorted. A large, bulky bandage covered the left side of his neck.

"How may I help you?" asked Nurse Bounds as she entered.

The stranger quickly stepped back from the bed and responded.

"Oh, yes. Hello. I came over from Mississippi to verify my uncle's identity. My name is Calvin Luther and, yes, this is definitely my Uncle Jake. He looks pretty rough. What happened to him, do you know?"

"Well, I think the doctor should give you those details. We will have to get some information from you before I can discuss his condition. Privacy, you know." Nurse Bounds was not a policy breaker or bender.

"Yes, of course. But, I can assure you that this *is* my uncle, and I'm the closest next of kin."

"Let me page Dr. Hawkins, and I'll also get the unit secretary to get some information from you. She'll be right with you." Ms. Bounds checked the IV pump and monitors briefly and then left and headed toward the nurse's station.

Calvin eased back over to his uncle's bedside and leaned down next to the unconscious patient's ear.

"Uncle Jake. It's Cal. Everything will be okay. I'm here to take care of you. Who did this to you? Do you hear me? Uncle Jake, do you hear me?"

Jake's eyelids began to twitch ever so slightly, as if he was trying to open his eyes and see his visitor. But, just as quickly the twitching stopped. Cal tried again.

"Uncle Jake. Can you hear me? It's Cal." His uncle lay motionless and did not respond.

"Don't worry," he whispered into Jake's ear. "I'll find whoever did this and make them pay. Someone will have to answer for this. Don't worry. They'll pay for this."

CHAPTER FOUR

Agent Keys

Atlanta
1998

J asen and Jade drove to Atlanta and found the regional field headquarters of the FBI. They entered the reception area after passing through metal detectors and being frisked by guards.

Jasen spoke first.

"We need to speak with an agent."

The attractive receptionist asked if they had an appointment.

"No," Jasen responded.

"What's the nature of your business?" The receptionist probed for more detail.

"We have some information about some suspected criminal activity that I think the FBI will be interested in," Jasen said, trying to not share more than necessary.

"Oh, okay. May I have your names?"

After completing the formalities, they were finally escorted to a small conference room and asked to wait until an agent could join them.

Jade and Jasen had discussed in advance how much information they would share with the FBI. For now, they had decided to keep to themselves the secret of the intruder killed by Jade in her house on Windermere Cove. Only the two of them and Willie Campbell knew about that night, and there was no evidence that it ever happened.

Whoever the man worked for could only speculate as to his fate. It was a crime of self defense covered up in a state of infidelity and shock. Best to leave well enough alone, for now. But, the attack by Jake Luther and Jade's subsequent counterattack had to be shared. Jade's mother was dead; Jade was a minor at the time. Jade was ready to confess and release her emotional burden. She would tell her story to the FBI agent in intimate and graphic detail. It would be a long, overdue catharsis for Jade.

Special Agent Elizabeth Keys was cordial and professional as she introduced herself to the strikingly handsome couple. Jade quickly observed that Agent Keys was quite attractive and wondered if Jasen was noticing, too. Elizabeth Keys was a slim, petite woman with shoulder length, wavy black hair, and Jade correctly assumed that she was probably close to her own age of forty three. She noticed that the agent was not wearing a wedding band. Her figure was well-proportioned, and Jade knew that there had to be a man in her life. She was too much of a looker to still be unattached. Jade looked at Jasen and noticed that he was not staring at the agent. She smiled to herself.

Keys listened attentively to the stories of the mysterious rooster and its revealed secrets and Jade's brushes with death. They relived the attempted theft of Willie the rooster, the discovery of the key, Jasen's abduction in Greenwood, his torture and eventual rescue, and then Jade's abduction in Aruba. They handed copies of Jake Luther's secret ledger sheets to Agent Keys who read them with keen interest, especially the Swan Lake names. She asked an assistant to run the names through their computer files and to cross reference the names with KKK activity in the Mississippi Delta area back in the 1950s and '60s.

"Are there other copies of these sheets?" asked Agent Keys.

"No," answered Jasen. "That's the only copies."

Jade did not look at him, knowing he was lying.

Jade looked at Jasen with mixed emotions as she then took an envelope out of her purse and handed it to Agent Keys. The agent opened the envelope, reached in, and pulled out the one hundred thousand dollars in cash. None of it had been spent. Jade explained how her deceased mother had apparently discovered it in the rooster and hidden it in her cuckoo clock for so many years. They did not know the owner of the money but presumed it was Jake Luther's. They wanted to do the right thing. It wasn't theirs.

Agent Keys studied their faces intensely as they narrated all of their intriguing adventures. She sensed a deep, genuine caring and connection between the two. She was impressed with their sincerity and apparent credibility. Thoughts of their procrastination in going to the authorities caused her to flirt with accusations of obstruction of justice, but she felt a connection with them and did not want to go down that road. She knew that both were still likely targets of organized criminals. Those suspects were the bad guys, not Jasen and Jade.

Their stories were enough to fill a mystery suspense novel, but something was nagging at Keys. Her investigator instinct was keen. She had not missed the eye contact and body language when they went over certain parts of their intense circumstances.

"I know this has been difficult for both of you. You've shared a lot of information, but somehow I keep getting the feeling that you're leaving something out. Are you telling me everything? Please, I need to know everything."

Jade and Jasen looked at each other then quickly back at Agent Keys. Jade spoke for them.

"Yes. We're telling you everything that we can remember. I mean, a lot has happened. I think we covered it all. Right, Jasen?"

"Yes, of course. I think so," he said as he looked at Agent Keys and nodded.

Keys stared at both of them and weighed their choreographed body language. She continued to make extensive notes. As the two-hour long meeting was ending, she told them that once the report was typed, they would have to sign it for authentication. She said that she would initiate her investigation based on their details, call the Mississippi Highway Patrol to verify the Swan Lake events, and then call them the next day.

Jade expressed her anxiety over their safety. There were likely more kidnappers or assassins out there looking for them. They had glaring targets on their backs. She wanted some type of protection. Agent Keys said that she understood but until the stories could be verified, no protective custody or security could be authorized. She gave Jade her business card and told her to call anytime day or night if something happened. She would send help immediately. Meanwhile, she told them, "Watch your backs." Jade looked at Jasen, then back at the agent and smiled but it wasn't a happy smile.

As she stood and turned to leave the conference room, Keys turned and looked at the couple now holding hands and staring at each other. "Oh, by the way. I'll catalogue the money you brought in. The law is clear: since the owner is apparently unknown and if no one legitimately claims the money within six months, it'll be yours. Just thought you'd like to know." She smiled and left the room.

They left the FBI office with mixed feelings of having immense weights lifted off their shoulders but at the same time a nervous and realistic fear. Jasen had a gun at home, and he told Jade that he would buy her one the next day. He said that he would take her to the shooting range and teach her how to use a firearm. They would be ready for their next attacker, if there was one. As they drove back to Lawrenceville, Jasen repeatedly assured Jade that together they would prevail. He reminded her of her Choctaw heritage and her unyielding strength that she had inherited from Jean and her grandfather. And they were even stronger together. Nothing could or would change that.

The skies were darkening as they took the exit off of I-85 to the Lawrenceville Highway. Jasen looked in the rearview mirror and noticed a large black sedan following close behind them and matching their speed and every lane change. He did not say anything to Jade at first but finally felt compelled.

"Jade, don't turn around but I think that black car behind us is following us. Look in your side mirror. Do you see it?"

Mouth agape, Jade glanced at Jasen then quickly turned her head and looked in the side mirror. "Yes, I see it. Looks like a single driver. I can't tell if it's a man or woman. No passengers. Does that black car remind you of anything?"

Jasen wrinkled his mouth and grimaced.

"I was hoping you wouldn't mention that. Yes, it reminds me of Calvin Luther's car, the one I was tossed into by his thugs in front of the Crystal Grill. But, Cal's supposed to be in jail. Jade, our nerves are frayed. We're just being paranoid."

"Like we don't have reason to be paranoid!" Jade said. She was correct.

"Okay, okay. You're right. I wish I had my gun right now. Let me try something. I'm going to take the next exit and see if he follows."

Jasen took the exit and watched incredulously as the black sedan followed close behind them.

"Damn it!" he blurted aloud. "He's still behind us."

Jasen reluctantly decided to continue the cat and mouse game. He pulled into the gas station at the end of the exit ramp and stopped at the first vacant pump. The black car also pulled into the station and pulled to a stop at the pumps opposite them, somewhat out of view. Jasen looked blankly at Jade, not processing what his next move would be if they were confronted by the person who was following them so closely. They could not see the driver who was blocked from their line of sight by the pumps.

Nervous, Jasen filled the gas tank. He was prepared to make a hasty exit if anyone suspicious approached him. He could not see the person in the black sedan next to them but he caught a glimpse of the driver's door opening and someone getting out. He cautiously stooped down and peered around the side of the pump to get a look at the driver. Then, in the next second, a familiar figure stood within arm's length of his face. Jasen jumped back, startled.

"Well, hello, Mr. Prospero. I didn't see you hiding behind the pump."

It was Special Agent Keys! Jasen rose from his semi-concealed position and flushed in embarrassment.

She was smiling but immediately sensed his cautious posture.

"I'm sorry. I didn't mean to startle you. Please, forgive me. I guess you're a little surprised to see me here."

Jasen agreed. "Yes. *Very* surprised. What in the world are you doing out here away from your Atlanta office? We thought we were being tailed by someone."

"You were. Me. I followed you after you left headquarters. My apologies if you were spooked. I guess you took my advice—watching your backs. I followed you because I just wanted to be sure you two made it home safely. I could get in trouble for this, but I felt lousy about not being able to approve any kind of protection for you two. I guess I felt a little guilty, too. Anyway, I'm glad you're safe and I assume almost home?"

"Yes," Jasen responded. "We live just about two miles from here. Wow! I can't believe you followed us. Above and beyond, Agent Keys. Above and beyond. Thanks. We appreciate it."

Agent Keys stepped over to their car and peered into the passenger window at Jade. She waved as Jade rolled the window down. Jade was equally surprised to see the agent and expressed her thanks for believing and caring about their safety. Jasen assured her that they were fine and didn't think they needed the escort the rest of the way home. Agent Keys assured them that she would be in contact the next day. As she headed back to her black sedan, she reminded them that they had her number.

"Call me if you need me, anytime."

***

Just as promised, Elizabeth Keys called the next morning just after ten o'clock. She had done her homework and discovered more than enough information to support the story of Jasen and Jade's wild and harrowing encounters from Mississippi to Alabama to Georgia and then to Aruba. She had corroborated the Swan Lake ordeal with the Mississippi Highway Patrol. The rookie officer Darrell Washington had arrested the Klansmen at the secret cabin and found plenty of evidence in the cabin of heinous activities that had been going on for years. The cabin had been secured as a crime scene. Cal Luther and his thugs had only spent twenty-four hours in lock-up, as an unknown source had secured each one's $250,000 dollar bail. Jade and Jasen quickly looked at each other with heightened anxiety. The Mississippi Bureau of Investigation had taken charge of the case and was gathering more evidence in anticipation of arraignments.

She told them that the Aruban Police had finally identified the man who abducted Jade from their hotel room. His name was Martin "Marty" Vosper, a registered Klansman in Mississippi. Apparently, he was known as the "Bone Stealer" due to his skills at kidnapping and other more gruesome talents. "The data sheets stated that he'd done two stints for kidnapping and assault at Parchman Farm, the Mississippi State big house, not that far from the city of Greenwood. Regardless, the next step is to see who in Mississippi he worked for. No one has come forward and requested his remains. The FBI here will take over further investigation of the late Mr. Vosper."

Jade was anxious and more than curious about Big Jake Luther. "Did you uncover any records of what happened to Jake Luther in Eutaw back in 1961? Is there

any evidence of a connection between Vosper and Jake Luther? I mean, we know Cal Luther is his nephew. But, is Cal the ring leader? Or is Jake alive? I have to know."

"I understand your concern, Jade," Agent Keys said, trying to sound sympathetic but not really able to fully appreciate the toll from Jade's recurring nightmares over the past thirty-five years. "I have some agents from the MBI in Jackson working on the Jake Luther piece of this. They will be pumping Cal Luther for more information, but I'm told that the Klan over there has some big shot lawyers. So far, Cal is not singing. From what I've learned, there is no obvious indication that his uncle is still alive. I am trying to pull some old files from 1961. Apparently, the Alabama State Police investigated a John Doe incident in Eutaw around the time of the attack on your mother. I've asked for the details, so I'll let you know."

Jade was unable to relax after Agent Keys's call, but she and Jasen were more than satisfied with the obvious thoroughness of her investigation. They had to return to their jobs in a few days. Both had taken vacation days when they headed over to Greenwood, but now they had to meld back into reality. Jade felt secure when she was around Jasen but knew she had to resume her life. She would have to go back to New York and work out a notice before returning to her home on Windermere Cove. She knew she could get her old job back at the telephone company. She hoped that Cal Luther and his gang, now freed, were in enough trouble without risking more attacks on her or Jasen. Hope was all she had for now.

CHAPTER FIVE

Private Eye

The flight back to New York was a mixed bag of rattled nerves and cautious relief for Jade. She felt safer in New York with her friend Beth Pendergass, but at the same time she knew that if her pursuers could track her to Aruba, they had the means to find her anywhere. Every stranger that looked at her might be her next assailant. Her paranoia was consuming her, a tiny nibble at a time. She was a prisoner to her imagination and fears. Remember your strength, she reminded herself. Strong women scare weak men. You are strong. You tame lions.

Surely, Cal Luther was running out of henchmen to do his filthy deeds, she thought. The money and copies of the secret KKK ledgers were now in the hands of the FBI. Jasen had secured copies, and he alone knew where they were. The rooster's secrets had been revealed. If Jade was still a target of the Klan, it was for revenge alone. She now had nothing that belonged to her mother's old nemesis Big Jake. But, he didn't know that. He was dead, wasn't he? Cal and his gang had to know that the MBI had evidence of their nefarious activities, past and present. Surely, she reasoned, the worst was behind her and Jasen.

Jasen had returned to his teaching at the University of Georgia and had listed his house on Windermere Cove by a local realtor. He and Jade had decided to live together in her house next door for the time being. Marriage had not even been discussed. Surviving would-be assassins, torture, and kidnappers had overwhelmed them over the past two weeks.

"No big deal," she laughed to herself. "Happens to everybody, right?" She tried to lighten her anxiety. There was plenty of time to talk about their relationship. First things first. Stay alive for now.

Jade and Beth caught up on the unbelievable events that had shrouded Jade's life. Beth commented that things like this only happen in movies or books, not to real people. She admired Jade's fortitude and resiliency but did not envy her spine-tingling brushes with death. They talked a lot about Jasen and his fortuitous entry into her life so full of highs and lows, challenging ordeals and miraculous victories. It was easy for Beth to see why Jade loved him. They both agreed that finding a full-packaged man with Hollywood looks, a kind heart, intelligence, and courage was a rare find. Physically, Jasen was quite a looker from most females' perspectives. His dedication to weight lifting accounted for his muscular arms and calves. His well-defined bone structure and broad shoulders complemented his sculptured arms which could easily be seen through his shirt. His trunk was slender for a somewhat tall man at six feet two inches, and he carried himself well. He always seemed to sport an elegant and slightly tanned face shaped by a chiseled jaw. His dark brown, barely combed hair was eye-catching with its few lighter-colored highlights in the front. Jade often mentioned Jasen's generous full head of soft hair and how it seemed to attract mesmerized stares from admiring women. She had told Beth that it was really his amazing smile that seemed to underscore his gentle features and project a warm and caring inner soul.

"Girlfriend," said Beth, "You have to hold on to that man. He's a keeper, an endangered species. I can't wait to meet him."

***

Jasen called the next day.

"Jade, I have some updates from Agent Keys and some intriguing information from that old guy in French Camp who helped us with the carriage. What do you want first, the bad news or the good news?"

Jade's heart skipped a beat as she wasn't prepared for more bad news. "I don't like the sound of that. Okay, go ahead. Bad news first."

Jasen continued.

"Agent Keys found some very interesting files courtesy of the Alabama State Police. It's about Jake Luther back in 1961. She said that they investigated an attack on a John Doe who was found bleeding and near death beside a diner in Eutaw, Alabama. Sound familiar?"

Jade's hands began to tremble as she waited for the rest.

"This doesn't sound too good so far. What else?"

"Well, he was taken to Druid City Hospital in Tuscaloosa and spent several weeks there in intensive care. They finally identified him. It was Jake."

Jade gripped the phone tightly and sat down as Jasen confirmed that her worst nightmare had come full circle.

"The investigation into what happened to him hit a dead end, no pun intended, as there were no apparent witnesses to the attack, which you already knew, of course, and Jake was unable to provide any information. Obviously, only you and your mom knew the truth. Seems he suffered some type of stroke after arriving at the hospital and was unable to speak. Get this—a nephew by the name of Calvin Luther came over from Greenwood and positively identified him as the one and only Jake Luther."

"Don't keep me guessing, Jasen," Jade pressed. "Did he survive or not?"

"That's the bad and good news, sort of. He spent a month at the hospital, slowly recovering but not regaining speech. He had a lot of residual effects from his stroke. He was discharged to a rehabilitative hospital in Jackson, Mississippi, where he spent six weeks in treatment. After he was discharged, he fell off the grid. I mean, he just flat out disappeared. Gone, vanished, without a trace. The Alabama State Police wanted to get more information from him if possible so they could close the investigation, but they also lost track of him. He just didn't exist anymore after that. The files Agent Keys looked at were in cold case storage."

"So, that's it? He survived, went through rehab, and then just disappeared, vanished? That's crazy. Why would he disappear? Is he still out there or not? Is he dead or not?" Jade asked incredulously in frustration and disbelief.

Jasen had more.

"I don't think it's necessarily a closed case. There was a young detective involved in the initial investigation of Jake's attack—a Marcus Bianco. He apparently took a very personal interest in solving the Eutaw incident, for some reason. He was the investigator of record who followed up on Jake. Curiously, Agent Keys told me that Mr. Bianco is now a private investigator in Jackson, Mississippi."

Jade was becoming impatient.

"Jasen, sweetie, you're losing me. What does a private detective have to do with us?"

"I know you well, Jade. You won't be able to sleep until you know what happened to Big Jake. I suggest that we contact Mr. Bianco and see if he can help. I think hiring a private investigator might be a good idea at this point. He'll be interested I know, because he closed the file on Jake as a cold case. He'll want final closure, too. Plus, when we fill in the thirty-five year gap, he'll be more than interested!"

Jade felt more uneasy than ever.

"I think you're right. I need to know the truth. And we both need to know who's really behind all of this. Are you going to contact the detective?"

"Yes," Jasen responded. "I'll let you know what he says."

"Jasen, you mentioned the retired history teacher from French Camp. What does he want with us? I hope he doesn't want you to give up those beautiful pearls. Does he want both of us?"

"Not you. He wants me. Seems he found another strange message among those memoirs that Chief Leflore hid under the carriage seat. He thinks I'm some kind of secret cipher expert. Whatever. I told him I'd come take a look at what he found. And one more interesting bit of information—the old gentleman—his name is Phineus Blount—told me that someone vandalized the carriage house last week. He said that various items were taken, including some inventory papers from a file drawer. The memoirs from the carriage seat were among the stolen files, but fortunately they were only copies. Mr. Blount has an extra copy, and he sent the originals down to Jackson at the Capitol Museum. Just another piece of intrigue and mystery or totally unrelated—who knows? Leflore's secrets may be attracting someone else's interest. Anyway, I'm game at helping Mr. Blount. Who knows? Maybe we'll be famous one day! Ha, ha."

"Jasen," Jade said seriously. "I think our safety is more important than deciphering secret messages, at least for now. Can you hold off until we don't have to look over our shoulders anymore? Please, hire that detective and see where that leads. There is plenty of time to rewrite the history books in Mississippi. Okay?"

Jasen conceded. "You're right. I'll see if Mr. Bianco is available. I'll talk to you after I track him down. I love you, Jade."

***

A tall, middle-aged man with black hair highlighted by grayish sideburns entered the domed-ceiling atrium of the Liberal Arts Building on the campus of the University of Georgia in Athens and walked over to the receptionist's desk.

The attractive student volunteer looked up at the stranger as he approached. She was drawn to his distinguished-looking black hair and his dark brown eyes that she silently graded as sexy. He was old enough to be her father, she thought, but he reminded her of a movie star, a very handsome one.

"May I help you?" she asked with a warm smile.

"Why, yes, miss. I'm looking for Professor Prospero. We spoke on the phone and he should be expecting me."

"Your name?" asked the young lady who stared into his eyes.

"It's Marcus Bianco," he responded, handing her his business card.

She studied the card and then looked up at the strikingly attractive visitor. Raising her eyebrows and smiling, she pointed to a bench across the atrium.

"Please, have a seat over there on the bench and I'll see if he is available. I think he just finished his last class." She lifted the phone and dialed an extension.

"Professor? Hi, this is Jennie at the front desk. There's a Mr. Bianco here to see you. His card says that he's a private investigator. Are you expecting him?" She paused, listening, then said, "Yes sir, I'll tell him you're on your way. Thanks."

She called out across the atrium. "Mr. Bianco. He'll be right with you." Bianco smiled, nodded, and then looked at his watch.

Jasen came down the wide hallway toward the atrium in less than five minutes. He walked over to his visitor and extended his hand.

"Mr. Bianco? I'm Jasen Prospero. Thanks so much for coming over from Jackson."

"Marcus Bianco. Pleasure to meet you, professor." The handshake was firm but brief.

"Please, no formalities," Jasen said. "Call me Jasen and I'll call you Marcus if that's okay with you."

"Fine by me. Jasen it is."

"Great. Please, let's go to my office and I'll continue where I left off from the phone conversation."

He turned and led Bianco back down the hallway toward the faculty offices.

As they walked, Jasen provided small talk. I hope your flight was uneventful. Any problems?"

"No. Everything was perfect. Thanks."

They walked into Jasen's small office, and Jasen asked Bianco to have a seat in the guest chair in front of his unassuming small desk.

"Marcus, I really appreciate your willingness to help me and Jade. She's still in New York winding down her job there. She's relocating back to Lawrenceville with me."

"I understand. Refresh my memory, Jasen. You and Jade are not married, correct?"

"That's right. We're significant others, I suppose you could say. We haven't discussed marriage yet. I'm recently divorced. Jade's been single for quite a few years. We were neighbors and that's how we met. I realize that I went over everything pretty fast on the phone, so I'll go through this again, if you prefer."

"Sure, I think you should. It sounds like you two were somehow meant to hook up, maybe. Truth is, I don't believe in coincidence, especially when it comes to love and romance. Everything happens for a reason.

"It can't be just an accident that mysteries 130 years old were solved after you two met. Sounds a little far-fetched to me. But, it's quite an interesting tale that you shared. The entire story is quite unusual. Before we revisit your Choctaw Indian intrigue, can you fill me in on Jade's encounter with Mr. Luther?"

"Okay. I understand that you were the detective that investigated Jake Luther's attack way back in 1961 in Eutaw. I told you on the phone about Jade. She was only six years old when all of that happened. You had no way of knowing the true story at the time in your investigation. Jake Luther was the aggressor. He was interrupted in the act of raping Jade's mother, Jean, when Jade stabbed him in the neck. Jade saved her mother that day.

"Luther was a very vile, evil, and disgusting man. He had repeatedly sexually assaulted and continually harassed Jean when she worked for him in Greenwood, Mississippi. So no matter what you might have imagined back in '61 about his injuries, it's probably a shame that he didn't die from his wounds. All these years, Jade has assumed that he indeed was dead. It was a shock for her to learn that he survived, but at the same time, she lived the past thirty-five years thinking she was a killer. Her past has haunted her. Nevertheless, she is unbelievably strong and psychologically intact, I think, considering all the tragedies life has dealt her.

"Jade and I obviously stumbled into criminal activities in which Jake Luther and his nephew Calvin have been involved, up to their eyeballs, I think. The person that you investigated back in 1961 was no saint. He tortured and murdered innocent people. The nagging questions that we need help with are these—is Jake Luther still alive? If so, is he behind the attacks on us? If not, who is and why? Why did Jake fall off the grid back in 1961? Is there more to this than a stolen rooster and dirty money?

"We need your help, Marcus. We can't keep looking over our shoulders wondering what's coming next or who our enemy is. Sooner or later our luck is going to change. Please, can you help us?"

Bianco had listened both intently and with admirable curiosity.

"I've wondered all of these years about Jake Luther. I followed the case closely hoping that in time he would be able to regain his speech or somehow be able to reveal what happened back in that alley in Eutaw. Obviously, from your accounting, even if he could talk, he would lie.

"I must confess to you, Jasen. I really never thought he was an innocent victim. His nephew Calvin was suspicious from my first encounter with him. I am not totally surprised to learn that they were active in KKK she-nanigans. My gut tells me that someone is trying to prevent you two from learning some very deep and dark secrets about something or somebody, probably somebody that was or is a public figure and very powerful. I think you and Jade have been caught up in a web of crime that will shake some real big coconuts out of those Greenwood, Mississippi trees, so to speak. This will likely be a pretty dangerous gig if I accept it, you understand?"

"Of course," Jasen agreed. "I understand. Will you help us? Please."

The detective leaned back in the chair and touched his index finger to his lips. He stared deeply into Jasen's eyes and dropped his hand to his side. He stood up and reached across the desk, extending his arm and hand.

Jasen rose and gripped the detective's hand firmly. He held his breath, anticipating the answer.

"Professor. You've hired yourself an investigator. It's time I made a visit to Greenwood."

They smiled at each other as they shook hands.

CHAPTER SIX

Where's Big Jake?

Greenwood, Mississippi

The summer weather in north-central Mississippi was uncomfortably hot and humid as Marcus Bianco drove down Main Street in Greenwood toward Cotton Row. His first task was to see if Bigelow's Cotton Exchange was still operating. He knew that Jake Luther had managed the exchange back in the sixties, and he had rehearsed in his head his concocted story of why he was looking for Luther.

In his thirty years as a private investigator, his first rule of thumb was always foremost in his mind: *share minimally and trust no one.* It had served him well.

He was pleasantly surprised to see the Bigelow sign on the corner building as he turned onto Cotton Row along Howard Street. He parked in the first empty space he came to two buildings down the block. As he walked back toward the exchange, he passed three men who were smoking and apparently surveying activity along Cotton Row. They were dressed in faded blue jeans, plaid long-sleeve shirts, sun-faded baseball caps, and dirty cowboy boots. Hired goons came immediately to Bianco's mind. In his custom-tailored wool suit and highly polished wing tips, he contrasted noticeably with the rough-looking men whose penetrating stares followed him until he entered Bigelow's.

"Hello," he said to the young woman seated behind the only desk in the small reception area that also contained two armless wooden chairs. A sign on her desk read "June Rivers."

She looked up at him and smiled. "May I help you?"

"Why, yes ma'am, uh, Ms. Rivers, you can. My name is Kelly, Michael Kelly. I represent Cotton States Mutual Insurance Company. I'm a benefits adjustor." He handed her a business card that looked quite authentic, thanks to his secretary Angie back in Jackson.

"I'm looking for someone, a Jackson Mason Luther, to be specific. He was named as a beneficiary by one of our life insurance policy holders who, sadly, passed. I was told that Mr. Luther works here, or at least, he used to work here. Could you possibly help me locate him?"

The receptionist looked down at the business card then back at him and was quick to respond.

"I'm sorry, Mr. Kelly. I think he *did* work here years ago but I have no idea of his whereabouts now. I never knew him."

Bianco stared into her eyes and noticed her pupils suddenly constrict. She was lying.

"My father is the manager here. He might be able to help you. Can I get him for you?"

He hesitated but felt confident he could keep up his pretense.

"That would be great. Thanks."

"Please," said the receptionist, "Have a seat while I go fetch him for you." She disappeared through a closed door behind her desk and returned less than a minute later.

"He'll be right with you, Mr. Kelly."

Bianco nodded and smiled at the quite attractive receptionist. "Thanks."

Two minutes later a late-fortyish man barged out of the door behind the young lady and headed straight for Bianco. He extended his hand as Marcus stood up.

"Mr. Kelly, is it? Hi, I'm John Rivers. I see that you've met my daughter here," he said. "What can I do for you?"

"Well, like I told Ms. Rivers, I'm trying to locate a Jackson "Jake" Luther. He's the named beneficiary of a deceased policy holder for my insurance company, Cotton States Mutual. All I know is that he once listed this exchange as his business address, but that was quite a few years ago. Any idea where he might be now? He's due a settlement."

The manager was studying Bianco's sophisticated facade and looked again at the business card that his daughter had given him.

"Who may I ask was your policy holder?" asked Rivers.

Bianco responded cautiously, "I'm sorry but I'm not allowed to share that with you unless you're next-of-kin. Are you related?"

"No, no. I knew of Jake but he's apparently been gone from Greenwood for a long time. I'm not really sure what happened to him. I was still in high school, if I recall, when he worked here at Bigelow's. The only story I ever heard was that he got sick and he just up and disappeared. Strange. There have been two other managers here before I stepped in ten years ago. I can give you their names. Maybe they could help. I'm sorry but that's all I know."

Bianco's thirty-plus years of detective experience told him that the answers were likely prefabricated denials from both father and daughter, but it told him that he was getting closer to the truth. Just how far locals would go in protecting the facts about Jake Luther gnawed at Bianco's suspicious detective side. The plot was thickening, he told himself. He had to tread lightly and stay alert. He hoped that his cover was working, but doubt was creeping in.

"Well, yes. If you can give me those names, I'll be on my way."

Rivers leaned over June's desk and secured a pen and a writing pad. He jotted down the names and handed the note to Bianco.

"Here you go, Mr. Kelly. The first name is Harlow Bartram. I am sure that you can find him in the Commander's Club. It's in the alley just behind Cotton Row. It's a private club but just tell the security man at the front that I sent you. He'll let you in. The second name is Calvin Luther. He's the nephew of Jake, but I think he's been working out of state for a while. Haven't seen him in months."

Bianco felt his heart skip a beat. He met Calvin back in 1961 when Jake was in the hospital recovering from the Eutaw attack. Rivers had no way of knowing that Bianco knew a lot more about Calvin Luther *aka* Calvin Caliban than he could possibly guess. He wondered silently where Calvin might be hiding out since Jasen's and Jade's encounter at Swan Lake and then being bailed out of jail. Rivers was cleverly acting ignorant about Jake's diabolical nephew.

Bianco was convinced that John and June Rivers were being intentionally evasive about Jake, and he was eager to poke down the next rabbit hole.

"Okay. Thanks so much for your help. I'll keep looking. Wouldn't want Mr. Luther's benefits to go to waste. I appreciate your assistance."

Bianco smiled politely at June and shook John's hand.

He headed out the front door and turned to look back over his shoulder. June was lifting the telephone receiver and dialing. He decided to walk the short distance to the Commander's Club, which was just behind Bigelow's. He glanced to his left down the sidewalk and saw the three shifty-looking locals staring again at him. As he rounded the corner of the building, he noticed that they were walking in his direction.

The Commander's Club was identifiable only by a small sign above a solid white door. The building had no windows and was sandwiched between two warehouse structures. Bianco tapped on the door below the warning: "Private. No Trespassers."

A giant man opened the door and nodded for Bianco to come in. He was an expected visitor, no doubt, courtesy of June's phone call. Bianco stepped inside and suddenly was aware of the security man frisking him from behind.

"Hey! Watch it. I'm not packing. I work for an insurance company."

Bianco lied and was hoping that the goon would miss his small pistol stuffed inside his right sock. The frisking ceased.

The detective then walked into a dimly lit room filled with empty tables and chairs. A long bar with a backdrop of an equally long mirror hugged the left side of the room. The room suggested to Bianco a redneck version of a French *boite*. He turned to look back at the silent bouncer who pointed toward a door in the rear of the large room. The brawny man then walked past Bianco and led him to the door marked "Private." He knocked once, opened the door, and motioned for Bianco to go in. He closed the door behind Bianco and faded back into the shadows of the gloomy outer room.

"Please, come in. Mr. Kelly…is that right?"

He was greeted by a goateed, portly man who was smoking a stogie with an overpowering bouquet of cheap tobacco. He was seated at a desk across the room that appeared to be a private office. Bianco was somewhat amused that the very Southern club owner preferred such inexpensive smokes over classier Cuban cigars. The peculiar man appeared to have stepped right out of a William Faulkner novel, and except for the cheap stogie, was the quintessence of an ego-studded, Southern aristocrat in his white linen suit and Kentucky black bow tie. Obviously, Bianco surmised, this was Harlow Bartram.

"Yes, that's correct. Mike Kelly. I'm with Cotton States Mutual Insurance Company, but I presume you already know that, uh, Mr. Bartram?"

"Yes, I see that you understand how things work in small towns. We're a 'close' sort, if you get my drift. Please, Mr. Kelly, have a seat and tell me what I can do for you." He pointed to the chair in front of his oversized oak desk that displayed assorted piles of sloppily arranged papers, a clear-glass ashtray, and a small highball glass partially filled with whiskey, Bianco guessed.

"I assume you know why I'm here. You knew Jake Luther. I need to find him or his next of kin. He was a named beneficiary of a deceased life insurance policy holder. Do you know where I can find him? Or if he is still alive? No one seems to know." Bianco studied the poker face of the rotundish man who puffed away on his smelly cigar.

"Yes, you're correct, Mr. Kelly. I did know Jake Luther. He was quite well known around here. Not really sure what finally became of him after he had some kind of unfortunate stroke or something like that. I took over as manager at Bigelow's after he left. Did right well, as you can see. Took over this club several years ago. Life is good here in Greenwood. Yes sir, quite good.

"I think you know about Jake's nephew managing the exchange for a while, too. Calvin never talked about his uncle after that stroke. I used to see Calvin in here a lot but haven't even seen him in months.

"I wish I could help you, Mr. Kelly. My advice is that you track down Calvin. He should be able to tell you about his uncle. That's about all I know. Is there anything else I can help you with? (pause) You know, you just don't look like the insurance-man type to me. But, I suppose you can't always judge a book by its cover, right?"

Bianco knew that his pretense was wearing thin. Time to exit stage rear, he thought to himself.

"Okay. I'll take your advice, Mr. Bartram. I appreciate your time. Sorry to have inconvenienced you." He stood and headed to the door.

Bartram had also stood and fleetingly took notice of Bianco's hiked right trouser leg that revealed the bulge in his sock of his partially concealed pearl-handled pistol. Bianco felt the hiked fabric and gently shook the leg, hoping that his weapon had not been seen.

When Bianco opened the door, the tall greeter was standing there waiting. Bartram made a gesture to the bouncer that Bianco could not see. The giant man nodded slightly and closed his boss's door. He escorted Bianco through the dining area and to the front door. Bianco was beginning to feel relieved that his façade had not been cracked. But, he was feeling empty, having learned nothing other than Greenwood was full of suspicious characters that were protecting secrets for unknown reasons. His interest in solving the Jake Luther mystery had only grown keener. He needed to find someone in Greenwood who he could trust.

The greeter opened the front door and waited for Bianco to exit. Similar to Bartram, he made a hand sign that Bianco could not see and slammed the door, almost propelling the detective out into the alley.

Suddenly, there they were. The three rough-looking creeps who had stared holes through him on Howard Street stood in front of him in a semicircle. As they closed the distance, Bianco saw no avenue for escape. He had a sinking feeling that he had worn out his Greenwood welcome.

The huskiest thug in the middle took the lead.

"You ask too many questions, Mr. Kelly, or whoever you are. You need to get the hell out of Greenwood *now* and don't look back."

Bianco did not see this encounter ending peacefully.

"Hey, fellas. I'm just an insurance guy doing his job. Is there a problem?"

"Just what part of 'get out of town' do you not understand, mister?" said the beefy man.

Bianco at age fifty-nine was not as agile and quick as he once was or wished he could be, and he knew three against one would likely get nasty for him. He smiled and began to walk around the men. The one on his left grabbed his arm and propelled him toward the other two. Bianco thought briefly about reaching down for his concealed pistol but did not want to give up his cover or trigger a shoot out. He staggered into the grasp of the spokesman for the group and without warning received a sledgehammer fist directly into his mid gut. The blow caused him to double forward and gasp for his next breath. He fell to his knees and fought away the urge to vomit.

One of the other assailants put his mud-covered boot against Bianco's shoulder and shoved him to the ground. The other two began to kick and punch him repeatedly from both sides. The pointed toes of their boots smashed into ribs, bones, and muscles, sending searing jolts of pain in all directions. He was tempted to fight back but decided to curl his wounded body and protect his head and internal organs. The leader approached him, cocked his leg and released a final jarring and rib-cracking kick into his side.

"I'll say it just one more time, mister. Get the hell out of town, *now!* Next time I assure you we won't be so gentle."

The three men peered down at him then turned and walked down the alley in the opposite direction of Howard Street.

Bianco's assaulted and pain-riddled body was curled in the fetal position anticipating the next blow. When he heard fading footsteps, he rolled to his side and looked down the alley. The attackers had disappeared, and he struggled to sit up. He had been pummeled by fists and cowboy boots and was certain that the last kick had broken ribs.

He stood slowly, held his side, and regained his bearings. He looked around and saw no one else in the alley. His head-to-toe pain was intense and throbbed with each step and breath as he cautiously headed back to his car parked around on Cotton Row. He thought to himself about his conversation with Jasen. His prediction had been right. It *was* turning into a dangerous gig.

He might have to adjust his fee, he chuckled to himself, making his side hurt even more.

As he wiped blood from his lip, he knew he was onto something. A lot of people were protecting the truth about Jake Luther. He needed a friend in Greenwood. He doubted that it would be local law enforcement. It was time to regroup.

CHAPTER SEVEN

Jade

New York City

J ade had given notice to her supervisor and was preparing to move back to Lawrenceville. She felt safer in New York with her friend Beth and was more relaxed by the day as she had not sensed that she was being followed or stalked. If Cal Luther and associates were still after her, they had apparently not traced her to New York. The nagging fear of a new attack resurfaced as she thought about her return to Georgia. Calvin knew where she lived. Would someone be waiting on her when she returned? The thought haunted her. What about their request to the FBI? Would the agency provide some type of protection for her and Jasen? He had told her that Agent Keys had still not authorized security. He cautioned her to not get her hopes up either.

Jade said her goodbyes to Beth and headed to LaGuardia for her flight to Atlanta. Jasen had called before she left with the good news about Private Investigator Bianco agreeing to help close the loop on Jake Luther. She knew that they had to eliminate the head man that had orchestrated and targeted her and Jasen. Neither of them felt confident that Calvin was the top boss. If it was Jake, their hired detective must find him somehow. Bianco had told Jasen of his plans to go to Greenwood, but Jasen had not received any status update in several days.

***

Airport check-in and weaving through the long security lines were uneventful, but Jade could not shake her paranoia. Every man she glanced at seemed to stare intensely at her. Were they just being lecherous, oversexed men? Was one of them following her? She couldn't resist constantly looking over her shoulder. She even played cat and mouse games by ducking in and out of newsstands and small retail stores just to see who might follow her. No one took the bait. She began to feel like she was overreacting, but her near-death experience in the trunk of that somersaulting, crashing car in Aruba was reason enough, she thought.

As time to board her flight approached, Jade decided to make one last restroom stop. She stood and walked toward the ladies' room, making note of a tall man in a suit who had also stood and began following just behind her. She quickened her pace and turned her head to look back just as she entered the restroom. The stranger was only ten steps behind her and still headed in her direction.

She ducked into the restroom feeling comfortable that he would surely not follow her into the ladies' room. A quick inspection of the restroom told her that no one else was there except a woman who was washing her hands and just leaving. She chose the middle stall, sat down, and listened anxiously for footsteps or sounds of anyone entering. She hurriedly relieved herself and stood to leave.

Just as she started to exit the stall, she heard someone enter the restroom. The clomping sounds on the tiled floor suggested heavy shoes or boots, and the pace was slow and deliberate. Jade's hand froze on the handle of the stall door, and she had not yet unlocked the door latch. The footsteps came closer to the row of stalls, seeming to stop briefly in front of each one. Then whoever it was stopped directly in front of her stall and stood silently. She could see black shoes that appeared to be a man's.

She slowly backed away from the door, her heart racing and her mind struggling to calculate her next action. She held her breath. Then, the door began to shake and rattle loudly as someone had grasped the outer handle and jiggled the door.

She hesitated but decided to respond.

"Excuse me," she said, voice quivering. "This stall is occupied."

The shaking stopped but no one spoke. She held her breath again. Seconds passed. She backed farther into the stall and pushed her back against the wall. Suddenly the stall door began to shake again, this time so violently that Jade feared the door would be forced open or off its hinges. The door shook and shook as more seconds passed. She was paralyzed with fear and could not find her voice. Then, the shaking stopped for a second time.

The clomping of footsteps resumed and faded slowly into the distance as the unknown person seemed to be exiting the restroom. Jade finally took a deep breath but had not moved from her frozen stance. She listened carefully but could not hear anything. No breathing. No conversation. No footsteps. Nothing. Her flight was probably boarding. She had to get back to her gate. She needed to reach down deep for strength and courage.

She cautiously unlatched the stall door and very slowly opened it. She quickly surveyed the restroom but saw no one. She thought it strange that the restroom had not been full of other female travelers.

She walked briskly out of the restroom and nearly tripped over a yellow sign that said "Closed. Out of Order." It had not been there when she entered earlier. She hurried into the wide corridor of the terminal gate area. She looked in all directions but saw no one focused on her. At her gate area, passengers were boarding. She scanned the area for the tall man in the suit but did not see him. Maybe he had already boarded. But, she had no idea of who had tried to enter her stall in the restroom. It may not have been him. She never saw a face. Her palpitating, racing heart was still pounding against her sternum and her hands were trembling noticeably.

She got in line and boarded her plane. As she placed her carry-on into the overhead bin and settled into her window seat, she tried to view the passengers without looking too obvious. No one seemed to be looking her way. She did not spot the man in the suit. She took a deep breath and settled back in her seat for the two-hour flight.

***

Jade was beginning to feel safer and less paranoid as she headed to the baggage claim area at Atlanta-Hartsfield. Jasen would be waiting on her there. Her protector. She hoped for good news about FBI security. The restroom mystery had shaken her more than she cared to admit to herself. As she took the down escalator to baggage claim, she turned and looked back up. She froze again.

There he was. The man in the suit from LaGuardia five persons back! She quickly looked away as her heart sped up. Her impulse was to run down the escalator, but it was packed with other arriving passengers heading down to retrieve baggage. The escalator speed seemed to be in slow motion as she anticipated getting off and locating Jasen. *Move, escalator, move!* She silently admonished the moving steps.

As she got to the baggage claim level, she briefly looked back up at the suited stranger, who was staring directly at her. She stepped off the escalator and headed briskly in the direction of the baggage carousel. Then she saw him—Jasen! She ran the last few feet and almost leaped at him. He embraced her tightly.

"Hey, hey! What's the running all about? Did you miss me that much?" asked Jasen.

They kissed softly. She smiled and said, "If you only knew."

"You looked like you were running *from* something instead of *to* something, or am I imaging things?" he asked.

"Very savvy, professor. I think I'm being followed." She turned and looked for the stranger in the suit. He wasn't there. Jade was operating on a full adrenalin rush.

"I had the most chilling experience back at the LaGuardia Airport. I thought this guy in a suit was following me. I went into the ladies' room and then someone tried to break into my stall. It was nerve wracking to say the least. Then, I thought he followed me down the escalator just now. But I don't see him. God, I'm a nervous noodle!"

Jasen was trying to soak it all in. "Calm down, calm down, my love. You're going too fast. What guy? Who? Where? What are you talking about? Let's get your luggage and then you can start all over. You're safe. I'm here. Calm down. And I have some good news for a change. I'll tell you on the way to the car. Come on. Show me which suitcase is yours."

***

As they headed to the parking deck, he looked at her and smiled. "Well, it's sort of good news, anyway. Agent Keys called and has agreed to provide partial protection for us, at least temporarily, until the Jake/Calvin connection is sorted out by Bianco."

"*Partial* protection?" Jade responded. "What the hell does that mean? Either they protect us or they don't."

Jasen had anticipated her reaction. "It means we aren't important enough for a twenty-four-seven babysitter, but the FBI will keep a man outside our house when we are there, *if* we request it. They won't follow us everywhere we go, again only if we request it in advance. I mean, I can understand. We are not on the protected witness list, at least not yet, hopefully never."

Jade listened with an unsettled sense of satisfaction. "I guess it's a start." She thought about her interesting trip back home from New York. "Jasen, did you tell Agent Keys that I was in New York and would be travelling back home today?"

"Of course I did, why?"

"Just wondering," Jade said.

Jade held tightly to Jasen's hand all the way to his car in the parking deck. She could not stop the urge to constantly scan their surroundings as they walked. In her mind, she was being stalked.

As Jade settled into the front passenger seat, Jasen opened the trunk to store her luggage. He was suddenly aware of someone behind him. He slammed the trunk lid and cautiously turned to look. There stood a tall man in a suit. Jasen did not have a chance to react before the stranger spoke.

"Oh, I'm sorry. I didn't mean to sneak up on you. Are you Jasen Prospero?"

Jasen did not recognize the stranger, and his mind was racing with thoughts of another assault or worse.

"Good God, man. Who the hell are you? Yes, I'm Jasen Prospero. What do you want?" Jasen was prepared to defend himself and Jade if necessary.

"Relax, Mr. Prospero. Please. My name is Carlos Hermes, Agent Hermes. I'm with the FBI." He quickly flashed a FBI identification. "Agent Keys assigned me to provide security for you and Ms. Colton, your passenger there, I presume," pointing to Jade.

Jasen was still in high caution mode and was hoping that the man was who he said he was. He decided to trust the man.

"Yes, that's Jade Colton." Jade was staring with her mouth agape as she tried to assimilate what was going on behind the car.

"Why didn't Agent Keys notify us that she was assigning you to us?" Jasen asked.

The agent responded, "I'm not sure that she hasn't tried. Anyway, I picked up the detail in New York at LaGuardia and have been watching Ms. Colton's back since then. So far so good."

Jasen was a little incredulous. "Why didn't you introduce yourself to her? She was convinced you were a stalker. I think you scared the bajeemies out of her."

"Sorry, Mr. Prospero. I didn't mean to scare her." He grinned wirily.

Jasen pressed for answers. "Did you follow her into the ladies room, by chance?"

"No, of course not. Why would I do that? Why do you ask?"

"Well, she said someone gave her quite a start by trying to break into her stall in the restroom. If that wasn't you, then who was it?"

"Interesting," mumbled the agent. "Well, now you guys are safe. I came over to ask if you wanted me to follow you home. If so, I'll just follow behind you until you get back to Lawrenceville."

Jasen turned and looked at Jade who was still trying to decide what was happening behind the car.

"It won't hurt. Sure, why not. Thanks, Agent Hermes. Please tell Agent Keys that we appreciate the concern." He got in the driver's seat and filled Jade in on her mystery man in the suit. She listened and began to feel a little more at ease. She looked again at the FBI agent who was walking away and wondered who she could trust and what other surprises might lay ahead.

They headed out of the airport exit and onto the interstate. Jasen looked in his rearview mirror and noticed a black sedan following close behind them. Hopefully, it was Agent Hermes.

Jade sat close to Jasen, holding onto his arm.

"Jasen, what about Bianco? What's he up to and why haven't you heard back from him?"

"Good question," responded Jasen. "I think he was headed to Greenwood but not sure what day. If he's been there, he hasn't called to update me. I think I'll give him a call as soon as we get home and get you unpacked. We have a lot to do, my dear. You know, I really hope Bianco doesn't need us to come to Greenwood, and we still need to get back to that little retired history teacher in French Camp. Solving riddles intrigues me, you know. I'm extremely curious to see what he's found and also to learn more about the break in."

Jade rolled her eyes and then peered over at Jasen. "I'll say it again, Mr. Full-of-Adventure. Our safety is first. Fun can wait." Sometimes the boy in him overshadowed the man, she thought to herself.

He chuckled at her intensity. "You're so right, as usual, Ms. Corona Extra. I just keep thinking that your distant relative, Chief Leflore, might have left me more than a pouch of pearls for my redeeming him. Just a hunch, that's all I'm saying. Let's do *this*, though. If we need to join Bianco over in Greenwood, let's make a quick stop at French Camp and take a look at the other message that Leflore left behind. Okay? It's on the way."

Jade looked at him and shook her head slightly. She laughed softly and said, "I love you, professor." She kissed him on the cheek, and then sat back, pushing her head against the headrest and reflecting on her far-from-ordinary life.

CHAPTER EIGHT

When You Need a Friend

Marcus Bianco needed time to rethink his strategy to learn about the mysterious disappearance of Jake Luther. Someone was going to a lot of trouble to prevent him from learning too much. And he wondered why the MBI had not been able to locate Jake. It was beginning to smell like more than just a simple cover-up of the evil dealings of one old, disabled, missing Klansman. Bianco sensed that he was probably dodging land mines and wading into a swamp filled with vicious, vindictive alligators. There were apparently some Delta secrets that neither he nor the pursued couple, Jade and Jasen, had even imagined. He needed to find an ally, someone in Greenwood that he could trust. He needed a friend.

"Jasen?" said Bianco. He had pulled into the Greyhound station parking lot and stopped to use his mobile phone.

"This is Marcus Bianco."

"Everything okay, Marcus?" asked Jasen. "Where are you? I was just about to call you."

"Yes, I'm okay but things sort of got off to an interesting start here in Greenwood. Some not-so-friendly local yokels let me know that I'm not welcome here, asking too many questions. I think I may have touched a nerve or two asking about the elusive Mr. Luther."

"Are you okay? Did they do anything to you?"

"Hey, I'm a tough old bird. Took a few punches and several cowboy boot kicks in my ribs, but I'll live to fight another day. Not to worry."

"Damn it, Marcus! This may be even more dangerous than we suspected. Did you go to the local police? What's your next move?"

Bianco responded, "I don't think we can trust the police from what you told me before. I need to find someone that I can trust. You mentioned an old timer, a black café owner that helped you out of that Swan Lake jam. Can you give me his name and where I might find him?"

"I thought we talked about him, Marcus. Hmmm, maybe not. Anyway, his name is Willie Campbell. He's the proprietor of the Crystal Grill over on Carrollton Street. He and his sons saved my lucky ass that night at Swan Lake. I would have had a bullet in my head if not for them. If there's anyone you can trust over there, it's Willie Campbell. He's been in Greenwood most of his life, so I suspect he knows who's who and what the scuttlebutt on the streets is these days. But, I suggest that you ask to meet him somewhere out of the public eye—too many snoops and unknowns hiding in the shadows around that county, if you know what I mean."

"Yes," agreed Marcus. "I echo that. So, I'm heading over to find Mr. Campbell. I'll let you know what he says. And, Jasen, watch your back, okay?"

"You sound like Agent Keys. We're doing our best."

Bianco remembered that he had forgotten to ask about how things were going in Georgia. "Oh, Jasen, did Jade return from New York?"

"We're together right now. I picked her up at the airport and we just got home. Interesting development—Jade thought she was being stalked at

LaGuardia and at the Atlanta airport. Turned out to be a FBI agent that was assigned by Agent Keys to provide security—at least he said he was with the FBI. He followed us home, I think."

Bianco was more than curious. "That's strange. I spoke to Agent Keys yesterday. She didn't mention anything about assigning a security detail. Are you sure everything is okay?"

"Sure," responded Jasen. "He seemed legit. I haven't noticed him outside so I assume he's left for the evening. Relax, Marcus. We're fine. I need to help Jade unpack. Call me tomorrow. Okay?"

"Okay, Jasen. Good night. Be safe." Bianco stared at his phone with an uneasy feeling before ending the call.

Jasen walked into the bedroom where Jade was unpacking.

"Okay, what did Bianco find out?" asked Jade, hoping for some better news. "Any trace of Big Jake?"

"Bianco apparently stepped on a swarming yellow jacket nest. He got roughed up by a 'welcoming committee' of locals for asking too many questions, but he's okay. This entire investigation gets muddier and more dangerous by the minute. He's headed over to talk to Willie at the Grill. I'm beginning to feel a little guilty about dragging Marcus into our mess. I think there is someone behind this who will go to any length to prevent us or Marcus from uncovering the truth, whatever the truth is. "Oh, Marcus also said that he spoke with agent Keys yesterday and she didn't mention anything about providing protection for us. Odd. I would have thought she would have told him. Jade, where is her business card? I'm going to call her and verify this agent Hermes."

Jade froze for a second and looked up at Jasen. "Surely he is who he said. Here we go again, being paranoid!" She looked on the nightstand and found the agent's card. "Here you go. Please, call her so we can sleep soundly."

Jasen took the card and headed to the kitchen phone to call.

***

"Hello? This is Jasen Prospero. I'm trying to reach Agent Keys. Is she available? Sure, I'll hold."

The front doorbell suddenly chimed and broke the edgy silence of the early evening.

Jasen called out to Jade. "Jade! Can you come and get the door? I'm holding for Agent Keys. And check to see if it's someone you know before you open the door."

"Okay, I'm coming," she responded from the bedroom.

She walked into the hallway, glanced at Jasen, and then peered through the door's peephole. It was Hermes. She hesitated, looked back toward Jasen in the kitchen, and then cautiously opened the door and greeted the visitor.

Agent Keys had picked up the line and listened to Jasen's query. As she responded, Jasen felt a sudden wave of nausea and a sinking feeling in his abdomen, and he paled in disbelief.

"I see," he said. "So, you're telling me that you have not yet assigned a security detail? Then exactly who is this guy who says he is Carlos Hermes? He had a FBI ID." He listened and couldn't believe his ears. "Hermes is *what?* You're sure?"

Jasen suddenly realized that Jade had responded to the door chime and had opened the front door.

"This is *not* good news, Agent Keys. Can you hold on just a second?" He put the phone down on the countertop and stepped into the hallway.

Jade was facing Jasen and standing near the front door, which had now been pushed closed. Behind her was the tall, suited man who had claimed to be Agent Hermes.

"What's going on?" asked Jasen with only a hint of panic in his voice.

Jade was calm but was wide-eyed and frowning.

"Jade, step over here," directed Jasen. She did not move.

"Jasen, he's got a gun crammed into my back." She was sorting through her options and forced herself to keep control and hide any fear.

The impersonator looked at Jasen and jabbed the barrel of the gun more firmly against Jade's ribs.

"I suggest you hold it right there, Mr. Prospero," ordered the stranger. "Don't do anything you'll regret because my trigger finger might overreact."

"Obviously, you're not Carlos Hermes." Jasen spoke loudly as he turned slightly back in the direction of the phone receiver lying on the kitchen counter. He hoped Keys could hear. "Who are you and what do you want?" he fired back at the man.

"Who I am is not important. What I want is what you and Ms. Colton have refused to hand over to my associates. Do you think you two have nine lives? Luck runs out sooner or later. My mission is simple. Give me that damn rooster and anything that you two may have found inside it. Hand it over and I'm out of here. It's that simple."

Jasen had few chips to play. "Look, mister whoever-you-are. Jade and I have nothing to hide. You can have the rooster. I don't know what you're talking about if you think we found something inside him. He's just a mounted trophy, nothing more. Please, take him." Jasen turned to step back into the kitchen and retrieve the colorful bird off the kitchen table.

"Hold it, Mr. Prospero. Walk this way. Ms. Colton can get the rooster while I keep this loaded gun in her back." He pushed Jade forward and into the kitchen. Jasen stood near the door opening and observed, knowing that any aggressive move by him could jeopardize Jade's life.

The intruder ordered Jade to pick up the rooster. Keeping a cautious eye on Jasen, he reached for the phone on the counter and slammed it back onto its cradle. Shuffling along in short steps, he maneuvered Jade back toward the front door. With the gun still digging sharply into Jade's back, he demanded that Jasen open the front door. Jasen complied and slowly opened the door. Both he and Jade simultaneously let out a loud, long audible gasp. Their recurring nightmare screeched at them. On the front porch stood Calvin Luther!

***

Even though Jasen had suggested that he meet with Willie out of the public eye, Marcus Bianco strolled into the Crystal Grill amid the rush of diners just sitting down for their early evening meal of the tasty Southern comfort food for which the café was famous. He looked distinctly out of place in his business suit that was ruffled and dusty from his attack in the alley in front of the Commander's Club. He approached the hostess podium and looked at the young, attractive black woman who was checking her table chart.

"Yes, how many in your party?" she asked as she looked up at the tall, handsome detective.

He leaned toward her and whispered, "Oh, I'm not here for dinner. I'm looking for your owner, Mr. Campbell. I'm a friend of a friend and have some very important business to discuss with him."

"Oh, I see," she said staring into his dark brown eyes as if she wanted to see more than he was telling. "Your name?"

"Marcus Bianco. Just tell Mr. Campbell that I represent Jasen Prospero and Jade Colton. I think he'll understand."

"Yes, sir. Excuse me and I'll see if he's available." She turned and headed down the middle hallway to the back of the restaurant and disappeared into an office. She returned in less than a minute. "He'll be right with you."

Bianco stepped away from the podium and said, "Thanks."

Willie came ambling down the hallway toward the front of his popular grill, now filled with patrons ordering their favorite dishes. He approached Bianco, stopped, and said very quietly, "Please, wait one minute. Come down the hallway and don't look around. My office is the last door on the right." He turned and walked away. Bianco did not speak to him and did as he was instructed. He looked at his watch and after a minute he headed toward the hallway that also led to restrooms. He did not look around at diners and tried to appear casual as he passed the restrooms and knocked softly on Willie's office door. The door opened immediately and he quickly entered, closing the door behind himself.

"Please, have a seat, Mr. Bianco," said Willie. "Sorry for the cloak and dagger stuff. Too many folks around here who don't know how to mind their own business." Willie sat down at his desk as Marcus settled into the wooden guest chair. "So, I assume you've been hired by my Georgia friends, Jasen and Jade, correct?"

"Yes, that's right, Mr. Campbell…"

"Just Willie, please."

"Oh, okay…Willie, yes…I run a private investigation firm down in Jackson…Bianco and Associates. I've been doing detective work now for over thirty years since I left the Alabama State Police. Jasen and Jade have engaged my services to help track down the source of repeated threats on their lives. I think you were intimately involved in one of those attacks over here in Greenwood."

"Yes indeed. Close call for Mr. Prospero. Me and my sons took care of some renegade remnants of the local KKK in Leflore County that seemed to think Jasen knows more about them than I think he does. At least, I think we took care of them. They got bailed out of jail, and I doubt the judiciary process here will move very fast to prosecute them. Too many good ole boys in high places here that are easily persuaded by one thing—money. The KKK has some pretty slick lawyers, too, so I kind of doubt that we'll see much justice done for a while. What exactly are Jade and Jasen asking you to do for them, Mr. Bianco?"

"Call me Marcus, please. Well, they think that you might be able to help with solving the mysterious disappearance of Jake Luther. You're familiar with him, I assume?"

"What an understatement, Marcus! I worked for that monster years ago, the same time that Jade's mother Jean worked for him. He was a big shot Klansman around the Delta area and probably one of the most dangerous men you've ever met. You name a crime and he's committed it. Hard-core criminal, mean to the bone and deeper.

"Folklore around the Delta has it that the Luthers here in Greenwood may be remotely related to an early-nineteenth-century road bandit named Samuel Mason. His full name was Samuel Luther Mason. His mother, the story goes, was a Luther from Kentucky. Some local history buffs say that Samuel Mason was probably one of the nastiest, most dangerous criminals that ever haunted Mississippi territory highways. From my personal encounters with Jake, I would tend to believe there's definitely a relation. Anyway, true or not, the Luthers have quite a nasty reputation in the Mississippi Delta.

"Jade's mother Jean was a friend of mine. From what she shared with me, she lived many a nightmare at the hands of that beast—Big Jake Luther. My friendship with Jean nearly cost me my life, too. That gang of Klansmen took me, like they had many other blacks, to their hideout at Swan Lake. Torture is too kind of a word for what happened there. Jake could have killed me right there if he had wanted to. To this day I don't know why he spared me. Thank God that he did.

"Miss Jade and her friend Jasen might have been history if I hadn't been around for them. Strange how everything came full circle after all those years. Not to mention the mystery of the Malmaison rooster and how Jasen solved that riddle and the one over in French Camp. Why or how Jake Luther got attached to that rooster in the first place is even more of a mystery. Worst thing that could have happened was Ms. Jean stealing that bird away from Jake."

Marcus now knew he was in a safe harbor. "Willie, I told Jasen that I needed to find someone over here in Greenwood that I can trust. I think I've found him."

Willie looked intently at the detective. "Marcus, you can bet your last penny that I'd do anything for Miss Jade. *Anything.* She's like a long lost granddaughter to me…well, different skin color, but you understand." He grinned but then felt a pang of sadness as he thought of his deceased friend Jean.

Marcus could sense the strength and integrity of Willie Campbell and was impressed with his endurance through obviously very turbulent trials in his life. "Let's get back to Mr. Luther. Do you know what happened to him, Willie?"

"Talk about mysteries! That is one question that no one has ever answered around here—what happened to Big Jake Luther? Biggest problem is that anyone who has asked in the past has either regretted it or in a few cases has disappeared too."

Marcus was incredulous. "What! Disappeared? I can personally attest to the regretting it part, but just asking about Luther can make one disappear? Who *was* that guy? I mean, who is protecting him or hiding the truth about him? This is crazy. He must have been associated with someone or something with enormous power or influence. Interesting! I *am* intrigued."

Willie continued. "Way back in '61, talk on the street was that he had had a terrible accident and stroke while out of town. Then there were stories about him being in a Jackson rehab facility or something like that. Finally, folks just quit talking about him. His only living kin was his nephew Calvin. Locals learned real quick not to ask Calvin about his uncle. Those that got to nosey, well, like I said, they regretted it. Jake was my boss right before he disappeared, but colored folks around here knew better than to poke in white men's business. You just learned to leave well enough alone. So, after all these years, I have absolutely no idea what happened to him or if he's still alive. He'd be in his seventies by now."

"Quite a story, Willie," Marcus concluded. "You do understand, though, why Jade sent me here, don't you? She needs some closure, and she and Jasen need to be able to go on with their lives. I mean, they may be in constant danger until I solve this puzzle. Someone out there thinks that Jade and Jasen are sitting on some very incriminating information. They aren't safe until this mystery is unraveled. And time may be running out for them."

"I hope you're wrong about that, Marcus. I certainly don't like to think about that possibility."

Willie glanced toward his office door as he heard a very soft "Knock, knock."

"Excuse me, Marcus," he said as he rose from his chair and shuffled over to the door and opened it.

It was Meisha, his granddaughter.

"Gramps. There's a phone call for you from a FBI agent in Atlanta by the name of Elizabeth Keys. What should I tell her?"

Willie looked a little confused and turned to look back at the detective.

Marcus had stood up and anxiously responded, "She's the one helping Jade and Jasen. She's probably looking for me. I think you had better talk to her."

"Thanks, dear. I'll pick up. The line that's flashing?"

"Yes, sir," said Meisha.

He picked up the receiver. "Hello, this is Willie Campbell." He listened and then responded. "Yes. Mr. Bianco is with me. What can we do for you?" He listened intently and slowly looked up at Marcus whose face was drawn and painted with anticipation.

"Oh, I see." He listened as Agent Keys went on. "Yes, ma'am. I understand. I'll tell Mr. Bianco. Thank you."

He replaced the receiver and sat down firmly in his old chair, leaning back and looking up at Bianco whose overly curious face was asking "what happened?"

"It's Jade and Jasen. They're missing."

"Damn!" said Bianco as he pounded his fist on Willie's desk.

"Agent Keys isn't sure but someone impersonating another FBI agent may have taken them. Keys has issued an APB for them but there are no good leads to go on. She has a hunch that they may be headed to this area. Anyway, she's coming over immediately and has Atlanta agents trying to sort out what happened over there. One minute she was on the phone with Jasen, then he put the phone down, and the next minute the phone went dead. She thought she may have overheard an abduction in process.

"Mr. Bianco, you've got some investigating to do, and fast. My friends are missing. I hope we're not too late this time."

CHAPTER NINE
Bianco and Associates

Marcus Bianco had quickly discovered that tracing the whereabouts of Jake Luther was far more of a challenge than he had ever imagined. He needed reinforcements and backup. He could not protect, and now rescue, his two clients while simultaneously digging deeper into the secret lives of evasive Delta criminals. The FBI agents were good allies to have and were finally accepting the obvious dangers that had entrapped Jade and Jasen. But, he was feeling a little like Willie Campbell—too little, too late.

He called his office in Jackson.

"Angie, Marcus here. Look. I'm swimming around in a Delta swamp full of real nasty animals that don't take prisoners. I need some backup."

"Swimming in a swamp? What are you doing in a swamp, Mr. Bianco? Angie asked naively.

Marcus knew better than to tease Angie, but it entertained him to hear her reaction.

"Angie, I'm *not* swimming in a swamp. It's a metaphor."

"A meta-what? What's a metaphor?" Angie was an adequate secretary but did not always appreciate or understand her boss's levity.

"Angie. Listen. I'm sort of in over my head here. I want you to track down Danny. He needs to get to Greenwood as soon as he can. Tell him to meet me at the Crystal Grill on Carrollton Street and to bring extra artillery. Got that, Angie?"

"Yes, boss. Danny, more artillery, Greenwood, Crystal Grill, ASAP. Got it. Anything else?"

"Yes, one more thing. Get in touch with my wife. I need some updated information on the rehab facility there in Jackson where a patient by the name of Jake Luther was treated. Tell her to see if she can find out exactly where he was discharged to back in 1961. She'll know what I'm talking about. I don't think I pursued it back in '61 when I was investigating him."

"1961? That's before I was born." Angie responded. "You're sure she'll know?"

"Angie, please, just do it. He was a patient of hers. She'll know. I'll call back tomorrow. Gotta go, Angie. Thanks, and chop, chop."

She looked at the phone as the line went silent. "Chop, chop?? Wonder what he wants me to chop?"

***

James Daniel (Danny) Malone had worked for Marcus Bianco and Associates for ten years, and Marcus trusted him like a son. He had urged Danny to join his investigative firm after encountering him while the rookie cop was working with the Jackson Police Department as a street patrolman. Marcus was not fooled by Danny's tough-guy persona and quickly sensed an underpinning of decency, persistence, and honest ambition. He had needed a second investigator to assist him with more cases than he alone could do justice. Danny was the perfect solution, and they had bonded together into a well-oiled detective tandem. Danny seemed to have developed a sixth sense when it came to reading the lies in clients' eyes. He needed Danny to come help him sniff out the rotten secrets that were protecting Jake Luther.

Angie was efficient, as always, locating Danny easily, and relaying Bianco's instructions. She told Danny to tell Bianco that his wife was unable to get details about Jake Luther's disposition back in 1961. She said that Marcus would know what she meant.

Danny arrived at the Grill about ten that night. Bianco had enjoyed a tasty dinner courtesy of Willie's cook, but his mind had been on Jade and Jasen. There had been no update from the FBI back in Atlanta, and he knew Agent Keys would not be arriving in Greenwood until late the next day. If Jade and Jasen had been abducted by Luther and his thugs, he agreed with Agent Keys that they would probably head back to Leflore County. That was assuming his clients were still alive. He confidently felt that they wouldn't be killed unless the crooks got what they wanted from them. He knew that they would continue to play dumb or stall as long as possible. At least, he hoped so.

Bianco, Danny, and Willie spent the next several hours rehashing the facts and assumptions about Jake and Calvin Luther. Danny suggested a different approach to discovering the fate or whereabouts of Jake. Obviously, someone or some group had gone to extreme lengths to cover up Jake's disappearance. Relying on his past experience as a savvy police-man, Danny had decided to visit the local hospital and see if he might find an ally that could point their investigation in the right direction.

His assumption was that not everyone in Greenwood was on the KKK's or another disreputable organization's payroll, even though the contrary seemed more accurate to Marcus. Danny decided that he would test his "charm" the next day at the Greenwood Hospital. Danny's wavy blond hair, gorgeous blue eyes, beach body good looks, and infectious smile would hopefully work to his advantage. Around Jackson, Danny Malone was considered a real lady killer and the hottest eligible bachelor in the investigative business. Marcus frequently tried to be matchmaker, but matrimony was not in Danny's vocabulary.

Both Marcus and Willie agreed that looking for possible healthcare workers that may have provided care, or may be currently providing care, for a mysterious, elderly stroke victim was a long shot but might be less risky. Danny said that his story would be "what if I needed home nursing care for my stroke victim grandfather." In a small community, there would probably be very limited resources for a private duty nurse or therapist experienced in stroke rehab. Marcus thought it was a brilliant idea. Danny's ingenuity constantly impressed him. Of course, he told Danny, testing the theory might depend upon Jake still being alive.

***

Danny spent the next morning at Greenwood Hospital Outpatient Services being punted from one department to another. His persistence paid off when he finally met a friendly and quite attractive nurse in the Neurology Clinic. He turned on the Malone charm, as idle chitchat accentuated with warm smiles and undressing eyes broke the ice. He learned that she was not married, and he sensed that his baby blue eyes were meeting her approval. He finally got to his intended task.

When he asked the young nurse about the availability of experienced healthcare workers for a homebound stroke victim, he hit pay dirt! She told him that Leflore County had very few private duty registered nurses; in fact, she was familiar with only two that provided home care full-time. One, she told him, was experienced in stroke rehabilitation. Danny had difficulty in hiding his reaction.

He had told her that he was looking for help for his elderly homebound grandfather who was recovering from a severe stroke. He got the private duty nurse's name and address and even managed to get the young nurse's phone number, just in case, he told her, that something else came up. He left the clinic, skipping and humming through the waiting area.

His only concern now, if he located the other nurse, was whether she would read through his fabricated facade and share information about a private patient.

Danny was beginning to feel like a charmed (in addition to being charming, he bragged silently to himself!) private detective. The experienced rehab nurse, June Svenson, answered when he called the number that his young acquaintance had provided. She understood his concern and explained her availability, her fees, and a little information about her background. She told him where her office was if he wanted more information. It was only two blocks from the hospital, so he charged out of the clinic and headed confidently to pursue his theory. When he arrived, she greeted him and offered a chair near her desk. Danny kept up his charade, telling her that she sounded like she was exactly what his grandfather needed. Then he began to probe.

"Ms. Svenson, I checked with the Baptist Spine and Brain Injury Rehabilitation facility down in Jackson about resources here in Leflore County for stroke victims. They referred me to the local Neurology Clinic here; that's where I got your name. Interestingly, the referral coordinator mentioned an unusual stroke patient that they treated years ago. She said that someone here accepted the transfer but she couldn't remember the name. It couldn't have been you; I mean, it was thirty years ago, I think. You look so young." His Malone charm continued.

Ms. Svenson smiled and flushed a little red. "Why, thank you, Mr. Malone. You're so right. But, if it was thirty years ago, it had to have been my mother. She was the only nurse around here in the sixties that knew anything about stroke rehabilitation. Do you know the name of the patient they mentioned?"

"No, no. I was just curious. I mean, if I knew who it was, I guess I could get a recommendation or something. But, I'm sure that you are more than qualified. The clinic strongly endorsed you."

"Well, I don't know if it's the same patient, but my mother provided care for years to a home-bound patient referred from the Baptist facility in Jackson; he was recovering from a severe injury and a stroke. I know because she handed his care off to me. I don't think she knew him even though he was from this county. He's over in Itta Bena living in a house on Lakeside Lane down on Roebuck Lake. Actually, it's the very last house on the street. It's less than ten miles from here, and I check on him once a month now at his son's request. He still has major neurologic deficits but is doing well for a guy in his seventies. He gets around in a wheelchair. Mother told me that he regained speech ten years after his stroke, very unusual. She thought it was kind of miraculous. He's a little difficult to understand, but at least he can communicate now."

"Well, Ms. Svenson, to be frank, it might help my family's decision if I get a reference. Would you mind telling me his name or where I might contact him or a relative?" Danny was really out on the tip of the limb now.

"I don't know, Mr. Malone." She knew she was sharing more than she should. "As I said, he lives over in Itta Bena, but he is an extremely private sort. I've told you more than I should have. Honestly, he and his son are quite eccentric. I mean, they have always paid for his care in cash, never checks or asking me to file insurance claims. Paid my mother cash, too. But, who's to argue with cold cash! Hey, I just do my nursing thing and don't ask questions."

Danny wasn't backing off. "You said he has a son? You're sure?"

"Yes, at least he says he's the son. He makes all of the healthcare decisions for sure. And he pays me."

"Well, I know it's a little irregular, Ms. Svenson, but I know my family. They want to be sure that grandfather will be in good hands. I'll tell them that the Baptist facility gave me their number so I could get a reference. The son will never know that you and I met. If you have a number that

I can call, that will be fine. Okay? I'd really appreciate it. Please. I'd be so thankful." He flashed his blue eyes at her and smiled sheepishly.

June Svenson fell for the brilliant acting, accepting the apparent sincerity in his voice. She hesitated but finally agreed.

"Mr. Malone. I certainly want your family to trust me. Okay. Here's the phone number that I have for the son. His name is Calvin. Calvin Morris." She read him the number and he jotted it down on the back of his business card.

"Calvin Morris, is that right?"

"Yes, that's correct," she responded.

Danny knew he might have hit the mother lode. Calvin—it couldn't be a coincidence, even if the last name was a lie. He knew that Jake Luther and his nephew would have used false names to enable Jake to fall off the grid so many years ago. He had to get back to the Grill and share his news with Marcus. One step closer to the truth. But, he knew it was also one step further into an unchartered field of land mines.

CHAPTER TEN

Bad News Good News

When Danny bounded into the Crystal Grill with his good news, Meisha greeted him and informed him that her grandfather and his boss had reassembled at Willie's home over on East Claiborne Street. She told him that she had also directed Agent Keys there. She gave him the address and a large piece of lemon icebox pie to go. He turned to leave but stopped, turned back and embraced her with a gentle hug. She was a little startled at the young detective's reaction but smiled with satisfaction as Danny hurried out the door to share his discovery with Marcus and company.

Willie met him at the front door and escorted him to the den in the back of the modest but well-kept house. He entered the room and saw doom and gloom looks painted on everyone's face.

Danny was on a roll and not prepared for any bad news.

"Hey, why the glum mugs? Did somebody die?" He immediately realized he had said the wrong thing.

Marcus looked up at his energetic, excited assistant.

"It's Jade and Jasen. No one has been able to locate them or trace them, Danny. Oh, I'm sorry. Danny, this is Agent Elizabeth Keys from the Atlanta FBI."

Danny walked toward her and extended his hand.

"Please, don't get up. I'm Danny Malone. Pleasure to meet you, Agent Keys."

Bianco went on to update Danny.

"When the FBI got to Ms. Colton's house over in Lawrenceville, they found her house had been ransacked. That crazy stuffed rooster that started this entire misadventure was smashed and torn apart feather-by-feather. Obviously, the thugs were hell bent on finding something and were more than a little pissed off. But, it gets worse. They found blood in the entry hall. No sign of Jasen or Ms. Colton. Both cars still in the driveway. Gone. Without a trace."

"Well, that's *not* good news," quipped Danny. "I was hoping this little committee meeting of Bianco and Associates was going to be a tad more upbeat. Okay, then. What's next?"

Agent Keys spoke up. "Mr. Malone. I have all of my available agents looking for your clients. We have a good lead, but so far no luck. A neighbor across the street saw a white van speeding away from Ms. Colton's house last night, and he said a black sedan was following close behind. The neighbor, a Mr. Chambers I think, was unable to get a tag number but he said he was pretty sure it was a Mississippi plate. Just a white van, late model. Not a lot to go on. How about you, Mr. Malone? Any luck tracking Jake Luther?"

"Interestingly, I think I may know exactly where the phantom Mr. Luther is living."

"He's alive!?" exclaimed Marcus.

"According to my source and if my assumptions are correct, he's alive and well, sort of, in Itta Bena, west of here. The home health nurse that checks on him monthly doesn't have a clue as to his real identity. But, I'm 99 percent sure it's the one and only Jake Luther. If it's him and he's the ring leader, then I think we may know exactly where to find our missing couple or at least who's abducted them."

Suddenly there was a spark of optimism in the room. Willie stood and walked toward Danny and patted him on his back.

"Young man, I certainly hope you're right. Who would have thought— that scoundrel living all these years within spitting distance of his den of hatemongers and hooligans. Actually, Mr. Malone, I would rather he not be alive. One of the most sadistic, vile, racist men in the Delta. I was hoping for Ms. Jade's sake that she had doomed him to his grave years ago. But, if he's alive and behind all of the abductions, stalkings, and who knows what else, then we need to head over to Itta Bena *now* and end this nightmare for those two fine people, Jasen and Ms. Jade."

"Hold on, hold on, Mr. Campbell," interjected Agent Keys. "I share your desire to end their nightmares, but we have to do this in a legal and organized way. We can't just blast our way into a house that we think is hiding Mr. Luther and be judge, jury, and possible executioner. First, we need confirmation of who's living in that Itta Bena house. Mr. Malone, did you get a name or phone number?"

"Only the alleged son's name, probably an alias, but…" he reached into his shirt pocket and extracted his business card. "Voila! One phone number at your service."

She smiled pleasingly and took the card. "I'll call Atlanta and get a trace on the account name. You're right, probably a bogus name but we'll see. If you're correct about Luther living there, then I need to bring in a few more agents before we drive over to Itta Bena."

"Elizabeth. You don't mind if I call you Elizabeth, do you?" asked Bianco.

"Please, Marcus. Call me Liz," she responded with a semi flirtatious smile and a slight gleam in her dark brown eyes. Not fully realizing it, she was growing fonder of the handsome, married detective.

"Seriously, Liz, do we really want to gamble with two lives and wait on FBI reinforcements? I think Mr. Campbell has some able-bodied sons that can back us up, right, Willie?"

"You betcha, Marcus. Just say the word. My boys can be here in ten minutes." They had already proven to be worthy and formidable rescuers at Swan Lake.

Agent Keys studied his face then looked into the intense eyes of the two detectives. She knew that officially she should follow FBI protocols, but she feared that further delay would jeopardize the fate of two people who had become her personal mission.

"Okay, you win," she acquiesced. "Let me call my office first and check out this phone number. Mr. Campbell, call in those backups Marcus mentioned. We have a job to do at a house in Itta Bena."

CHAPTER ELEVEN
The House in Itta Bena

The ride from Lawrenceville to Itta Bena seemed agonizingly long for the bound and gagged abductees. Eight hours in the back of a dark van with no padding was both physical and mental torment for Jade and Jasen, propelling their level of anxiety, anticipation, and fear past eleven on a scale of one to ten. The two abductors in the van had stopped only twice along their escape route from Lawrenceville.

During the first stop, the driver filled the gas tank while the second watched their two prisoners who were pressed against the side panels of the van. A short distance from the gas station, each captive was escorted separately under the cover of darkness into the roadside brush and allowed without privacy to relieve their painfully full bladders. Jasen weighed his options when his hands were temporarily untied but thought twice about challenging the thug with his gun aimed at his head.

He had had more than enough of the brutality from Cal Luther and his goons. His jaw and nose still throbbed from the vicious blow delivered by the man who had called himself Carlos Hermes and had been masquerading as a FBI agent. As Cal began to rip Jade's rooster apart and fling pieces at Jade, Jasen instinctively rushed toward him. Hermes stepped between them and caught Jasen with a tremendous right hook that sent Jasen reeling backward and crashing against the wall. His nose had gushed with bright red blood that covered his upper lip and then cascaded into maroon puddles onto the hall floor. Jasen reached for his crushed nose and pinched the nostrils attempting to slow the deluge of blood. His jaw throbbed but he didn't think it was fractured. Jade tried to move toward her assaulted lover but was stopped in her tracks and restrained by Hermes. She watched helplessly as Jasen tried to regain his senses.

Fleetingly, she speculated to herself about her neighbor, Earl Chambers, the self-appointed neighborhood watch captain. He usually knew everything that was going on in Windermere. Where was he when she *really* needed him?

"Jasen! I'm sorry." She tried to loosen Hermes powerful grip on her arm but to no avail.

Cal looked at the outmanned couple with disgust. "You two never learn, do you? There *is* no way out of this for either of you. Resisting will only get you shot."

Looking toward the sham agent Hermes, he said, "Victor, get these two pathetic love birds tied up and into the van. I'm sick of looking at them grovel and whine. Gag them, too. As soon as I satisfy myself that the information is not here, we'll head back to Mississippi. Get 'em out of here!"

***

Agent Keys got verification from Atlanta in less than thirty minutes that the phone number supplied by Danny was assigned to an account in the name of Calvin Morris. They all agreed that the name "Calvin" was much too coincidental. It had to be Calvin Luther. Keys finally committed.

"Okay, gentlemen. Saddle up. We have some rescuing to do. Mr. Campbell, are your sons available?"

"Already called 'em, ma'am. They're probably out front as we speak," Willie said with a tooth-filled grin.

"Okay, then. Let's do this," she said confidently. "Marcus, I'll ride with you and Danny. Willie and his sons can follow us. I'll brief you on the way about my plan, unless you have your own."

"Liz, you're in charge," Marcus responded. Keys did not notice as he winked at Danny and nodded once.

They exited out the rear of the Grill and headed to Marcus's car parked on the side street. Turning onto Carrollton, they saw Willie climbing into a four-door truck where his sons waited. The two-vehicle caravan headed west to Itta Bena.

***

The basement of the house was cool and as dark as a bottomless mineshaft, and it reeked of staleness, mold, and damp mustiness. Sitting on a small bluff above meandering Roebuck Lake, a branch of the Yazoo River, the old, declining house had absorbed more than its share of river moisture over the years. The captives were still gagged and now bound back-to-back on opposite sides of a wooden beam that was supporting the uninsulated floor above their heads. The scratching and scurrying sounds that they could hear were uncomfortably near them, and Jasen guessed that there were likely rats or mice exploring and curious about the intruders in their murky, dark domain. They could hear muffled voices and constant sounds of something rolling in the room over them, as if someone was nervously rolling something in one direction then back again, over and over. It seemed like the monotonous sounds had continued for hours.

In the darkness Jasen could barely see the side of Jade's face as they both strained against their bindings to find familiar eyes. She suddenly released a very stifled screech through her tightly gagged mouth when something she could not see crawled across her foot.

Jasen was fatigued from the long ride while bound in the back of the van but was convinced that he could muster some reserve. His body was strong thanks to his obsession with exercising and weight lifting at the fitness center. He guessed that it was likely midmorning, but the basement had no windows or light source unless the door at the top of the stairs opened. They had been almost thrown down the stairs before being bound.

As their minds were spinning madly and searching for strength and answers, the door at the top of the stairs opened then closed just as quickly. Someone with heavy shoes or boots banged down the wooden steps and approached them. Both Jasen and Jade held their breath in anticipation of bad news. In the next instant, a bright flashlight flicked on and pointed at Jasen's face. For several seconds he was blinded by the intense beam.

"You two having fun down here?" snarled the unseen stranger. He briefly focused the light on the frozen, intense face of Jade.

"The man upstairs sent me down here to get you two primed for your 'tribute.' So, if your memories have returned and you want to tell me what secrets you're keeping from us, well…he might go easy on you." He chuckled devilishly. "Not! I think he's ready to concede that you two will never talk. The only question now is how fast you want to die? Quickly or slowly?"

He walked around to Jade who was straining with pleading eyes to find Jasen. They were completely and painfully defenseless and at the mercy of cutthroat goons. As he steadied the beam from the flashlight on Jade, he very slowly moved it up and down, inspecting her from head to toe, stopping it briefly at her chest.

"My, my. It'll be such a waste. Your girlfriend here is a real beauty. Can't say that I've ever seen such a toothsome red-headed lady. Such silky skin, too," he continued as he stroked her cheek. "Maybe I'll just have to have a little fun with your lady friend before I take you two upstairs."

In disgust Jade turned her head sharply away from the filthy hand touching her face.

Jasen's pounding heart was about to rupture and explode in his chest as an inner rage fought an overwhelming impulse to kill the vile stranger. He would not sit back and let a monster ravage his soul mate right in front of him. He sensed that the attacker was releasing Jade's bindings and was likely forcing her toward another dark corner of the rat-infested basement. He could hear Jade's muted cries for help beneath her gag and the sounds of her being dragged, and he knew what was about to happen. The sounds of bodies wrestling and a slap told him that Jade was not submitting without a fight. His rage had peaked.

A miraculous burst of strength from an adrenalin surge suddenly defeated his tight rope trappings. His hands slipped away from the loosened ties, and in a flash he was freeing his bound legs. Jade's attacker had met unexpected resistance from the woman that had learned to tame the lions in her life. He was unaware of Jasen's escape from his bindings. His only thought was of his conquest of Jade.

It was eerily dark except for the attacker's flashlight that he had discarded as he struggled with a prey that wasn't allowing him to have his way easily. Jasen ripped off his mouth gag, stood, and wobbled unsteadily as he refocused and gained his bearings. He followed the dim light and Jade's grunts of determined resistance to the back corner of the basement and like a starving lion pounced with all of his two hundred pounds onto the back of the surprised assailant. He locked his arm around the villain's neck and with a tremendous effort pulled him away from Jade.

His opponent began to spin and spin in an attempt to free Jasen from his back. He was quite a husky man and without warning countered Jasen's choking neck hold with a smashing stomp onto Jasen's right foot. It had the desired effect, as the force of the huge foot hammering Jasen's caused him to relax his choke hold. The excruciating pain radiated up his leg, and he was sure bones had been crushed. The huge man broke free of Jasen's hold and smiled satisfyingly as Jasen danced away on one foot trying to cope with the throbbing pain in the injured one.

The unyielding thug suddenly remembered the .38 revolver that was holstered on his belt, and he reached for the loaded gun. Jasen, balancing on his good foot while trying to avoid pressure on the other, was only a few feet from his adversary. With a sudden sense of impending doom, he saw the man drawing the weapon. He braced himself instinctively, anticipating the shot but sensing that he could not move quickly enough to avoid a bullet. In a split second, Jasen leaned a few degrees to one side, and the shooter violently arched his back. His head jerked upward along with his trigger hand. Reflexively, he dropped the .38, and it bounced harmlessly away across the floor.

The would-be killer dropped to his knees and slowly fell forward, his head slamming like a dropped bowling ball against the concrete basement floor. A long-handled pick ax was imbedded deeply and directly in the middle of his back. Behind him stood Jade with her loosened mouth gag dangling around her neck. Jasen stared incredulously at his courageous, tight-faced lion tamer.

She stared down defiantly at the dead attacker.

"All I've got to say is 'Don't mess with Delta Jade Colton!'" She stepped over her fallen foe and walked over to her hobbled hero. They hugged briefly, and she said, "Let's get our lucky butts out of here."

"Not so fast," said Jasen as he reached down and massaged his crushed foot. "The only way out is up. We don't know who's up there or what they've heard. I'm surprised no one has rushed down to see what's going on down here."

Jade leaned down and picked up the dead man's .38.

"You taught me how to shoot these things. I'm ready. Let's do this.

CHAPTER TWELVE

A Requiem

Jasen put his ear to the door at the top of the stairs and listened for conversation or any signs of movement. He thought he could hear classical music but it sounded faint and several rooms distance. He cautiously turned the doorknob and slowly pushed the door open into the hallway. Jade was behind him with the .38 cocked and ready.

They eased silently into the hallway and quickly surveyed both ends. No one was waiting or expecting them, they hoped. They saw only a dark, empty hall. Jasen correctly assessed that the nearest exit and escape route was at the end of that hall.

He motioned to Jade and stealthily headed in the direction of the music as Jade followed just on his heels. They tiptoed past two rooms and saw no sign of more house guests or captors. The music appeared to be coming from the next room at the end of the long hallway. Jasen recognized it as Mozart's *Requiem in D Minor*. He turned and looked back at Jade and wondered if she knew the piece. His love for classical music would likely be a surprise to her, and he briefly thought about how much more she really did not know about him.

He suddenly felt the irony of someone in the house relishing Mozart's last but never completed masterpiece—intended to be a tribute to the deceased wife of the person who commissioned him to compose it. He remembered how Mozart obsessed with the project even on his death bed and had concluded that he was writing his own death tribute. Now someone was preparing for a tribute to someone else's death—theirs! But, as far as Jasen was concerned, the tribute would be for their captor's death.

His foot still screaming in pain with each step, Jasen with Jade at his side now inched closer to the room that was bellowing the Latin lyrics of the Mozart classic. Jasen took the .38 from Jade, and he thought briefly about just escaping out the front door. But he decided to confront his captor. He whispered softly, hoping only Jade could hear him.

"I'll do this. Stay close." She did not argue but nodded and took a deep breath.

Gun in hand, cocked and ready, Jasen turned quickly and stepped with a slight limp into the room. At first glance he didn't see anyone. As he scanned the dimly lit, very large room, he noted three walls of bookcases with shelves bulging with books of all sizes. Someone seemed to be a very avid reader or a collector at best.

Jasen remained postured in a ready-to-fire stance. Then, suddenly he could see the back of someone in a wheelchair positioned behind a large desk on the far wall. The unknown person seemed to be alone in the room. He was staring at a turntable that was spinning slowly around and around as it echoed across the room the *Requiem's* most serene movement "Lacrimosa." Jade entered the room and, peeping around Jasen's shoulder, saw what he was mentally weighing. Jasen looked at her and shrugged.

They crept catlike one step at a time toward the wheelchair and its occupant, trying to remain undetected. As Jasen neared the desk, the old wooden floor beneath his shoes suddenly creaked and popped loudly. Both of them froze in their steps.

"Well, finally! I've been expecting you two," said the mystery man in a voice that was unusually slow and somewhat distorted. He very adeptly spun his wheelchair around and faced his two captives.

***

As they neared the outskirts of the small town of Itta Bena, Elizabeth Keys had laid out her plan. Danny was confident that the last house on Lakeside Lane was hiding the mysterious Jake Luther. Bianco agreed with Liz's plan for Danny to knock on the door posing as a Mississippi River Gas Company utility worker investigating a report of a gas leak. Hopefully, he could gain access and get an idea of how many people were in the house. And with luck, he might even see their target.

Danny found some workman's clothes and a baseball cap in Marcus's trunk that was well stocked with "costumes" that they had used in their investigative work. He even found a fake handheld meter device that he would feign as a gas detector. His boss was resourceful when it came to being prepared for any and everything.

They passed south through the main part of town and turned back east toward Roebuck Lake. Marcus mentally made note of a black sedan passing them and heading toward the river. He could make out three men in the sedan. A block ahead of them the sedan turned left onto Lakeside and disappeared from view.

As Marcus turned slowly onto the street paralleling the lake, he did not see any other cars. He parked one block from the end of the street, not wanting to attract attention from possible lookouts at the house. Willie Campbell and his four sons had followed the FBI agent and the detectives and pulled their truck just behind Bianco's car. Marcus walked back to the truck and briefed the Campbells on the plan. He told Willie to just sit tight for the time being.

Danny glanced back at Marcus and Liz as he walked toward the house. He felt for his gun concealed in his left shoulder holster and hoped that he wouldn't have to use it. He silently rehearsed his lines, knowing that this time his boyish charm was not going to get him past kidnappers or ruthless murderers. He took a deep breath, climbed the steps to the very fusty looking house, and rang the doorbell.

***

The man in the wheelchair appeared old with a full head of white hair and a heavily wrinkled, leathery face. Jade stared at him, open-mouthed, but not recognizing him as her mother's fiendish boss in Eutaw from so many years ago. His left arm, supported by a sling, was propped against his lower chest, and in his right hand he held a 9-mm Parabellum Luger pointed deliberately at the duo.

"Please, Mr. Prospero," he warned, "I would advise you to refrain from discharging that gun. I am an expert marksman and can get off several rounds from this semiautomatic pistol before you can squeeze that trigger. Let's be sensible. Put down your gun and I'll do the same." His muddled speech suggested someone who had suffered a significant neurologic event or brain injury.

Jasen was no sharpshooter but was not a novice either when it came to guns. Nevertheless, he recognized the standoff and did not want to risk his or Jade's life against a German luger in the hand of an evil-appearing villain who was old but obviously unpredictable. He hesitated, not wanting to give up his only defense. The stranger might just shoot both of them anyway. His mind reeled with uncertainty.

"Both of you, please, have a seat and we can discuss your situation," he said, pointing to two armless chairs five feet from his desk. "You really have no choice. My nephew and his friends greatly worsen your odds. As a matter-of-fact, they're right behind you."

Jasen and Jade turned in disbelief and shock as they saw Calvin standing behind them in the hallway with two goons who were grinning and aiming guns at their backs. Thoughts of escape and victory over their nemesis evaporated with their next heart beat.

"Please," said the old man. "Have a seat." He reached for the turntable and lifted the arm from the slow-spinning record.

"I hope you have been enjoying the requiem mass—one of my favorite Mozarts. I played it in your honor."

Jasen and Jade dared not imagine what the villains would do to them once they discovered their dead crony in the basement. They sat down as Calvin walked over and took the .38 from Jasen's hand.

"Very wise of you, Mr. Prospero. Or should I just call you Agent McCoy?"

Jade quickly looked at Jasen, then back at the old man with a very puzzled look. She looked again at Jasen who stared into her eyes but said nothing and gently shook his head.

"I know about your secret identity, Agent Ethan McCoy. I must say that you have done an expert job of concealing your double life, and I can tell by the bewildered look on Ms. Colton's face that she does not have the slightest clue as to what I'm talking about. You see, Ms. Colton, there is much more to your friend than meets the eye. I sincerely hope that the truth does not upset you. Then again, what difference would it make? Your journey together ends today in, of all places, Itta Bena, Mississippi, and not all that far from where your life began, my dear.

"Let me fill you in, Ms. Colton. It wouldn't be fair to send you to your grave without sharing the truth. The man you have known as Jasen Prospero is secretly employed by the US Treasury Department. Yes, that's right—a bona fide secret agent man. For years now, he has been investigating me and my organization. You were, to put it bluntly, simply a means to a possible end in his search."

Jade looked stunned and confused. Her mind wasn't prepared for more lies and pretense. *It can't be true,* she thought to herself. *Jasen's a kind and special person.* She thought that their serendipitous love was special and meant to be. She looked at him and he shook his head again, silently mouthing "not true."

The old man continued.

"Look at me carefully, Ms. Colton. I am Jackson Mason Luther. Your mother and you knew me as Big Jake Luther."

Jade stared at him with a cascade of colliding emotions that were spinning like a giant cement mixer in her head. Her recurring nightmare was now sitting directly in front of her. It was him—her mother's evil attacker that she thought she had killed when she was only six. He was alive!

Jake was now poised to reap his long-postponed revenge. And the only man that she thought she could trust was apparently concealing a lie. Her world was flipped completely upside down. Her life was unraveling and being shred into pieces exactly like the rooster, which she had guarded for so many years.

"You must have thought that you sent me to my grave that day back in Alabama. As you see, my dear, I am alive and well, that is if you consider my disability as being well. However, I did suffer a hell-on-earth thanks to your vicious attack on my neck. I survived by some miracle but have endured months and even years of treatment and rehabilitation. My apology if you find my words somewhat difficult to understand. It took almost five years before I could walk with assistance and over ten years to learn to speak again. This chair just makes life a little easier, but I can walk now without it.

"You and your mother took a lot more from me than just that wretched rooster. You took away my dignity, you robbed me of many good years of life, and you stole information that I must recover and protect. I execute the orders and wishes of others that will go to any lengths to protect a legacy. I have pursued what's rightfully mine and theirs for many years, albeit delayed due to my injuries and disability. Until I regained my speech, I could not communicate what had to be done. You have been an elusive target, partly a fault of my own, sending bungling idiots to find you. My nephew here, Calvin, has painfully disappointed me with his failures. Finally, he did something right and brought you here.

"And that child molester, stepfather of yours, Mr. Winters, couldn't even steal a dumb, dead rooster apparently because his perverted interest in you distracted him from his task. He claimed that he did not know where your mother had hidden the rooster. He just couldn't resist getting his revenge against your mother, and now it appears that he's going to be incarcerated for quite a while. Fitting."

Jade looked at him with tears forming in her eyes.

"Yes, that's correct, Ms. Colton. Her car didn't drive off into that ravine by accident. I'm sorry to have to tell you that. She did not have to die. All we needed was what was in that rooster. No one had to die. I've come to the conclusion that you two either don't have the information or are the most stupid couple I have ever encountered. Regardless, it doesn't matter anymore. Your boyfriend and you know too much about me and my friends. I have no choice but to kill you. And, no, killing a US Treasury agent does not bother me. It would give me considerable pleasure, for sure.

"Which brings me back to your friend here, Agent McCoy, or Jasen, whichever you prefer. I don't know what all he's told you, but judging from your reaction, it's not much. He could tell you, I'm certain, if you two had more time. But, since time is almost up, I'll fill in the blanks.

"For the past several years, the Feds have been interested in persons in very high places who are alleged to have links to questionable business activities. For some reason, the Treasury Department suspected these persons—the names are not important as far as you are concerned— might be involved in an international money laundering operation. The investigation apparently, by some stroke of luck, led your handsome friend here to my organization in Greenwood. But, I think that's where McCoy here hit a dead end. My organization went underground. I had disappeared. No one knew if I was dead or alive.

"I must boast that I have done a masterful job of protecting others and keeping snooping eyes out of their and my affairs. And I think that's where you, your mother, and the notorious magical rooster entered this little game of deception and pursuit. Agent McCoy uncovered your connection to me and to the dead Choctaw Chief. Since no one could find me, you simply became a clue that might lead McCoy to me. In addition, I know a lot more about your distant Indian chief relative and his hidden secrets than you realize. It's why I took the rooster. Now, McCoy is going to help me solve one more mystery before he dies."

Jasen looked up at Jake, intrigued at his remarks. He wasn't certain but he wondered now about the theft at the French Camp carriage house. Was Jake behind that, too?

"I assure you, Ms. Colton, you and your college professor becoming neighbors was no accident or coincidence. Everything happens for a reason, even 'falling in love.' Your life was planned even before you were born, I assure you. And hiring that private investigator—brilliant! A very clever way to further protect your cover, McCoy. I must say, however, your detective friend does not make a very convincing insurance man."

Jade's mind was on information overload. Jake's story sounded totally preposterous. Nothing made sense. Why was he manufacturing lies about Jasen? He was her protector. Her soul mate. The only man that understood her. She trusted him. Jake had to be lying for reasons she could not fathom. It was all more than she could sort or comprehend. Now certain death was awaiting them, but, she had to know the truth. She looked at Jasen, begging him for answers. His eyes brightened with a slight gleam, and he smiled as if to say, "Trust me, I love you." What she didn't know was that his secret identity was about to be tested.

Jake placed the Luger on his desk and retrieved a paper from an open file folder lying on his desk. He turned in his wheelchair and maneuvered it with ease from behind his desk, rolling it toward Jasen. He held the paper in front of Jasen and handed it to him.

"I need your expertise one last time before your die, McCoy," said Jake. Up close, his drawn, craggy face, worn down by years of debilitation, accentuated a body that looked much older than he was. "Please, take a look at this and tell me what you think it means."

Jasen took the paper that exhibited a highlighted handwritten note. He immediately recognized it as Greenwood Leflore's characteristic hand-writing style, all small case, no punctuation. The note confirmed that one of Jake's thugs must have vandalized the carriage house in French Camp. There were obviously no secrets of which Jake was not aware. Their every movement was known. Did everyone they've met in Greenwood work for Jake Luther? How did he know so much about them? So many questions without answers. Jake Luther's superiors must be more power-ful than he could have imagined.

"Where, may I ask, did you obtain this note?" asked Jasen, knowing the answer already.

Jake smiled proudly and said, "Let's just say that I have my methods. Just look at the note and tell me what it means. I don't have to say 'please' because if you don't decipher this, my colleague Victor over there will be forced to do something that you won't like."

Victor walked over to Jade and grabbed her tousled auburn hair, jerk-ing her head forcefully upward and back. He put a box cutter with its exposed shiny razor's edge against her throat. It was déjà vu all over again for Jade. Damian Winters, her mother's ex-husband, had threatened to slash Jade's throat the night of his thwarted ambush at her house on Windermere. Jasen's daughter Ariel had saved the day, but she knew that there would be no Ariel this time.

Jasen also knew that time was running out. He had to make a move.

"Okay, okay. Just relax. I'll do what I can but not while your goon holds that blade against Jade's throat."

Jake stared into Jasen's eyes briefly and then motioned for Victor to back off. He withdrew the cutter and forcefully pushed Jade's head forward in disgust. He snarled at Jasen and backed up one step.

Jasen began to read the note again and decided he needed to improve his odds. He held the paper closer to his eyes.

"I need a magnifying glass. I think there may be some finer print embedded within the larger print." He was ad-libbing.

Jake hesitated as he studied Jasen's eyes. Finally, he snapped his fingers at Victor. "Go look in the kitchen drawers by the refrigerator. I think there's a magnifier in one of them. Go! Now!"

Just as Victor exited the room, the front doorbell buzzed loudly. Cal looked at Jake for direction. The doorbell buzzed for a second time. Whoever was at the door was not being patient.

"Damn!" exclaimed Jake. "Who the hell can that be at this time of the day?" He nodded at Victor's sidekick. "Go see who that is and get rid of them. Go!"

Jasen and Jade looked at each other briefly. Jasen went back at pretending to study the note. Only Jake and Cal holding the .38 now stood in their way. It was time.

"Calvin," said Jasen. "Come over here and look at this word and tell me if you see what I see."

Cal warily stepped over to Jasen's chair and leaned toward the paper and peered down at the note. Before Cal could suspect anything, Jasen quickly dropped the note and floated it toward the floor. As Cal instinctively bent down to catch the note, Jasen reacted like a hungry puma pouncing on its unsuspecting prey.

He grabbed Cal's wrist with a vise-like grip, hoping to cause him to drop the gun. Jasen quickly stood and they wrestled for control of the .38, which was pointing erratically in all directions. Cal refused to yield to Jasen's powerful grip and relinquish possession of the gun.

Jade instinctively moved her head to one side when the gun was suddenly pointed at her. A shot exploded from the .38, and she felt the bullet's heat sear her cheek as it sped by and into the wall behind her. She sprang from her chair and backed away, realizing her momentary luck. At the same instance, two gunshots echoed back to them from the front of the house. Victor and his companion must have confronted an unwelcomed visitor at the front door.

As Cal and Jasen battled feverishly for control, Jake suddenly realized that he had left his Luger on his desk. He spun his wheelchair around and propelled himself like a paralympian champion toward the weapon. Jade saw his amazing athletic move but was too far away to intercept him in time.

Jasen and Cal continued to spin and stagger like drunken dancers as they fought for an advantage. Jake reached his desk, leaned forward and grabbed the Parabellum Luger. Just as he wheeled the chair around in the direction of Cal and Jasen, Cal's .38 fired a second time with a thunderous report. The projectile zoomed just past Jasen's ear with tympanic rupturing speed and sound.

Big Jake's body instantly froze. The bullet had drilled a perfect hole between his eyes and ripped part of his skull from the back of his head, splattering bone, blood, and gray matter across the desk. He slumped forward as the Luger dropped from his hand and fell to the floor.

Jade surged with renewed energy and raced to pick up Jake's gun. She swirled around just as Jasen twisted Cal's wrist violently, snapping bones with a very loud cracking echo. Cal screamed loudly and dropped the still smoking .38 to the floor. He dropped to his knees, screaming out in pain as he grasped his contorted, dangling hand, which was grotesquely hyper-extended and pointing up his arm. The enraged adversary looked up at his challenger and growled, "You're a dead man!" He attempted to stand and lunged to retrieve his .38. Jasen calmly responded, "No, I think you have that backward."

Before his next breath, Jasen raised his leg and coiled his still throbbing, crushed foot. Just before the infuriated Calvin reached the gun, Jasen slammed his foot with the force of a sledge hammer into the side of his head with an emphatic skull-splitting finale. Cal's body crumpled to the floor and he lay motionless.

Jade pointed the Luger at the lifeless body and for a fleeting second thought about pulling the trigger. Instead, she lowered the gun and smiled at Jasen who was just regaining his bearings after his apparent victory. They both looked at the slumped, partially exploded head of Jake Luther, and Jasen suddenly realized the irony of the evil Jake being shot by his own nephew after thirty-plus years of "not even existing."

Before they could celebrate the finality of defeating their unrelenting pursuers, they realized that something had happened out in the hallway. They looked at each other realizing that they may not be home-free. Victor and his buddy had surely heard the blasts from Calvin's .38 but had not returned to investigate.

Jasen grabbed Jade and pulled her around to the other side of Jake's desk where they crouched down out of sight. Both were armed and ready for a shoot out if necessary. Cal's body lay in the middle of the floor with his deformed twisted arm at his side.

After a long minute of no other sounds from the outer hallway, they heard an unfamiliar voice calling from just outside of the large room.

"Hello? Jasen? Jade? Are you two in there? Hello?"

Jasen peeped above the desk and saw a blond man wearing work clothes and a baseball cap standing in the door opening with a gun in hand. It wasn't Victor or his goony friend. Jasen did not recognize him.

"Stop right where you are. We're armed. Who are you?" asked Jasen from his semi-concealed position.

"Hey, relax, man. I'm the Calvary. Danny Malone, PI. Are you Jasen?"

Jasen stood cautiously but did not drop his aim at the stranger. "PI? You don't look like a PI. Do you work with Bianco?"

"You got it, man. Please, put the gun away. We came to rescue you two but it looks as if you are doing a pretty good job by yourselves. By the way, I took care of the two front door greeters. They pulled a piece on me when they heard the gunfire in here, but I was a split second quicker. They're history, I'm afraid."

Jade finally stood up, took Jasen's hand, and in a rush of euphoria sensed new life flowing through her body. Her thirty-year nightmare had ended... she hoped. But, she thought to herself, Jasen had a whole lot of explaining to do.

CHAPTER THIRTEEN

The Double Life

Lawrenceville, Georgia
1998

Their journey back to Georgia with Elizabeth Keys was a mixed bag of emotions: elation over the conquest of the monstrous Jake Luther and his gangsters and at the same time confusion and uncertainty about the revelation of Jasen's double life. Jade replayed over and over in her mind Jake's words: "Becoming neighbors and falling in love with Jasen was not an accident or coincidence. You were simply a means to an end. A means to an end." The words haunted her and shrouded her in sadness. Was it true? Was she just a pawn in a large impersonal government investigation? She couldn't accept the thought. She would have to hear the truth when they returned to Windermere Cove.

"You two put on quite a show back there in Itta Bena," said Agent Keys. "I don't think I've ever known two people cheating death and winning as many times as you have. Uncanny. With the Luthers and their Klansmen gone, it's time for you two to get back to a 'normal' life."

Jasen looked at Jade with raised brows, then rolled his eyes and twisted his mouth. He knew that in time there could be others who might target them, even more powerful others. Elizabeth was unaware of Jasen's larger but top secret role in the Greenwood activities. He knew he would have to reveal his cover to her eventually but decided to wait until he and Jade had had a chance to reconcile the past year and a half of their lives. Jade waited for him to reveal the truth, but he remained silent.

Keys continued. "I must say that I was quite impressed with young Danny Malone. Marcus speaks highly of his talents and he demonstrated them very ably today.

"Speaking of Marcus, that is one handsome man! Too bad he's married…oh, sorry, back to Danny. He didn't even have a chance to wait on me, Marcus, and the Campbells to join him. Taking out both of those goons at the same time. Impressive. Quick Draw, that's what Marcus calls him. And you two didn't leave much for the rest of us to do except clean up the mess. Five dead bad guys with you two and Danny pretty much unscathed. Not bad considering what could have happened." She couldn't help but notice their deafening silence.

"You're both being pretty quite. Are you sure you're okay?" she asked.

Jasen answered for them. "Just worn out from the ordeal. It was a little intense for a while. We'll be fine once we get some rest and reality sets in. Thanks for being there for us, Elizabeth."

"No problem. Except I didn't do anything, but we *did* have a good plan. Just didn't need it, thank goodness. Sometimes things just seem to work themselves out. If I didn't know any better, I would guess that you two are pros!" she smiled jokingly and refocused on her driving.

Jade wanted to say something but instead stared blankly out the window into the evening darkness, trying to imagine how any of the last eighteen months could possibly have been only an orchestrated Shakespearean play with Jasen and her as actors on a stage.

✳✳✳

Agent Keys insisted on escorting them inside when they finally arrived at Jade's house on Windermere. She had warned them that her agents who responded after their kidnapping found that the house had been ransacked, presumably by Calvin Luther in his maddened search for the rooster's secrets. Jade stopped as she approached her den and stared incredulously. "Oh, my God!"

"I'm sorry, Jade. I tried to prepare you. Calvin was on a mission, but I think most of what you see here is the result of his outrage and refusal to accept defeat by you two. If he had only known that the secrets were already in federal hands. What a shame. Can I stay and give you two a hand at straightening up this mess?"

"Thanks, Elizabeth, but I think we'd rather be alone now," responded Jade. "We have some matters to resolve." She looked at Jasen who turned and looked away. "Thanks for getting us back safe and sound. We'll be fine."

"Okay, I understand. Just remember—if you need anything, just call. I *will* need both of you to come to the Atlanta office tomorrow so we can debrief you and get signed statements. Let me know tomorrow when you're ready. Good night." She turned and let herself out.

Jasen picked up several sofa pillows and stepped over broken lamps as he walked over to the overturned sofa. He righted it and cleared an area to sit down.

"Jade, come sit down and let me explain everything." He replaced the pillows and sat down.

She hesitated only for a second and walked over and sat beside him. "Okay, Jasen, Ethan or whoever-you-are. This had better be good."

For the next hour Jasen recounted the last eighteen months of their roller coaster affair. He started at the end.

"Jade, no matter what's spinning around inside your head and your heart, I want you to know that I love you and nothing can change how I feel about you. I'm sorry if you are feeling betrayed or used or whatever you're thinking. How I feel about you is genuine and sincere. Please believe *that* even if you want to hate me for hiding my other identity, I had no choice. Just listen and I hope you'll see. We're a team now and we have unfinished business. Don't judge me until you hear the truth. Okay?"

She looked deeply into his soft brown eyes and wanted so badly to believe him. But, constant betrayals and lies had plagued her entire life. She knew, or thought she knew, Jasen Prospero but had no inkling about who Ethan McCoy really was. How could she trust a man with two identities and she only knew one? "Okay," she said softly.

As she listened she studied the face and body language of a man with deep convictions. She sensed the moral dilemmas that he struggled with, including his marital indiscretions. He told her that that was not part of the plan. His official and secret orders were to only meet her, befriend her, and somehow get her to help entice Jake Luther out of hiding if he was still alive. The thought was now bitterly distasteful, he told her.

She was bait in the government's eyes. Just saying it made him nauseous, he confessed to her. He was not supposed to fall in love with her. But, he did and more. He became obsessed with her. She unknowingly controlled his every thought and desire. It wasn't contrived. It happened and he couldn't stop it. Destiny, coincidence, a job assignment...call it whatever you want, he told her. But, falling in love with her was real, not manufactured. He could have taken a different turn at the crossroads when they met, but he *chose* her. He could have refused the assignment. But, he didn't. Everything else happened because it had to.

After listening and weighing on his every word, she fought an overwhelming urge to hate him and everything he stood for. She had been duped and humiliated. Men had used her all of her life. Jasen was no different. Her mind screamed loudly and painfully. Run away from him as fast as you can and never look back. Her heart was trying to tell her the opposite.

She looked again into the eyes of someone she thought she knew but now realized she didn't. The very idea of being used as "bait" provoked her anger and resentment. She had relinquished her trust to someone she thought was genuine and real. Someone she had looked for all of her life. But, he was like all the rest of the men in her life. Jerks. Pretenders. Exploiters. How could he say he loved her? She was a fool all over again. She realized that she was like her mother—an easy mark for ill-intended suitors. The gullible, vulnerable beauty. She hated herself at that very moment more than she hated him.

She stared more intensely at him and weighed his pleading eyes, which were searching for the right words.

An uneasy silence begged for a response. Finally, the words he had feared broke the tense night. Jade had decided.

"I want you to leave, Jasen," she said calmly as she looked into his eyes.

He looked back with lips tightened. "Jade, please forgive me. I did what I was trained to do. What I had to do. But, I love you. We can work this out. Please."

"Please leave, Jasen. Now! Get out of my house! Just leave." She stood and walked to her bedroom and slammed the door.

He thought about going to her and trying to help her work through the confusion. But he knew it was not the time. He felt the cutting pains of his betrayal and searched for redemption. He knew it would not come tonight. He walked out the front door into the cool darkness of the Georgia night, wondering if he would ever find a way to right his wrongs.

***

Jade buried her face in her soft pillow that soon became a wet, salty river. Her tears flowed from something stabbing her heart like a bone-deep loss of a lifelong sought joy. She wept with memories that flooded her consciousness. Sleep refused her.

She remembered his fresh, soft touch on her skin and the manly smell of his satisfied desires. She remembered the nights of awakening in his reassuring arms and tasting the sweetness of his lips. She remembered the tenderness of his voice whispering in her ear "I love you." She remembered his gentle hugs and his caressing breath on the back of her neck. She remembered the look on his face when he saw her naked body outside of his sunroom window. She remembered a cold, snowy night when two souls became one. She remembered the dreams of physical longings fulfilled and the nightmares of death unleashed. She remembered the indescribable joy of his comforting presence. She remembered his kind and gentle spirit. She remembered his gift of unconditional love.

Now he was gone. The solitude of the night slowly fell upon her like the final curtain of the final act. What had she done?

She strangely began to feel even closer than ever to the man she knew as Jasen. As far as she was concerned, Ethan McCoy was a temporary invention of the US Treasury Department. Someday that person would be gone, but Jasen Prospero would still exist. One of them had betrayed her but she did not know how she could ever trust either one of them.

Her mind rewound, and she saw her son's bedroom and his lifeless body beside the shotgun. She missed him so much. She tried to push the memories of the horrors of Damian deeper and deeper and farther away from her thoughts. She tried to forget the day she saved her mother from the jaws of Jake Luther. She tried to forget the countless empty, lonely nights without her husband James. She tried to erase the memory of her mother's fiery death at the bottom of a dark, forbidden ravine.

She tried to deny all of the assaults on her life, nightmares that could not possibly have been real.

The men in her life were her recurring nightmares. She thought Jasen had saved her from them. Now, he was just another of so many. Ironically, she longed for his naked, muscular, masculinity to be lying beside her, holding her, consoling her, fighting off her demons. But he was gone. She rolled to her side and brushed the streams of tears from her cheeks. Life was not fair. She closed her moist eyes and drifted back into another time. At last, an overwhelming fatigue overcame her memories, her desires, and her torment. Sleep came.

Part Two

CHAPTER FOURTEEN

The Old Natchez Road

Bandits

Frenchman's Camp (Present Day French Camp)
Mississippi Territory
1812

The middle aged clerk/innkeeper looked up briefly and just as quickly went back to his work on his inventory journal, as the three strangers charged into the front door of the log cabin stand.. In addition to supplying basic commodities for frontiersmen, traders, and hunters, the tiny post also accommodated Natchez Road travelers overnight in the small room that had been added to the rear of the one-room main house. The room could sleep four on old frayed and musty cots that were arranged side-by-side without privacy. Weary travelers gladly accepted the smelly cots over the hard ground outside.

One of the unrecognized men walked over to the innkeeper's desk with his heavy leather boots pounding and echoing against the rock hard, heart-of-pine floor that was covered with the trail dust of many prior patrons. His face portrayed an arrogance and authority that hinted at trouble for the unwary. He was a tall, husky man with a chiseled and hardened face who was oddly dressed in filthy buckskin galligaskins and a dark shirt covered by a brown, knee-length coachman's coat. A very dusty black Stetson with a silver band adorned his square head.

Holstered pearl-handled British New Land Calvary pistols, most likely stolen, complemented his bulky gun belt, which held spare flints and powder.

"Who's the owner of this pathetic excuse for a stand?" demanded the stocky man.

The innkeeper looked up, away from his work, and responded somewhat rudely, perturbed from the interruption. "If you're looking for Mr. LeFleur, he's not here just now. He's out hunting with his sons. I'm Josiah Duke, the innkeeper and stand manager. How may I be of help?"

"My name is Samuel Mason, and if you are not familiar with that name, I strongly suggest that you put away whatever you're doing and gather this list of supplies, now!" he said, as he flung the paper list into the face of Duke.

Josiah Duke was not intimidated, having had more confrontations with frontier scoundrels than he could remember. Remote stands *could* be prime targets for the countless brigands and land pirates along the Old Road, but oddly, the stands were rarely raided or robbed. Even the most cutthroat and notorious pirates respected the necessity of the sparse posts that resupplied both the honest and dishonest travelers with water, food, and other necessities for surviving the rough, unsettled frontier. The basic code of the frontier trader was to accommodate everyone. Even the nastiest of the nasties were likely to pay something if they got vital supplies, which enabled them to continue their nefarious and sometimes murderous assaults on unsuspecting prey that dared venture up and down the 444 miles of the Old Natchez Road (Trace) from Natchez to Nashville.

"Keep your shirt on, Mr. Mason. I was in the middle of performing inventory on everything," said Mr. Duke. "Let me see if I can get your stuff together." He stared at Mason's shiny pistols and then looked over his broad shoulders at his two weasely looking companions who appeared to be Kaintucks, judging from their attire. They stood on either side of the door and rested their shooting hand on their own holstered flint pistols. Duke stepped out from behind his old spindle-leg desk and went to his task of gathering Mason's items.

Josiah had seen their kind many times and knew that they would not hesitate to use their weapons if he did not follow their boss's instructions. He was a seasoned trader and had learned the secrets to surviving in a hostile frontier. Whoever this Samuel Mason was, Josiah lumped him in with the rest of the countless, unsavory southern land pirates with their gang of brigands—mean, ruthless, and totally irreverent to life if you stood in their way.

Duke tried to lighten the tense, thick atmosphere. "So, Mr. Mason, what brings you and your friends to Frenchman's Camp?"

"None of your damn business, Duke! Me and the boys here are headed down to Natchez. Just get the list done and we'll be on our way. No more questions, got it?"

Duke had his suspicions. No doubt. Land pirates, brigands. They all looked alike. And he had heard of the Natchez-under-the-Hill part of town, which was a haven for robbers, murderers, brothels, and criminals of all sorts. He surmised that was more likely their destination. He hurried to complete the task, hoping Mason meant what he said—that they would soon be on their way.

"Sure thing, Mr. Mason. No more questions."

Duke packed the supplies in two burlap sacks and placed them in front of the two shifty-eyed characters by the door. They glared at him without saying a word or moving. Their trigger hands still rested on their undrawn pistols.

"Here you go, Mr. Mason. Everything on your list. I threw in some extra tobacco, sorghum, and jerky, 'cause I like your two men here," Duke said sarcastically with a very insincere grin, which revealed gaps from several missing teeth."

Mason glared at Duke and plopped two gold coins down on the innkeeper's desk, turning and clomping noisily across the wooden floor and past his two guards. He did not speak or even acknowledge Duke's prompt compliance. The two hostile-looking gang men lifted the burlap sacks, turned, and followed their boss out the stand door. The three strangers mounted their horses that had been tied out front, and they galloped off, leaving a cloud of dry, dusty trail dirt in their wake. Duke had followed them to the door and breathed easier as he watched them retreat back toward the Old Road just west of the trading post.

"Good riddance," he uttered, inaudible to the strangers. "Please, *don't* come back!"

***

Louis LeFleur and his sons Benjamin and Greenwood approached the trading post on foot from its eastern exposure and noticed a rising cloud of dust swirling on the trail off to the west. Louis recognized the trailing dust as the mark of horsemen riding away from his establishment. Each of his sons carried two limp, dead rabbits by their long ears in their left hands and held rifles in their right. Louis carried only a rifle, a handsome Harpers Ferry Model 1803 made popular by Captain Meriwether Lewis several years earlier.

"Looks like Duke has had some visitors," observed LeFleur. "Judging from the dust cloud, it appears they left in haste. Hope our man is okay. Greenwood, scurry on to the stand and see if he's in one piece."

Twelve-year old Greenwood LeFleur quickly handed his two rabbits to his brother, pushed off in a fast, youthful run, and hurried into the post's front entrance. Before Louis and Benjamin had caught up, Greenwood poked his head out the door. His broad grin told Louis that Duke was fine. Louis and Benjamin followed Greenwood inside and found Mr. Duke sitting at his desk with his nose buried again in his inventory journal.

"I see you've had some customers. Any problems?" asked LeFleur.

Duke spoke with confidence and calm. "Nothing I couldn't handle. Three highwaymen is my guess. Two looked like Kaintucks. The leader said he was Samuel Mason. I figure he's just another John Murrell-type pirate. Had quite an ego. They got some supplies, left two gold pieces, and high-tailed it back toward the Old Road, probably to ambush the next poor souls that are fool enough to use that trail. Word is that it's buzzing with robbers from Natchez to Nashville, but especially closer to Natchez."

LeFleur said, "I know of this pirate Mason. They call him the "Wolfman." Chief Pushmataha told me that Mason and his gang have been quite active along the road ever since Merrell and his brigands got captured and locked up. You know how nature abhors a vacuum. I was down at LeFleur's Bluff last month and heard the local traders talking about this Sam Mason. They said he had been actively operating north of Natchez in cahoots with the Harpe brothers and had been seen around Natchez-under-the-Hill. As vicious as the Harpe brothers are known to be, they say Mason makes them look like kittens. You're likely correct about the Kaintucks. Mason and his clan once lived around Diamond Island in Kentucky. He probably recruited a lot of Kaintucks into his gang. Ironic, since they were once the prime targets of the Murrell gang. If you can't beat them, well…you know the rest.

"They may be on the run. I heard that he and his goons were rooted from their hideout down near Rocky Springs by the Exterminators— Captain Thomas Young's vigilante bounty hunters from Mercer County, Kentucky. They have been pursuing this murderous bunch for years. The traders said that Mason had to leave behind several large caches of gold in his hasty escapes. Apparently, the Mason Gang has robbed enough caravans and honest Kaintucks headed home to accumulate over two hundred million dollars in gold and other treasures. Probably an exaggeration. Now, the word on the Trace is that some of Mason's treasure hoard is buried somewhere near Rocky Springs. Or maybe, some say, he may have hidden part of the gold north of here near Walker's Crossroads when he stopped at George Colbert's Tavern last year. Either way, he hasn't made it back to his gold—too many bounty hunters looking for him and his treasure around those areas. Two thousand five hundred dollars on his head right now."

Greenwood and his seventeen-year old brother Benjamin were listening to their father's tale of the Mason Gang with youthful curiosity, and both looked at each other and smiled when Louis mentioned the lost treasures. They were particularly attentive to the Walker's Crossroads piece of the tale, because they had hunted buffalo, deer, and rabbit extensively in that area, even though it was in Chickasaw territory. Treasure hunting. Hmmm. That sounded like a beckoning challenge to the young brothers.

Louis sensed his sons' keen interest in the story and was quick to add a fatherly warning.

"Don't get any ideas, boys. You don't want to get anywhere near that murderer and especially his spoils. He'd just as soon kill you two as he would grown men. You may be part Choctaw, but he won't care. He's brutal—scalps everyone he kills, just like the Apaches and Creeks, and carries the scalps in his baggage like trophies. Not to mention that he's been known to gut his victims, fill their carcasses with stones, and throw them in the swamps for gator bait so they are never found. Don't do anything stupid. Are you listening, boys?"

The brothers tried to keep a serious look, nodded, and remained silent.

Louis reminded them about their rabbits. "You two need to get those rabbits skinned and give them to your mother. I can taste the rabbit stew already!"

They turned, disappeared out the stand's front door and went to their task.

Louis walked over to Mr. Duke and asked to see the inventory journal. "I think I need to get back down to Natchez and get some more supplies. We're getting a touch scarce on a few things. Sure hope those boys of mine stay away from Mason and his like. They don't always appreciate the real dangers around these parts."

Duke knew the two sons well. "Mr. LeFleur, I don't think you need to worry about those two. They're tough as bison leather and can handle themselves well. Not to worry, sir."

***

They were both thinking it, but Benjamin spoke first. "What do you think, Greenwood?"

"About what?" Greenwood responded, knowing exactly what his brother meant. He focused on his rabbit skinning, not wanting to appear too anxious.

"The gold, of course. I say we look for it." Benjamin exposed his façade of older brother bravado perfectly.

Greenwood was game. "Well, we do know Bissell and the Walker's Crossroads area probably better than any other Choctaws. Choctaws and Chickasaws have hunted in every inch of that territory for many years. Benjamin, come to think of it that may not be too far from the Noxubee silver mine. I wonder if Mason ever stumbled upon the mine. That would be bad for us Choctaw. Our tribes have worked that silver mine for decades. Sure would hate for it to fall into a pirate's hands."

Benjamin was impressed. "So, brother, how do you know so much about the silver mine? Have you been there?"

"No, but Chief Mushulatubbee told me all about it when he was here at the Council House at a tribal meeting. The mine is in his Noxubee district and his tribe has mined a lot of silver from there. The Chief told me that there is a lot of concern about the US Government taking the mine from us. In Washington City, he told me, President Jefferson had lobbied for treaties to relocate our tribes out of our ancestral Mississippi homeland. I think President Madison is pushing for the same thing. Do you think that will ever happen? How could the government force us to leave? This is our home. We were here first. And now, the country is on the verge of a new war with the British. Major Donly told me that most Indian tribes are prepared to help the British. The Choctaws and Cherokees are still friends of the US Government. Father said that we cannot trust the British."

"Little Brother, you're sounding like a politician. What is Major Donly teaching you up there in Nashville? I thought he was just a government post rider."

"I've been under his tutelage for six months now, Benjamin. Yes, he is a post carrier, but he's a great teacher, too, especially when it comes to history and political science. The best part of his service is my tutor, his beautiful daughter Rosanna. Too bad that Father didn't send you away for schooling."

"I've learned all I need to know from our Choctaw brothers and from the land, Greenwood. Guess I don't share your hunger for education or your ambition. And how can you keep your thoughts on learning if your loins are always thinking about his daughter? Knowing you, my brother, I wouldn't be surprised if you become chief some day or maybe even president of the entire country! Now, let's get back to the gold. When do we leave?"

"I have only one month left before I return to the Donly's. I suggest first light tomorrow," said Greenwood. "We'll tell Father we're going hunting again."

"Agreed!"

They returned to their rabbit skinning and preparing the meat for their mother.

***

The morning sun was barely visible, filtering through the tall loblolly pines and assorted hardwoods of the Mississippi frontier when the LeFleur brothers bridled their painted colts and quietly rode off to the west and then north on the Old Road. Josiah had mentioned that Mason and his brigands were headed south to Natchez, so Benjamin and Greenwood felt confident that they would avoid trouble on their day-and-a-half ride to the Colbert stand at Walker's Crossroads near Bissell.

After a long day's ride, the summer sun dropped in the western skies and dusk settled on the deeply shaded trail. Benjamin looked at Greenwood and motioned for him to pull up.

"I think we need to camp for the night, little brother. We can start early tomorrow and be there before midday."

"Okay with me, Ben. Let's head down that side trail and find a clearing." He pulled the reins on his colt and trotted east. Benjamin followed just behind.

After a few hundred yards, Greenwood suddenly brought his mount to a quick stop. Benjamin's colt trotted up beside him and stopped also.

"Do you hear that? Greenwood asked. "Lot of voices booming from around the next bend in the path. I smell a fire, too. Let's tie up and go check it out."

"Okay, but I have an uneasy feeling about this. Let's not get too close," said Benjamin, the brave but suddenly now cautious one.

Their Choctaw heritage served them well when it came to stealth and trail knowledge. They approached the increasing sounds of shouting, banter, and laughter, and they stayed low, using trees and brambly brush for concealment. An opening was faintly visible in the darkening woods only fifty feet ahead, and both boys quickly fell prone on their bellies, remaining undetected.

In the clearing, a fire was popping and cracking with white smoke bellowing toward the clear, heavenly, early night sky. The men were standing around the fire that was fueled by green, unseasoned, and wet wood. They all held bottles likely filled with home-brewed whiskey frequently tipping the vessels to their lips and taking another generous gulp. The loud, raucous language suggested that all had consumed excessive quantities of their favorite spirits.

The brothers were frozen with caution in the bosky forest and dared not move or make any noise. They tried to listen and decide if the men were friend or foe before making another move.

The conversation from around the campfire was difficult for the brothers to follow and seemed to be more inebriated blatherskite than anything substantive. But when the words "gold" and "Wolfman" echoed back toward them, both lifted their heads slightly off the ground and pointed an ear, hoping to hear more. One of the men around the fire was detailing a location, but only Greenwood was able to clearly understand what he said.

The big, husky man said, "I told you to bury it two hundred north, one hundred west, then two hundred north, starting behind the northwest corner of George Colbert's tavern. Did you follow my orders exactly?"

Another man that Greenwood could not see answered. "Yes, sir, Mr. Mason. There was a huge white oak at that spot, so I dug the pit just behind the oak. Covered it with a large stone. No one will ever find it 'cept us, guaranteed. Just like at Little Sand Creek where I started at the northwest edge of the ridge."

It was now clearly apparent to both brothers. They had crept within fifty feet of the murderer Sam Mason and his band of thieves! The gang had not headed south to Natchez as Mr. Duke said.

Greenwood glanced over at his brother whose face was now etched in surprise and shock. The warnings from their father replayed in their minds as visions of their scalped heads floating in a nearby swamp helped quickly determine their next move. Still on their bellies, they slowly inched backward, exactly reversing their tracks, being careful not to make any noise or be discovered.

When they reached a tree line, which was more than 150 feet from the gang, they pushed upright to stand in the darkness, then turned and ran like hunted rabbits in the direction of their horses. Then, just as they reached sight of their tied painted mounts, two figures holding rifles stepped out of the heavy underbrush and stood directly in their path.

"Hold it right there, boys," growled the more ugsome-appearing of the bearded ruffians. "Where do you think you're going?"

Greenwood and Benjamin instantly froze as panic filled their minds and paralyzed their limbs. Ben's uneasy feeling was now their stark reality.

CHAPTER FIFTEEN
Treasure Hunters

Ben naively started to reach for the knife tucked in his belt but was quickly dissuaded when the two men aimed their rifles in his direction. There was no escape.

"You boys look like Choctaws or Chickasaws. You're not lost, I'm sure. You redskins don't get lost around these parts. You weren't spying on our camp were you, boys?" the grisly looking one asked.

Ben answered. "No, mister. We're Choctaws. We were just scouting for a place to camp for the night. We're headed north to hunt."

"Your English is pretty good, boy," the bandit observed. "*Issish iklanna*, half breed, I bet." He said it with disgust and spat on the ground.

"Yes sir, we are *itibapishi toba*. Our father is French-Canadian. Our mother is Choctaw. Missionaries taught us English. If it's okay, we'll be on our way. We did not mean to intrude on your camp." Benjamin took a step toward the colts.

Greenwood's tongue had gone mute. He could only stare wide eyed as his anxiety raced out of control. He was frozen with paralysis.

The bandit sneered back at both of them. "Not so fast, Frenchie-Choctaw boy. We need to see what our boss thinks about you two. Toss those knives out of your belts and turn around. Head back to the camp. No tricks.

The brothers did as ordered by the two gang members and walked back toward the flickering, popping fire in the distance.

The leader looked up when his men advanced toward the campfire with the two brothers just in front of rifles aimed at their backs.

"Looks like you two found some half-breed spies. What are going to do with them?" asked the leader commandingly. The gang of bandits around the fire laughed loudly and tipped their whiskey bottles a little skyward.

Their captor answered, "Mr. Mason, we brought them to you for you to decide." Mason made all decisions for the gang.

Benjamin spoke in a pleading voice. "Please, mister. We're just headed north to hunt and were looking for a place to camp for the night. We don't want any trouble. Just let us go and we'll forget we saw you and your camp. We have nothing, just our small horses, our hunting rifles, and knives, and a small amount of food and water. Take it all if you like. We just want to get back on our journey."

"Sorry, boys. Samuel 'Wolfman' Mason don't take no chances going up and down the Natchez Road. You two just happen to be in the wrong place at the wrong time. Your journey ends here."

He looked toward their bearded captor. "Tie them to a tree somewhere in the woods away from here and smear some sorghum and blood on them. I suspect by morning the flesh and muscles will all be chewed off their spying half-breed bones. Get to it!"

Two of the brigands grabbed the LeFleur brothers by their arms and pulled them away from the campsite and into the dense, dark grove of trees and thick brush, while a third man followed with a rifle pointed at the boys. About a quarter of a mile away they found two trees close together in a small opening and tied Ben and Greenwood securely to the tree trunks with leather bindings that had been stripped from bison hide. They gagged their mouths with filthy, smelly pieces of ragged remnants of handkerchiefs and then made shallow cuts in their forearms with a Bowie knife, just deep enough to draw a small flow of blood. One of the louts smeared the blood across their faces, covering cheeks and forehead completely. "War paint," he said as he laughed. The third man that had held the pointed rifle dropped it when the boys were safely secured to the trees. He reached and retrieved a small bottle of sorghum syrup from his back trouser pocket. He grinned as he slowly poured a stream of the thick, sticky syrup over their heads and then splashed some on their shirts and pants. The three men stepped back and laughed at the horrified look on the brothers' faces.

"Nice meeting you, Injun boys. Have a nice trip to your happy hunting grounds!" The three laughed again, turned, and disappeared toward Sam Mason and the rest of his gang into the dark, moonless night.

***

Benjamin and Greenwood looked at each other and realized that the ogres of fear and helplessness had grimly suffocated the usual courage and determination, which they had inherited from their Choctaw mother. Their father's warning had gone unheeded, and now they faced a challenge to survive that they could have never imagined. Bound, gagged, and dressed as fresh bait for predators in the remote Mississippi wilderness, the brothers searched their souls for hope and their unseasoned minds for a means of escape.

Greenwood struggled with the leather bindings that anchored his arms and hands tied behind the tree and began to feel a bit of looseness. His hands were small with slender fingers, and the sweat and blood from his arms had trickled down and moistened his hands. Ben noticed that his younger brother was working with focused resolve to loosen his bindings. He had tried to do the same but found that his restraints were so tight that restricted blood circulation had numbed both of his large hands. Any further movement seemed to only tighten the leather straps more. His upper arms throbbed with sharp pains with each heartbeat when he made any effort to loosen himself.

Minutes turned into hours as Ben and Greenwood saw chances of survival spiraling further and further to a slow but certain death. A surreal quietude had descended on the remote wilderness, broken only by the occasional muted, heavy breathing of the brothers as they struggled to free themselves but now drained of strength and near exhaustion. Greenwood had made minimal progress in working his hands free when the eerie stillness of the night surrendered to sounds of something or someone approaching. Snapping and cracking sounds of twigs and small tree limbs breaking were commingled with the softer rustling sounds of footsteps treading on the leafy floor of the forest. The brothers looked at each other with renewed fear competing rapidly with anxious anticipation. Greenwood felt a terror-induced rush of rejuvenated energy and feverishly fought the leather ties, knowing that their precious time was running out.

Then, the dim and stark darkness of the calm, dense woods revealed the intruders. Two very large adult wolves appeared in the small clearing and slowly approached their defenseless prey with cautious curiosity. To the tree-bound brothers, the wolves were the *Shampes* (giant monsters of the woods greatly feared by the Choctaws). The scent of fresh blood and strong sorghum sweetness had lured the ravenous predators to an inviting and easy meal.

The wild beasts inched closer and closer to Ben, ignoring Greenwood for the moment. Both wolves drooled and snarled, showing their razor-sharp incisors as Ben writhed and tried to move against his tight bison bindings. One beast came breath-to-breath with Ben's face and began to lick and taste the sweet syrup and blood. He instinctively retreated back a few steps when Ben shook his head from side to side, hoping to discourage the next step. The wolves sensed the vulnerability of their prey and both stepped toward Ben, revealing a gaping maw of glistening, wet teeth bared and ready to sink into the exposed neck.

At that exact instant, Greenwood suddenly felt his hands slip free from the sweaty, leather straps. He saw the beasts with open mouths spiked with fanged, saliva-coated teeth targeting his brother's neck. As he brought his arms around to his face, he threw his foul-tasting mouth gag to the ground and screamed loudly in Choctaw at the hungry, drooling animals.

"Issa! Issa! Kucha Nashoba! Issa, Issa!" Then, he began to yip repeatedly in a high, shrill cry that both wolves and coyotes understand. He yipped again, this time louder and even shriller. *"Issa, Issa!!*

The two wolves stopped their advance and looked with some confusion at Greenwood who was now flailing his arms wildly and continuing his wolf-like yips. He quickly leaned to the ground and picked up a small broken tree limb and sailed it spear-like at the beasts, scoring a direct hit between the eyes of the wolf closest to Ben. Both wolves jumped to one side and immediately backed up several steps, then turned and retreated into the dark underbrush. Greenwood scrambled to untie the bindings around his legs, knowing that the predators would likely return after regrouping. He was surprised that only two wolves had shown themselves, remembering that they typically travelled in packs of six. He hurried to release Benjamin, who stood and embraced his brother with a manly hug.

"*Yakoke*, thank you, my brother," said Benjamin, still reeling from the shocking reality of his frightening brush with being ripped and torn into bloody pieces of flesh by the wolves. He was impressed with Greenwood's timely yipping that had stalled the attack on him. "Let's get out of here before *Shampe* returns!"

The young Choctaws sprinted into the woods in the opposite direction of the wolves retreat, knowing that the dangers of the unchartered wilderness could still be just one step out of the bleak, hostile darkness.

***

Ben and Greenwood discovered quickly that advancing through the forest growth that had been thickened from the unusually heavy summer rains was challenging, and they were worried that the beasts may be tracking them. They had intentionally moved away from the Mason camp and the dangers of a second capture. Ben told Greenwood that he thought they were headed in the direction of the Old Road but was not certain. They pushed their way through the thickets and underbrush as the late night wore on and began to echo early dawn aubades of aroused, warbling song birds. Anticipating a new day, the sun, still below the horizon, began to faintly lighten the early morning sky in the east and obscure the starry heavens.

They stopped for a moment to be sure there were no sounds save their own footsteps rustling through the thick brushwood. Then, as they were about to resume their escape from the harrowing nightmare back near Mason's camp, they heard familiar sounds of a trotting horse. They must be near the Natchez Road or another trail, Ben said to Greenwood. But, who was approaching? Had Mason and his gang caught up with them? They had outsmarted the wolves, but had they been followed by the brigands? The brothers dropped to their knees and halted in their tracks as they held their breath.

The horseman and his galumphing horse came closer and closer. The sounds stopped. Ben and Greenwood pressed down almost prone in the brush and could barely see the horse and its now dismounted rider through a slit-like opening between the trees. Suddenly, the face of the horseman was highlighted by a narrow ray of the rising sun filtering through the trees. Ben, with eyes widened, stood.

"*Aki! Aki!* Father! Father!" Over here. We're over here!" Louis LeFleur had found his sons.

***

Louis embraced his sons but did not speak at first. His anger over their disobedience was muffled by his relief and discovery of their safe being. Riding on his chestnut mare, he finally spoke as they walked behind him.

"From the filth of blood and a strange odor of sweetness on your faces and clothes, I can only guess that you were prisoners of someone who threw you to the vultures for your bones to be picked bare. We will discuss this later. For punishment, I should make you two walk back to the stand. You need to spend the time thinking about your poor decision."

The brothers looked at each other with shame and the dread of a long walk home.

LeFleur continued, "But, I found your colts on the Old Road headed home. I could only assume that you were dead or in serious trouble. God has mercifully granted you more time. You have lived to be tested another day. Wisdom has eluded you. In time, you will learn to tame your youthful temptations."

The brothers again looked at each other and knew that they would be given additional chores when they returned home, but they also knew that their father was a just man. The ordeal alone had been sufficient punishment. They were hungry and dry-mouthed and had not dared ask Louis to slake their thirst. They wondered how long it would be before their father would stop and let them rest. They were a full day's journey from home by horseback. On foot, it was much longer. By midday, they finally saw their horses a short distance down the trail. Louis had tied them to a tree and was surprised that they had not run off. Ben and Greenwood ran ahead of their father's mount and untied their colts.

They both smiled broadly at Louis as he climbed down and smiled back at them.

"You brothers need a rest. Sit down. You need *oka*." He handed his leather water pouch to Benjamin who took two gulps of water and handed it to Greenwood. Finally, they both felt a warm surge of thankfulness and relief. They would be safely back home by dusk.

The next day back at Frenchman's Camp, as they attacked their extra chores, Greenwood and Benjamin did not talk a lot about their terrifying night at the hands of Sam Mason and his brigands. Embarrassment and Choctaw pride overruled any temptation to relive the details or even brag about their fortuitous escape. God had protected them, they told each other. Youthful excitement and curiosity over undiscovered treasures had not come without a price. They had been impetuous and had learned hard lessons from the dangerous, forbidden frontier. Any idea of finding Mason's hidden gold was now only a fleeting and whimsical thought, at least for Benjamin. But, Greenwood had overheard the land pirates' secret. He would protect it, for now, until the right moment. No one but him must know.

***

One month later Greenwood left Frenchman's Camp to return to his studies under Major Donly in Nashville, a service that would extend over the next five years. The nightmare of having been captured and then tossed out as fresh bait for predators by the Natchez Road's most notorious bandit now behind him, Greenwood was anxious to return to Nashville and see Donly's youngest daughter Rosanna again—he preferred to call her Rosa. He had become captivated by her youthful beauty, which contradicted her tomboyish zeal, and she seemed to have developed an infatuation and fondness for him also. They were much too young to understand love, the Major had told him. Just enjoy your childhood and friendship, he said. And, please, he added, control your desires and keep your hands in your pockets! Greenwood was convinced that someday he would marry Rosa.

The stagecoach left the stand at Frenchman's Camp early in the humid, awakening morning air and turned onto the Old Natchez Road headed north. The journey always took three and one half days, and Greenwood settled back on the uncomfortable pinewood bench seat, dreading the pounding that was to follow. The Old Road was notorious for pot holes, large tree roots, mud holes, and jaw-snapping bumps from washed-out ruts, and he tried to brace his feet against the opposing seat base to help absorb the unpredictable bounces and jolts that were sure to come. He was alone in the coach compartment, and topside a shotgun-carrying guard sat beside the driver who whipped the two horses to their task of covering one third of the three hundred-plus mile journey to Nashville before dusk. Greenwood hated frontier stage coaches and vowed that someday he would own a luxurious carriage that would be the envy of any traveler. He closed his eyes and imagined soft, overstuffed seat cushions that would pad his heavy body. *Yes,* he thought, *someday I'll own that carriage.*

Greenwood felt more secure on his trip home with the armed guard, who his father had hired, beside the driver. But, anxiety crept in when the coach neared the area where he and Ben had ventured off the Old Road and stumbled upon the Mason gang. Surely, he thought, they were long gone and hopefully not hiding in the ghostly shadows of the dense groves of pine and hardwood trees that lined the trail, poised to savagely ambush another stage coach with travelers that were bold enough to risk the adventure. Greenwood had also brought his loaded rifle with him and would not be afraid to shoot at any threat. He prayed that God would protect him.

After brief stops at three stands along the Natchez Road, Greenwood had been joined in the coach at Tockshish's Stand by a twenty-five to thirtyish-looking man who was also travelling to Tennessee. He said that he was a simple frontiersman from Lincoln County, Tennessee, and had been down in Natchez doing some trading. He had traded his horse for a few gold pieces and decided to make it back to Tennessee by coach. He had stayed at the last stand for a few days doing some hunting before resuming his return home to his wife Polly and his two sons John and William. He said that he, like many other frontiersmen, planned to join the Tennessee militia under General Jackson when he returned home.

Greenwood was entertained for the rest of his trip by the tall, lanky man dressed in leather hunting attire and who was a rather witty raconteur with captivating tales of East Tennessee (his birthplace and where he was raised), bear fighting and other hair-raising adventures that he spiced with colorful backwoods language. Greenwood laughed at his story of playing hooky from school after getting into a scuffle with a classmate. He said that his father wanted to whip him but couldn't catch him. He was swift afoot and outran his father. Never got the whipping, he said, but he had to run away from home. Greenwood thought to himself that with his gift of gab the man would make a good statesman or politician.

"I'm doing all the chatting. Tell me about yourself," the storyteller said. "I would guess you'd be part Indian. Choctaw?"

"Yes. I am part Choctaw, part French-Canadian. My name is Greenwood LeFleur. My father is Louis LeFleur. He operates the stand at Frenchman's Camp back down the Road. I am on my way back to Nashville to continue my schooling under Major John Donly."

"Well, if that ain't a coincidence. I spent the night at your father's stand once. My father also had a tavern and inn on a stagecoach route up near Morristown, Tennessee. Now, I want you to understand, son. I have absolutely nothing against Indians. And, from all I have heard, you Choctaws are easygoing, peace-loving folks. I could be a bitter man when it comes to Indians. My grandparents were attacked and killed in their home by some renegade Creeks and Chickamauga Cherokees back in Rogersville back in '77. My father said it was a savage chief who called himself Dragging Canoe that led the massacre. Dragging Canoe wounded my uncle Joseph and took my Uncle James hostage. Uncle James spent seventeen years as a Creek prisoner. He came home when I was eight. My father was the lucky one—he was off serving in the Rifleman's Militia.

If he had been killed by the Creeks, I would never have been born. Odd how things work out, you know. Not that I'll ever leave any mark on history or anything.

"I have always had a soft spot in my soul for poor settlers and native Indians who have been tread upon by the government's liberal use of land grants. Someday, I'd like to be a land manager. I think President Madison and even Jefferson have been pushing for removal of tribes like yours to Western lands. Can't say that I agree with them. I never liked big government stepping on the little man. Just ain't right. And I can tell you right now, if General Jackson ever gets to be President, God help the Indians!"

Greenwood was fully engaged in his fellow passenger's ramblings. It was exactly what Major Donly had been teaching him. If his new acquaintance was not a politician, he certainly should be. The stranger's tales had helped disguise the monotony of the trip. He had forgotten to ask his name.

"Mister, I may be only twelve years old, but I have a very strong feeling that one day you'll do some important things for this country. I think you'll be famous, but I do not know your name."

"Sorry, young Greenwood. Got so wrapped up in those yarns from my mountain days as a boy, I forgot to mention my name. David Stern Crockett, at your service, Mr. LeFleur." He reached and gripped Greenwood's hand firmly. "Friends just call me Davy. It was nice meeting such a bright and promising Choctaw. I have a feeling also. I think someday you will do your Choctaw tribe proud. You seem to be a very determined and confident boy. Let me share with you my most favorite bit of advice. It goes like this: 'Always be sure you are right, then go ahead.' Another way of saying that is simply to just let your heart be your compass and you can't go wrong. That's my half-a-penny's worth—it has kept me an honest man. If your heart says you're right, you can't go wrong. Good luck, young man."

***

A curtain of evening twilight was falling on the sparsely settled countryside of the northeastern Mississippi Territory where densely forested trails surrendered to gentle, rolling fields with assorted crops that were planted, tended, and harvested by the local Chickasaw tribesmen. The next stand at George Colbert's Tavern was barely visible to Greenwood in the ghostly crepuscule far across an empty, unplanted field. He was weary from the ten-hour trip and anxious to eat, refresh himself, and find a cot at the inn for a welcomed night's rest. He had remembered that Saleechie Colbert was known for her hearty wild game cooking, especially deer and bear meat, but yearned for a taste of her roasted wild boar. He told Mr. Crockett who said that he had also enjoyed Mrs. Colbert's cooking on previous stops at Colbert's. They both eagerly anticipated their next stop along the Old Natchez Road.

After enjoying Mrs. Colbert's savory dishes and her gracious hospitality, Greenwood was preparing to excuse himself from Crockett's company and find a cot to bed down upstairs for the night when they were approached by a tall, imposing stranger with shoulder-length black hair. The muscular man was fair-skinned but with his high cheek bones, square forehead, and dark penetrating eyes, Greenwood felt certain that the man was at least part Indian.

He stopped near their table and extended his hand to Crockett.

"I heard you were here, Mr. Crockett. Someone told me that you are interested in joining the Tennessee militia under General Jackson. Allow me to introduce myself—Colonel George Colbert. I am Chief Tootemastubbe to my Chickasaw brothers. I am the co proprietor of this tavern. My brother James does most of the work around here. I see you've been rewarded with some of my wife's, Saleechie's, best cooking."

David Crockett stood and shook hands with the tavern owner.

"Very nice to make your acquaintance, Colonel. Your reputation precedes you, sir. I am aware of your service with General Washington in the Revolution, and I assume that your commission was one of *your* tributes."

"Well, yes. You're correct. But, I wanted to tell you that I have also served with General Jackson in some of the recent Creek wars. Jackson is a born leader, truly destined for greatness. I heartily agree with your desire to enlist in his militia. He can use more good Tennesseans."

"I have something to confess to you, Colonel," said Crockett. "You may not remember me from my use of your ferry service across the Tennessee River. I've traveled up and down the Old Road a number of times. I must say that crossing the rapid currents of the Tennessee River is hands down the toughest, indeed, most treacherous part of the journey. Your ferry has made it considerably less challenging, but, frankly, sir, your transit fee is too high for the average traveler. You must have forgotten my violent and loud protest the last time I crossed. Or perhaps, everyone protests the Ferryman's fees, so they all run together." Crockett laughed.

"Anyway, Colonel, you are quite the businessman. Just look at your tavern here—quite the success. Hearty food, rest, beautiful Indian women to entertain lonely frontiersmen. I trust Mrs. Colbert's food charges are more reasonable than your ferry fees." He grinned and slapped the Indian chief on the back.

Tootemastubbe was not amused. He turned and looked at Greenwood.

"So, who's your young traveling companion, Crockett?" asked Colbert. He extended his hand, gripped the young man's hand tightly, and squeezed.

"I'm Greenwood LeFleur, Chief Tootemastubbe. I'm headed back to Nashville to resume my studies with Major John Donly."

"LeFleur?" said Colbert. "Then you must be one of Louis LeFleur's sons down at the stand at Frenchman's Camp. I heard he has several young Choctaw warrior sons. I met him once at a council meeting at Pontotoc Creek. You look fit, boy. Can't be tough enough if you're going to ride up and down the Natchez Road. I hear the highwaymen are unusually active these days and more ruthless than ever. Wolfman Mason stopped here recently. Son of the Devil, for sure. My advice: stay as far away from him as you can. Indians aren't the only ones who scalp their victims. Good luck to you, Greenwood. My respects to Major Donly when you get to Nashville. He and I go way back."

"Thank you, sir. I'll do that," said Greenwood who was now staring at a beautiful nine-inch dirk dagger hanging from Colbert's belt. It had a Gaelic twist knot handle and a large, deep-blue ruby gemstone adorning the end of the handle. Greenwood couldn't take his eyes off of the shiny, black, hard scabbard with silver finished trim in which the dagger rested. He thought it odd that a Chickasaw chief carried such a magnificent Scotsman knife.

Colbert saw the youngster's keen interest in his dagger. He slid it out of the scabbard and handed it to Greenwood.

"Go, ahead, LeFleur. Check it out. It belonged to my father. He was a bonafide Scot. Came over here to America in 1736 on the *Prince of Wales* to find a better life. He settled in the Carolinas but eventually married into the Chickasaw tribe. He lived with Chickasaws so long, I think he thought of himself as more Chickasaw than Scot; but, he had this authentic Gaelic Celtic dirk that was his favorite knife. Any Scot worth his bitters always carried a dirk. It's saved me more than once from a scoundrel or two trying to outsmart me. Sharp edge. Be careful.

"Crockett will appreciate this—I defended myself once from none other than General Andrew Jackson himself with this dagger. Jackson was, dare I say, a little upset with my fee of seventy-five thousand dollars to ferry his two thousand man militia across the Tennessee at my landing last year. He lashed at me with his sword when I refused to back off of my fee. I dodged and he only managed to notch a groove into one of the black walnut columns on my stand's porch. He backed away when I pulled this dirk and threatened to fling it at him. We both had a good laugh afterward. By the way, I never got full payment from Jackson."

Greenwood wondered silently if the chief was serious or just another clever yarn spinner like Crockett. He inspected the beautiful knife and smiled with envy at such a show piece. He slowly handed it back to Colbert. The chief took it and reset it into the black scabbard. He looked up at the wide-eyed LeFleur and smiled back at him. He unfastened the scabbard from his belt, took Greenwood by the hand and placed the dagger in his palm.

"This is my gift to you, Mr. LeFleur. Guard it with honor and remember your Chickasaw cousins. We were not always friends, you know, but now, together, our peace-loving tribes will prosper. Make your tribe proud of you, my boy."

Greenwood did not know what to say. He stammered, "But. Sir, I can't, uh, uh. Thank you, Chief. I will guard and protect it forever. You are much too kind to me."

"You looked very tired, Mr. LeFleur. I suggest you find an empty cot upstairs before these ruffians here grab them all. Good night. Peace and perpetual happiness to you and to you, too, Mr. Crockett."

He turned and walked out of the tavern and into the still, dark night.

Greenwood walked away staring at and admiring the chief's gift. He had *already* found a treasure.

He found an empty cot in the single room on the second floor of the clapboard siding stand and tavern. As he closed his tired eyes, he was barely aware of the raucous laughter and music from the rowdy, drinking travelers in the tavern below him. He became keenly aware of his sore muscles and joints that had been pounded by the repetitive bouncing and shaking of the old stage coach. He clutched his gift close to his chest, and he thought again of his dream carriage as he drifted quickly into a welcomed sleep.

Greenwood awoke suddenly from a deep slumber sometime after midnight and looked around the dark room. He could faintly see Mr. Crockett, the coach driver, and the guard on cots nearby. An out-of-tune symphony of abrasive, very loud snoring from all three filled the small room. Greenwood slowly and quietly sat up on his cot. He knew that this night might be his only chance to search for Mason's gold. He had not even thought of what he would do if he found it. First things first. He thought of Mr. Crockett's advice. He was not sure of how right he was, but he knew that he was being drawn outside by a force that he could not control. Tucking the dirk into the front of his belt, he silently tiptoed down the stairs and slipped out of the inn into the forbidden hours of darkness. He found a lantern by a small shed near the tavern. He lit it and nervously searched the shed, finding a small shovel leaning against the wall with several other tools.

He had burned the details of the gold's burial site into his memory and started at the left rear corner of the tavern. He could only hope that his steps matched closely the brigand that had hidden the treasure. Two hundred north, one hundred west, two hundred north. He counted silently to himself. The steps led him across an empty field and then into a thick grove of pines and hardwoods. He now stood in front of a very large white oak tree. His chest pounded with anticipation as he turned and looked back through the dense grove of trees that were shrouded in a sinister calm. No other sounds were audible above his lubb-dubbing, palpitating heart.

He circled the large oak and looked down at a very large round stone that rested slightly against the base of the tree. It was just as the bandit described and the site appeared undisturbed. With some effort, he rolled the large rock to one side and began to dig. He had exceptional strength for a twelve year old but did not need it as the dirt was quite loose and easy to scoop and toss aside. Within ten minutes he had evacuated a generous pit almost two feet deep and wide. It was an empty cavity. He began to sense that the treasure was gone or never there in the first place. He was too late, he guessed.

He stopped and began to imagine the evil murders and mutilations of innocent travelers that the stolen spoils might represent. Mr. Crockett's words echoed hauntingly in his head. Was he right? Was he wrong? What was he doing? Suddenly, the fear of discovery enveloped him like a trapped animal covered by a heavy, weighted net. He felt the need to turn and run away from the shallow pit. Was he digging his own grave? He forcefully thrust the shovel into the hole in full surrender. Before he could turn, he heard the sound of the shovel ricocheting and clinking against metal. He stiffened for an instant, then reached down into the hole and grabbed the shovel. He drove it back into the hole and heard the metallic clink again. His mind reeled with anticipation as he frantically dug deeper and deeper, exposing the surface of a large metal box. It was there. He had discovered Sam Mason's treasure!

Greenwood was able to shovel and loosen the dirt from around the metal chest within several minutes and noted handles on each end. If filled with gold, it would be very heavy. He lay prone over his freshly dug crater and firmly gripped the handles. As strong as he was, he could not lift the metal box. He tried again but could not budge the chest from its earthen pit. He collapsed back to the ground with his arms dangling down into the cavity. So close but now with no hope of raising the heavy spoils. Then, he suddenly heard the soft rustling of footsteps approaching. He stiffened again and held his breath.

"Need some help, Greenwood?"

Greenwood turned his head and looked up with surprise and the sudden feeling of the fox being caught in the hen house. It was Davy Crockett who was now standing beside him peering down into the shallow hole.

"Looks like you dug up a buried treasure chest or something. Here, let me help." Crockett fell to his knees and leaned into Greenwood's freshly dug hollow.

"I'll grab this handle and you get the other one."

Greenwood did as his travelling friend suggested. They both strained and grunted, and soon the chest began to slowly rise from its secret tomb. With a final heave, the heavy box was hoisted up and out of the pit, and they sat it on the dirt piled next to the hole. Sitting back on the bare ground with his legs crossed, Crockett smiled without judgment at Greenwood.

Crockett raised the lid of the chest and looked at the incredulous Choctaw whose wide black eyes were fixed on the contents of the chest.

"I guess I underestimated your resourcefulness, Mr. LeFleur. I won't ask how you discovered the whereabouts of a buried treasure, but it sure looks like you have someone else's cache here. Correct?"

Greenwood was still staring at the chest full of gold and silver coins and jewelry and didn't really know how to explain his shared secret. Maybe the truth would work, he thought.

"It's a very long story, Mr. Crockett, but I'll give it a try."

He went on to explain his bold adventure with his brother as they set out to look for the infamous pirate Samuel Mason's buried treasure rumored to be in the area of Colbert's Tavern, and how he had overheard the location of a hoard of gold, then how he and Ben were captured by the brigands but had escaped and miraculously lived to look for treasures another day. Crockett listened with admiration when Greenwood described how he bravely drove off the attacking wolves.

"Quite a yarn, young man. So, tell me. What are your intentions with this cache here? You know where all of this came from, right?"

His conscience was twitching noticeably as he answered.

"Yes sir. I know. It's blood gold."

Crockett stood and looked at the kneeling Greenwood. As he turned to leave, he said, "I know you'll do what is right. Remember—first, be sure you're right, then go ahead."

He disappeared with barely a sound back into the pitch black, late night Mississippi forest and headed back in the direction of the tavern.

***

Two days later Greenwood LeFleur arrived at Joslin's Stand on the Natchez Road near Nashville where he was met by the Major and young Rosa Donly. Greenwood and Rosa locked eyes and smiled affectionately at each other.

"Welcome back, Greenwood," said the Major, very sincerely. "Hope you enjoyed your break from your studies. I'll get your bag. You can give us a full accounting of your summer on the way home. Time to get back to schooling. Rosa, show Greenwood where the buggy is tied up."

As they walked to the buggy, Greenwood debated silently with himself on where he would start with his accounting of his summer adventures. He wondered, with a touch of sadness, if he would ever see Davy Crockett again. But, without any doubt he knew his secret would be safe.

***

Twenty years later...

Manuel Sanz, far removed from his roots in La Guairá, Venezuela, had become an entrusted servant of the Choctaw's great chief two years after the Dancing Rabbit Creek Treaty was signed in 1830. Leflore assured him that he would be rewarded with a permanent home and a land plot of his choosing on the estate if he succeeded in his dangerous assignment. The chief had not forgotten his harrowing experiences as an adventuresome twelve-year-old boy and had vowed to himself and to God to never fall prey to evil temptations again. He needed Manuel to follow his directions carefully and evade any attempts that might force him to reveal the truth. Leflore had made Manuel rehearse the script ten times, a script that he finally memorized and was to use if stopped or questioned.

Manuel and his companion, a bulky and muscular slave named Jefferson Campbell, were hopeful as they neared Frenchman's Camp on the Old Road. It was their second and longest journey in the past month that had been necessary to complete Leflore's instructions. Their task was growing a little closer to completion when two horsemen suddenly appeared on the narrow road in front of their wagon. One fired a rifle shot into the sky of the vanishing daylight.

"Pull up there, you two!" one of the men shouted, pointing a rifle at Manuel and Jefferson.

Manuel commanded, "Whoa, mules. Whoa!" He pulled the four-mule drawn wagon to a gradual stop.

"What're you two slaves doing in these parts? You've wandered away from the cotton fields. Running from your master I would guess."

"Oh, no, sir," answered Manuel. "I'm a freed man from South America. Have my papers with me to prove it. My friend and I work on the Greenwood Leflore plantation over near Carrollton."

"So what's in the wagon that requires four mules to pull it?" asked the man who was still pointing his rifle their way.

"We had to haul a heavy load of cotton bales down to LeFleur's Bluff. Needed the mules for that. Then, we picked up the bodies of some of

Colonel Leflore's Choctaw relatives that did not move to the Oklahoma territory. They were stricken with the pox and died. The Colonel wanted them brought home so he could give them a proper burial on his own land. Eight poor souls back there in the wagon."

"You don't say," quipped the rifleman. "I think I'd better have a look for myself." He dismounted and began to walk to the rear of the wagon.

Manuel was ready.

"Mister, I don't know if you've ever been around the pox. It behaves like the plague sometimes. Can spread like a wild fire dancing in a dry forest. The doctors down in Jackson told me and Jefferson here to handle these coffins as if they are full of the most deadly poisonous snakes in the world. They said that we should not open them for *any* reason or we'd most certainly get the pox. They're going straight to their graves. I just thought you ought to know that, mister."

The rifle-toting highwayman had already climbed up on the wagon and was studying the eight pine wood coffins, which were stacked two high and four across. Choctaw names and skulls and crossbones were inscribed on each coffin, and each said "Danger! Smallpox. Do NOT Open!"

The stranger stared at Manuel's cargo.

"So, why didn't you just burn these heathen bodies?" he asked.

"Oh, no, sir. The Choctaws don't permit that," responded Manuel.

The stranger looked up at his sidekick who had backed his horse away from the wagon but continued to train his rifle on Manuel and Jefferson. The leader slowly climbed down from the wagon and then quickly remounted his horse. Both of the highwaymen turned their mounts and galloped off like 'scalded ticks jumping off a coon dog's back,' as

Jefferson recounted it later to Leflore. They didn't look back as they raced their steeds across an empty field and disappeared into the twilight forest.

Manuel looked at Jefferson and smiled with extreme satisfaction.

"The Colonel is a very smart man. He was right. The fear of the pox turns the bravest jackal into a panicky field mouse.

"Jefferson, let's keep going. Get up, mules!" he shouted as he flicked the leather reins. "We'll stay the night at Frenchman's Camp."

"The Colonel will be most pleased when we get back to the Big Sandy Place. Our secret will never be discovered. Never."

Part Three

CHAPTER SIXTEEN
Return to French Camp

1998

Phineus Blount welcomed his Georgia guest into the French Camp Carriage House and directed him to his office behind the showroom that displayed the well-preserved grand carriage owned by the famous Choctaw Chief Leflore.

"Very kind of you to drive over from Georgia, Mr. Prospero. Travelling without Ms. Colton, I see. Hope she is well."

He continued before Jasen could respond. "I *thought* you might be interested in more Greenwood Leflore intrigue. Guess I was correct. Anyway, I think I mentioned to you that I found a very interesting note amongst the secret memoirs left by the late chief, but I'm not really sure what it means. You seem to have a knack for understanding how Leflore thought. So, are you game?"

"Yes, of course, Mr. Blount," Jasen responded. "But, I've already seen the page. You may not believe how that happened." He wasn't completely comfortable with Phineus Blount's story about the carriage house break-in. How did the page end up in Jake Luther's possession? How did Luther and his associates even know about Jasen's and Jade's first visit to French Camp? Something didn't add up. He decided to be vague about how the page fell into his possession.

"It's a long story, Mr. Blount, but someone else wanted to employ my alleged 'talents' at decoding secret messages. It's complicated but suffice it to say, I have in my custody the copy that was apparently stolen from your files. Small world, I guess."

"That's strangely coincidental, wouldn't you say? Blount remarked, quite casually. He smiled at Jasen. "So, have you decoded it yet or do you have any idea what it means?"

Jasen wasn't going to reveal anything until he had concluded that Blount was really who he said he was. If the night had a thousand eyes, the recently deceased Jake Luther had a thousand spies. He remembered Marcus Bianco's basic investigative strategy: share minimally and trust no one.

Jasen decided to share minimally with caution. "Best I can make out is that the note was part of some kind of diary or log that Leflore kept. Why he hid this particular page and not the entire log is intriguing. Obviously, there's something here that he did not want to share with anyone, including his heirs. Personally, I think Leflore truly thought that the secrets he had hidden away in that damn rooster would never see the light of day. I also think he thought that if, by chance, the secrets under the driver Mr. Cross's seat *were* discovered, it would be because of God's divine plan.

"The Chief was a very religious man. Call it redemption for his past sins or whatever history might want to record; I think he went to his grave protecting something that had a very profound effect on his life. That's about all I can say right now, Mr. Blount. I'm working on another theory, but I'm not ready to conclude anything more." He was lying. In addition, he was getting a gnawing feeling in his gut that his alter ego Ethan McCoy needed to extend his secret investigation to French Camp.

"Very interesting deductions, Mr. Prospero," said Blount. "I'm sure that you understand that my interest is purely for the historical significance of these priceless memoirs. I have a close relationship with the Mississippi

Historical Society and with the Mississippi Band of Choctaws. You *do* understand, correct?"

"Indeed, Mr. Blount. Indeed, I do." He hesitated to ask but decided to go for it anyway. "Out of curiosity, you don't happen to know anyone over in Greenwood, do you?"

"Why, no, I don't. Why do you ask?" Blount said with no hint of deceit.

"Just curious, that's all. Before I go, is there anything else that you discovered in those memoirs that might tie to this mysterious page?"

"No, I'm afraid not. Just the one odd note that had nothing to do with Leflore's accounting of the Rabbit Creek treaty signing. I *do* hope you can shed some light on this mystery, Mr. Prospero."

"Yes, well, I'll let you know, Mr. Blount. It was very nice seeing you again." As he turned to go, he stopped, turned back, and looked at the old man. "By the way, I would assume that you have put all of the valuable documents in a more secure place now, yes?"

"But of course, Mr. Prospero. But of course." He walked to the door and watched Jasen drive off, then picked up the phone and dialed.

CHAPTER SEVENTEEN

Strength in Numbers

FBI Regional Field Office
Atlanta

"**P**lease, come on in, Jasen," said Agent Keys as she directed him into her office. "Jade is not with you?"

"No," responded Jasen. "She's catching up on her work and sorting out a few things in her mind."

"Oh, I see. Well, I did as you requested, Jasen, and asked Mr. Bianco and Mr. Malone to fly in from Jackson. They should be here any minute now. It'll be nice to see those two again, especially Marcus," she said with a hint of a smile.

"Excuse me? responded a curious Jasen.

"Oh, nothing. They're just my kind of people." She looked away before Jasen could read her face. "May I offer you something to drink while we're waiting?"

"Yes, thanks. Maybe a bottle of cold water."

"You've got it. I'll be right back."

Jasen smiled to himself, amused by Elizabeth's apparent interest in Bianco. He knew she was single but wondered if she realized that Marcus was happily married to a physician back in Jackson. At least, he *assumed* the marriage was sound. He hadn't discussed the detective's personal life that much with him.

It was still unimaginable to him that both Marcus and his wife had been involved in Jake's Luther's near death experience at the hands of Jade back in 1961. Marcus's words at their first meeting echoed in his head: *I don't believe in coincidence. Everything happens for a reason.* It was the same thing that Jake told Jade just before he died. He fleetingly wondered if he and Jade would have still met even if he had not become her neighbor. He shook his head vigorously trying to expel his existential rambling thoughts.

"Here you go, Jasen," said Elizabeth, handing him the water. "The receptionist just told me that Marcus and Danny are on their way up. Care to give me a head start on what this is all about?"

"If you don't mind, I'd like to go over this just once. It's a little complicated. Let's just say that I think it's time that we join forces—strength in numbers, so-to-speak."

Elizabeth looked confused, as she thought they already had joined forces, but she would wait and hear the rest when he was ready.

The receptionist escorted the two detectives into Elizabeth's office, and everyone exchanged greetings and handshakes. Jasen was silently amused when Marcus greeted Elizabeth. Her face lit up with a broad smile when he gave her a firm hug and said, "Liz, how are you?" Danny smiled and looked away with raised brows but said nothing.

Marcus took control and said, "Okay, the gang's all here. Somebody clue me in. Jasen, I think you asked for this meeting. We're all ears."

Jasen looked at them, as they leaned forward in their chairs in anticipation. He took in a deep breath.

"Let me begin by saying that what I am about to share with you is top secret, highly confidential—need to know only. I am taking some risk in doing this, but it's time we all know the same thing. This entire Jake Luther ordeal is a lot more complicated than I have told you. Jake and his organization have had *double* motives for their relentless pursuit of me and Jade. And, I have a *double* identity. I am more than a simple college professor who got caught up in a tangled web of KKK revenge against a mother and her daughter who just happened to be my neighbor."

Elizabeth raised her hand to her mouth and raised her brows at Jasen's revelation.

"To cut to the chase, I am working undercover for the Treasury Department. My cover moniker is Ethan McCoy. It's a long story, but I was recruited over five years ago to aid in the investigation of a very sensitive case, partly because of my knowledge of Mississippi Choctaw history and partly because of my real-life role as a college professor. That role allows me access to confidential databases that have proven invaluable in a long, drawn-out investigation into an international money laundering scheme that may reach all the way to the US Senate and possibly even to the White House. Yes, that's right…all the way to the top. That's why I should not even be talking to you about this.

My cover had been concealed very well until someone—an insider perhaps—tipped Luther and his henchmen about my connection to Jade. There are many people who will go to any lengths to protect certain Washington secrets. My life may not be worth a wooden nickel anymore. Pulling you into this may put your lives in jeopardy, too, but I felt that we have to work through this together. Forgive me."

Jasen scanned the faces in the room. They were suddenly wearing "I'm confused," "Are you kidding me?" and "What in the world is he talking about?" masks.

Marcus interrupted. "Jasen, I'm not sure how you're going to tie this and all of what has happened into one neat little package with a pretty bow, but just how does this relate to Choctaws, hidden treasures, mysterious stuffed roosters, the KKK, and your, uh, friend Jade? And how can *we* possibly fit into an international political scandal or whatever you're involved in?"

"Like I said, Marcus, it's complicated. Let me start with my cover name, Ethan McCoy.

"Just a little over five years ago, I learned that my graduate school research work and publications on Greenwood Leflore and the Mississippi Choctaw tribes had come to the attention of someone in the federal government in DC. I have absolutely *no* idea how that happened, but it did. I don't think anything about one's private life is private anymore. The Internet has connected our lives, private or public, to the world in ways we could have never imagined. Some predict it will get worse.

"Regardless, someone profiled me and the next thing you know, I'm being recruited to become a part-time, undercover federal agent. I couldn't say 'no' especially when I learned about the perks—I was promised a lot more than a tenured college professor could ever make. I know what you're thinking—how in the world would a college ethics professor be recruited as a federal agent? I asked myself that same question a hundred times. Seems kind of hokey or even improbable, but it happened. Ordinary people get recruited all of the time by government agencies. Trust me. Of course, I like to say that I'm a little *more* than ordinary, but, hey, that's my opinion." He smiled.

"It's was only because of my so-called expertise in Choctaw history and Greenwood connections that I think I was profiled. The case for which I was chosen involved trying to make sense of a loose association between elements of the KKK, like Jake Luther, and assorted mysteries that circulated around about Chief Leflore, hidden treasures, and other rumors about criminal activities in the Delta. Someone at Treasury speculated that Washington politicians might somehow be connected to Greenwood no-good. But, that's pure conjecture—no proof of any connection has surfaced to date.

"The Treasury Department was heading the investigation because of evidence of years of difficult-to-trace money laundering transactions between sources outside of the United States and possible powerful forces in high places in the US. The tainted dollars were finding their way to strong lobbyists and organizations that were backing some long-standing political empires that were perpetuating land grabs and other controversial activities in the South.

"This country may have made significant advances on the civil rights front since the sixties, but I assure you—bigots, hate groups, segregationists, and crimes against minorities and certain ethic groups are all alive and well. Apparently, some of those involved now hold very prominent public offices. A front-page scandal is not something that these figures can afford, so I'm sure that you can understand why I've tried to fly under the radar and remain anonymous.

"What you may have thought was simply a ruthless man like Jake Luther seeking revenge over a secret stolen away in a stuffed rooster was far more than that. Jade and her mother unknowingly and innocently got caught up in a very sticky international web of criminal activity that could conceivably send many politicians scurrying for cover. This will make more sense to you when I share details later.

"So, the politically explosive investigation is one thing. Jake Luther, as I said, had double motives. He has been working for and probably protecting some power mongers in Washington, and he may not have even known the names of the persons he had been protecting. He only knew that the names on the list stolen along with his pet rooster might lead to the top, and if that happened he was a dead man. He had to get that list back but as we know, Jade's mom apparently discovered it and hid it away in a cuckoo clock for nearly thirty years. Jake's severe injuries and stroke after Jade's defensive attack left him incapable of organizing a sophisticated search for the rooster, and Jean and Jade were not all that easy to trace either.

"Enter Jasen Prospero into Jade Colton's life. Yes, it was part of my assignment, but let me say this for the record—I love her and would do anything to protect her, anything. Jade has been under the impression, I think, that stalkers and abductors were just after her rooster, her mother, or her. Actually, when Jake Luther somehow learned of my real identity, I became the primary target, not Jade. We just got tangled up in this together. Jake had two goals: find out what Jade knew about his network of associates and find out if I had learned anything about his superiors. I think he finally concluded that we knew very little about either but was certainly going to try and eliminate any possibility.

"Jake's other motive for the unrelenting pursuit of Jean and Jade? It was purely a selfish one. He had hidden the one hundred thousand dollars along with the list of his KKK friends and dirty money recipients in the base of the rooster. He wanted his money for sure, but he was convinced that the rooster was hiding more secrets of the great Chief Leflore. Jake's stealing that Malmaison rooster was quite a coupe for him. Remember: the cause of the fire that destroyed the mansion was never officially determined. He knew of all the legends that had persisted around Leflore's plantation for over a hundred years. Legends about hidden gold, other treasures, secret documents, and other skeletons in the cupboard that Leflore had shared with no one. No one, so the story goes, except for an old black farmhand that seemed to be unusually close to Leflore.

"Myths, legends, rumors, folklore? Yes, all of the above, but the stories have persisted for more than a century. Jake Luther, I was told, forced some of the information from some farmhands that he terrorized. He accepted the stories as true and finally got possession of the rooster, which he thought would eventually lead him to a great fortune. Jake Luther was many things, but basically, it was all about greed. He was a treasure hunter, and Jean and Jade got in his way."

The story was beginning to seem like it had no end. Danny Malone had heard enough.

"Jasen," grumbled Danny. "This is the most preposterous tall tale that I've heard in a long time. Exactly where do we fit into this web of deceit and intrigue and this ridiculous story about gold, treasures, or whatever? We're private detectives, not treasure hunters. And, I for one did not sign on to start busting heads with federal agents or powerful politicians that can order a hit on any or all of us and not even blink an eye. You remember what happened to anyone that got too close to uncovering the truth about those high-powered lawyers Ryan and Maggie Nelson and their shady real estate deal back in Jackson, don't you? Are you recruiting us to be Treasury agents or what?"

"I can understand your skepticism, Danny. It *does* reek of a pretty far-fetched story. The money laundering scheme, though, is very real, and *very* dangerous. Luther was only one of many agents that have assisted with hiding the dirty money. His death does not end my investigation. It just starts a new chapter. And, I can use some help.

"There are other leads in Mississippi with which I think you and Marcus can help. But, to address your Doubting Thomas mind regarding treasure hunting, I believe I have something here that may get your attention. That is, if you're up for some real adventure and a possible share in the spoils?"

Danny sat taller in his chair and let that thought soak in.

Jasen reached into his shirt pocket and extracted a folded document.

"Just before Luther got a head full of that .38-caliber bullet, he had asked me to try and decipher this strange message that was hidden away apparently for eternity until Jade and I made that little sojourn to French Camp. This was one of many secret documents that Chief Leflore had purposely hidden away from everyone for reasons we do not understand. Jake had someone steal this from the French Camp files. Anyway, I never suggested to Jake that I understood the message. I lied. I think I have a pretty good idea of what Leflore intended to keep secret forever. Unless, again I'm thinking like he may have, unless God intervened and revealed the secret. Divine intervention or dumb luck—call it what you like—I have the message and I think I have the meaning."

Elizabeth, Marcus, and Danny scooted to the edge of their chairs.

"Well, you have our attention now, Jasen," Danny said. "What's it say?"

CHAPTER EIGHTEEN

The Note

J asen continued with his discovery.

"Greenwood Leflore, corrupted from the French 'LeFleur' to the English 'Leflore,' was a very interesting figure in the early history of Mississippi and Indian treatment in general in the early nineteenth century. I think his place in the history of the Choctaw Nation is still controversial, but I've learned that there was a lot more to that man than history books record."

"Come on, come on, Jasen." Danny was past being patient. "What's in the note? Your suspense is cutting me to the bone!"

"Okay. Sorry, Danny. I was just providing some editorial background. Let me read you the note first, then I'll give you my slant on it." He unfolded the document and prepared to read.

"It's dated August 12, 1865. Interesting, as he died in bed on August 31, 1865, just about three weeks after writing and hiding this note."

"Jasen!" exclaimed Danny. "Read!"

"Okay. Okay. Here goes."

"My years and the date are one
If right go ahead he said
The Tennessee traveler
He died with the truth as will I
God spared me from the Shampe neshobas
And led me to Tootemastubbe
and Little Sand Creek
blood stained and wrong
now under LeFleur's oaks
my dirk protects the six
forever with God
I started poor because that was right
Success came and
I give thanks."

Jasen looked up and saw the blank faces.

"Okay, Mr. College Professor genius. Is that it? What the hell does it mean?" asked Danny with obvious disappointment. "Is that supposed to be about a treasure? I'm afraid you lost me. Who's Shampe and Tootsie-tubby? What's a *neshoba?*"

"It's Tootemastubbe. And *neshoba* means wolf in Choctaw. I must admit," Jasen countered, "without some extensive research, the note is pretty vague and veiled in a dying old man's memory. Fortunately, I dedicated a massive amount of my graduate school time to researching Choctaw history and their great chiefs. I think what Leflore wrote here was a confession of sorts. Like a lot of older people do in their declining years, I think he was reflecting on something that happened in his youth.

"At first, I was struck by the reference to his years, i.e., his age and the date are one. He was sixty five and died in 1865. But, if he was reliving an event, then is he referencing his age at the time? He wrote the note on August 12, so I am assuming it was something that happened when he was twelve years old, not age sixty five. Of course, he could have meant age eight (August) or age eighteen (*1865*), but I think he meant twelve."

Elizabeth had kept silent through most of Jasen's ramblings but was gaining a new respect for the diversity and intuitiveness of the teacher/federal agent/treasure hunter.

"Jasen," she asked. "What would lead you to believe that this is anything more than an old man enveloped in the throes of dementia? It almost sounds as if he was hallucinating. I mean, he's says he's seeing some Tennessee traveler, something that's blood-stained, something called *Shampe neshobas*. It's all very strange."

"I can understand how you might think that, Elizabeth. However, you might change your mind after I explain." Jasen was confident in his deductions and continued.

"Please, bear with me. Here's how I'm looking at this. In 1812, Leflore lived with his family in his father's inn, which was in present-day French Camp, Mississippi. French Camp is situated on the Natchez Trace, known in the late 1700s and 1800s as the Old Natchez Road. In the early 1800s the Trace was plagued with notorious highwaymen who robbed, tortured, and murdered unwary travelers. Rumors and myths have persisted even to this day that some of the bandits left unclaimed, buried caches of gold, silver, and jewelry, all stolen from hapless travelers. It's not totally unthinkable that Leflore somehow could have stumbled upon some of the lost treasure. This would fit with the legends and myths around Leflore's home at the Malmaison plantation that endured for over a century. Myths that Jake Luther accepted as truth.

"He describes being spared from the *Shampe neshobas*. In Choctaw lore, the *Shampe* was the name for a feared beast of the wilderness. Whatever happened to him, you can imagine that as a boy of twelve, it was most likely a very traumatic event. How that would have led him to 'Tootemastubbe' is a little vague, for sure, but I think I know what he meant. Tootemastubbe was the Chickasaw name for a famous tribal chief, also known as Colonel George Colbert. I researched Colbert. Among many things that he did, including operating a ferry across the Tennessee River near Cherokee, Alabama, he, curiously, co-owned with his brother James Colbert a tavern and inn around 1812 along the Natchez Trace—Colbert's Stand. I think Leflore is saying that something led him to Colbert's Stand. It makes sense because he obviously traveled up and down the Trace between his home at French Camp and his tutor's home in Nashville—known facts about Leflore. The reference to Little Sand Creek has me stumped. There are multiple creeks called Sand Creek in Mississippi. In addition, creek beds that existed over 150 years ago may not even exist now. I'm still researching that."

"But, Jasen," probed Marcus, "how would Leflore have known about any buried treasure at Colbert's Stand or Little Sand Creek or whatever ?"

"Good question, Marcus," responded Jasen. "Your guess is as good as mine. However, I discovered something very interesting when I randomly searched databases for information about 'lost treasures.' The legends of hidden caches of gold that I mentioned were published years ago in a very obscure historical newsletter. It was sheer luck that I stumbled upon the newsletter. I would guess that very few people have ever read it. The gold story is mentioned almost as an afterthought and wasn't felt to be credible information."

"Okay, genius," quipped Danny. "Why would *you* think it may be credible?"

"Well, Danny, I'll tell you. The writer mentioned two locations where caches were rumored to have been abandoned—one is just north of Natchez, near Rocky Springs. The other is near Bissell, Mississippi. And guess where Bissell is located?"

The others looked at him in wide-eyed anticipation.

"Bissell is a tiny suburb of Tupelo along the Natchez Trace, of course. And guess where Colbert's Stand was located? That's right—Bissell! Somehow, Leflore must have known about the rumors. Wishful thinking or whatever, even back then people would have wanted to believe in buried treasures and striking it rich. Maybe Leflore knew something that no one else knew. We'll never know. Which brings me back to the note. It certainly sounds as if the Tennessee traveler mentioned knew Leflore's secret. The identity of the Tennessean was not that difficult to figure out. I simply looked up famous Tennesseans and famous quotes. Actually, I had heard the quote before. You'll never guess who."

The silence was deafening as they waited for his next twist in his now captivating narrative.

"He died along with 256 Texian heroes at the Alamo. His most famous quote is "Be sure you're right, then go ahead." That's right, Davy Crockett, the legendary King of the Wild Frontier!"

"What! exclaimed Marcus. "You've got to be kidding."

"Actually, Marcus, you could be right. There is absolutely nothing recorded anywhere in historical documents or personal letters, memoirs, etc. that suggests Greenwood Leflore knew or ever met Davy Crockett. But, if this note is anything more than a figment of Leflore's imagination, it certainly sounds as if they met at least once. If Crockett helped Leflore or knew about a treasure, he took the secret with him to his grave at the Alamo where his and the heroic Texians' ashes are buried.

"That interesting bit of unknown history is neither here nor there. Is this note really about buried gold? I think the part that references Tootemastubbe and Little Sand Creek could be the locations or former locations of gold caches buried by Sam Mason, the infamous highwayman in the early 1800's. Blood stained basically means blood money. The note then suggests that something, presumably the gold, is buried under LeFleur's oaks. Finally, my dirk protects the six? I'm not sure what this means. A dirk is a Scottish dagger. Why would an Indian chief have a Scottish dagger, much less use it to mark a treasure site or six of something?

"In the nineteenth century, stolen money or gold was commonly called 'blood gold' because it usually meant someone died at the hands of the robbers. It was tainted treasure and Leflore knew it. He knew it wasn't right so he left it buried to be forever with God. He could have been instantly a rich young man, but instead he chose to do the right thing and stay 'poor.'

"Maybe you all have some ideas. Believe it or not, I think the Malmaison gold legends are probably true. Only time will tell. Anyway, that's my story."

The room was hauntingly quiet and his audience as still as mannequins in a department store as they were still digesting his intriguing interpretation of the 130-year-old secret note. Danny interrupted their whirling, spinning minds.

"Jasen, you can certainly spin a yarn. I'd love to go on a treasure hunt with you, but I'm afraid I'll have to burst your bubble. From what you told us earlier, we've got some more serious business hanging out there. I want to know how we fit into an investigation into top brass politicians and what makes you think we can even help? The Luther gang is history. I would rather get back to investigating cheating husbands and wives and crimes of passion back in Jackson. I'm not too keen about pinning a target on my back for thugs working for elite, corrupt politicians to shoot at. I'm afraid you've got to convince me, Mr. Prospero or Agent McCoy, whichever it is."

"I understand, Danny. But, don't say that I didn't give you a chance to share in the gold. But, you're right. There are higher mountains to climb. The gold can certainly wait, well maybe, if it's really there.

"Oh, yes, did I mention how much gold is alleged to have been buried and forgotten? The historical newsletter mentioned that rumors circulated for years that over 200 million dollars in gold coins and other valuables were never accounted for. The Bissell stash alone was estimated to be worth 250,000 dollars when it was buried. I did the math. In today's dollars, that's about 5 million dollars." He looked at the surprised faces in the room.

"But, here's the kicker," Jasen said. "I suggest that all of you grab your seats tightly. If Leflore somehow stumbled across the entire cache of 200 million dollars, we're talking, at the current price of gold, a lost treasure that would now be worth 3.5 *billion* dollars—that's billion with a 'b'!"

He had Danny's attention now.

"Holy crap! Now that might be a good reason for going on a treasure hunt!" exclaimed Danny. "When do we start? That's a lot of gold, wow!"

The others in the room looked at each with raised brows and echoed the "wow!"

"However," Danny interjected. "Paint me just a little skeptical. Sorry. I think this entire Leflore, buried treasure thing is simply too good to be true. A great story for a fiction novel but just too unreal for me. Somehow, I just can't get too excited about some vague note left by an ancient, dying Indian chief. Can we come back down to earth for a minute and talk about your investigation? I think that two of us in this room are a little out of our league in such a high profile investigation. Not saying I'm not man enough, understand. I'm not a federal agent. Just a lowly PI."

Jasen looked at a smiling Marcus, then back at Danny. "Okay, Danny. Then how would you like to come to work for the Treasury Department? I'm actually here to recruit you and Marcus. You don't realize it yet, but you could be the key to solving the biggest government cover-up of the century. And it all started with a stolen rooster in Greenwood, Mississippi, in 1961."

CHAPTER NINETEEN

Liz and Marcus

"Liz, I appreciate the invitation to join you for lunch," said Marcus. "I assume that Jasen put you up to this to try and convince me to seriously consider his offer, correct?"

Elizabeth smiled at the tall, handsome detective who sat down across from her at Taverna Mikos in Atlanta's Buckhead. She focused on his generous black hair with distinctive grayish sideburns and his dark brown eyes. His manly physique suggested an outdoorsman or a devoted student of physical fitness. She guessed that he was likely in his fifties and admired the absence of a middle age stomach bulge as he sat down. Her mind was drifting into unchartered waters, and she pinched her hand to bring her back to reality.

"Well, yes and no, Marcus. We may need you to work on your associate Mr. Malone. He sounds a little reluctant to join the 'team.' Actually, I confess. I just wanted to get you alone for a few minutes." She smiled again and peered intensely into his dreamy dark-brown eyes.

"Why, Agent Keys. Whatever do you mean? I'm a married man."

"Yes, I know. Too bad. But I'll settle for just getting to know you a little better."

He studied her smile and pupils and reminded himself of his professional modus operandi—share minimally and trust no one.

"Okay, Liz. What would you like to know? I'm just a garden variety private eye trying to eke out a living deep in the Heart of Dixie. Danny and I have done well back in Jackson, and I must say that I really enjoy what we do. Normally, our cases are a little less risky than this Jake Luther nightmare. I mean, it's unusual that I get beat up or even physically threatened. Like Danny said, domestic squabbles mostly."

"Such modesty, Marcus," observed Elizabeth as she sipped her Chardonnay. "My sources tell me that your agency is the best in the state and that you personally are the number one 'Guy Noir' of Jackson, Mississippi. I can hear your radio ad now—'A dark night in a city that knows how to keep its secrets, but on the eighth floor of the Plaza Building a light is on, and one man is still trying to find the answers to life's most persistent questions—Marcus Bianco, Private Eye.'"

"Nice, Liz. Somewhat overstated though, I assure you. A fan of Garrison Keiller? Me too. And how do you know that I'm in the Plaza Building?"

"Marcus, my dear man. I work for the FBI. I know everything. Well, not quite, but I *did* do my homework on you. I must say, I'm impressed *and* enchanted!"

"I guess I should say 'thanks' but I'm still struggling with why we're having lunch together. I think Danny got his feelings a little hurt. He may be a little jealous, too."

Elizabeth looked pleased. "He's a big boy. He'll get over it. I just wanted you all to myself, even if the attraction is one-sided. I hope you'll forgive my boldness. Anyway, can we just sit back and savor the moment? I'm starving. Let's order."

As he looked down to study the menu, he thought to himself, *What makes her think the attraction is one-sided?* Just as quickly, he knew he had better keep that secret to himself.

***

They ordered lunch, and then Liz tried to continue her agenda. Marcus deflected her attempt to discuss more business, as he thought he should try and learn more about the interesting FBI agent.

"Since you invited me here, how about telling me more about yourself? If we're going to be working closer together, I'd love to know more about the 'real' Elizabeth Keys."

Superficially, he guessed silently, any red-blooded male could easily be persuaded to pursue her come-on. She was a looker, by any standard, pleasingly petite and slim. Her wavy black hair stopped at her shoulders and was side swept with some side fringes, creating a subtle picture of innocence and sweetness but with style. Her soft brown eyes were difficult to read, Marcus thought to himself. Even dressed in her business attire, she was comfortable to the eyes but far from the stereotypical fantasy female. Marcus read her as strong and independent and genuinely relatable. He wondered about her single status but not for long.

"I'm flattered, Marcus, that you're interested," she responded. "I guess you've wondered about why I'm unattached. Or maybe you haven't. Anyway, the FBI is my life. I was married ten years ago for six months to a real jerk. Not a period of my life that I'm particularly proud of. I prefer my independence and my work. Sometimes, I *do* think about settling down again, but not unless I meet Mr. Perfect, which will likely never happen. For now, I'm happy in my home near here, actually. I piddle in the garden and love to read novels, mostly psychological thrillers. I love the suspense. It helps me in my FBI role in dealing with weird criminal minds."

"Family?" he asked. "I mean siblings, parents, etc."

"Two brothers. My parents are deceased." She looked down and flashed a hint of sadness. "Victims of a head-on collision five years ago. Drunk driver. He's serving time, as he should. Anyway, I'm not particularly close to my brothers. Their careers took them in different directions—one to New York, the other one to San Francisco. So, I'm pretty much my own girl here in Atlanta. Married to the FBI and happy."

Her eyes told him that she was lying. He was correct about judging her as independent but wondered about her emotional strength. She was lonelier than she admitted. He was still cautious of her interest in him, and he didn't even want to go down that road just yet.

"Enough about me!" she said with the grin of an infatuated teenager. "I lured you to this luncheon. Tell me about the 'real' Marcus Bianco."

He smiled and stared back at her without saying anything.

"Well, are you just going to stare at me? Tell me about yourself, Mr. Private Eye."

"Okay, but you might find it boring. I've been a successful private investigator for almost thirty years. Successful because I've kept business and pleasure separate. And I've found that sharing minimally avoids misunderstandings or malice. So, please forgive me if I seem rude. It's just who I am."

"Please. I'm not trying to be nosy. You're an interesting man and I'm attracted to you. However, I'm a realist and I know you're a married man. I'm not asking for a biography, just curious about how you ended up in Jackson, Mississippi, and married a doctor. And, no, I am not a husband stealer. I told you, I'm dedicated to my job."

He hesitated but decided to open slightly more.

"I'm an only child. I met my wife Carol when I worked as a young detective for the Alabama State Police. I was investigating the John Doe stabbing in Eutaw, Alabama. You already know that that turned out to be Jake Luther. We would have never guessed that his attack was at the hands of six-year-old Jade Colton. Carol was the physician who treated Jake's injuries. I asked her out on a date and, well, thirty years later we're still together. She's an emergency room medical director and leads a typical busy physician's life. Her job is the reason we settled in Jackson, well, actually in Madison, a suburb north of Jackson. We don't really see much of each other in a typical week. I think that's why we get along! Just kidding. No children. She couldn't for medical reasons and we never talked about adoption. Danny Malone is about as close as I've come to having a son. He's bullheaded but has a very soft heart. Our agency in Jackson has done very well, as you learned. I was hired by Jasen and Jade when they learned of my past involvement in the unsolved Jake Luther case. The rest, as they say, is history."

She had not taken her eyes off of him and sat leaning forward with her hands together and resting under her chin.

"We have a lot in common, Marcus Bianco," she said.

"Really? What would that be?"

"Well, both of us have black hair, brown eyes, are investigators, live in the suburbs, are helping Jasen and Jade, and are looking for something else in life."

"You're mostly right, Liz, except for the looking for something else. Exactly what would that be?

She leaned across the table, touched his face very softly, and slowly circled her index finger around his lips. She paused a second before she spoke.

"Perfection, Marcus, perfection."

***

As they were enjoying their baklava, Marcus tried to steer the conversation back to business.

"Liz, just how much do you know about the investigation that Jasen has been secretly involved in? I mean, he certainly had me fooled. No way I would have ever suspected him as any kind of spy or agent. Did you know?"

"Marcus, the FBI is a very large bureaucratic agency. I told you that I know almost everything, but I had no inside knowledge of Ethan McCoy or what or who he was investigating. Believe me, I was just as surprised as you were. Everything looked like a vindictive stalking of Jade because of a KKK nutcase's revenge, and Ethan, Jasen, got caught up in it. Jasen's role is a great example of how one government agency like the US Treasury Department can operate so independently of another like the FBI. You wouldn't believe the competitiveness of federal agents. Everyone is out for guts and glory. You'd think that we would work together on high-profile cases, but, unfortunately, that's not how the government works. Self-indulgence. Self-interests. Personal agendas. Too many mega-egos. Just look at the top. Congress and the President hate each other's guts. Bipartisanship? What's that? Government agencies don't talk to one another. Why, I think they even spy on each other! It's all about politics, control, personal ideology, and protecting secrets. Like Guy Noir's city, Washington is a city that knows how to keep its secrets.

"So, I must say that I concur with Jasen's request. I have been approved to work more closely with him and other Treasury agents on this money laundering scandal. However, due to the high-level positions that some of the suspected targets hold, the investigation is going further underground than it was. Jasen's cover may have been compromised. His life is in more danger than he knows, although I think he suspects it. And I am worried about Jade also. She doesn't know what she doesn't know, but those protecting the secrets that Jake Luther died with don't know what she doesn't know, either. She's still a target, I think. We all are. That's why we have to work together and build a façade that the pursuers can't breach."

"Pursuers?" asked a puzzled Marcus.

"Those that will go to any extreme to protect the ones at the top of the food chain. I suspect that they would make Jake Luther look like a summer breeze. What I am saying, Marcus, is that we are in this together, and that includes you and Danny, like it or not. We've got to plan smarter, work smarter, and hide who we are smarter. I need you—please, don't take that the wrong way—Jasen needs you, and Jade needs you. So, for now, mum is the word. Go back to Jackson and flush out all those cheating spouses, Mr. Noir. Jasen and I will be in touch. Damn! There I go again- *need*ing you, *touch*ing you, keeping secrets—do you think something Freudian is going on between us, Detective Bianco?" She smiled again with forbidden visions frolicking like sprites in her head. He smiled back but was not ready to accept her pretense. Trust no one, not even the FBI, he told himself.

CHAPTER TWENTY

The Stronger of the Species

Lawrenceville, Georgia

"Jade? It's me. I miss you," he said. They had not talked in over a week. He decided to call hoping she would answer. She did.

"How did the meeting go?" Jade asked distantly. "Did you tell them everything?"

"It went well and yes, they now know everything," Jasen responded. "The real challenge is how a Treasury agent, the FBI, and two private investigators can work on this together and still keep it a hush-hush investigation. We don't know who Jake Luther's superiors are and how much they may know about what we know, which is very little.

"Plus, you and I can't risk doing anything alone until this mystery is solved. I'm still worried that what's left of Jake's gang back in Leflore County may still seek revenge and may even know about Jake's suspicion of a buried treasure. We're potential targets for many reasons until we sort out all of this intrigue. I'm now on a six-month sabbatical from my teaching job. Treasury has asked me to devote 100 percent of my time to unraveling Jake Luther's suspicious connection to Washington politics. This operation is about to become more dangerous than we've bargained for, Jade, and I'm worried about your safety."

"Jasen. I'm still struggling with your cruel deception, how I feel about you, and about our future together. Somehow I don't feel like I know who you really are. I thought I could trust you with anything and everything, but I can't ignore the fact that you took advantage of me. You humiliated me. I love you and I hate you at the same time. If we had not faced death together so many times, I think I would never want to see you again. I'm fighting my feelings for you every second, every minute of every hour. I just don't know what I want anymore. I need more time to deal with my heart. I hope you can understand. I wish you had not called."

"I can only say that I'm sorry and that I love you. I never expected to be affected by you like I was. But, Jade, neither of us is safe. We need to stay together and find some answers. Also, I know you don't care, but I went back to French Camp and talked to that little old man at the Carriage House about Leflore's strange note. He wanted to know what I thought it meant. I played dumb. I don't know why, but I think he was somehow involved with Jake and company. I don't trust him. I think he believes that there really is a buried horde of gold and he wants to find it before someone else does. I can't imagine how gold lost over a century ago could be connected to a present-day political scandal but I think it may be. Call me nuts but there's more to this than we could even make up."

"Jasen, stop it! You're driving me crazy with your obsession about some make-believe buried treasure. It's 1998. Let's deal with today. The past is the past. I've made up my mind about how to confront my enemies head on. I can't go back to work. I'm resigning from my director position."

"Resigning!" exclaimed Jasen. "You can't resign. You aren't independently wealthy, are you? What will you do?"

"You won't agree with my decision, but I'm going to work for the FBI. I've got a lot personally invested in this wild and crazy ride we've been on, and I owe it to my mom. It's because of me and Mom that you and I are at this new crossroad. Your agency used me as bait to lure Jake out of hiding. Now I want to work on this in an official role. I've been through some nasty, harrowing escapes to get to this point. I'm tired of being a target. I want to do the targeting. I've met with Elizabeth Keys and she's supportive of my joining forces with her. I've accepted a consulting role with the Atlanta bureau as a communications specialist. It's a done deal."

"Jade, for heaven's sake, you're a director for the telephone company, not a trained federal agent. This is insane!"

"I've made up my mind. I think I've proven that I've got the moxie to do whatever I want to do. It's the Choctaw in me. Jasen, get over it. I'm taking an orientation course and firearms training next week. If we end up working on this together, I'll deal with it then. For now, our personal relationship is on hold. One voice tells me that you're just a damn good actor with a mesmerizing, handsome face and a superhero body. The other says you're the most wonderful guy I've ever met. But, I'm not doing this for us. I'm doing it for Mom."

"You're a strong and determined woman, Jade—one of a hundred reasons that I fell in love with you. I just don't think this is a good idea. We're playing with fire and someone is going to get burned. It's a high stakes poker game now, and I don't think we've seen the worst of the bad guys yet. *Please*, don't do this."

"I told you it's a done deal. As soon as I finish orientation, we start a new chapter in this investigation. I've been baptized under fire. Nothing scares me anymore. Please discuss it with Elizabeth if you need to. And don't call me. I'll see you when I see you. Good-bye, Jasen."

Jasen stared at the phone as the line went dead. "Damn it!" he said to himself. "She's going to get herself killed." He already missed her and closed his eyes and saw her special smile. He wished that he could touch her and hold her in his arms. He wanted to protect her and keep her out of harm's way. But now he couldn't help but wonder who might really be the stronger.

***

"Agent Keys, this is Jasen. I just had a conversation with Jade. What's going on? She told me that you have agreed to hire her in some kind of consulting role. Is that true?"

"Well, hello to you too, Jasen. Yes, she's absolutely correct. We need someone with knowledge of sensitive and sophisticated telecommunication systems, and Jade convinced me of her insider expertise on the technical issues. I needed a fresher approach to connecting the dots between Greenwood, Jackson, and Washington. I liked Jade's ideas, and she convinced me of her commitment to finding the truth. She's invested a lot of sweat and blood in this mystery, just like you have. I like her. She's a tough, gritty, and strong woman. But, I don't have to convince you. I know how you feel about her, although she has a long way to go now in ever believing you again. Trust is not automatic; it has to be earned. You lost it, and you're going to have to re-earn it. Do you have a problem with my decision?"

"I don't have a good feeling about it, that's all. Yes, Jade is a tough woman, but she's not a pro. She's an amateur. This situation is going to get more dangerous. I just don't want to lose her. I need to protect her."

"That's odd, Jasen," Elizabeth said. "She thinks she's doing this to protect you. She has a sense of invulnerability, and that can be detrimental. I told her that. She fired back something about destiny, fate, born to do this, whatever. Anyway, she convinced me. She's on my team now, and I consider her an asset. With you, Marcus, and Danny working one angle and me, Jade, and my team working another, I think we have a decent chance of splitting this money laundering, political power-grab, buried treasure mystery wide open. Are you trying to back out?"

"No, of course not, Elizabeth. I've got five years invested in this. It's time we kick this up a notch or two. I'm ready. Just please promise me that you'll watch Jade's back. If I ever get her back, I never want to lose her again."

"Don't underestimate yourself, Jasen. I have a good feeling about you two. Be patient. Now, let me get back to planning our next move. I'll be in touch. I suggest that you head over to Jackson and meet with Marcus and Danny. They're working on a new scheme. We all have a lot of homework to do. Jade and I will meet up with you in Jackson. And, oh, give my regards to Marcus," she said smiling broadly as she hung up the phone.

CHAPTER TWENTY-ONE

Jade and Damian

FBI Regional Field Office
Atlanta

E lizabeth Keys was impressed with the confidence displayed by Jade Colton as she observed her training session in the firing room in the basement of the FBI building. Jade exhibited no reluctance to fire the weapons, and Elizabeth got a sense that Jade was a natural marksman as she scored higher than any other rookie she had ever seen. Her instinct was right; Jade was tough as railroad spikes and seemed to have a natural tendency to succeed and take charge. Elizabeth reminded her that despite her firearms skills, she would not be allowed to carry a weapon as a consultant, at least for now.

The two weeks of orientation had passed, and Jade was officially approved by Elizabeth's superior to begin her consulting role and assist with the alleged money laundering scheme whose trail had gone cold after Jake Luther's death. Elizabeth and her team were scheduled to meet with Jasen, Marcus, and Danny the following week. Some of them would be assigned to investigate some possible leads in Washington, and Elizabeth needed a sound plan. She was anxious to begin putting the pieces of the puzzle together but needed everyone buying into her ideas.

She had said goodbye to Jade within the past hour when the receptionist buzzed her with a phone call.

"This is Agent Keys. How may I help you?"

"Agent Keys, this is Gene McGregor. I'm the interim warden over here at the Atlanta Federal Penitentiary. I have something that I think you might be interested to know."

"Yes, Warden, what is it?"

"One of your clients, a Ms. Jade Colton, was involved in an assault attempt a while back by one of my prisoners, Damian Winters. He's been incarcerated here for some time after being convicted of assault with intent."

"Yes," responded Elizabeth. "I'm very familiar with Mr. Winters. And Ms. Colton is now working for me. What's this about?"

"Well, due to the previous attack on Ms. Colton, I thought you needed to know that Mr. Winters has been released from my prison. It may not seem right, but his lawyer got him off on some weird technicality. I don't know if he would try anything, but I just thought that someone needed to give Ms. Colton a head's up."

"That's not good news, Warden. How did this happen? We thought he was locked away for good. Good old American justice." She sighed in disgust. "Sometimes it just plain sucks. Thanks, Warden for the tip. By the way, when was he released?"

"Two days ago. He's required to remain in the Atlanta area according to his probation officer. I just hope he's not stupid enough to get into trouble again. Then again, some criminals never learn. Good luck, Agent Keys. Just thought you needed to know. Thanks for your time."

"Thank you, Warden. I'll alert Ms. Colton. Good-bye."

She hung up the phone and shouted out to her secretary. "Betty! Get Ms. Colton on the line as soon as you can. She left here about an hour ago.

She should be home within the next thirty minutes unless she stopped on the way. Keep trying her home phone number until you get her. She doesn't have a mobile phone."

"Yes ma'am," responded Betty.

***

As she drove away from the FBI offices, Jade reflected on her latest circumstances and her new career. She was far removed from her home-town of Greenwood, Mississippi, and ironically chuckled a little to her-self as she remembered her childhood innocence being stolen away from her by Damian Winters so many years ago down in Jackson. The very thought of his predatory perversions and his twisted sex games that he played with her when she was a trusting toddler conjured a nauseating disgust that shrouded her decency and gave her prickly, goose-fleshing chills.

At the same time, she could chuckle even more as she savored the revenge that she and her mother had crafted with the fire ant attack and Ariel's attack on him with her golf club. She thought of him hopefully rotting away in the federal penitentiary nearby and wondered if his fel-low inmates had given him ample payback like most child molesters that ended up in prison.

From their Itta Bena adventure, she knew that Damian was responsible for her mother's death, as she and Jasen had suspected. Jake Luther had confirmed it before his nephew's bullet ripped through his brain and sent him to a well-deserved but long overdue hell. Little by little justice was being served.

She smiled briefly and then felt a ripple of melancholia fluttering in her bruised heart as she thought about her mother's last moments before going over the railing into that deep ravine. She didn't know why, but she felt a sudden urge to go back to the fatal scene. As if being pulled by some unknown force, she took the next exit off of the interstate and headed back to North Atlanta and the winding county road that her mother had traveled that fateful night.

Early dusk darkness was beginning to replace the fading late afternoon daylight as Jade turned onto County Road 30 just at the outskirts of Duluth, north of Atlanta. Just as she made the turn, she noticed a red pickup truck approaching rapidly and turning just behind her. The truck sped up and was following less than a car length behind her. At first, she didn't give the truck much thought, but the narrow gap between her and the truck began to make her a little uneasy.

"Damn tailgaters!" she said aloud. She tapped her brakes lightly as a signal to the driver that he was following too close. He didn't back off. Instead he seemed to inch even closer to her rear bumper. She accelerated to widen the distance but the truck matched her speed. *Who is this maniac?* she asked herself. Suddenly, she noticed a sign warning of dangerous curves ahead. She had no choice but to slow down.

Her heart pounded and raced now as the combination of a dangerous road looming ahead and a tailgating fool in a pickup truck forced her to lean forward slightly and grip the steering wheel with both hands. As she turned carefully into the first S-curve of the county road, she looked into the rearview mirror and could only see the intensely bright headlights of the truck.

Unexpectedly, on the opposite side of the road, an oncoming vehicle with its headlights on high beam was entering the curve but was crowding the center line. For a brief second Jade was blinded in both directions by both the oncoming lights and the truck lights behind her. Sensing a sure head-on collision, she reflexively jerked the steering wheel to the right but immediately felt the right side of her car sliding off the pavement and losing control.

Steep drop-offs on both sides of the road spelled major trouble for inattentive or unlucky drivers. She reacted just as her tires were running out of flat surface on the shoulder and at the last possible second was able to bring her car back into her lane. The truck had backed off several yards but quickly sped back up and nearly kissed her bumper again.

Jade could only think of getting off the dangerous road, but she saw no shoulder on which to pull off and no side roads. She knew she couldn't stop, especially if the person in the truck might be more of a threat than the winding road. She continued down the darker than dark road, which was bordered by thick densities of hardwood trees and heavy brush.

For a fleeting second, Jade thought she was reliving what had happened to her mother on the unforgiving, pitch black, narrow road. She began to regret her decision to return to the site where Jean had crashed into that deep ravine. She dared not accept the possibility that she could end up like her mother. She looked again at the glaring headlights filling her rearview mirror. What was happening? Where was her escape? *Who* was following her?

The truck accelerated again and matched her speed. Suddenly and without warning the driver slammed his truck into her rear bumper. The force jolted her, and her head jerked forward then backward just as rapidly. The headrest absorbed the pounding rebound from the back of her head, but her neck tightened, sending electrifying spasms down her upper back and arms.

The unrelenting pursuit continued through the next two snakelike curves, but Jade astutely managed to gain separation between her and the truck. She tried to get a glimpse of the truck's driver, but the high beams obscured all but an outline of a man behind the wheel. Jade's mind rushed with thoughts of somehow outfoxing the driver behind her, but she knew that time was running out. They were approaching the final hairpin curve on the narrow county road that was guarded now by a new metal railing that overlooked the ravine, the deadly ravine that had suspiciously devoured her mother that hapless night.

As they entered the dead man's curve, the truck unexpectedly sped up and pulled into the outer lane. It quickly pulled even with Jade's car, and Jade suddenly got a glimpse of the driver. He was grinning at her with his familiar evil snarl as he briefly took one hand off of the wheel and made a slashing gesture across the front of his neck then blew her a kiss.

Both vehicles slowed slightly as they approached the first bend in the curve, just thirty yards before reaching the metal railing that protected the ravine. Then, Jade surprisingly slammed on her brakes and watched the truck zip past her. She had totally fooled him, and he could not react or match her move as he saw the dangerous curve ahead. When he finally realized what she had done, he slammed his foot with all of his weight on the brake pedal, but the heavy truck had too much momentum. Its driver now helpless to control his machine, it continued on into the treacherous curve, smashing violently into the guardrail and ripping a gaping hole in the barrier before finally coming to a screeching, rocks-and-dirt-flying stop. The front tires had slipped a few inches over the precipice's edge, and the truck had luckily stopped just on the brink of certain disaster.

Jade had anticipated an opportunity at becoming the pursuer instead of the pursued. She sped up when she saw the truck come to a sliding, dirt-gripping stop just a split second before going off into the ravine. She knew she could not hesitate and had to reach him before he could reverse his predicament. She floored the accelerator and plowed like a mad, unrelenting bulldozer into the right rear side of the truck, having just barely enough momentum to finish the job.

She clearly saw the wide-eyed and horrified look of the stunned driver just before the truck slipped off the cliff's edge and tumbled sideways into oblivion. The dark abyss of the ravine swallowed the somersaulting truck like a hungry giant beast. The ebony, moonless sky lit up in blinding bursts of white and orange as the truck crashed into the rocky bottom and burst into sky-reaching flames.

Miraculously, Jade had stopped her car just inches before reaching the road's edge. She exited her car and stood looking into the same ravine that had brought an end to her mother's life. She had always been convinced that Damian had killed Jean, and Jake had verified it. Now justice had finally come full circle. Damian Winters had met his match. He would burn in hell forever. Delta Jade Colton felt no regret. Life was all about choices. That night on the Georgia back roads north of Atlanta, Damian had made the wrong choice.

CHAPTER TWENTY-TWO

The Plan

Eighth Floor
The Plaza Building, Downtown
Jackson, Mississippi

Elizabeth Keys had suggested it, and Marcus and Jasen had agreed. The new team needed to meet and review everything that had happened over the past few months and years. Jasen's undercover probe had yielded little about the Greenwood connection to the money laundering schemes and evolving Washington scandals. Even his carefully planned entry into the mysterious life of Jade had only clouded the intrigue and well-masked activities of Jake Luther and associates. Bianco was anxious to regroup and help Elizabeth come up with a plan. He couldn't believe that an unpretentious Mississippi private eye and his sidekick were now neck-deep in a major national political cover-up. He silently wondered if his life would ever be the same again.

Jade and Elizabeth had flown to Jackson together, and Jade had engaged only in small talk, mentioning nothing personal about Jasen. Elizabeth had observed with curiosity as Jade's pretense of Jasen as a mere business colleague contrasted strikingly with the lover's passion that she had seen before Jasen revealed his secret identity. The two were meant for each other, she thought, regardless of Jasen's background and deceit. Sooner or later, she suspected, Jade would realize it, if she hadn't already.

They took a taxi to downtown Jackson and exited in front of the Plaza Building on North Congress Street. Across the one-way street, the high white brick wall that surrounded the governor's mansion caught Jade's eye, and she turned and looked north, seeing the gold eagle-capped dome of the state capitol building only a few blocks away. She thought of Jasen's strong convictions about the long, lost buried gold, and it made her smile. She looked back at the Plaza Building. Marcus had quite a view from his eighth floor office, she guessed. They took the elevator to the eighth floor and followed a sign that pointed to Suite 808, Bianco and Associates.

Angie greeted them as they entered the smartly decorated reception area with mahogany paneled walls that looked more like a high profile LA lawyer's suite than a small-city private detective's office. The crimson tufted leather club chairs were handsome and masculine. Angie was sitting behind a small cherry desk adorned only by her name on a wooden sign, a telephone, and a small desk lamp.

"Good afternoon," Angie said cheerfully. "May I presume that you are Agent Keys and Ms. Colton?"

"Yes," answered Elizabeth. "So nice to meet you, Angie," she said as she glanced at the name on the small sign. "Thank you so much for your assistance with our flight and hotel accommodations. Marcus said that you are the consummate Girl Friday."

Angie smiled and blushed slightly. "Aw, he's a good boss. I don't know what that means, but I love working for him and Mr. Malone."

Jade spoke up. "Is everyone here? I think we're right on time."

"Yes ma'am. They're all in the conference room. I'll tell Mr. Bianco that you're here. Please, have a seat." Angie stood and walked from behind her desk and disappeared behind large double mahogany doors that led to the back offices and conference room.

Jade walked over and sat in the closest club chair, while Elizabeth walked slowly around the reception area and studied the interesting oil paintings on the paneled walls. The room was immaculate, free of dust, and a few magazines were stacked neatly under an antique occasional table.

"A man after my own heart," observed Elizabeth, smiling broadly as she studied the artwork.

"You mean he's *after* your heart or has the same taste?" asked Jade who couldn't help but pounce on the double entendre. She chuckled noticeably.

"Very funny, Jade. I assure you, Marcus is *not* after my heart. I can't seem to get to first base with that gorgeous man. He's got exquisite taste in art, though. Just look at these paintings. And this office décor. I told him over lunch that we were both after perfection. I think he's already there. My, my. Lucky Mrs. Bianco." Jade looked at her smile and could only imagine what wheels were turning in her head.

She stood as Angie reentered the reception room and spoke. "Please, come on back ladies. The guys are ready for you." They followed her through the large doors and into the conference room where Marcus, Danny, and Jasen were waiting.

The three men stood as Elizabeth and Jade walked briskly into the lavishly adorned room, which looked more like a corporate board room than a detective's office.

Marcus spoke first. "Welcome, ladies. I trust the flight was okay. Please, have a seat. Can Angie get you something to drink? Water? Coffee? Soda?"

Both women shook their heads, and Elizabeth quickly shook hands with Jasen and Danny then turned and smiled at Marcus. She took a step toward him and gave him a tight hug. Danny and Jasen looked at each other with raised brows and smiled.

"Well, how's my favorite private eye doing, Mr. Noir?" Elizabeth said as she backed away and smiled again at Marcus. He was caught off guard and flushed a little red.

"I'm fine, Elizabeth," he responded. "Just fine. Please, have a seat."

Jade had walked to the opposite side of the conference table from Jasen, who followed her every step with slightly pleading eyes that seemed to be silently saying "I'm sorry. I've missed you." She did not look at him and sat down, seemingly not curious about the Elizabeth/Marcus hug. Her thoughts were all about Jasen. She did not speak to him, but she looked at him briefly, not smiling.

Danny, noticing the tense body language in the room, decided to push the conversation straight to business before the two couples drifted off into rocky waters.

"Okay, then. Well everyone, why don't we dive right into what brought us all together. I think Agent Keys has come up with some good ideas. Let's get this team up to date. I think we need to start with Jasen. He started this investigation, and I for one am confused. I want to know what's really behind this cat and mouse intrigue. So, can we maybe start at the beginning? *Please?*"

Marcus was anxious to move the meeting along, too. "I agree, Danny. Jasen, can you recap your last few years of the investigation? I don't think all of us have heard all of the details. The floor's yours. Go for it."

Jasen had come prepared and passed around a one-page summary of his investigation. "This will help you follow along as I go over my activities over the past five years. Please, interrupt me if I go too fast.

"I think I've already covered the history of how and why I was recruited by the Treasury Department, so let's skip that. My original assignment was to trace a multimillion-dollar money stream that was flowing from Colombia, South America, to Greenwood, Mississippi, of all places. Someone seemed to think that I had connections to Greenwood because of my historical publications. Anyway, how valuable I am to their investigation is now moot. I'm in way over my head, good or bad.

"The Treasury Department had obtained secret documents from an undercover informant who infiltrated a Colombian drug cartel as a falcon or spy. The documents detailed large cash payments to the KKK in Greenwood that had been ongoing for years. The money, largely from illegal sales of cocaine and marijuana in the US, its largest market, was traced to a large drug cartel in Atlántico, Colombia, that was funneling wired payments to an anonymous account that eventually was found to be controlled by, yes, you guessed it, Jake Luther. The challenging part was trying to understand the connection between major league drug cartels in South America and the Mississippi Delta's KKK activities. The Atlántico cartel was one of the most active and successful in South America in the 1970s and 1980s. With its international reach, at its peak operations it brought in over 400 million dollars a week. The Capos (drug lords) were probably the wealthiest citizens in South America. They had tremendous success at laundering their money by purchasing massive amounts of land that became highly profitable cattle ranches, among other things. Interestingly, the Atlántico cartel was largely put out of business by 1993 when most its members had either been imprisoned or assassinated.

"The entire investigation took a bizarre turn when Treasury discovered that the money did not stay in Greenwood, at least, not all of it. Periodic deposits in one-hundred-thousand-dollar increments were being diverted to multiple accounts in a bank in Falls Church, Virginia. That ultimately led to a friend of a friend of a friend of an aide to Senator Roger Trevane.

Coincidentally, mega land purchases in Mississippi were made by a former law firm partner of Trevane over the past ten years. That's when lights, sirens, and bells went off in DC. Nothing to date has linked any of the payments or land purchases to Senator Trevane, but Treasury is still trying to put all of the pieces of this international puzzle together.

"From Virginia, most the money has been wired regularly to an offshore account that is totally off limits to any prying eyes. No one knows the identity of that account holder."

Danny Malone, like the others in the room, had listened politely but was struggling to fit Jasen's intriguing narrative into the wild escapades that had entrapped Jade and her Greenwood connection.

"Please help me out here, Jasen. How did this complicated scheme lead you to Ms. Colton and how does any of this even tie to a long dead Choctaw Indian chief? I think you tried to answer that once before, but please, refresh my memory."

Jasen responded. "You already know part of the answer, Danny. Jade's mother's connection to Jake Luther eventually led me to Jade."

Jade leaned forward in her chair and peered into Jasen's eyes. If looks could kill, he would have been history. Jasen felt her piercing stare but resisted looking back at her.

"I still don't follow," said Danny.

"It's complicated, my friend. Jade has blood lineage back to Greenwood Leflore, and Jake Luther was interested in Leflore for more reasons than you can imagine. Haven't I already gone over this?

"It's beginning to look like Greenwood Leflore had more buried secrets than some highway robber's gold. Basically, Danny, it's all about land grab—land that once belonged to the Choctaws' chief but is now the prime target of somebody in Washington, somebody with ambition, money, and power. Add those up in political circles and you've got trouble. Money does not just talk, believe me, it *screams*! And the ambition to have more money is highly seductive. The power that follows corrupts you and finally consumes you like a raging forest fire. It's the age-old theme of politicians that began with George Washington's administration. I think we have stumbled into the political scandal of the century. The money trail leads far beyond Greenwood, Mississippi. This investigation is about to become a little more than just dangerous. It could be world changing."

"Come on, Jasen," said Danny. "Aren't we being a little overly dramatic here? World changing? How?"

Elizabeth joined in. "Jasen, I agree that this may be big, but I'm not sure I share your view. The FBI has tried for years to find evidence of criminal activities involving the Trevanes, all to no avail. Either they're not behind any of this or they're very skilled at covering their tracks."

"I appreciate your skepticism, Liz and Danny, but I think you'll be surprised once we crack through the layers of deceit. It's no secret that Roger Trevane has his eyes on the White House. He's already one of the most powerful and influential senators that his party has ever had in Washington. He has worldwide clout, trust me. Plus, his wife, Charlotte, has her hands in more lobbyists' pockets that you could imagine. The Trevanes are building a legacy and will do anything to get there. The main challenge has been finding a smoking gun. Anyone who seems to be investigating Trevane either ends up missing or having a convenient 'accident.'

"We know what happened to Jade's mother, and she had no inkling whatsoever that her old boss was anything more than a wicked and ruthless Klansman."

Jasen glanced at Jade who looked away and distantly out the window.

"And I guess you heard about Jade's encounter with the deceased Damian Winters. Thank God, Jade outsmarted him. Elizabeth said that the FBI could find no connection with Damian other than being a crony of Jake Luther. Correct, Liz?"

"Yes," she answered. "Correct. Jade passed her first real test as an FBI consultant. We're lucky to have her as part of the team."

Marcus had been silent until now but decided to probe Jasen more.

"So, Jasen, where do we go from here? Obviously, there are still unknowns in Greenwood who may give us a new lead, but how do we identify them and how do we avoid becoming a disappearing act again? I don't want another Swan Lake dance, and I know Jade doesn't want to end up stuffed into another car trunk."

Jade nodded in agreement and glanced over at Liz who seemed goo-goo eyed as she smiled and stared at Marcus. "That woman!" she thought to herself. "She's in love with a married man." Then, suddenly she remembered her own emotional ride with Jasen. She was in no position to judge. She still struggled with accepting what had happened. But, she knew she loved him in spite of his pretense. She wondered to herself if trust could ever be found again. Or was love enough?

Jasen continued. "Liz and I have talked in detail about our next move. Treasury and the FBI have decided to join forces and have approved our team. The key is remaining just out of sight from the apparent multiple layers of Trevane protectors that seem to be everywhere. Liz has come up with a plan, so I'll let her explain."

"Thanks, Jasen," said Elizabeth. "We'll all be operating totally under the radar from this point on. Our agencies will deny that they even know us. Jasen, Jade, and I will be assigned to DC. Marcus, you and Danny have some more digging to do back in Greenwood. And I don't mean for buried gold. You two need to come up when one of your clever disguises since your faces may be familiar to your targets. I'm sure you can do that. Here's my list of your targets." She handed Marcus a file.

"Your goal is to find the connection between the wired KKK money and anyone of importance in DC. Luther's dead but I suspect he left some crumbs behind in Itta Bena that will help. Just be careful, guys. I wouldn't want anything to happen to you." She smiled and looked at Marcus as if she specifically meant him.

"The three of us will be headed to DC. Jade will be working on the phone tapping angle of known associates of the Virginia bank account owner. Jasen will be digging into the land purchase history and how it relates all the way back to the Choctaws. Just an FYI, we think the land issue has ties to plans for more casinos in north-central Mississippi. There's billions to be made for those who control that land once owned by Greenwood Leflore. You might also be very surprised to learn that Roger Trevane's family tree has a branch that traces back to the Mississippi Choctaws. Just another reason to wonder what Trevane may be involved in."

"Okay, any questions?" asked Liz. "We'll talk more about contacting each other later. I'm also passing out the information on our new aliases. Study it well. We'll have a conference call next week before we start our new plan. Unofficially, it's called Operation Blood Gold. The enormous amount of laundered money that may be involved did not happen without casualties along the way. It's tainted and we won't stop until we solve this. Good luck to us all."

***

The flight back to Atlanta was uneventful. Jasen and Jade were on the same flight but did not sit together. Both wondered to themselves about the next chapter in their roller coaster affair. Jade leaned her head back on the headrest, closed her eyes, and drifted back to the white sandy beaches of Aruba and the touch of Jasen's hand holding hers.

CHAPTER TWENTY-THREE

Starkville after Dark

The Campus
Mississippi State University
Fall 1998

An ominous darkness had fallen on the unusually quiet campus as Ariel Prospero and Ernestine Marshall left the Sanderson Student Activity Center on a Monday night the week before fall classes were scheduled to start. The old activity center had been razed to make way for a new modernized center that had opened in the spring. It was an exciting time for the two junior sorority sisters and best friends. Far from the security and comforts of their Georgian homes and families, the two young women walked south down George Perry Street toward President's Circle and the center of the sprawling campus. They laughed and giggled as Ariel relived her neighbor Jade's and her father's strange and interesting escapades and escapes from dangers over the past year.

"I can still hear the crack of my Big Bertha driver on Damian's head," said Ariel. "I didn't have a clue about who he was, but I knew Jade was in trouble. Goodness, I'm surprised I didn't kill him. That would have been *real* ugly. I mean, I really slammed him hard with that club."

"Did you really never tell your mom about that night?" asked Teenie.

"No, I never did. I told Dad the next morning but he said he wouldn't tell her until later. The divorce sort of made it a moot point. Mom was always insanely jealous of Jade for some reason. She never trusted Dad about anything."

"Are you okay with the divorce—I mean, did it surprise you?"

"It didn't surprise me one bit," responded Ariel. "Mom was very unhappy—she *had* been for a long time. I guess I'm more surprised that they stayed together as long as they did. Parents! Go figure. I never understood why two people who were so miserable tolerated each other for that long. You know, divorce is pretty common now. Don't get me wrong—I *hate* divorces. I don't think I'll ever commit to any man unless I know he's the one. In fact, even the very thought of marriage scares me."

"Okay, girlfriend, what's your secret for knowing who's really the 'one'?" Teenie wasn't dating and had never had a serious boyfriend.

Ariel looked at her friend and smiled. "I really don't have a magic formula, but I can sort of imagine a guy that's like my dad."

"You mean tall, muscular, tanned, and handsome?" Teenie asked as she grinned.

"Don't be so shallow," quipped Ariel. "I mean, yeah, that would be nice, but I'm talking about what's on the inside. Jade told me that her mom had convinced her that most men are simply jerks—selfish and superficial. She told me that my dad seemed different. Kind, intelligent, caring, principled, concerned more about others than himself, and gentle on top of that. She said that was how she saw him. I have to agree. He and I are very close. I'm glad he's found some happiness now. He deserves it."

"I admire you, Ariel. I wish my Dad and I had that kind of relationship. He's always too busy keeping up with his grocery empire. I'm curious. Do you think you *really* know your dad? I mean, Mom told me once that everybody has two personas—the one you see and the one they keep secret. Have you ever wondered if your dad has a secret side? I mean, what's with all of this mystery and intrigue that Jade is wrapped up in? How did your dad ever get involved in all of that? Is he just an innocent acquaintance or is something else going on there?"

"Your imagination is going a little crazy. My dad is a straight shooter—what you see is what you get. Jade, however, is another story. Her life has more mysteries, kinks, twists, and turns than any suspense thriller that I've ever read. But, I think she's really a neat lady. We kind of bonded. She gave me that t-shirt—you know, 'Strong Women Scare Weak Men.' I hope I'll be strong like her."

"You're already pretty strong if you ask me. By the way, what happened over in Greenwood that night last year that you followed your dad and Jade? And why in Heaven's name did you even follow them over there in the first place? You never told me why. I can't believe you never told me more details about Jade and your father and what happened."

"Well, truthfully, Dad asked me to promise to keep tight-lipped about his personal life. Believe me, I've wanted to share this for a long time. You have to promise that this stays just between us. Dad told me before he left that he was on the verge of solving some of Jade's mysteries about her distant relationship to some old Indian chief and that he needed to find out what was behind all of the nut cases that seemed to be stalking Jade. I think he had appointed himself as her protector. And there was that really weird thing about that rooster, which Jade kept in her kitchen. If you knew the entire story about that rooster, you'd never look at roosters the same way again!

"Anyway, Mom had already announced that she was divorcing him and had moved out. I was 100 percent behind Dad helping Jade. When he told me that he was driving over to Greenwood, I guess my curiosity got the best of me. I followed them. It was kind of dumb, in hindsight, but I didn't see any danger at the time.

"Then, this tremendous thunderstorm hit, and my car stalled on the flooded highway just outside of Greenwood. I was really freaking out—single young female, all alone, in an unfamiliar city, stranded in an unbelievable storm. Out of nowhere Jade shows up with a black man—I mean, smack dab in the middle of KKK country. My mind was going crazy!

"Then, I find out that Dad had been abducted by some maniacs or something. Jade told me to stay behind—she and her friend Willie—the black guy—were headed to some lake to find Dad. It was like a nightmare. I told Jade that there was no way I was staying behind. It was *my* dad and I wanted to help. So, I hopped in and off we went to a place called Swan Lake. It was exciting but, again, it was pretty stupid of me to go along. The men that abducted Dad were armed and dangerous Klansmen."

"Klansmen?!" exclaimed Teenie.

"Honest to God, yes, real live KKK. Dad never shared all of the details but I'm pretty sure that he was tortured."

"Tortured!" cried Teenie. "You never told me that. What happened"?

"Well, we all crept up to this remote cabin where we thought Dad was being held. Jade, Willie, and Willie's four sons pulled off a hair-raising rescue, guns blazing and all, and saved Dad from being murdered. Jade pulled one of my tricks and KO'd one of the bad guys with my golf driver. She packs a mean swing, believe me. Anyway, Dad was rescued, we were all fine, and the bad guys were hog-tied and left hanging upside down from the rafters. Willie called the authorities, and we all lived happily ever after!"

"Ariel, if you weren't my best friend, I'd say that you just made up this entire story. Come on, is this *really* what happened? I think your imagination is on overdrive. Come on, really! Things like this don't happen in *real* life, you know. I mean, I'm still trying to digest this. I think you need to write a book about it. Sounds like a best seller."

"You're right, Teenie. Sometimes I have to convince *myself* that it really happened, but it *did*. Believe me, please. Jade and Dad got themselves into a really big mess. I can't imagine anything worse happening. I just hope it's all behind them."

They continued walking along President's Circle and saw a bench on the grassy area in the center of the circle. They headed over and sat down. A short distance behind them, a black van without its headlights on pulled up to the curb and stopped. Neither girl had noticed the van.

"Do you think your dad and Jade will get married? asked Teenie. "I think they make the perfect couple."

"I think you're getting ahead of yourself *and* me. And, no, I have *not* asked Dad about his intentions with Jade. He's helping her unravel her distant past, that's all. Sometimes, though, their relationship seems off and on. They did go to Aruba together, interestingly. I think he may move in with her when our house sells."

"Doesn't that bother you?" asked Teenie.

"No, it's not my place to judge my father. It wouldn't surprise me if they live together. Just before I left to come over here, he told me that he and Jade had uncovered some information about possible criminal activities over in Greenwood. He said that they were going to the FBI. He contacted an Agent Keys in Atlanta, I think he said. I think he realized that whatever is going on, they needed professional help. I haven't talked to him in a few days so I need to check in with him and see what's going on. Sometimes Dad does act a little mysterious, but he has a lot on his mind. Commuting back and forth to Athens everyday takes its toll on him."

Teenie had heard enough about the two Js. "Changing the subject, aren't you happy that we decided to rush with Chi Omega two years ago? It's been terrific as far as I'm concerned. When we were freshmen, I thought XO was kisses and hugs, not a Greek sorority. I love the hootie owl mascot, don't you?"

Ariel smiled and said, "Yes, I remember how nervous I was about rush week two years ago, but it wasn't as bad as I thought it would be. Now we're the ones dishing it out to the new girls. I like being on this end a lot better than the newbie side, but it's nothing compared to what my dad went through.

"I think we joined the best sorority. The girls have always been so nice and caring. They really are like true sisters. I think Phi Mu would have been okay, too, but I feel good that we made the right choice. I've always loved the campus here, too. Things will start hopping again next week and especially when the football games start. The Bulldog Bash has had some great concerts, don't you agree? And all of the after game parties have been fabulous. My Dad warned me about the Cotton District before we started here, and he told me to never go there alone. I really don't think he actually knew the truth about all of those eateries and bars. I never felt threatened there, did you?"

"No, never," replied Teenie.

"I can't wait for Derby Days again in the spring. Gosh. We're juniors already. Can't believe how fast the time has gone by. I'm ready! How about you?"

"Ditto, girlfriend!" She gave Ariel a warm hug and smiled. "I still can't believe that you gave up that golf scholarship, but I can understand. You're so smart, getting that academic scholarship, too. And making the Dean's List every semester—you're unbelievable! I guess with classes, cheerleading, Chi Omega, looking for 'Mr. Right,' and all of the other distractions, your plate has been full. But, it's a waste; you were a great golfer. Did I say that you're pretty, too?" She laughed.

Ariel smiled at her loyal best friend. "We'd better not lose track of time. We're supposed to be back at the XO house by nine. It's a little past eight now. Don't you need to stop by the bookstore? It's around the corner. Let's go."

They headed around the Circle and noticed several small groups of students exiting the bookstore. They didn't, however, notice the slow-moving black van inching around the Circle behind them.

"Go on in, Teenie, and get your supplies," said Ariel. "I'm going to the ladies' room right inside. I'll wait for you on the sidewalk right here. Okay?"

"Okay, I'll just be a minute."

***

Teenie had a short list and found everything quickly. The checkout line, though, was unexpectedly slow, and she knew that Ariel was probably wondering what had happened to her.

Finally, she charged her items, grabbed her bag, and headed out the front entrance anticipating a pacing Ariel.

At first glance, she didn't see anyone on the sidewalk. She looked right then left. Ariel was nowhere in sight. A black van with no lights was moving slowly westward down Bully Boulevard away from the bookstore, but Teenie didn't notice.

Surely she isn't still in the restroom, thought Teenie to herself. Maybe she went into the store looking for her. Teenie looked up and down the sidewalk again. No one was in sight. She headed back inside, first stopping in the restroom. It appeared to be empty. She checked all of the stalls but saw no one.

"Ariel? Are you in here?" There was no response. She walked back into the store and quickly scanned up and down all of the isles. It was getting near closing time and the store was mostly empty except for the few workers at cash registers. She walked up to the front register.

"Did you happen to notice a petite, very pretty girl with shoulder-length dark hair? She's wearing a maroon sweat shirt and jeans. She's my room-mate. We seem to have 'lost' each other."

"No, sorry. I think most everyone has gone," answered the clerk.

"Okay, thanks anyway."

Satisfied that Ariel was not inside, she hurried back out the front and was hopeful that Ariel would be waiting. She saw no one. The sidewalks were vacant except for a group of male students about a block away, heading toward Fraternity Row.

Teenie was getting nervous and trying not to panic. Her heart was now racing as she paced back and forth in front of the bookstore. She debated with herself about her next step. She dared not think that something nefarious had happened. She knew Ariel was independent and strong. Maybe she had walked on back to the Chi Omega house. Yes, that's it, she thought to herself. She must have gotten impatient and gone back alone. *But, why would she leave me alone,* thought Teenie. That didn't com-pute in her mind. It was beginning to sink in that something wasn't right. Indeed, her gut tightened with a nauseous, empty feeling.

"Call the campus police?" she asked herself. "Scream for help?" No, that didn't make sense. She looked down Bully Boulevard toward Sorority Row and started walking briskly in that direction. The fast walking turned quickly to running. She ran fast, then faster and faster, soon passing the group of male students casually headed to a fraternity house.

"Where's the fire?" quipped one of the boys.

She ignored the group and ran past them like a thoroughbred horse being whipped by his jockey. She finally reached the XO house and was nearly gasping for more breath. She charged inside hoping to see Ariel sitting in the lounging area and prepared to tease her and ask, "Where have *you* been?" The only person in sight was Nicole, the house monitor, who was sitting at the reception desk, looking down as she read a book. Nicole looked up as Teenie approached her.

Teenie was wide-eyed and out of breath as she stopped at the desk and leaned over with her hands on her hips.

"Why are you panting, Teenie? Have you been jogging or something?"

"No, Nicole! I ran all the way here from the bookstore." She paused and tried to take in more air before continuing. "Ariel and I got separated. Is she back? Have you seen her? Please tell me you've seen her."

"No. I've been right here for the past hour. If she had come in, I would have seen her. What's going on?"

"I'm not sure, but I'm worried. She was waiting for me outside of the bookstore. When I came out, she was gone. I couldn't find her. I'm worried, Nicole. I'm afraid something bad has happened. My best friend has vanished. Ariel is gone."

Part Four

CHAPTER TWENTY-FOUR
A City That Keeps Its Secrets

Washington. D.C
Offices of Senator Roger Alan Trevane

I t was a day not unlike most in the Hart Senate Office Building that was home away from home for many US Senators and their large cadre of staffers that organized the senators' busy schedules and filtered and processed the unrelenting volume of mail and other communications from constituents back in their home states. There were six other office buildings around the US Capitol that provided administrative space for senators, but the Hart complex was the newest. The senators were protected by multiple layers of security that began at the entrance to the impressive office complex, continued at three outer offices, and ended with a final personal secretary—all providing more than ample separation between annoying lobbyists, nonessential visitors, potential nut cases, and the respected, powerful politicians.

Only the most veteran and powerful senators and a few committee chairs were assigned the most prestigious suites in the US Capitol building itself. The luxurious suites were invisible and inaccessible to the public. Affectionately tagged "hideaways," the twenty or so suites were secretly tucked away on the third floor of the Capitol, not too far from the Senate chambers, and all enjoyed commanding views of the sprawling Washington Mall or the Supreme Court Building.

Senator Trevane as the Senate Majority leader hands-down had the grandest and most elegant suite of all with its stupendous view of the vast Mall. An unassuming darkly tanned man in a baggy brown suit had presented appropriate credentials and made it to the senator's grand final outer office in the Hart Building and stood in front of Lois Burnham's desk.

"Good afternoon, Ms. Burnham," said the visitor. "I have an appointment to see Senator Trevane." He handed her his business card and smiled quickly and briefly. She scanned the card and immediately recognized the logo and name.

"Why yes, sir. He's expecting you. Please," she said, pointing to a large, red leather wing backed chair, "Have a seat and I'll let him know that you've arrived."

The visitor sat down and had just picked up a copy of the current *Washington Post* when Ms. Burnham returned and approached him.

"Please, Mr. Xavier, walk this way." He rose and followed her into a spacious suite that led to a private office at the far end. She held the door open as he entered, and the door closed behind him. He was greeted, not by the senator, but by a young man in an impeccably tailored navy suit adorned with a small American flag lapel pin. The young man extended his hand to the visitor.

"Mr. Xavier, good afternoon. My name is Chris Gentry, Senator Trevane's personal aide. Please follow me if you would be so kind." He turned and walked across the room to a highly polished wood paneled wall and flipped the wall switch upward then down again. The panel glided silently to the right, revealing an elevator door. The aide inserted a key into a slot located to the side of the elevator, turned it, and the doors opened, showcasing interior elevator walls decorated in crimson damask.

"Excuse me, Mr. Gentry," said Xavier. "I thought *this* was the Senator's office. Where are we going?"

Gentry responded, "Senator Trevane has several offices, Mr. Xavier. He prefers seeing you in his most private suite. The elevator will take us down to an underground tram that will take us to an office that very few people even know exists. He must really trust you," said Gentry who winked and smiled.

Frederic Ivan Xavier, known only to Senator Trevane by his actual name of Richard Jordan, did as instructed, impressed and entertained at the same time with all of the security and cloak and dagger charades. They were soon on a two-car tram that navigated easily through a well-lighted, white-tiled tunnel. Xavier guessed that the tram would lead to the Capitol Building, but Gentry was not offering a narrated tour. They exited the tram after a short ride and took another elevator that was accessed by Gentry's key. Within a minute the elevator door opened into a darkened red-carpeted corridor that led past several doors on the right side and to a set of double doors at the end of the corridor. Gentry knocked softly on the door, and it opened almost immediately.

They were greeted by a tall, gaunt but striking man who had a formidable mass of white hair topping a narrow, angular face. His penetrating, steely blue eyes and tailor-made dark gray suit complimented by a red designer tie projected a man of self-confidence and importance. He was standing in a small outer vestibule that connected to an enormous suite. His tanned face suggested ample outside activities, most likely golf or tennis thought Xavier. Gentry backed into the outer corridor as he closed the door, leaving the other two men in privacy.

"Richard, my man, or should I call you Xavier? I really hate that name but I suppose it helps protect your real identity. Anyway, I'm glad you made it through the security maze without a hitch. Come on in. Can I pour you a drink?" The senator walked into the majestic suite and over to a large ornate, granite-topped bar and retrieved two highball glasses and began adding ice to one.

"Bourbon, straight up," responded Xavier. "Thanks for seeing me. I assure you that I would not have insisted if this wasn't important." Xavier scanned the room and began to feel like he must have been escorted into a suite right out of one of Napoleon Bonaparte's four French mansions.

"Does anyone else know why you're here, Richard?"

"Not a soul, Senator. The pretense was that it's a family matter, that's all."

"Good," Trevane said. "You know how sensitive these issues can be. I have to remain anonymous and can never be even remotely connected to Greenwood matters.

"So, Richard, tell me. What happened to our man in Greenwood? Luther was the most important link to our Colombian friends. Who's taking his place?"

Xavier answered. "It's difficult to know exactly what happened. All we know is that both Luther, his nephew, and three of his security guys are dead. Federal agents were involved but the actual record of what went down has been quashed. I was hoping that you could pull some strings and find out. That's why I insisted on meeting with you personally. From everything I know, we are the only two who have any idea of the Greenwood-Washington connection. I had rather keep it that way."

"Yes, I understand. But pulling strings is the last thing I should do. I can't be connected to anything that those clowns in Greenwood bungled. But, I need you to probe deeper and see if you can find out if the cartel had other contacts in Luther's operation. I know Luther covered his tracks well, but he surely trusted someone other than his nephew."

"Yes, sir, I would hope so. Trouble is that Luther had no other living relatives or known confidants. None, that is, except for two 'terminators,' and one of them was killed in Aruba trying to protect Luther's operation. I've tried to contact his brother, Stefan Vosper, but no luck so far. I know Luther hired both of them at times to arrange convenient 'accidents' for certain people. They called Marty, the dead brother, the 'Bone Stealer.' Stefan earned the nickname the 'Bone Crusher.' It seems his scrap metal business has some impressive machines that can 'crush' the evidence into a small ball, if you get my drift."

"Please, Richard. I don't need to know these details. Just get back to Greenwood and dig around until you find out who's involved and how much they know about the money and the impending land acquisition. We're on the verge of capitalizing on a multibillion dollar gambling and gaming empire.

"That dead Indian chief Leflore was sitting on more than some mythical hidden gold treasure over which Jake Luther became obsessed. Leflore had no idea that his cotton empire granted to him by Andrew Jackson would eventually fall into the hands of non-Choctaw Mississippi land owners. I worked behind the scenes for years when I was in the Mississippi Senate to divert that land from the Choctaws to my anonymous real estate connections.

"The lawyers were quite clever, considering the historical significance, in discovering the flaws in that Rabbit Creek Treaty that Leflore finagled. If we pull this off, no one will be able to beat me at anything. Money is the means to all ends. With the kind of money I'm talking about, I will absolutely be the most powerful man in the country, maybe even the world.

"You have to protect me at any cost, Richard, and you know what that means. Anyone who is even remotely close to connecting Luther and his money to Washington has to meet with some very unfortunate luck. And I do not need to know who or when. Just do whatever it takes. I trust you, Richard. In fact, you are the only living person that I trust. Let's keep it that way. Pull this off and the Virginia account is yours. When we're done and in the White House, you'll be richer than you ever dreamed and can happily fade away into the proverbial sunset."

Trevane shook Xavier's hand and patted him on his back. "Good luck, and remember, we never had this meeting. I don't know you, and you don't know me. Why, I don't even know your name!"

***

"Stefan. Where the hell have you been!" exclaimed Xavier. "I left you several messages over the past two days. Why haven't you returned my calls?"

"Sorry, Mr. Xavier. I've been a little preoccupied. My brother's death cannot go unavenged."

"What are you saying, Stefan? What have you done? We don't need more attention drawn to Luther's death and what's left of his band in Greenwood."

"I don't care about that, Xavier. Marty was my only brother. We were very close. That couple in Georgia is responsible for his death. Someone has to pay. I have Mr. Prospero's daughter. It'll get his attention, no doubt."

"Stefan, we don't need another killing or whatever you're up to that might draw in more feds. Where do have her? What are you going to do with her?"

"Let's just say that she's somewhere where the sun don't shine and where no one can find her. I'm going to use her to lure that creep back this way. Then, he's going to pay for what happened to Marty. Don't try to talk me out of this. Marty deserves retribution."

"Well, for God's sake, leave me and the rest of us out of this. We have a bigger agenda, and a lot is at stake. I don't know you, and you never heard of me. Don't ever forget that. If I need you to take care of anything back in Greenwood, I will contact you the usual way. Whatever you're up to, just do it quickly and get back to your junk yard in case you're needed. And, remember, Stefan…clean up any mess you make, understand?"

"I understand." He grinned broadly as he ended the call. His thoughts shifted back to his captive and what he would do to her next.

CHAPTER TWENTY-FIVE

The Crypt

The stark darkness, 100 percent absence of any light, and the total quietness permeated the deathlike, dank stench of her surroundings. Her hands were bound behind her back and were rubbed raw and bloody around her wrists from her struggling to release her bindings. She remembered only being grabbed from behind while she lingered on the sidewalk outside of the bookstore, waiting for her friend Teenie. Her abductor had smothered her face with a chemically laced cloth, covered her head with a dark hood, and in a flash, her consciousness vanished.

She awoke with a startle in the darkest-of-dark places, like an unlighted coal mine miles and miles underground, with which only her imagination could grapple. She had never given any thought to being wide awake and at the same time being totally unable to see her own body and arms at her side. She had suddenly become aware of her hands bound behind her back when she instinctively tried to raise a hand toward her eyes. Was she dead? How could she be alive and it still be so dark?

She sat up and instinctively shouted. "Where am I? Help! Someone help! Can anyone hear me?" Her frantic voice echoed off of the walls of her imprisonment in a painful reverberating roar. No sounds came back other than her pounding heart. She madly searched her mind for explanations. What was happening? Where was she? Who abducted her? Why? Her mind raced faster and faster, begging for answers. She found none.

She had fleetingly thought that she might be buried alive and in a coffin, but sitting up had temporarily dashed that fear. She stood slowly and cautiously. When completely upright, she breathed slight relief. She couldn't be in a coffin. But how could any other place be so dark? And the air seemed thin and was getting staler by the minute. Suffocation fears shrouded her but were quickly repressed.

She carefully began to take baby steps forward. She reasoned that she was in some type of room without windows and probably underground, judging from the moldy, decaying smell and utter darkness. More horrors of critter company sped through her thoughts, and she thought she could hear the faint squeaking of scurrying four-legged beasties. She felt no sensations of smaller creatures crawling on her skin, but she shook her torso back and forth just in case.

She relaxed her body and listened for further sounds. Suddenly, she felt a sharp pain in one of her wrists behind her back. It was a biting sensation, and she reflexively screamed and shook her body and bound hands tied behind her back. Something let out a high-pitched screech, and she heard the patter of a creature scampering away from her. She had company. It was a rat who had gnawed at her raw, blood-covered wrists. Her fear factor soared as she could only imagine being overwhelmed by a pack of hungry, plague-infested rodents. She fought off sheer panic as she tried to refocus.

Nothing made sense. What was happening? Why? She needed to find answers but most of all she needed to survive. She remembered her friend Jade's conclusion that she was a strong woman. *Find your strength,* she demanded silently to herself. *There has to be a way out. Rein in the negative fears. Don't let panic win. Get control. Live!*

She inched forward in the inky black darkness, hoping that she would not step on the unwelcomed co-occupants of her terrifying entrapment, and she continued to try to free her tight bindings. She guessed she had gone about five feet when she bumped against something solid. She turned her back and with her bound hands felt a cold, stone wall that was slightly moist. She turned to the right and with her back against it crept along the wall. She sensed a corner, turned, and continued along another wall for about ten feet where she found the next corner. After several feet in a new direction, she felt a long seam in the wall and what seemed to be a metal door hinge.

"A door!" she exclaimed loudly. She inched a few feet farther and felt the other edge of the apparent metal door. For a moment she irrationally dared think of escape and had visions of finding a door handle or a door knob. With her bound hands she was unable to reach more than waist high. No knob or handle was evident. She correctly surmised that that door could only be opened from the outside. She suddenly remembered the rough metallic edge of the door hinge and reversed her steps. She groped again for the hinge and felt the ragged, sharp metal edges.

She pressed her back against the door and by touch and feel pushed her bindings to the hinge and began to move her hands up and down. Her raw bloody hands stung with an intense, sharp pain, but she needed to free her hands if she had any hope of escape, as remote as the thought sounded to her.

Locked in an apparent rectangular room underground with a metal door that could only be opened by someone from the outside—the stark reality suddenly overwhelmed her mind like the last shovelful of dirt being thrown over a freshly planted coffin. The odds of escape seemed impossible. Hope was turning to despair.

Her father had taught her to always have a plan B. She didn't even have a plan A. As she continued to rub her bindings against the sharp-edged hinge, she began to wonder why her life was being snatched away from her. She was too young to die. What had she done to deserve her plight? Thoughts of final resignation battled with her dwindling will and strength and pushed harder and harder, deeper and deeper, to overpower her.

Then, suddenly, she began to feel an eerie calming as her thoughts drifted to what may be on the other side. Would she go down a brilliant white tunnel? Who would be waiting for her? Maybe heaven is like what she had been taught in Sunday School. She stopped her frantic efforts to cut through her bindings, slid very slowly down the wall, closed her eyes, and sat motionless, waiting.

***

Stefan Vosper had left a message on Jasen Prospero's answering machine.

"I've got your daughter, and if you ever want to see her alive again, you will follow my directions precisely. I will call back at exactly 8:00 a.m. tomorrow. Your daughter has little time left. If you do not answer and if you go to the police, your daughter will die." *Click*.

Jasen Prospero and Elizabeth Keys listened to the message three times hoping to get some clues from the voice or background noise. They had rushed back to Jasen's home in Lawrenceville after Jasen had received a frantic-sounding phone call from Ernestine Marshall. She told Jasen the mysterious circumstances of Ariel's disappearance. She told him that she had contacted the campus police who had decided to wait until the next day to make it an official missing person case.

"Policy," the officer told Teenie. "College students often go missing for short times," he said. "Give her time. She'll surface." Teenie failed at convincing the officer that something bad must have happened to Ariel. She couldn't wait on policy and tracked down Jasen who she finally reached when she remembered Ariel mentioning FBI Agent Keys in Atlanta.

Jasen knew that Teenie was right. He didn't want to think that Ariel could possibly get mixed up in his secret investigation, but he was not surprised that Jake Luther's demise would not go unheeded by ruthless associates once they learned the truth. Elizabeth had assured him that her report about the Itta Bena shootout would be marked "top secret" and would be sealed. Jasen had incorrectly assumed that Ariel's circumstance was connected to Luther's death. He was unaware of the "Bone Stealer's" brother.

"Why do you think someone has abducted Ariel?" Jasen asked Elizabeth.

"Well, I'm thinking like you. Somehow word got out that you were involved in Luther's unfortunate death—or should I say 'fortunate'—whatever. Anyway, you've been tracking this band of thugs for a long time. I think someone decided that if they can't take care of you, i.e., eliminate you, then they'll use Ariel to get to you. Obviously, they're betting on your vulnerability. Makes sense. You and Ariel are so close."

"I'd do anything for her, you've got that right. We've got to get her back. We've got to play this smart, though, Liz. Let's talk through this. I won't sleep until he calls back tomorrow. Damn it! I hate myself. I never thought that Ariel would become a target. If something happens to her, well…I'd rather not think about that. We'll get her back. Somehow. We have to."

***

The doorbell dinged at exactly 7:45 a.m. Jasen opened the front door and froze for a brief second. He had not expected this. It was Jade. He stared at her stunning beauty highlighted by warm rays of the early morning sun, and he felt his heart skip a beat. He stared and grappled for words.

"Well, good morning to you, too," she said. "Are you going to just stand there and stare at me like an idiot or are you going to let me in?"

He quickly thawed his awkwardness and responded. "Oh, of course. Please come in. I guess I'm just surprised to see you. Surprised but glad." He smiled and stood aside as she entered.

"I heard about Ariel, Jasen. I want to help," she said as she walked into the den and saw Elizabeth Keys sitting on the sofa. "Oh, Liz! I didn't know you were here. Been here long?"

"I spent the night, Jade."

Jade looked at her with raised brows then glanced at Jasen.

Liz responded quickly. "Relax, Jade. I slept on the sofa. Jasen's not my type, anyway." She chuckled. "Now, Marcus, on the other hand, well, yes…my Mr. Guy Noir." She was smiling from ear-to-ear.

"Okay, then," Liz said. Let's get back to business. We're expecting an eight o'clock call from the abductor. I'm glad you're here, Jade. Jasen can use the support."

"So, what's this all about, Liz? Who took Ariel and why?"

"We're not exactly sure but will soon find out. Apparently it's a revenge abduction—payback for Jake Luther? Not sure. You know as much as we do. Can I get you a cup of coffee while we get ready for the call?"

***

Ariel sat in her entombment leaning against the cold, metal door in the utter darkness that she was imagining to be like a bottomless, cosmic black hole. She felt dizzy and sleepy as she guessed that she was running out of time and out of life-sustaining air. The oxygen was nearly all consumed, and carbon dioxide was winning the battle of the gases. She had relived all of her fondest memories, starting from her toddler days, and was mentally ready. *Que sera sera,* she thought.

"I love you, Dad," she said aloud in her dark, empty tomb. She closed her eyes, relaxed her muscles, and faded silently into another world.

Immediately, she saw a brilliant white light shining from the end of a long passage. A blurry image seemed to be gesturing to her to walk toward the light. Her new world all at once was at peace, and she felt amazingly safe and loved. She stood and looked at her now unbound hands that were smooth and healed, then walked toward the light, which grew brighter and brighter with each step that she took. She was not afraid. Closer and closer she came to the light, and beckoning arms extended toward her. She felt a refreshing breath of cool air, and a gentle wind swept across her face. One more step. Then she would be safe forever.

She reached for the extended arms. In a fraction of a second, the passage was immediately pitch black. Her eyes were still open but she saw nothing or no one. Suddenly, she felt movement of the door that she had collapsed against earlier and realized she was still sitting. The door was being pushed against her, and she instinctively moved aside. She shielded her eyes when out of the darkness a seemingly very bright light shone across the room. It was only the beam of a flashlight, but to her eyes, it was brighter than a midday sun. She slowly reopened her eyes as she focused to see the source of the light and who had entered her apparent crypt. She no longer felt safe, as a suffocating fear pressed against her chest. She couldn't breathe.

"Where are you, Missy?" beckoned a man who was scanning the tomb with his flashlight. The beam finally glided to her spot partially behind the opened, very thick metal door. He shined the beam at her face, and she quickly covered her eyes.

"Aaaah, there you are. Guess you were beginning to think I wasn't coming back. Not much breathable air ten feet under the old chief's mausoleum, is there? Too bad he's not here anymore. He could have kept you company. Ha! This old crypt's been empty for some time now. Grave robbers. Some very unhappy Choctaws, so the story goes, took his body out of here years ago and buried him facedown in an unmarked grave. Nobody knows where that is. Too bad. I hear he was a pretty darn good Indian chief."

Ariel was eerily beginning to feel more like the living again as the fresh air from the open tomb door began to filter in. She felt an encouraging surge of her youthful spirit.

"Who are you and why did you kidnap me?" she demanded. "Why am I here? And why are my hands tied? What kind of monster are you! Please, let me out of here!"

"Screaming at me will not win you any favors. You're here because of what your father did to my brother. If he agrees to my terms, you might have a chance of getting out of here alive." He lied.

"Please, just untie my hands. They hurt so *bad*," Ariel pleaded.

"You'd like that I'm sure, but I'm afraid I can't trust you just yet." He walked over to her and reached out to caress her face. She jerked away, partly defensively and partly in disgust.

"Testy, aren't we," he snarled. "In case you haven't noticed, I'm in complete control. You'll do whatever I ask. You don't really have a choice, now do you?"

Ariel looked back at his face, which was barely visible behind the bright beam of the flashlight trained on her face. He was clean-shaven and had very short hair, almost like he had partially shaved his head. From her sitting position on the floor, he appeared to be medium height and wore all black clothing. His appearance was not nearly as menacing as his growling animal-like voice. She thought again of her t-shirt—"Strong Women Scare Weak Men." At that very moment she knew she had to dig deeper and find her strength.

"If your dad is smart, he'll be waiting for my call soon. Then you might be able to see the light of day again. For now, just cool your pretty little charming personality."

She could sense that he was studying her body and imagining having whatever he desired. It sickened her at the very thought. She would *never* let him touch her, even if it meant getting killed. Never!

"I imagine that you might be a little thirsty," he said as he threw a plastic bottle of water at her feet.

"And exactly how do you expect me to drink that with my hands tied behind my back? And I need to pee too. For God's sake, whoever you are, untie me!"

He aimed the light at her face again and grunted. "You look pretty smart to me. Figure it out."

As he turned to leave and rotated the flashlight back to the door, Ariel momentarily noticed that the tomb was not empty. She could see a short-legged, old wooden table centered in the room. Her guess was that the coffin of the body that once occupied the crypt probably rested on the table. The wheels in her head began to turn.

The "Bone Crusher" closed the door behind him with an echoing, pounding sound, and Ariel's world immediately turned black again. She wanted to scream out but decided to not waste precious air. A veil of deathlike quietness filled the crypt but could not drown out the thumping and pounding of her beating heart.

CHAPTER TWENTY-SIX

The Call

Holding her coffee cup, Jade sat down in an overstuffed leather chair and studied the faces of Jasen and Liz who sat across from her on the sofa. The intensity told her more than she cared to know. She thought about her special night dining with Ariel almost two years ago and Ariel's creative bravery in subduing the deranged Damian. She knew her mother Jean would have been proud, and she was glad she had made Damian pay for what he did to Jean. If she had a daughter, she would be just like Ariel. She wondered for a moment about Ariel's mom Caitlyn and if she knew what had happened. She had sensed from Jasen earlier that Caitlyn had mostly faded from their lives. *So strange,* she thought.

She imagined a renewed relationship with Jasen, if she could ever trust him again, and what it might be like to be Ariel's step-mother. The pain of James Jr.'s suicide had been repressed deeply, but it haunted her sometimes on lonely nights. She took a sip of the hot coffee and refocused.

"Jasen, please tell me if you have a plan," Jade said. "Ariel is so special and I know you are blaming yourself. Surely, this is connected to Big Jake's death. But, what about the guy in Aruba? And what about the nameless dead attacker that we buried in the concrete slab next door?"

Jasen looked up, quickly realizing that Liz knew nothing about their winter storm encounter with the knife- and gun-wielding home invader. He had never explained his strange insistence and reason for burying the body and not reporting it, other than hiding their affair from Caitlyn.

Liz perked up and quickly digested Jade's questions. "What's this about burying a body next door? Jasen, I don't think you ever mentioned that in any of our conversations or reports." She sat back and waited for his reaction.

Jasen responded without hesitation. "It was all about protecting my deep cover with Treasury. It's not pertinent now, so, please let's concentrate on Ariel. I'll fill you in later, Liz. Please. It's almost eight. And, yes, Jade, it could be any of those reasons."

Liz looked back at him with some puzzlement and decided to let it rest for now. "Okay, but I want details later."

Sharply at 8:00 a.m., the call came in. Liz had arranged for her office to set up a trace, and all the equipment was in place. After three rings she motioned for Jasen to pick up. She was listening on another headset.

"Hello?" said Jasen with a hint of nervousness.

"Listen carefully," said a deep and very distorted voice. He spoke quickly. "I'll only say this once. If you want to see your daughter alive, follow these directions: Take Malmaison Road north of Carrollton, Mississippi, and go exactly eleven miles to a dirt road on the left. It's marked by a small sign that says 'To Malmaison.' It leads to the ruins of the mansion. I'll be waiting there. Come alone. I have associates who will be observing you. No weapons. Wear a white t-shirt and shorts, no shoes, no belt, no hat. Be there at 5:00 p.m. today." Click. The line went dead.

Jasen and Jade looked hopefully at Liz. She looked back in disappointment.

"It was less than thirty seconds. Not enough time for a trace. It was a pay phone, we think. I'm sorry. Whether he is calling from the

Carrollton area or not is hard to say. It'll take us nearly eight hours to get there if we drive. He could be anywhere in between. And who knows if he's even holding Ariel there. He wants *you*, Jasen. He's not really interested in Ariel, I hope. I mean, for goodness sake, he could be right under our noses. Anyway, we need to move. I think we'll head to the Atlanta airport and take the Bureau's Leer jet to Greenwood. We can't risk not meeting his deadline. We'll discuss the plan in flight."

"Liz," said Jade. "He said to come alone. Are you sure it's safe?"

"No way, Sweetie, that I'd risk Jasen going alone. I have some thoughts. I'll explain on the plane. I assume you want to go since you're on my payroll, correct?"

"Of course, I want to go. Jasen needs me. We both need to get Ariel back. I feel like I'm as much to blame as Jasen."

Jasen stood and walked around the coffee table to Jade. She stood and looked at his strong and determined face. He saw that special look in her beautiful green eyes, reached out, and hugged her gently. She put her arms around his broad back and squeezed him tightly.

"Thank you," he said. "Thank you."

***

The sleek jet landed at the small Greenwood Leflore Airport less than an hour after wheels up in Atlanta. Agent Keys had alerted Marcus and Danny who were driving up from Jackson after coordinating their next steps at unraveling the Jake Luther network when they arrived back in Greenwood. They offered any support needed. Liz asked them to contact Willie Campbell and gather some intelligence about the now vacated vast Leflore estate. If anyone knew the area, Willie did. She asked that he await her phone call once they arrived in Carrollton.

Liz had gone over the plan several times during the short flight. Jasen would wear a small microphone on the button of his shorts, which also incorporated a tracking sensor. She elected to not let him wear an ear bud for two-way communications. She couldn't be sure how extensive Jasen might be searched or how sophisticated the abductor or abductors were.

Liz felt that it was less risky if Jasen drove from Carrollton to the old mansion site completely alone, convinced the caller meant what he said. She, Jade, and another agent would follow fifteen minutes later in a plain white van with a local plumbing company logo. The Jackson agents had borrowed the van on short notice without difficulty. They would remain a safe distance from the turn to the mansion ruins. If Jasen got into trouble they could converge on the site quickly. From what Willie Campbell told them, there was only one road to the ruins and back out.

Liz had also arranged for a local Civil Air Patrol helicopter at the airport to be on standby in case they needed air coverage. She chose the CAP over local enforcement because she didn't know who she could trust. Jake Luther seemed to have most of Leflore County in his back pocket and on the take. Marcus and Danny were en route to Greenwood, but not close enough yet to join them.

Jasen had committed to turning himself over to the abductor only if Ariel was released and allowed to drive away in his car. He was gambling that the abductor would keep his word and release Ariel. They all knew that they were likely dealing with seasoned criminals who might also decide to shoot Jasen and Ariel on the spot. It was a catch 22. Jasen saw no other option.

"By the way," Liz told them. "We've been checking out as many angles as we can on who may be behind this. Obviously, Luther had associates in many places and some in high positions. Any of them could be after revenge. The Vosper character that threw Jade in that car trunk in Aruba, we learned, has a brother in this area. He owns a scrap metal yard on the eastern outskirts of Greenwood and just happens to have an impressive rap sheet. Seems he is known around the criminal circles as the Bone Crusher. If you recall, his brother was known as the Bone Stealer. I have two agents from the Jackson office headed over to his junk and scrap metal yard as we speak. Who knows, he may have been very close to his brother and is more than just a little pissed off at you and Jade.

"Like I said, we are playing every angle. But, I'm like you Jasen. This entire mystery, links to our deceased Chief Leflore, and constant abductions, assaults, and intimidations suggest that there are some very powerful predators calling the shots in this apparent undeclared war. I think we're just chipping around the edges of something very big. Once we get Ariel back, we have to dive deeper into this deception. We need to get to DC ASAP. I think the answers are there."

CHAPTER TWENTY-SEVEN

The Bone Crusher

A riel had anticipated the next visit by her captor. He had arrogantly underestimated her resolve and ingenuity to "figure it out." The brief recharging of her entombment with fresher air and the challenge of getting the bottled water had helped her find the inner strength that she knew was there. Challenged by the creep's retort, she had worked her way back to the sharp edge of the door hinge, and with a final surge of adrenalin, she managed to slowly saw her rope bindings almost all the way through. Then with all the strength left in her young muscular arms, she ripped apart the final strands and was finally free.

She fumbled in the dark and finally located the bottle of water that had been thrown at her feet. At first, she gulped the room temperature, refreshing water but quickly decided to back off. She had no idea how long she might need it. She decided to pour a few drops on her burning wrists. The pain eased only slightly. She had to relieve her aching bladder, which proved to be a challenge she had never imagined as she worked her way in the dark to the far corner of the crypt, pulled down her jeans and panties, and squatted. More immediate relief. Being all alone in a 130-year-old, dark crypt, modesty was not an issue.

Her resourcefulness had already kicked in, and she remembered her quick thinking the night she whacked the living daylights out of Damian Winters. She had already decided on a substitute for her golf driver. The base table that Leflore's coffin must have rested upon appeared to be wooden from the brief glimpse she had of it as her abductor left. The old wood was probably soft or deteriorated. She worked her way slowly to the center of the tomb, appreciating humbly how blind people "saw" their world—totally by instinct, feel, and use of other senses. After a few feet, she bumped into the table and knelt down to find a corner and one of the legs or possibly a side board. Hopefully, she prayed to herself, she could find a piece to pry loose. It would be her new club.

The old wood turned out to be softer and more pliable that she had expected. She easily snapped off one of the short legs but immediately sensed that it would be too short to allow much leverage against her taller foe. She worked her way around the table and felt the side boards, which were at least eight feet long. She went to work on the board nearest the leg that she had snapped off. It easily separated from the nails that had once held the table together, which had supported a coffin and body. She worked slowly hoping that the board would not break before she had an acceptable length. Suddenly, it snapped before she reached the end at the next leg. But, she ran the length with her hands and guessed that she had about a five-foot board that would make a decent club. Most of the board was still solid enough to wallop with some force, she thought and hoped.

She didn't know how long it would be before the growly voiced captor would return, but she felt her way back to the metal door and slid her back down the cold surface, put down the improvised club, and sat, drawing her knees up to her chest. She hadn't thought too much about food over the past unknown number of hours. In total darkness, time was basically nonexistent. Now, she realized how long it had been since she had eaten. Her stomach growled like her abductor's voice, and her hunger pangs surged, making her temporarily forget about her raw arms.

***

She had rehearsed her moves over and over for what seemed like hours when she finally heard the crypt door beginning to open. She picked up her improvised wooden club, stood, and pressed her back tightly against the cool stone wall. As the door opened, she slowly and silently pressed her petite body behind the opening door.

The Bone Crusher gradually shifted his flashlight around the room. "Okay, my pretty. Where are you?"

She saw the light nearing her location, but she was effectively concealed behind the door. When he did not immediately see her, he walked over to the coffin table, noticing that it was collapsed on one end and had a partially broken-off side board.

He tried to assimilate what he saw and uttered, "So, what do we have here, little lady? Did you have an accident?" He walked around to the other side of the table, and then she made her move.

She bolted like a spring-loaded cat from behind the door and charged at him with her makeshift club cocked to her side and slightly behind her head. He sensed movement in the room and began to turn toward her, the light lagging behind his body movement. Ariel aimed for his head, and the board smashed with a reverberating *whamm* against his left temple. His head recoiled violently backward. He staggered away from her, grabbing the side of his head, and collapsed behind the end of the coffin table. The flashlight rolled away from him and shone toward the open door. The element of surprise had caught him completely off guard.

Ariel bounded toward the door and up the steep stone stairway that led to the family mausoleum at ground level. She saw daylight through a partially open wrought-iron gateway and ran toward it, almost leaping back into the real world. She stopped momentarily, looked behind her, and suddenly realized that she had not locked her abductor in the crypt. It was too late to go back.

She scanned her surroundings that were mostly dense underbrush and tall hardwood trees and pines. She saw what looked like a narrow pathway and resumed her escape, not knowing where the path would lead or if the captor had accomplices lurking around.

It appeared to be late in the afternoon, and she knew she could be easily seen. She thought of just hiding in the heavily forested countryside, but her instincts said to run as far away as possible from her horrific underground prison. She ran up and down the meandering path that followed a rolling hill terrain, stumbling at times over tree roots that crisscrossed the narrow dirt path. Faster and faster until she was almost out of breath. She paused and leaned against a large tree trying to catch her wind. Her heart beat like a loud drum against her sternum, and her heavy breathing replaced the silence of the deep woods.

She resumed her winded sprinting, and she could see daylight at the end of the path about twenty five yards ahead. It opened into a clearing, and she could see the ruins of a chimney that had toppled into a rubble of soot-covered bricks. She ran faster and faster toward the clearing. Without warning, out of nowhere, he appeared just at the end of the path. It was the Bone Crusher.

Ariel tried to stop. She stumbled forward, then staggered right and left. Her momentum carried her within a few feet of her abductor who had a stream of blood dripping down the side of his head. He did not hesitate as he lunged for her and grabbed her arm, clamping his massive hand tightly around her bloodstained wrist. He pulled, almost dragging her into the clearing, and she had no strength left to resist.

"Guess I didn't give you enough credit, missy. You pack a mean wallop for a such a skinny thing. But, I assure you, it'll take more of a blow than that to stop me. Good try, though." He growled at her and grinned.

He continued to pull her in spite of her weaker efforts to break his vise-like grip. As they entered the clearing, she noticed a black van parked nearby. She had a split-second flashback of being grabbed and thrown into that van in front of the campus bookstore.

He held her arm tightly and opened the side door of the van, retrieving a rope. A gun was lying beside a pile of other supplies that she guessed he used in her abduction and who-knew what other unfortunate souls that got in his way.

"Turn around!" he commanded in his raspy growl. "Try to run again and you'll get a bullet in your back." He twisted her body around and wound the rope around her throbbing wrists. He tied the knot extra tight, and she cried out in pain.

"Stop! You're hurting me," she cried.

"Get in the van and shut your damn mouth," he commanded as he picked up the gun and shoved her into the van.

"I'm expecting company any minute now. One peep out of you and it'll be the last sound you ever make. I'll be standing right here." He slammed the door shut and stood by the van waiting.

***

It was one minute before 5:00 p.m. when Jasen pulled his car into the clearing. He stopped ten yards before reaching a man who was standing by a black van. At his side the stranger held a .38 caliber handgun pointed at the ground. Jasen killed the engine and sat in his car studying his unknown foe. He scanned the surroundings for others but saw no one else. Other than the scant ruins from the once magnificent mansion of Greenwood Leflore, there were no dwellings, only a wooded countryside and a path that led south of the clearing.

"Get out of the car. No funny business or your daughter dies."

Jasen stepped out from the driver's side of the car and closed the door.

"I need to see Ariel…now!" he said.

The abductor aimed the .38 that he held in one hand at Jasen's head while sliding the side panel door of the van open.

"Get out!" he snapped at Ariel.

Ariel scooted to the edge of the door and stepped down. The abductor grabbed her arm tightly and held her close to his side. She resisted only slightly.

"Dad!" she exclaimed. She had concluded in the crypt that she would never see him again.

"Ariel, are you okay?" asked Jasen anxiously.

"I told you to keep quiet," he said. "No talking. You can see she's okay," he said looking at Jasen.

"Just let her go. You've got me. That's what you wanted. Let her go."

"Not until I have you secured. Take off your shirt and shorts and toss them aside. Then open your trunk. Do it now!"

Jasen hesitated, knowing that he would be giving up the one-way communication and tracker button.

"I said undress. Do it!" He was getting agitated and waved the gun at Jasen.

He stripped to his boxer shorts and threw his shirt and shorts to one side of the clearing. Then he opened the driver's door and pulled the trunk release. Jasen saw that his options had evaporated and could only trust that the abductor would release Ariel as promised if he cooperated.

"Now, climb into your trunk."

"Not until Ariel is out of sight. Let her go!" demanded Jasen.

"I don't think that this is a negotiation. I have a gun. You don't. Get in the trunk and I'll let her go."

Jasen looked at his daughter and said, "Don't worry, sweetheart. I'll be okay. Just get out of here as fast as you can."

The abductor continued to wave the gun at Jasen who walked to the back of his car. The Bone Crusher pushed Ariel toward the back of the car as Jasen climbed in.

"Lie down on your side and turn your back to me. Do it!"

"Please let her go. She's done nothing to you. Let her go," pleaded Jasen as he rolled on his side.

"You two are so close, how sweet," mocked their adversary. Without warning the crusher suddenly shoved Ariel into the trunk, and she landed awkwardly on top of her dad. The trunk lid slammed shut with a resounding, loud thud, rocking the car slightly.

"How's that for being close!" He laughed through his snarling teeth.

The Bone Crusher was determined to get his pound of flesh and more. He opened the driver's door, settled into the seat, and started the car. He turned the steering wheel sharply and sped off through a small opening in between two bushy trees. It led to a hidden road that Jasen had not noticed. Jasen had no way of knowing that it was another exit from the old estate. Liz, Jade, and the other FBI agent would be approaching from what they thought was the only entrance and exit. Willie Campbell apparently never knew that Chief Leflore had a secret back road to his estate.

The abductor had planned his escape cleverly. He felt proud as he sped down the narrow dirt road that would lead back to the far western end of Malmaison Road, close to the northern fringes of the Greenwood city limits. He slapped the steering wheel with his palm.

"Hot damn!" he exclaimed. "No one outsmarts the Bone Crusher."

CHAPTER TWENTY-EIGHT

Crushed

L iz, Jade, and the other agent had listened to Jasen's encounter with the abductor and decided to move toward the dirt road leading to the ruins where Jasen was ordered to get into the car trunk. The sounds became muffled and inaudible after Jasen had tossed his clothes aside. Liz was willing to take the risk and try to block the abductor's exit from the estate. She ordered the agent to speed toward the turn to the Malmaison ruins.

She had just received a call on her mobile phone from the two Jackson agents that had gone to Stefan Vosper's scrap metal yard. They had seen no sign of him or anyone else. They had left the junkyard and were almost to Carrollton to rendezvous with Liz. It raised Liz's suspicions that Vosper might be the abductor. She realized too late that she should have told the Jackson agents to stay near Vosper's junkyard in case he returned.

She and Jade looked at each other with almost frantic concern when they heard a voice transmitted through the concealed button microphone, the voice that had ordered Jasen into the car trunk. A criminal known as the Bone Crusher who just happened to run a scrap metal business where junk cars and other junk metals were crushed and recycled…if their adding two and two made sense, Jasen and Ariel were in deep trouble. It was time to move in.

They turned onto the small dirt road that led to the old ruins, fully expecting to be detected by accomplices or to meet the abductor driving Jasen's car with Jasen locked inside the trunk. They screeched to a stop in the small clearing near the pile of the old, blackened chimney bricks. Jasen's car was not in sight, only a black van with its side panel open.

All three exited their own van hurriedly and ran over to the black van and peered inside—it was empty. No Ariel. No Jasen. No abductor. They looked at each other and knew the obvious.

"There's got to be another way out of here. Willie was wrong," said Jade.

"He's got at least a ten-minute head start," said Liz. "He could be back in Greenwood by now. We need to move and move fast."

Jade knew that Liz did not have to state what she was thinking. The three would-be rescuers charged back to their van and sped back the way they came in, leaving a mushrooming, thick cloud of red dust and leaves in their wake.

***

Stefan Vosper felt a sense of deep satisfaction as he pulled up to the gate to his junkyard only eight minutes after escaping from Malmaison. The long five-foot-high metal gate was still closed just as he had left it, and the padlock appeared secure. He exited from the driver's seat, leaving the car idling, and hurried to the gate. He took a key from his pocket and removed the lock, then pushed the gate forward. Jumping back into the car, he pulled into the yard and drove the car to an open area near a small school bus–sized open steel container that held random pieces of scrap metal waiting to be crushed. A crane beside the crusher dangled a four-foot-diameter, round magnetic disk that easily transferred large pieces of metal into the crusher.

He scurried back to the gate, closed it, and secured the padlock. He walked briskly to the crane, climbed up into the operator's stand and started the motor. The long arm of the crane began to easily turn toward Jasen's car, and Vosper effortlessly lowered the magnetic disk over the car. It attached with a loud, banging sound to the roof of the car and grabbed it securely.

Vosper sensed that potential rescuers might be converging on his business, so he worked deliberately and quickly. Knowing that time was running out, he swung the crane arm holding the car around and toward the open crusher. Once over the container, he released the magnet, and Jasen's car crashed on top of the tangled pieces of scrap metal. Immediately, the four walls of the crusher began surrounding the scraps and the car. It efficiently did its intended job in less than two minutes. Jasen's car and the rest of the metal were reduced to a square bundle of compressed iron, steel, and assorted scraps less than three feet across.

The Bone Crusher had watched satisfyingly as his machine did its job. He sat back in the operator's seat of his crane and smiled. He had reaped his revenge for his brother's death. He felt no remorse for Jasen or Ariel. It was over.

CHAPTER TWENTY-NINE
Junk Yard Jade

The scrap metal junkyard covered more than five acres off of County Road 520 and had become more than a temporary home to rusted carcasses of junked cars, trucks, school buses, worn out refrigerators, rusted washing machines, and almost anything else made of metal for which someone no longer found a use. Stefan Vosper had already netted a handsome profit with his recycling business but still had months and months of unattended inventory. Some locals had complained of the small mountains of piled up debris and vehicles. Even on the outskirts of town, it was gaining the reputation as an unwelcome eyesore.

Vosper continued to ignore complaints and knew that legal authorities would never pressure him as long as Jake Luther controlled Leflore County. Now with Luther dead, there was sure to be a power struggle to control the local political machine. Vosper still had not felt motivated to hire assistants to help work down his massive inventory.

***

Liz and Jade's white van screeched to a stop in front of the wide metal gate outside of Vosper's junkyard. Seconds later, the two Jackson agents pulled up behind them, having been redirected back to Greenwood by Liz. Visible through the ten-foot fenced enclosure were multiple heaps of assorted scrap metal, wrecked vehicles, and other metal debris that had been dumped on the site for eventual crushing and recycling.

Jade leaped from the van as it came to a stop and ran over to the gate. She stood on her tiptoes and her fingers held onto the gate. She scanned the area, hoping to see any sign of Jasen or his car. She saw no activity or sign of workers stirring about the yard, not unexpected since it was early evening. She turned and looked back at Liz and the other agents who were now converging near the gate. One agent looked at the padlock and drew his revolver. The shot echoed off of the gate, and the lock split apart. He threw it aside and pushed the wide gate forward into the yard.

Jade and Liz entered first, Liz with her service revolver drawn and ready. Their eyes anxiously searched and scanned the piles of metal, and they noticed a small, silver Airstream trailer with no windows off to one side of the yard and a giant metal container in the center of several piles of scraps. Their faces froze.

Inside the container a large block of crimson-colored metal was clearly visible. They both recognized that it matched the color of Jasen's car. It had been crushed into an almost square locker-size block, unrecognizable now as a car. They looked grimly at each other and couldn't say it. They were too late.

But, Jade refused to accept the obvious. She motioned to Liz and pointed to the small trailer. If Vosper was inside, he had not chosen to show himself. They moved cautiously toward the trailer, as the other agents dispersed and began to search other areas of the sprawling yard.

With Jade tucked safely behind her, Liz approached the door to the trailer, grabbed the doorknob, and slowly opened the door. She held her revolver with both hands as she charged inside, ready to fire at any threat or resistance. The single-room trailer appeared empty except for a small desk, a worn office chair, a small desk lamp, a Mr. Coffee, a telephone, and several cardboard boxes stacked against one wall. Papers were randomly scattered across the desk with two dirty half-empty coffee cups near the edge.

Jade followed Liz in and also saw no evidence of Vosper or Jasen. It went unsaid, but they realized Vosper had likely escaped again. Jade's pulse raced and her brain flashed with conflicting thoughts and horrifying visions of Jasen and Ariel. She refused to accept the thought that the glob of crushed metal outside might contain the remains of the only persons that had given her purpose, hope, and a renewed zest for life. She had to know the truth. She had to find Vosper.

***

As Liz and Jade investigated the small office in the old Airstream trailer, they heard a volley of gunshots—two then two more close behind. They hurried out into the dusk dark evening and found cover by their white van.

Two more gunshots rang out, as they caught a glimpse of a pickup truck speeding in their direction from the rear of the yard, weaving in and out between mounds of junk. They could not identify the occupant or occupants of the truck as it roared toward the front entrance.

Liz made a split-second decision, jumped into her van, and started the engine. As the pickup truck gained, she moved quickly to cut off his only route of escape from the yard. She won the race to block the entrance, but it was too late for the fleeing driver to avert a collision. The small truck's momentum and speed catapulted it forward and T-boned Liz's van in a deafening crescendo of metal against metal as it decelerated from sixty mph to zero in a split second. The van's passenger side crumpled inward from the force of the collision, as Liz's body slammed against the driver's door and shook back and forth like a ragdoll. She slumped forward over the steering wheel unconscious.

The front end of the truck folded inward like an accordion toward the passenger compartment. The driver's head smashed against the front windshield, which suddenly resembled a magnificent glassy starburst. Miraculously, the driver pushed his body back to a sitting position and stared out the side window at Jade with a mixed look of shock and a vicious snarl. He should have been dead from the impact but only had a bleeding forehead wound.

He tried to open the driver's door but it was jammed from the impact. He tried the passenger side with the same realization. He was trapped inside and Jade was the only rescuer in sight. The other agents that had fired upon the fleeing driver were still far back in the scrap yard.

Jade saw her opportunity. If this was Vosper, he would never escape from her clutches. She could only feel an uncontrollable surge of hate and contempt for the one who had stolen the only ones in her life that mattered anymore. Killing him would be too good for him, but it was her only option.

She ran over to the tall crane that dangled the large magnetic disk near the gigantic compactor, which still contained the remains of Jasen's car. In his haste, the abductor had left the crane motor idling. Jade nestled confidently into the operator's seat and quickly studied the levers and controls. The arrows on the levers were mostly self-explanatory. The crane arm began to move, first in the wrong direction, which Jade deftly corrected. She was pleasantly surprised with the ease of operating the controls.

The driver trapped in the truck watched helplessly as Jade lowered the magnetic disk over the top of his truck. With a loud bang, it grabbed the truck, which swayed moderately side to side. Jade swung the crane holding the truck around to the compactor bin like a professional at the controls and pushed the magnet release switch. The wrecked truck with its now frantic occupant crashed beside the red block of Jasen's car. Jade redirected the magnet and lifted the red mass out of the compactor, dropping it gently to the ground.

Jade stared at the imprisoned abductor and mouthed "Go to hell" as she pressed the button labeled "crusher" that remotely activated the enormous and powerful metal crusher. As the four walls pushed inward against the small truck, Jade could see the driver madly clawing at the windows and headliner looking for any way to cheat death. It was over in less than two minutes as the efficient metal crusher reduced the truck and its driver to the size of a small foot locker, finally sending the Bone Crusher to what Jade considered a just reward. She wondered if she would be accused of murder. She was only acting in self-defense, wasn't she? It was pay back. She sat back in the crane operator's seat but felt no satisfaction. She needed Jasen. She needed to tell him how she felt. Tears flooded her cheeks as she closed her eyes.

***

The other agents arrived near the front gate where the truck had smashed unmercifully into Liz's van. They gawked at Jade who was sitting at the controls of the crane and swinging the wrecked pickup over the crusher bin. She maneuvered the machine with the confidence of someone more experienced, but they saw no reason to interrupt her task. They needed to tend to Liz.

One of the agents rushed to the driver's side and finally opened the door after considerable effort. The collision had partially jammed the door. He turned and shouted to the other agents.

"She's got a pulse. I don't see any obvious injury but we need paramedics. Call 911. Hurry! And get in touch with Willie Campbell, Bianco, and Malone!" He didn't want to aggravate a spine or neck injury, so he elected not to move her until medical help arrived. But, then he got a whiff of gasoline.

"Guys!" he screamed. "I smell gasoline. This thing could blow any minute. We need to get her out. Come on, help me. We need to secure her neck and back first."

They worked carefully. In less than a minute, they had extracted her and moved her a safe distance from the demolished van. They turned and looked back at the wreck just as a loud boom exploded upward toward the heavens. A fiery orange and blue flame mushroomed over the van into the night sky, lighting up the darkness. They reflexively turned away from the explosion and felt the heat and percussion wash against their skin.

Jade had dealt with Vosper and was jumping from the crane when she was suddenly propelled backward by the explosion and pinned against the monstrous machine. Her head crashed into the base of the crane, and she slumped into a sitting position, dazed and disoriented. She tried to stand but her ears roared with an intense, pulsating pressure against her eardrums. Staring in confusion at the ground, she heard a distant-sounding voice say, "Jade, are you all right? Jade? Are you okay?"

She was more disoriented than she thought. The voice sounded so familiar. She looked up and saw a blurry image of a man leaning over her and touching her shoulder. Then, she fainted.

CHAPTER THIRTY
Fried Green Tomatoes

Marcus and Danny arrived in Greenwood just after six that evening and were concerned that they had not heard back from Liz. They had prepared to be part of a rescue team if needed, but Liz had not called. Marcus decided to head over to the Crystal Grill and find Willie Campbell who had supplied skimpy information earlier about the old Malmaison property. Perhaps he had heard some news about Jasen and Ariel.

Willie welcomed the private investigators and part-time Treasury agents into his back office.

"So, Willie, you haven't heard from Liz?" asked Marcus.

"Not a word," responded Willie. "Either nothing's come down or they're up to their ears in alligators and can't call. I was considering heading out to the Malmaison site to see for myself, but I don't want to jeopardize their plans. From what Agent Keys told me, they're dealing with an unknown abductor with unpredictable behavior. What he's capable of and has accomplished is anybody's guess."

"Well," said Danny, "I'm all for heading over there. No news is not good news as far as I'm concerned. They may be in a real jam or a standoff or who knows what."

"Liz asked that we not ring her mobile phone in case it might tip the abductor. Let's give them a few more minutes. If Liz doesn't call us, we'll go," replied Marcus, who was thinking more about Liz than the others.

"Are you two hungry?" asked Willie. "I can get the cook to bring you some of my famous fried green tomatoes. Soul food will help calm you two down."

"I'm game," quipped Danny. "We missed lunch scrambling to get up here."

Marcus looked at Danny and shook his head. How could he think of food when the lives of their colleagues were dangling in limbo. "Go ahead, Danny. I'm not hungry."

Willie picked up his phone and dialed an intercom number.

"Meisha, bring Mr. Malone an order of fried green tomatoes, a fried chicken breast, and some sweet iced tea. Okay? Thanks, sweetheart."

They heard a knock on the office door within seconds.

"Now, that's fast service!" said Willie. "Come on in!" he shouted.

The door opened slowly and the grill's co-hostess took two steps into the room.

"Mr. Campbell," said the young woman. "You need to come up front. You're not going to believe what just walked in."

***

Willie had received a frantic call from one of Liz's agents who asked for assistance at Vosper's junkyard at the eastern end of County Road 520, but he had already learned about Stefan Vosper's dirty deed. The agent had shared his concern over his unconscious boss, Elizabeth Keys. He told Willie that paramedics were on the way. When Willie shared Liz's condition, Marcus ran out of the cafe with Danny Malone clutching his chicken breast in one hand close behind. Willie and his passengers followed Marcus and Danny in his Buick as they sped east on Carrollton and turned on to 520. They could see a mushrooming cloud of black smoke climbing skyward in the distance.

"Something's on fire and it looks like it's coming from that scrap metal yard," observed Marcus. He looked at Danny who was nibbling on his chicken breast and didn't say anything.

They arrived only seconds before the paramedics, spraying dirt and gravel into the air as they skidded to an abrupt stop just inside the junkyard's gate. Marcus vaulted from his car and ran over to Liz who was supine in the dirt with two agents kneeling over her. Marcus leaned over and felt her pulse. She was pale but not cold.

"Liz! Liz! It's Marcus. Can you hear me?"

She didn't move and her eyelids remained still and closed. Marcus took her hand and pressed it to his lips.

"Sir, sir, please move back," requested one of the paramedics. "Please move back. We'll take over."

They worked professionally and quickly as they carefully placed a stabilizing brace around her neck and rolled her onto a back board before placing her on a gurney and lifting her into the ambulance. Marcus stayed at her side and told the driver that he was riding with her to the Greenwood Leflore Hospital. They sped off as one paramedic assessed her vitals and told the driver to radio the ER with her condition and their ETA.

***

Jade tried to open her eyes and felt a throbbing pain on the back of her head. She was sitting with her back against the huge crane from which she had just jumped when the exploding van propelled her like a rocket into the monstrous machine. She suddenly remembered the last thing she saw or thought she had seen. She shook her head, trying to clear away the cobwebs and apparent hallucinations.

"Well, my dear. That's the first time that I remember my ugly mug making someone faint. Are you okay?" he asked.

She focused and looked up in the direction of the voice.

"Jasen!" she exclaimed. "Jasen! Am I dreaming? Is it really you? I thought…" She looked over at the red metal block near the crusher then back at him.

"It's really me, and, no, I was not crushed. And Ariel's fine, too. She's right here."

"Hi, Jade. Are you okay? Looks like you got banged pretty hard against that crane," said Ariel.

"I think I'm okay, but I must still be dreaming. We all thought that you two were goners, more victims of that madman. I'm afraid he's unable to tell me what happened," she said, looking very satisfied at the compacting bin. "Guess one of you owes me an explanation."

Jasen smiled. "It's a long story, Jade. Let's just say that Ariel and I make a good team when it comes to being in a jam. Let's get everyone back to town and I'll explain. You can't get rid of me, you know. We've got some unfinished business. Ariel, grab an arm and let's get Jade up and out of here."

They helped her up on her wobbly knees, then they all climbed into Willie's Buick and headed back to the grill. Danny followed in Marcus's car and was anxious to hear a report on Liz's condition, but he couldn't wait to get back to those tasty, fried green tomatoes.

CHAPTER THIRTY-ONE

Friends or Lovers

Marcus sat by her hospital bed and cupped her right hand gently between both of his as he stared at the unconscious FBI agent. The bedside monitors displayed steady readings of vital signs, as an intravenous solution of glucose dripped slowly. An oxygen sensor covered her index finger. Everything told her caregivers that she was in guarded but stable condition, but Marcus was anxious for some good news. He looked across the bed as a young physician walked in and began to examine Liz.

"Are you the physician in charge?" Marcus asked.

"Oh, yes, sorry. I'm Dr. Bailey. I'm covering the ICU today. Are you next-of-kin?"

"No. I'm her, uh, business associate, Marcus Bianco. I suppose I'm the closest thing to next-of-kin. I don't think she has any living relatives." He reached across the bed and shook hands with the tall, thin doctor. "Can you give me an update? Is she going to be okay?"

"Well, from what I've read in her chart, she doesn't seem to have any serious internal injuries. I think she most likely has had a pretty significant concussion. Her CT scan didn't show any hemorrhage, just mild cerebral edema. We're monitoring her intracerebral pressure, and so far it's not too high. She's getting IV steroids periodically, so I think it's just a matter of time before she wakes up. From everything that we've checked, I would say that she's a pretty lucky lady. Car crashes tend to whip the body and head around like a wet noodle in a hurricane."

"Thanks, doctor. Is it okay if I stay with her until she wakes up? It would help if she sees a familiar face."

"Of course, Mr. Bianco. No problem. You seem to be a good friend. She's lucky." He completed his examination and then made some notes in her medical record.

"We'll keep you informed if there's any change. Nice meeting you, Mr. Bianco." He turned and exited as he worked his way patient by patient through the busy intensive care unit.

Marcus settled back into the chair at the bedside and stared again at Liz. He wrestled mentally with his feelings as he looked down and rubbed his wedding band. He knew that Liz had more than a casual interest in him, but he also knew that his heart belonged to his wife Carol. He cared for Liz as a person and pushed any further feelings into the deeply hidden rooms of his mind. He just wanted her to be okay. He was just being a good friend, he reminded himself. Share minimally, trust no one. That was his mantra. Now he wondered if he could even trust his own heart.

***

The Crystal Grill was bustling with hungry dinner customers by the time Jasen, Jade, and the others made it safely back to Greenwood. They retreated to a small private dining room near Willie's office to enjoy some of Willie's favorite menu offerings. Danny Malone was savoring the last bite of his fried green tomatoes as he listened to the story of Jasen and Ariel's escape from a certain death-by-crushing at the hands of the psycho Stefan Vosper. Ariel's recounting of her bone-chilling kidnapping and imprisonment in the dark underground crypt made Danny shudder.

"The maniac got what he deserved," concluded Danny. "You're lucky, Ariel, that he didn't do more than throw you in that totally dark tomb, if you get my drift."

"I think he was a lot more interested in me than Ariel," Jasen said. "It was also pretty obvious that he never intended to let her go. She came so close to outfoxing him. Too bad his skull was so thick. Ariel still packs a pretty mean swing."

"So, Jasen. Exactly how *did* you get out of that car trunk before Vosper crushed it?" asked Danny.

"Timing, Danny, timing is everything. After Jade's nightmare ride in Martin Vosper's trunk in Aruba, I decided to install inside emergency trunk releases in my car and Jade's. Someday, I think these will be required by law in all new cars. Anyway, there's no way that Vosper could have known that I was way ahead of him. All we needed was a brief stop in order to get out of the trunk unnoticed. So, when he got out of the car to unlock his front gate, we made our move. Before he could return to the car, we had bolted free, closed the trunk, and run for cover. He had no clue that we were no longer locked in that trunk when he crushed my car into that neat, little red package.

"While he did his crane, magnet, crushing act, we were running back to the main road. We flagged down a truck, which was headed back to town and got dropped off here. The truck driver was a little hesitant to stop—I mean a guy in nothing but boxer shorts who was dragging a very attractive young girl with bloody wrists—who knows what he was imagining. Thank God he stopped and didn't ask questions. I told him that we needed to get to the Crystal Grill as quickly as possible. He did a double take at our appearance and just said, "Get in. You must be *pretty* hungry." Ariel and I looked at each other and grinned. We wanted to laugh so bad.

"The truck driver's look was worth a million by itself, but when we got to the grill and walked in the front door, the young girl at the hostess stand gasped and started to scream until I identified myself and asked for Willie. Of course, you and Marcus had already arrived, and you know the rest of the story. Jasen Prospero lives to fight another day. Talk about 'die hard.' Jade and I may already be on borrowed time. But, then, Liz keeps reminding us that there are no coincidences; everything happens for a reason. Actually, that monster Jake Luther said the same thing. Ironic, isn't it?"

"Speaking of Liz," said Jade, "has anyone heard from Marcus at the hospital? Here we sit feeding our faces and wallowing like fat pigs in mud in our own good fortune. We need to be praying for Liz. She absorbed quite an impact from Vosper's truck. Danny, can you call and see if you can get an update?"

"Sure thing, Jade. Marcus would have called if there was bad news, but I'll track him down and check on Liz's condition. Marcus didn't hesitate about riding to the hospital with her. I know they're friends but sometimes I get the impression that their relationship is getting a little, well, shall I say, complicated." He cleared his throat, rolled his eyes, and headed to find a phone.

***

Having excused themselves and retreated across the hall to Willie's office, Jasen followed as Jade went in. She walked over to Willie's desk and turned to face Jasen. He turned and looked at her with one hand still on the doorknob. She didn't speak but her dazzling green eyes locked onto his "what's this all about?" dark browns. Seconds crawled by like minutes. He released the doorknob and quietly walked toward her. She did not look away or move. Her face said all that he needed to hear—"I forgive you."

He took the final step in her direction and she leaned forward, falling into his open arms. Their lips met softly at first, just a butterfly kiss. Then he hugged her tightly and pressed his lips against hers, releasing weeks of bridled passion. She opened her eyes and looked at his face. She knew that she had been wrong to push him away for so many weeks. Things *did* happen for a reason. Their lives were intertwined. The secrets hidden away by Greenwood Leflore would have never been revealed if Jasen had not come into her life. Nothing could change what had happened. But she knew that nothing could ever keep them apart again.

They pushed apart slightly and stared at each other. Jade began to speak as a tear streamed down her cheek.

"I thought you were dead. When I saw your crushed car, I felt as if I had been pushed off the same cliff that took Mom from me. I'm not sure why I've been in denial. You are truly the only good thing that has ever happened to me, besides the birth of James Jr. When I lost him, I blamed myself. I was resigned to be alone forever. That was the only way I knew that I could never get hurt again. Then, you came into my life.

"I toyed with your emotions, and I apologize for that. I lied to myself about how you were affecting my heart. I flirted with you. I teased you. I used you. I wanted you. I didn't want you. I confused myself as much as I confused you. Finally, I completely surrendered to you. I trusted in someone when I thought it was impossible to ever do so again.

"Then, you told me that our relationship was only the assignment for a secret agent. I was your mission, not the love of your life. You can't imagine how I felt at that moment. It was like someone telling you that you are the most important thing in the world to them, but he really has his fingers crossed. You used me like I thought I was using you. We were just players on a stage, acting out different plots, except I thought it was the same plot. Somewhere in the middle of all of that acting, I think we both realized that only one plot would work. We really and truly fell in love with each other, but we were too distracted by the sudden treachery that intruded into our romantic bliss on that wintry night to realize what had happened. We were caught in a rip current that dragged us from one nightmare to the next. We survived because we held on to each other. Our bodies and souls were fused.

"This wild and crazy drama in which we're starring can't be a coincidence. We met at that mailbox on Windermere Cove for a reason. We made the next choice for a reason. I'm not the most religious person in the world, but this script was written for us, you and me, no one else. We're on a journey together and we can't stop until we get to wherever we're supposed to end up. Neither of us can do it alone. I know that now. Jasen, I love you, and I now know that I've always loved you. I've forgiven you. Please forgive me. Please…"

He had listened to every word while admiring her beauty and tenacity. She had grown stronger than any woman he had ever known.

"Jade, stop…stop." He smiled. "I forgave you at 'I thought you were dead.'"

She smiled back in her Jade way, then looked intently at the surrender painted on his face. He put his arms around her and lifted her gently off the floor. They kissed, and for a moment they did not have to wonder about what new nightmare might be waiting around the next bend when they left their quaint cul-de-sac back in Georgia.

***

Almost three days had passed, and he had not left her bedside except for brief restroom breaks and water. A nurse had offered him snacks at which he had only nibbled. He walked over to the large window and gazed down three stories below at the packed parking lot and streams of visitors headed inside with anxious questions and worry about their loved ones.

"Hey, you, over there. Detective Noir," a voice said. "Have you got a mirror? I think my hair is a mess."

Bianco turned with a jerk and looked at the hospital bed. Liz was trying to sit up as she continued.

"God, do *I* ever have a humongous headache. What happened and why are you here?" she said groggily.

He almost vaulted to the bedside and placed his hand on her shoulder.

"You don't need to try to get up, Liz. You've had a nasty accident. I would dare say that you're lucky to be here."

"Accident?" she said with a puzzled look. "What kind of accident? And, by the way, you look like hell. How long has it been since you shaved?"

Marcus rubbed his fingers across his stubby, coarse beard and realized for the first time that he had neglected himself during his long bedside vigil.

"Thanks for the compliment," he quipped wryly. "I've been sitting here for almost three days waiting on you to wake up. You took quite a nap, lucky lady. How do you feel?"

"Like crap or whatever is the most opposite of splendid. I'm afraid I don't remember much after Jade and I were waiting on Jasen back on Malmaison Road. Please tell me that Jasen and Ariel are okay. I have a vague recollection of someone getting crushed in an oversized trash compactor. Did I dream that?" She studied his face for a hint of any bad news.

She breathed a little easier when he smiled.

"Jasen and Ariel are fine. They somehow outsmarted Ariel's kidnapper and survived to fight another day. You were the victim of Vosper T-boning you and your van with his truck at about sixty mph. I think you were playing hero and trying to block his escape from his junkyard.

"The team was here in Greenwood for a day, but now everyone's gone back to Georgia except Ariel and Danny. Ariel's back in Starkville, safe and sound. Danny's still here waiting on news about you. Willie Campbell has taken him under his wing and has been fattening him up with the Grill's famous Southern cuisine and lemon icebox pie. I'll have a tough time getting him back to Jackson."

Liz looked at her IV tubing and monitor leads, then back up at Marcus. "So, you didn't answer my other question. Why are you here? Don't you have a wife back in Jackson?"

Marcus flushed slightly and smiled. "You were in critical condition for a while, Lizzy (he had never called her that before). You've been in a coma for almost three days. You needed a friend to watch over you. I guess you could also say that I've grown a little fond of you, in a friend-sort-of-way, you understand. No one has ever accused me of abandoning a friend in times of need. So, here I am. You have to admit that it was nice to see a familiar face just now, right?"

She was still foggy in her processing but alert enough to sense that she was peering through a facade of pretense.

"Yes, Marcus. You're right. It was nice to see a friendly face when I woke up. Thank you for staying with me. It means a lot." She reached out and pulled his hand into hers.

"Okay, my friend, my Detective Noir. Sit down here beside me and tell me what's been happening in the world over the past three days."

He sat on the edge of her bed and began. She didn't release his hand from her grasp as she lay her head back on the pillow and closed her eyes, soothed by his gentle, strong voice.

Part Five

CHAPTER THIRTY-TWO

The Commander's Club

Greenwood, Mississippi

"He's in his office, Mr. Xavier. Richard Jordan had never revealed his real name to anyone except Roger Trevane. Go on in. I think he's expecting you," said the very attractive woman who was one of the Club's "entertainers." It was still early in the afternoon, hours before the expected influx of local, affluent patrons who retreated to the Club almost every night to unwind from their high-pressure roles as business owners or corporate heads.

"Come on in, Fred," said the portly Harlow Bartram, who slowly exhaled the stinky smoke of his cheap stogie. "What brings you down to the Delta and away from your DC buddies?"

"A lot has changed, Harlow. We need to talk about Jake Luther, the late Jake Luther," he said as he settled into a chair in front of Bartram's large oak desk.

"Yes, too bad about old Big Jake. Can't say that I miss him, though. He had amassed quite a few enemies around Leflore County. I did my part, though. Protected him from some snooping private dick that kept showing up around here."

"I'm afraid that Jake and Calvin were their own worst enemies," responded Xavier. "Got a little too greedy. Greed has claimed many a victim. Nothing that you would understand, I'm sure, eh, Harlow?"

"Not a greedy bone in this sculptured body," replied Bartram who grinned and patted his protruding belly, which made the buttons on his shirt bulge as if they would snap off at any minute.

"Let me get right to the point, Harlow. Jake had taken full responsibility for dealing with the drug bosses down in Colombia. Unfortunately, his nephew was the only other person who knew the process of cleaning and relocating all of the money that they 'donated' to our cause. Jake's closest associates have been decimated. I need you to step up and fill the void. My contacts in DC will not be patient if the money flow dries up. Before you respond, let me assure you that your share will be tripled compared to before."

"Fred, my boy, you know how much I dislike dealing with those Latinos. I have a family, you know. Those capos are vicious cutthroats. They don't trust anybody. I need a few more security men if I have to take this on."

"Relax, Harlow. Go ahead and beef up your goon squad as long as anybody new understands the rules and avoids loose lips. You know the outcome if that happens.

"If you keep Rivers over at Bigelow's doing his part, then the money will be wired on schedule. So far, hiding the drugs in those cotton bales has worked like a charm. You just need to keep Rivers focused on the distribution of the goods. You make the wire transfers to the Virginia account on time and your job is done. Once a week is all I'm asking. The details are in this envelope."

He pushed it across the desk to Bartram.

"Keep this under lock and key. No one but you can lay eyes on this, understand? Anyone else that reads this is a dead man."

"Bartram picked up the envelope and responded, "I understand.""

"We have a slight glitch on the shipment end of the drugs. The cartel is still getting away with hiding the goods in their scrap metal shipments to Vosper's junk yard. Only problem is Vosper has gone missing. He got distracted with paying back that Georgia couple for causing his brother's demise. I have the feeling he may have also met his match. My sources can't find any trace of him, and his yard workers haven't heard from him in several days. I'm assigning a new man to take over the junkyard. The next shipment is due any day. But, that's not your worry. Just be sure Rivers picks up the goods as scheduled."

"I think what you're saying, Fred, is that I really don't have a choice."

"The rewards justify the means. Be a loyal company man and you won't cross anybody," said Xavier who stood and reached out to shake Bartram's hand.

As he watched the man he knew as Fred Xavier exit his office, Harlow Bartram tapped the envelope on his desktop and took another big draw on his pungent cigar. He smiled at the thought of his salary being tripled. For a moment, he didn't have to think about the capos' henchmen lurking in the shadows in case anyone strayed. And somehow, it didn't matter how he earned his windfall. Blood money, whatever. He liked being rich, but filthy rich was even nicer.

CHAPTER THIRTY-THREE

The Big Sandy Place

From the top of the ridge that once showcased Malmaison, former home of Chief Greenwood Leflore, now burned to the ground and just a small pile of bricks and brush Frederick Xavier, , aka Richard Jordan, surveyed the expanse of the former cotton plantation of the great Indian chief.

"You know, Leflore's slaves called this estate 'The Big Sandy Place,'" he said, not looking at the real estate representative who had met him to discuss next steps.

"I don't get it because I don't see any sand now. I suppose all of the unplanted cotton fields may have resembled fields of sand, who knows. Or maybe the soil was sandier than it looks now 150 years later."

"Difficult to believe that there were 15,000 acres of cotton fields below this ridge," said Mitchell Carlisle. "Almost a natural, unexplored frontier look now."

"So, Mitch. Tell me your thoughts. Can you get a visual of casinos and resort hotels here?'

"Fred, this ridge will be a perfect location. You can't tell but the Tallahatchie and Yalobusha Rivers are just off to the northwest. Those oaks are obscuring the view but by the time the structures go up, the panorama will be spectacular. The property will extend all the way to the rivers, which gives us the waiver required by Mississippi state law to host gambling and gaming here. But, just in case we need it, I understand we can get the same land exemption that the Choctaws got over in Neshoba County at the Pearl River complex in '96. In total, we've acquired fifty thousand acres of land, more than three times the original size of Leflore's property.

"I can see this being a prime destination for gamblers, sportsman, families, campers, golfers…you name it. Sharkey Bayou off to the east will be enlarged into a picturesque lake. I think, besides the casinos and luxury hotels, the plans call for a major theme park, three Robert Trent Jones–caliber golf courses, a water park, an upscale RV park, shopping outlets, something called a Mega-Bass Pro and Outdoor Store, a sandy beach for swimmers, and the lake will be large enough for skiing. The lake sloughs lead off and drain into the Tallahatchie. Those will attract great bass and crappie fishing. We've even penciled in a skeet shooting range, a firearms practice range, and annual Choctaw festivals and powwows. And if that's not enough of a grand vision, the magnum opus of the development will be a five-star thoroughbred horse racing track that will put the big three to shame. The LeFleur Derby will become the fourth jewel in a new 'quadruple crown.'

"Leflore's mansion will be rebuilt near the family cemetery as a tourist attraction similar to The Hermitage in Nashville. I see this entire development putting Mississippi back on the national, if not international, map.

"Tunica got a head start on us in '92, but I assure you that it will be dwarfed once we complete the entire project. Plus, we need to move quickly before Biloxi gets into the act. I hear that some Las Vegas mogul is working on something called Beau Rivage down on the Gulf Coast. It was supposed to be called Bellagio, but he decided to keep that name for his Vegas casino.

"The window of opportunity is open. We need to move forward with haste. I see this as holding its own against anything comparable. The old chief will probably turn over in his grave once this becomes reality."

"Ha! Interesting that you say that, Mitch. Don't you know the story about the grave robbers? Some angry Choctaws apparently took Leflore's American flag–wrapped body from his crypt years ago and buried him face down in an unmarked grave. A major act of disrespect. So, if he turns over, that'll be a good thing!"

"No kidding? Yes, that's very interesting. Anyway, Fred, I'm very pleased with the property. It'll hold everything we've planned and more. We're close to Memphis, so the access from Interstate 55 will be upgraded. Western visitors can easily come across the Mississippi at Greenville, and Highway 82 will become interstate quality. Getting here will be no problem. I heard, also, that someone has pulled rank and secured funding to upgrade the Greenwood Airport."

"Has anyone suggested a name for this ambitious development?" asked Xavier.

Mitch didn't hesitate. "I've been told that whoever controls the financial piece of this huge project has insisted on a name—*The Delta LeFleur Casino and Resort* and *The Golden Bay—Discover America* Park. I'm certain there will be plenty of other suggestions.

"By the way, Fred, I'm curious. This law firm that you work for…I mean, how did they pull this off? Someone must have connections in high places to get this off the drawing board, or even to have the vision. And, maybe it's just me and my suspicious side, but is there more to this land deal and audacious grand venture than meets the eye? I understand myths, rumors, and the grapevine, but the stories about gold, which may be worth billions, buried on Leflore's estate have circulated for decades. Do you know anything about that?"

"Mitch, I just do what I'm told. I don't ask too many questions. It's safer that way. My advice to you, my friend…stay focused on the real estate and just smile and stay quiet when you see your bank account balance. I strongly suggest you drop the buried gold talk. You'll stay healthier if you do, if you get my drift."

***

Senator Roger Trevane sat behind his massive desk in his opulent hideaway suite on the third floor of the US Capitol building with his reading glasses pushed down to the end of his nose. He had received a letter marked "Highly Confidential" and opened it with his twisted-steel-handle Gaelic dirk dagger. The note was brief.

"I will call at 10:00 a.m. Friday on our secure line. Important. FIX."

"FI$\overline{X}$" was the code signature for Richard Jordan, alias Frederick Xavier. He looked at the rare antique Italian wall clock to his left. He still had ten minutes.

"Ms. Ormon," he said into the intercom. "Would you please bring a cup of coffee? I'm expecting a secure call at ten. Please, no interruptions until I get back to you."

"Yes, Senator," she responded. "Of course. Right away."

The call came promptly at ten. Richard Jordan was always prompt and efficient, thought Trevane to himself.

"Good morning, Senator. My apologies, but as I said, this is important. I didn't want to discuss this with the law firm without you knowing first."

"All right, Richard. What is it? You need to be brief. This line is secure but sometimes I just don't trust that it'll stay that way. The

NSA is being given more and more leeway in snooping on anybody and everybody."

"Yes, I'll be concise. First, we need to break ground on the Greenwood property within thirty to sixty days. The bids are being finalized this week. I'm moving the money with your permission."

"No problem. Move it."

"Second, I'm worried about the junkyard being compromised. I learned that the FBI had a confrontation there with Vosper. He's missing. I think he's dead but likely didn't talk, so I'm not too worried that anyone has made a connection with the shipments from South America. It depends on how curious the FBI is about Vosper's associates. For now, I think no one has gotten wind of Luther's or Vosper's connection to anything outside of Greenwood."

"Just who and how many FBI or other agents have been nosing around there? asked Trevane.

"It seems like there are only five major players who have sniffed around in Luther's activities…a couple from Georgia—a college professor named Prospero and an ATT telecoms director named Jade Colton who has some connections to the late Greenwood Leflore and some apparent secrets that Luther had tried to hide. Long story.

"Then, there's a senior FBI agent" in Atlanta who's assisted them. Bartram has been visited by a private investigator out of Jackson. He and his partner keep showing up every time that the Georgia pair does. My sources say that these five may be gearing up for a DC investigation."

"What!" exclaimed the senator.

"Relax. Your name has never come up and won't. You've kept a very long arm's-length approach, and it'll stay that way."

"I'm counting on you, Richard. I have to do anything, I mean *anything*, to keep my name out of this. That means that everyone is expendable, including you. Clear?"

"Crystal, sir, crystal."

"Richard, I want the five you mentioned to disappear. I do not want to hear their names again or anything about them, specifically that they're in DC. Do what you do best, and soon."

"It'll be done, sir. One last thing. Our contact in French Camp has credible information about the location of the gold. Possibly all 200 million dollars of it—estimated now to be worth 3.5 billion."

"Get on it, Richard. It needs to be located before the earthmovers get in there."

Jordan had used up his time. "I won't contact you again on this line. If it gets compromised, we need another venue. I'll let you know."

"No, no more calls. Go through the firm for anything else. Good-bye, Richard."

CHAPTER THIRTY-FOUR

Unchartered Waters

Elizabeth Keys had responded rapidly to her treatment at the medical center in Greenwood and had flown back to Atlanta on the FBI jet. Marcus and Danny had made it back to their Plaza Building suite in Jackson and were organizing their next steps in their investigation of the remnants of Jake Luther's organization. It had become clear that Luther's ties to the local KKK were real but only a cover for other criminal activities that were apparently tied to a secret bank account.

Darrell Washington, Willie Campbell's third cousin at the Mississippi Highway Patrol who had helped Jasen, Jade, and Willie clean up the mess at Swan Lake, had provided useful intelligence to Bianco and Malone, but Marcus and Danny knew that another visit back to Greenwood was inevitable. They also knew that Vosper's death would likely result in others pursuing them. They began to be suspicious of anybody that even looked at them. Danny's nerves were unraveling.

In Georgia, Jasen and Jade had settled into a new luxury apartment in Atlanta's Buckhead community. Both agreed that staying in their Windermere Cove garden homes was tantamount to inviting more assaults if Jake Luther's unknown associates were intent on eliminating them. They also felt that being in Atlanta made the FBI office more accessible when they needed to meet with Liz. Their relocation was done under the radar, and only Liz knew about their move. Their Lawrenceville homes remained furnished with timers, controlling lights at night to make them appear lived in. Their former neighbors, Earl and Rose Chambers, the self-appointed watch captains of the community, were asked to contact the FBI for any unusual activity around Jade and Jasen's homes.

"Jasen, are you sure you're okay with me going to Washington with you?" asked Jade as she diced the onions, green peppers, black olives, and tomatoes for the meal she was preparing.

"Absolutely, my dear. Where I go, you go. Where you go, I go. We about to plunge into deeper, uncharted waters probably infested with meaner predators than we've already seen. I'm ready if you are." He took a sip of his Chianti, walked over to where she was cooking, and kissed her on the back of her neck.

"I love it when you do that," she said, turning her head and kissing his cheek.

"The food smells divine," he said. "I'm starving."

"It won't hold a candle to your mom's souvlaki, but I think you'll like it. Pour me some wine please. The food's about ready."

He filled both glasses and sat down. "We're meeting with Liz tomorrow and then I think we're off to the Treasury office in DC. Liz has arranged transportation. We can't take a chance on commercial flights. We'll also have agents with us at all times."

"What? *All* times? That could get interesting," she said with a grin.

"Well, hopefully they'll be in another room. Let's eat!"

She served him her Greek concoction and sat down beside him. "Professor Prospero, did I ever tell you that I love you?"

***

Frederick Xavier's secret contacts had provided him all he needed to know. He had previously arranged for his pros to arrange the vanishing act at their homes but worked quickly on an alternate plan to intercept the couple in Washington. If all went according to plan, it would appear to be just another tragic accident. Xavier's pros had mastered many variations of accidents and mishaps. In the past year, ten people that had gotten too inquisitive about Trevane's previous law firm partners and other business affairs had suffered convenient accidents or had vanished without a trace. Xavier felt confident of this outcome. He knew his boss would not accept any miscues.

***

They landed at the airport at dusk and taxied to an unmarked hanger on the opposite side of the airport terminals and came to a stop safely inside.

"Did you notice that small silver hanger at the end of the runway just before we turned?" asked Jasen.

"No," responded Jade. "Can't say that I did. Why?"

"Private hanger of famous writer Clint Canter. I hear he stashes some of his vintage classic cars there. Just like his alter ego Deacon 'Deke' Pax in his books."

"Did you say Deke?" asked Jade with a puzzled face.

"Forget it. It's not important. Speaking of alter egos, once we get to Treasury, we're disappearing. I mean, we're going deep undercover. Jasen Prospero and Jade Colton are about to become history."

"I don't like the way that sounds," Jade said. "I *like* being Delta Jade Colton."

"Relax, my love. It's just temporary. What can be erased can be unerased just as easily."

"I'm holding you to that, Professor," she said with a half-smile.

An unmarked black SUV was waiting inside the hanger, and the two agents walked down the plane's ramp and climbed into the vehicle. Another agent was waiting for them in the front passenger seat.

"Welcome to Washington," he said, turning and looking briefly at them. "Fasten your seat belts. DC traffic can be a nightmare."

The SUV merged onto the George Washington Memorial Parkway and sped up as it wedged in between two cars, leaving Jade and Jasen's driver little room for error.

"It's only a fifteen- to twenty-minute drive, even in traffic," Jasen said to Jade. "Liz has arranged a staging office out of which we'll work. We'll get new identities there. You'll be working with an expert phone tap and computer technician who claims he can hack even the most secure phone lines and every computer on earth. He's been working on listening in on several senators and congressmen that may have had connections with Greenwood, Choctaws, or land acquisitions in Mississippi. I'm anxious to see if he's had any luck."

"He may be an expert, but I've learned a trick or two at AT&T that I bet he doesn't know," bragged Jade.

"My odds on are you, Sweetie."

"Jasen, where do you think this so-called top secret investigation will go? You've been chasing money trails for years and never got past the Greenwood Klan. Instead of 'money trails' you've really been chasing 'monkey's tails.' What makes you or Liz think that we'll find anything in Washington?"

Jade continued, "Obviously, someone is very clever at disguising themselves. No one seems to have made it past the Greenwood piece of this and lived to tell about it. We're on borrowed time ourselves. Neither one of us should still be alive. It's like we have a guardian angel watching over us. I keep getting visions of our luck running out. When I got into this SUV, the hairs on the back of my neck prickled as if I'd had a mild shock. Weird."

"Jade, Jade. Oh ye of little faith. We've both said it. Our lives came together either by divine purpose *or* by coincidence, take your pick. Unless you don't buy the coincidence option. It doesn't matter. We were put together for a higher reason. We're meant to solve this mystery and correct some major wrongs. I have no doubt."

"There you go again, Professor Existential. I can't see anything we've done or might do being even a blip on anybody's radar. Come back down to Earth, my handsome superhero."

They both laughed and settled back into their seats for the short ride into the government district.

The driver veered left off the parkway past Lady Bird Johnson Park and merged into the free-for-all Arlington roundabout, managing to slip in between cars and take the middle lane to the Arlington Bridge. His passengers were fixed on the view ahead of the lighted Jefferson Memorial and the familiar iconic landmarks of the Nation's Capitol beyond.

Suddenly, without warning, a tanker truck in the oncoming lane to the left cut sharply toward the SUV. The truck's driver accelerated and almost leaped toward the oncoming traffic. Before the SUV's driver could react, the cab of the truck slammed into the left side of the SUV. The truck's mass and momentum crushed the SUV's side like tinfoil and catapulted it rapidly over the side of the bridge. The SUV nose-dived and pounded with a huge spray into the murky waters of the Potomac, disappearing in only seconds. The tanker truck screeched to a halt with one tire hanging over the edge of the demolished bridge wall and pointing to the swirling foamy water that marked the drowned SUV and its passengers.

The uninjured truck driver gingerly exited from the dangling cab and jumped down on the pavement. He looked down at the frothy, bubbling spot in the water and smiled. His job was done.

CHAPTER THIRTY-FIVE
Ambition, Seduction, Power,
and Corruption

Potomac, Maryland
The Wynstone Estate

Congress had adjourned for the late summer holidays, and Roger Trevane had retreated to his 10-million-dollar, 33,000-square-foot mansion near the Potomac River thirty miles north of the Capitol. The Trevanes had acquired the Wynstone Estate ten years ago from a Middle Eastern oil tycoon and had earned the reputation for owning the most magnificent real estate in Potomac, Maryland, a community well known for its luxury estates.

Wynstone was regarded as the area's most prestigious custom home and was a masterpiece of unparalleled European design and materials. It was a spectacular two-story stone-front mansion with a very wide circular drive and a five-car garage. Its crème de la crème was the two-story grand library that boasted custom-milled cherry and tiger wood paneling. The foyer was accented by double floating curved marble staircases, and the family room was an incredible two-story conversation piece. With two elevators, seven fireplaces, ten bedrooms, ten bathrooms, five half-baths, two media rooms, a bowling alley, an enormous gourmet kitchen, and an open floor plan, the mansion was perfect for impressing and entertaining the Trevane's friends, cronies, lobbyists, movers, shakers, and assorted dignitaries.

Senator Trevane was happy to have left the recessed backstabbing, name-calling political circus in the Capitol that had brought any hope of new legislation on healthcare reform to an embarrassing gridlock. A Republican House and a Democrat Senate had not compromised on any versions of a law that was already doomed to be unpopular with the public in any shape or form. It was the same old same old that had characterized the multiple attempts by Congress at passing palatable healthcare reform for decades. The first elected president that had run as an Independent had not been able to persuade either major party to accept any part of multiple proposed bills.

Trevane's wife, Charlotte Anne, glided silently into his private two-story library and study, which was located on the far right end of the medieval-looking estate. He had his back to the open doorway and was fixated on a computer screen that displayed a detailed spreadsheet of numbers. She tiptoed up behind him and clasped her hands over his eyes.

"Guess who?" she said coyly.

He reacted instantly, turning toward her and grabbing her arms at the wrists.

"Damn it, Charlotte!" he said almost screaming. "I told you to never sneak up on me. What are you doing!"

She winced in pain.

"Roger, please! You're hurting my arms. Let go…please."

He relaxed his grip, then turned back to his PC and turned the monitor off quickly.

"What are you working on, dear? You're on recess. Can't you leave work at the Capitol for once? We're supposed to be relaxing. Maybe we should have gone back to the lake house in Madison instead of coming here. I think you need to get as far from that abominable city as you can. And you really need to be back in Mississippi connecting with our constituents."

"They're getting more than their money's worth. I don't need to kiss those ugly Mississippi babies anymore. Roger Trevane *is* Mississippi. If I can control the US Senate, I can control anybody or anything. You had better prepare yourself, because we'll be swapping this address for a new one…1600 Pennsylvania Avenue. The Democratic National Committee has assured me that I'll be nominated next year. Our Independent Party President has proven to be the fool for which I pegged him. He'll never get reelected, and the Republicans are so divided internally, they'll never come up with a credible candidate. That Margaret Daley, ex-governor goofball has taken that party so far to the right, they'll never find their way back to the middle. We'll be a shoo-in."

"Roger, I'm not so sure that I want this. Being a powerful senator's wife is one thing, but I'm not sure that being First Lady is what I want. Actually, it scares the hell out of me. Enemies will ooze out of the woodwork. I just want to go back to a simpler life on Lake Madison in Mississippi."

"Charlotte, my dear. How in the world would you want to give up this place or not want eight years in the White House? There's nothing left back in Mississippi for us. The Trevanes were born to rule! Where's your ambition? Where's your soul?"

"My soul is in Mississippi. Roger, this is all about *you. Your* ambition. *Your* obsession with controlling your enemies and your friends. The days of kings, emperors, pharaohs, and monarchs in free societies are in the past. Sometimes I just don't understand what's driving you. You seem to think that you alone were put on this earth to change it and control it. That puffed up ego between your pointy ears is getting so big, I think your head is going to explode!"

"You'll never get it, Charlotte. Lawyer or not, somehow I think you've never gotten past your Holden County roots. I think you're the only one from that hick county that ever finished high school!"

"I've had enough of your insults, Roger. You're so full of it and blinded by power and an insatiable appetite for it, you can't even see straight. I'm going to bed. You're making me sick!"

She turned and huffed out of his domain and clomped noisily down the wide, white marble hallway to the elevator.

"Women!" he said in disgust. "Can't please them."

He turned back to his scrutiny of the spreadsheet on his computer, then picked up his cell phone and entered a private number.

One of his former law partners, Gerome Rainey, answered after one ring. "Hello?"

"Gerry, old man, how in the world are you?"

"Roger! I never expected to hear from you. I thought you were flying very low under the radar—the stealth leader of the US Senate."

"This is an unlisted mobile number that can't be traced to me or you. Don't worry, Gerry. I called to verify where the firm stands with the land deal. I heard from Fred but probably won't be accepting any more calls from him. I don't like leaving bread crumbs for someone to follow. He should be communicating directly with the firm or the real estate rep. I need to know if things are moving ahead. Time is of the essence."

"Yes, everything is in high gear, Roger. Fred said that you authorized the funds transfer. Bids have been finalized and we'll be ready to break ground within three weeks. The real estate firm is drafting a press release, and it'll appear that a foreign billionaire is behind the project. You're safe.

Not to worry. The funds had been cleaned and scrubbed in every way imaginable by Luther before he met his tragic end. I'm sure the accounts are untraceable.

"Fred has assigned the shipment receipts and payment tracking to that Greenwood club owner, Harlow Bartram. He knows very little beyond what Luther told him, so I wouldn't be concerned about him. He's very capable of managing the fund transfers. Is there something else bothering you, Roger?"

"Fred told me about a team of five that had encounters with Luther, probably the ones that killed him. Three of them are government agents; the other two are private eyes. They're still trying to figure out what all Luther knew and was involved in, and Fred's source says that they're headed to DC. He knows what he has to do to eliminate that little threat. Once that's done, we should be clear to proceed as before. Unless a Geraldo Rivera-type investigative reporter surfaces, I think we're *all* on the verge of joining the Billionaires Club. The potential payoff if we get this Delta project open is incalculable. The South has seen nothing like it…ever! The firm needs to keep the realtors on top of the timeline. And I fully expect that my offshore funds will continue to appreciate."

"You can count on it, Roger. The Virginia account has changed owners so many times, no one will ever trace its origination. In addition, you're going to love the balance on your next quarterly statements for the offshore account. At least, the owner Peter Hasbrough will love it. I'm the only person alive that knows that you and Hasbrough are one and the same. When you're ready, it will all be yours."

"In time, Gerry, in time. For now, it's not about the money. It's about what I can do once I control those kinds of funds. Nothing, absolutely nothing, will be beyond my grasp. If you do your job well, the DNC will assure my nomination. The country's political climate is ripe for a change. I see nothing stopping me from winning the White House.

Then, as the most powerful person in the free world, I will have every country's leaders eating out of my hand. Except for China and North Korea, but, I have plans for them too.

"President Roger Trevane will be everyone's choice as the leader of a one-world government—the only hope to save mankind from total annihilation. And, to think, Gerry, *you* were once *my* law partner. Do your job and maybe I'll make you czar of something or another."

"Roger, I'm never sure when you start all of your ramblings and having these grand delusions, whether I should take you seriously or just laugh out loud. Actually, you scare me a little bit, Roger. I worry about you. I think the turmoil in Congress may be stressing you more than you realize."

"Nonsense, old man," Trevane said. "I'm completely in control of my faculties. Charlotte says that power has gone to my head. That's crap. Every move I've made has been planned and calculated to the nth degree. It's what I was put on this earth to do. Nothing can stop me. Especially, a ragtag team of a few government agents and amateur detectives. Their numbers are up. The clock is ticking. All of the sand has run out of their hour glass. It's time for us to move ahead. Get 'er done, Gerry. Get 'er done. Good-bye."

***

"Fred? This is Gerome Rainey. When's the last time you spoke with the senator?"

"Just this week, Gerry. Why, what's up?" Fred Xavier responded.

"Well, I just talked to him. I know he's anxious to move ahead with the Delta project, and so am I. It's just his obsession with all of this. I mean, he's beginning to sound like a madman."

"Come on, Gerry." Xavier said without concern. "We both know how eccentric Roger can be."

"It's beyond eccentric, in my opinion. He's turned into a megalomaniac on steroids. All this talk of power grabs, winning the presidency, world ruler—it's pathologic." Gerome Rainey had never fully trusted his former law partner.

"We're all tense right now, Gerry. Roger sees his ambitious dreams about to become reality. Plus, we all worry about leaks and someone putting all of this together. The Colombian transactions have been working smoothly, but with Vosper out of the picture, we need to be sure of whom we can trust to not ask too many questions. The FBI and Treasury are too distracted with other scandals, so I think once the small team that was after Jake Luther is out of the way, we'll be fine."

Rainey agreed. "Roger told me that you were handling that. Any word yet?"

"Yes. I got a call earlier from one of my contacts. Two of the five somehow had an 'unfortunate' swimming accident. I'm not sure if the others have been located yet, but they should be soon."

"Fred, I'm glad you're on top of all of this. Roger is fortunate that you're such a master 'fixer.' What I fear the most is that Roger may be his own worst enemy. He has been seduced by the lure of power that all of his wealth has bought. You and I have profited handsomely from this, too, but we know when enough is enough. Roger seems to be obsessed with being in control of everything and everybody. History tends to repeat itself. Too much power corrupted even popes.

"Regardless, Fred, clean up the loose ends as soon as possible, I'll keep the project on track. Ironically, blood money or not, it'll be a very positive boon for the state of Mississippi. We just need to be sure no one ever knows who's profiting the most from it."

Fred, aka Richard Jordan, concluded, "I'll let you know if I need you, Gerry. Meanwhile, leave Roger to me. It's not him I worry about. It's Mrs. Trevane."

CHAPTER THIRTY-SIX

Liz's Guy

Greenwood, Mississippi

Marcus Bianco and Danny Malone had rehearsed their plan in Willie Campbell's office and were ready to head down to the Commander's Club when Meisha Campbell burst into the room.

"Meisha!" snapped Willie. "I told you to knock first. What's so important, dear?"

"Sorry, Gramps," she said, almost breathless. "These two strangers in dark suits came in and asked for Mr. Bianco. I pretended like I don't know him. When they turned to leave, I could tell that one had a gun. Did I do the right thing?"

"You most certainly did, my dear. Thanks. Get back up front in case they come back in and suspect something."

As Meisha left and closed the door, Marcus spoke up.

"I must admit that I'm a little weary of this good-guy bad-guy game. It seems that I've gotten on someone's 'most wanted' list, and I don't like it. At first, it was all about everybody protecting or hiding Jake Luther. Now someone wants to snuff out these two small town detectives," he said, looking at Danny.

Danny stood, wrung his hands, and said, "Jasen was onto something bigger than Luther hiding KKK secrets, just like he said. Now I don't know who to trust. I hope this plan of yours works, Marcus."

"At least we know that the bad guys are looking for us. They don't know what we know, so it gives us an advantage. We won't be ambushed. I'm ready to go on the offense. Danny?"

"I'd rather be spying on cheating husbands and wives back in Jackson, but, hey! Let's get this rodeo rolling."

"I'm ready, too, Marcus," Willie chimed in. "I've never liked that weasel Bartram or his stinking cigars. He won't like a black man knocking on his door at all!" Willie grinned broadly, revealing the gaps between his pearly white teeth.

***

Elizabeth Keys, fully recovered from her head trauma, was working late in the evening at her desk at the FBI Regional Field Office in Atlanta. She was preparing to join Jasen and Jade in Washington the following day when her phone rang.

"Agent Keys?"

"Yes, this is Elizabeth Keys. May I help you?"

"Yes, ma'am. This is Agent Gaines in Treasury in DC. We were expecting your two agents this evening but I'm afraid something has happened."

"What do mean? They were under full escort by FBI agents. What's happened?" Liz had not expected an attack on Jasen and Jade while being protected by other agents. She fought off a surge of panic.

"Well, ma'am. They were involved in a crash on the Arlington Bridge on their way here from Reagan National Airport. Their SUV went over the rails and sank in the Potomac."

"Good God, man!" she exclaimed. "Are they okay? Have they been rescued? Please tell me they're okay!"

"The Coast Guard has been searching for them. They sent divers down to the wreckage, but the river is pretty murky at night. All I've heard is that your agents were apparently not in the SUV. The driver's body was recovered—he's dead. The agent that was riding up front made it out alive, but he's in ICU at Georgetown. The Coast Guard and Potomac River Patrol are searching downstream for any signs of your agents. So far, no luck. I'm sorry, ma'am."

"Thank you, Gaines. I'll be headed to DC as soon as I can get a flight lined up. Please keep me informed if there's any news, good or bad."

"Yes, ma'am. Good night."

She hung up then dialed the FBI's private hanger at Atlanta-Hartsfield Airport that housed the FBI Leer jet.

"John? This is Agent Keys. Get the jet ready and file a flight plan to Washington. I'll be there in forty minutes. Okay? Thanks."

Liz then dialed Willie Campbell's number at the Crystal Grill in Greenwood. She spoke to Meisha and learned that Willie, Marcus, and Danny had just left. She needed to alert Marcus. She wanted him to be safe. Her "Detective Noir'" had been on her mind constantly since she had returned to Atlanta. She felt closer to him than she knew she should be, because his vigil by her bedside for three days had touched her heart. He belonged to another, but he was *her* Prince Charming, in her mind. She just needed to hear his voice. And he needed to know about Jasen and Jade.

***

Willie Campbell, who had disguised himself to look like a homeless vagrant, smell and all, knocked on the windowless white door at the entrance to the Commander's Club. The door opened almost immediately, and Willie was quickly scanned from head to toe by the very tall and bulky security goon.

"This is a private establishment, members only. Buzz off, you bum!"

"I has to see Mr. Bartram," Willie said in his fake uneducated voice. "It's an emergency. He'll want to see me. Please, sir."

"Who the hell are you? He doesn't associate with homeless rail hoppers. What do you want?" insisted the bouncer.

"I is Caleb Smith. I work over at the junkyard for Mr. Vosper. I has some good news about him. Mr. Bartram will want to hear 'bout what I knows."

Willie was sounding very convincing. He and Marcus had calculated that any mention of Vosper would perk the interest of Bartram, assuming they were *all* involved in the same clandestine activities that had to be protected at any cost.

The giant man frowned and stared intensely at Willie for several seconds.

"Wait here," he said and slammed the door in Willie's face.

He returned in less than a minute and opened the door. He unexpectedly saw no one waiting. Puzzled momentarily, he propped the door open, took two steps over the threshold of the doorway and stepped into the alley. Before he could react to what he saw, a force equivalent to a massive, swinging wrecking ball slammed into his forehead. In a instant, his eyes glazed over and rolled back in his head. He toppled and fell to the pavement, crashing like a lumberjack-felled giant redwood.

Marcus, holding a large iron pole, stood with Danny and Willie peering at the unconscious body of the huge bouncer.

"Now, what do you think his boss will say if he catches his bodyguard sleeping on the job?" quipped Danny.

Marcus chuckled only briefly. "Let's don't give him the chance of finding Lurch. Give me a hand, you two, quickly."

The three grabbed limbs of the downed guard and with considerable grunting, huffing, and tugging, dragged the body away from the front entrance and to the far side of the club.

"Tie him up, Willie," said Marcus. "Danny and I have a chubby, little man in a white suit to see."

They cautiously entered the club, which was empty of patrons at the early hour. No one else was immediately visible so they walked quietly and very slowly toward the door marked "Private."

As they crept step-by-step closer to Bartram's office door, the faint light from the opening front door suddenly diffused into the dimly lit room.

"Hey, you two, wait up!"

It was Willie who had quickly hogtied the bouncer and did not want to miss the confrontation with Harlow Bartram.

As Marcus and Danny turned and looked toward Willie, they could not see the door ahead marked "Private" slowly opening.

"Look out!" shouted Willie. "A gun!"

Instinctively, Marcus and Danny stooped and leaned to one side as they turned back toward Bartram's office door. A barrel of a revolver protruded from the partially opened door, and suddenly a flash of light and loud report exploded toward the front entrance. Willie grabbed his chest and fell to the floor.

Marcus looked back to see his friend fall and knew that he had been hit. In the next second he stood and charged with all of his weight into the office door. The gun discharged again but this time into the ceiling as Marcus had surprised Bartram with his quick response. Marcus's momentum propelled him into the office, and he barreled over the surprised club manager, knocking him to the floor. The gun flew from Bartram's hand in the opposite direction and bounced across the floor. With all of his weight, Marcus pushed one knee into the chest of the portly Bartram, pinning him against the floor. Bartram looked up at the muscular detective and knew he was no match. He sighed in surrender.

"Well, how are you, Mr. Bartram? I hope you haven't missed me." Marcus had not planned on Bartram having a gun. He needed to hear about Willie.

"Danny. Check on Willie. Mr. Bartram here is not going anywhere."

He looked back at Bartram. "You had better hope that my friend out there was not seriously wounded. I'd hate to mess up your cute little Colonel Sanders suit with bullet holes and blood."

***

Marcus, Danny, Willie, and Willie's four sons sat around the table in the private dining room across from Willie's office at the Grill, and Danny raised his wine glass to toast the successful evening.

"Danny," admonished Marcus. "I think it's a little premature to celebrate. We won a battle, not the war."

"Sorry, boss. It's been a good night as far as I'm concerned," argued Danny. "Willie's wound is minor—a through and through, muscle only. Bartram squealed like a poked pig in a BBQ joint, his security guard is still seeing stars, and Willie's boys took care of those hired terminators in the black suits. Plus, Luther, Calvin, and Vosper are history, too. I think, all in all, we've taken care of any further Greenwood threats. I'm feeling pretty damn good."

Marcus's worries had eased a bit, too, though he knew that it was probably only a matter of time before whoever was really behind the threats, abductions, murder attempts, and other crimes would send in reinforcements. They had wounded a link in the chain of mysteries but like Medusa, every time they cut off one head, another took its place. *Trust no one,* he reminded himself. *No one.*

"Danny," Marcus said. "We can't be celebrating knowing that Jasen and Jade are missing. Maybe even dead. Liz is on her way to DC to find out what's happened to them. Let's bring this party back down a notch or two."

Danny sat his glass down and lowered his head. "You're right, boss. I hope they're okay. They're survivors, so if there's any possibility that they might have survived that crash, I'll take that bet. If anybody is hard to kill, it's those two. Maybe you and I need to be in DC helping Liz."

Marcus's grim face quickly lit up, and the others in the room couldn't help but notice.

"I think you're right, Danny. I, uh, *we* need to be there with Liz. I'll call Angie to make the travel arrangements."

He turned and headed to Willie's office to use the phone. Liz had told him that he was her "Guy Noir." He smiled to himself. Then, he instantly removed his smile. *Reveal minimally,* he reminded himself. *Minimally.*

CHAPTER THIRTY-SEVEN

Erased

Its old motor sputtered as the small fishing boat hugged the tree-lined bank of the Potomac in the quiet darkness of the night. The boat's operator, whose bushy gray hair was mostly hidden by an old, faded Boston Red Sox baseball cap, had purposely moved down the river at a very slow pace, hoping to not attract the attention that a speeding boat might. Several miles upriver, boats with flashing red and yellow lights had filled the waters around and under the Arlington Bridge. A massive rescue operation was underway with nets dragging the waters and divers popping up frequently as they made multiple trips down to the wreckage of the black SUV.

The gray-bearded boatman looked down at the dark green canvas covering his precious cargo and saw no movement.

"You doing okay under there?" he asked.

"Snug as the proverbial bug," someone responded. "Where are we going?"

"Patience, my wet friend. We're close. I think you need to stay hidden until I clear the end of the airport property, in case any spotlights are aimed my way. I'm not churning up a wake, so I think we're pretty much a dot in the water. You're very lucky that I happened along when I did.

This old river can drag even the best of swimmers down and push you into its muddy bottom grave."

He covered the last half mile in a long ten minutes and inched along the bank until the river angled west toward the south end of the airport property. He had noticed the opening in the marshes earlier in the day when he was surveying the river, and he glided his small boat through the opening until it tapped the bank's edge. It came gently to a stop. He grabbed a rope tether and hopped onto dry land. The area was protected by high, marshy reeds and a small stand of river birch. In the moonless night, he was certain that he had not been seen. He tugged on the rope and secured it to a nearby tree.

"Okay. Time to go," he said as he lifted the canvas.

His passengers sat up and looked around curiously.

"Follow me," he said.

The boatman had strangely bought the story about their being undercover federal agents and the apparent attempt to kill them by what may have seemed by casual observers to be a tragic accident. They had convinced him that it was safer for them to appear as if they had drowned. Whoever had run them off the bridge would probably try to finish the job if they surfaced, they told him.

"You two are fortunate to have gotten out of your car and made it downstream as far as you did. When I saw you swimming beside the riverbank, I thought I was seeing river creatures in the darkness. I've seen a few manatees and even a gator or two in these waters. Started not to stop. Guess you're glad I did."

"We're in your debt, mister. Did you say there is a safe place for us to hide around here? Somewhere with a phone?"

"I told you not to worry. I'll take care of you. The place is just about two hundred yards in that direction," he said, pointing north.

"The place?" Jasen said to Jade. She shrugged her shoulders.

They covered the short distance in the darkness quickly, and the old man opened the unlocked rear door to the small silver building. He motioned for them in go inside the darkened structure.

"You'll find some dry clothes in the closet. Can't promise they'll fit, though. Make yourselves some coffee. You two look cold. Your lady friend there is shivering a bit."

"Thank you," Jasen said in his gentle voice. "Is this your place?"

"Let's just say that I've been known to hang out here sometimes," he said with a big grin. "I kind of like spy stuff and mysteries. You two seem like good spies to me. Just consider yourselves lucky."

They smiled at him as he turned to leave.

"Oh, yes," he added. "The phone's in the kitchen. Make yourselves comfortable and don't forget to turn off the lights when you leave." He closed the door and disappeared back toward his boat.

Jade, still soaking wet and shivering, scanned the unique apartment that they now realized was once an airplane hangar. Although tastefully decorated, it definitely had the ambiance of a man cave with little feminine flavor. Through a glass wall across the spacious living area, Jasen could make out several classic vintage automobiles.

"Jasen," said Jade. "Who do you think that guy *was* and how did he happen to come along at just the right time? Nothing happens by coincidence, remember? I'm remembering now that you pointed this hangar out to me as we were leaving the airport earlier. Didn't you say that this belonged to some famous writer?"

"Yes, indeed, I did. Clint Canter. I can't believe we're in *his* apartment. This is more than weird."

"Surely, that wasn't Canter, was it?" asked Jade.

"I seriously doubt it. Not the image of a famous writer to me. Maybe a hired hand. Anyway, it's not important. Let's get some dry clothes on!"

***

"Wow!" exclaimed Jade. "I never thought that dry, warm clothes could feel so good. I'm still shivering. This hot coffee is sooo good. I feel like pouring it over my head."

"Here," he said, wrapping a throw around her shoulders. "This'll help."

"Jasen, where in the world did you get those mini-breathing devices? I'm not so sure I could have held my breath long enough to get out of that SUV."

"I picked them up from the FBI technical department along with several other agent props the last time we met with Liz. I dropped them in my brief case never guessing that we'd ever need them. Dumb luck? Who knows. I suppose if we had *had* to, we could have held our breath, even though you didn't think you could.

"I also always carry a small window break tool and knife with me, just in case. That's just my 'always be prepared background.' Good thing I did. Cutting the seat belts and breaking the window out was slower going than I would have planned. Fortunately, I remembered the breathing devices. My sixth sense, I guess."

Jade was warmer now. "Hey, we'd better give Liz or someone over at Treasury a call, someone we can trust. I'll level with you, Jasen. I'm not 100 percent positive that Liz is all she says she is."

"Don't be ridiculous. She hired you, didn't she? Liz is Liz. Relax. And she's good looking, too.

"Hey! Watch it, big boy. You've got all you can handle right here." She laughed.

"When I was talking before the crash about being erased, I didn't exactly have this scenario in mind," said Jasen. "Regardless, this is working out better than I could have predicted. If we pull this off, whoever arranged for that tanker truck to plow into us has to be thinking that we're dead, swallowed by the currents of the Potomac. The Treasury Department and FBI will officially report us as deceased. We've been erased."

Jade shook her shoulders slightly. "I told you that I like being Delta Jade Colton. When do we get to be unerased?"

"Patience, my love. Patience. We have a date with the head of a snake. As soon as we figure out what rock he's hiding under."

CHAPTER THIRTY-EIGHT

The Firm

Jackson, Mississippi
Offices of Rainey, Marsh, Giordano, and Associates

The law firm had dropped the Trevanes' name from their logo and stationary years ago at Roger Trevane's request. Roger and Charlotte had been full partners in the early history of the firm but had successfully distanced themselves when Roger jumped into the political arena, serving as a one-term governor of Mississippi, and using that office as a springboard to the respected US Senate. Only a few people knew the real reasons that the Trevanes divested of their interests in the firm.

Trevane had mastered the secret of "bedding down" with all of the right movers and shakers that could guarantee his re-election as long as they got their wishes in return. It was the classic greasing of the palms that kept the DC political machine turning, and it created more and more power for the ones who played the game well. Not by the rules, just well.

Fred Xavier and Gerome Rainey were secure in Rainey's private suite as they discussed their options. The wheels were beginning to fly off of their grand scheme, and they knew that Roger Trevane would not accept more failures or miscues.

"What have you learned about Bartram's situation in Greenwood, Fred?" asked Rainey.

"My two men that I sent in to eliminate the two Dick Tracys ran into an unexpected welcoming party. Some blacks showed up out of nowhere, shanghaied them, and neutralized them before they could locate the detectives. Unfortunately, the gumshoes got to Bartram first. I don't know if he spilled his guts or not, but I fear the worse. I've had to tell the cartel to shut down shipments until we can find another intake point. They weren't happy *capos* about the news. If we don't find a redirect soon, we're all in danger of their wrath.

"Has the FBI tied any of this to us?" asked Rainey.

"I don't think so. Depends on what Bartram might have shared. He knew very little about the firm. Just that I freelanced for a law firm. I never used real names. If he shared my name, the FBI will be chasing their tails for weeks trying to find someone who doesn't even exist."

"You mean you're not really Fred Xavier?" asked Rainey.

"As far as Bartram, you, or anyone else is concerned, I *am* Fred Xavier. If Bartram told them about the drug shipments from Colombia, I don't think the drug lords will share much! The Colombian henchmen have already taken out that Rivers character at the cotton exchange. Not too many sources left breathing that can put all of this together."

"What about the agents that were headed to DC?"

"History. They tried to swim across the Potomac, imagine that!—didn't make it. That threat is over. Trevane is satisfied for now," said Xavier. "He wants to concentrate on the land deal and getting the Delta project going. He still thinks he's going to find a boatload of gold out there somewhere on the Leflore property. I think he's delusional. Or just blinded by power and greed. Either way, I'm taking this one day at a time. Trevane has plenty of contacts that can make you and me sorry we ever got in bed with him. I just want to finish this and go cash in that Virginia account, then disappear forever."

"So, what's next, Fred?"

"We get the bulldozers out there to Leflore County and break ground. Regardless of the drugs, we have more than enough funding to complete the project. It's a grand vision with a high probability of enormous profits for all of us. We just need to be sure that no one tracks the origins of our funds. Drug money, blood money…just doesn't play well in the newspapers. Do your job, Gerry. We can't afford any delays.

"I couldn't stop him from visiting the site, so Roger is planning on being there at the groundbreaking ceremonies. He says that he has to appear supportive of the project and his constituents. Personally, I think he's going to look for the gold. He got his hands on that secret note that the French Camp guy stumbled onto. He told me that he thought he had deciphered the note's meaning. I couldn't talk him out of it. Obsessed, that's what he is. Delusional and obsessed."

"Can't he just hire someone to look for this mythical gold? He's taking a big chance if he shows up there," said a cautious Rainey.

"Are you serious? Roger Trevane does not trust *anyone*, not even Mrs. Trevane. Or, should I say, *especially* Mrs. Trevane. Gerry, I strongly suggest that you and I come up with other options in case the sky crashes down on our heads. Keep me posted, Gerry. The world may not be a big enough place for us to hide if this breaks open."

CHAPTER THIRTY-NINE

Undercover

The Washington leads were practically nonexistent, as Jasen and Jade headed to Potomac, Maryland, on a hunch provided by Marcus after grilling Harlow Bartram. It was obvious to Marcus that Bartram knew very little about what organization or persons were actually behind the drug shipments. He knew nothing at all about any land deals, but gave up his contact, Fred Xavier—who Bartram thought directed money flows and accounts. As Richard Jordan had predicted, the FBI could find no such person, at least still living. Death records verified a Fred Xavier from Duluth, Minnesota, who died in 1946. It was apparent to Marcus that the man's real identity was kept from Bartram.

The only clue that Marcus felt credible was that this Xavier worked with or for a big law firm in Jackson. Marcus knew firsthand that the largest and most prominent firm in Mississippi was Rainey, Marsh, and Giordano. A number of his past clients had benefited from their services in large divorce settlements.

With considerable digging, Marcus stumbled upon a list of former partners in the firm. The names Roger and Charlotte Trevane caught his attention, as he knew that Roger Trevane had gained considerable advantages in political circles and was strangely both loved or hated by Mississippians who kept putting him back in his Senate seat term after term. The FBI had been unable to discover any phone records of recent activity between the law firm and Trevane's office. But, the past association was enough for Marcus. It was all circumstantial, but he said that he just had a gut feeling. Jasen and Jade needed to check out the Trevanes.

Nothing in Bianco and Associates' investigations or from Jasen's own research had connected Roger Trevane to Greenwood, KKK activities, or clandestine criminal dealings anyway, much less in Greenwood. But, to Marcus it seemed like a good starting point for Jasen. His celebration in learning of Jasen and Jade's latest escape from the clutches of the cold Potomac was short-lived, as he knew that any chance that the undercover agents might get a lucky lead was diminishing by the day.

Gaining access to the Wynstone estate would not be easy without proper credentials. Jasen and Jade, with new names and in their new disguises, however, looked the part. Jade sported a stunning platinum blond wig and a shimmering, sleek, midthigh designer dress. Her neck was draped in a string of imported white pearls. Jasen's hair was dyed jet black and combed straight back. His gray sharkskin suit looked custom-made and accentuated his muscular physique. The royal purple necktie and handmade, imported Italian loafers oozed richness.

At Elizabeth Keys's request, Clint Canter had graciously agreed to loan his temporary houseguests his classic 1937 Packard V12 Town Car, a gesture that Jasen nearly did a triple somersault over. It had a beautiful town car body and boasted the finest of coach work. It totally reeked of someone with big money, almost assuring an easy admission to the fabulous estate.

The 175-horsepower Packard engine hummed like a tamed beast and soared like a glider along the highway to Potomac, Maryland. Jasen felt like a teenager who had just borrowed his father's fanciest sports car. For a moment, he wanted to forget his job and keep on driving with no final destination.

They approached the locked wrought iron gate at Wynstone and pressed the button on the intercom mounted on a short stone column. Introducing themselves as dealers in classic vintage cars, they were thoroughly scrutinized by a wiry-looking security guard who viewed the unexpected visitors through the closed-circuit security cameras mounted on the gate. He informed the imposters that the Senator was not at home and that they would need to schedule an appointment if they wished to show the senator their car. They pretended that Trevane had invited them to come up any time, but the guard wasn't biting.

Hoping to at least talk to Mrs. Trevane, Jasen insisted that the guard notify her of the opportunity to see the car. Reluctantly, the guard buzzed Charlotte Trevane's room. She turned on the security monitor in her bedroom and studied the beautiful car and its handsome occupants. Surely, she thought, Roger must have met them somewhere and suggested that they visit sometime.

She decided to allow the guard to let them in. *Maybe,* she wondered, Roger was going to surprise her with the car. It was truly beautiful and he knew how she loved fancy cars. Maybe it was intended to be an apology for his rough treatment two nights before.

After formal introductions, she invited the pretentious couple into a sitting room off from the large, white marble foyer that showcased an ornate French provincial antique table holding an antique vase filled with a bouquet of large, freshly cut flowers and greenery.

Jade started the conversation after being served a cup of hot tea by a house servant.

"Mrs. Trevane, we were really hoping to speak with your husband about the Packard Town Car. He may not remember but we met him some time ago at a party, and he seemed to be very intrigued with our classic car restoration business. We were headed to a showing in upstate Maryland and thought we would pop in and show him an example of our work. He mentioned his love of old town cars. The '37 Packard is one of a kind. I think he'd love it."

"Yes, uh, Mrs. Givens, is that correct?"

"Yes, but please, it's Katie."

"Well, yes, Katie. I think you *must* know my husband. If he were here, he'd probably write you a check right now. It's a beautiful car, for sure. I'm so sorry that you missed Roger. He's actually on his way to Mississippi. We have a home on Lake Madison. He had to meet with some real estate people about a new project that they want him to bless—you know, as the senator representing that area."

Jasen's interest was tweaked. "I'm curious, Mrs. Trevane."

"Please call me Charlotte, Mr. Givens."

"Okay, Charlotte. Please call me Vince. What area would that be?"

"I don't pay that much attention to what he's in to anymore. He says that I actually don't pay much attention to him *period*. Oh, I'm sorry. I digress. I think he told me that some oil tycoon is developing a one-of-a-kind casino, resort hotel, and family theme park. That sounds like an odd mix to me, but, hey. Whatever."

"The area?" asked Jasen.

"Oh, yes, sorry. It's in the Delta somewhere. I think near Greenwood."

Jasen and Jade instantly looked at each other, mouths slightly agape.

CHAPTER FORTY
Delta Reunion

R ichard Jordan had his final orders from Roger Trevane: eliminate the private detectives in Greenwood and any others than may have gained access to Jake Luther's secrets that had been hidden in the now destroyed rooster, including knowledge of the gold. Jordan was told to personally make it happen. "No gofers this time!" Trevane told him emphatically.

He packed his weapons of choice—two semiautomatic Glock 20 Gen 4 pistols. He also always kept a backup tucked in his belt—a Beretta 9-mm Pico. No one other than Bartram, his security doorman, and a stripper at his club knew his face, a face known to them as Fred Xavier He would take care of those loose ends first. Phineus Blount in French Camp probably knew too much, also. Jordan needed to get the secret note, then Blount had to disappear. Afterward, Jordan would track down the others. No one knew his real name. Advantage: Jordan. He knew he couldn't fail.

***

Marcus, Danny, and Liz were just as intrigued as Jasen and Jade to hear about Roger Trevane's interest in the just publicly announced *Delta LeFleur Casino* project to be developed near Greenwood. No one could pin any piece of illegal drug shipments, money laundering, KKK shenanigans, missing persons, abductions, land deals, or any other criminal mischief on Senator Trevane. However, his name just kept coming up far too often, Marcus had said. Someone in Treasury continued to speculate about Trevane's involvement but still had found no smoking gun. Even bank accounts with unusually large balances seemed to be remotely connected to a friend of a Trevane staffer. But, if he was involved, he was a master at cover-up.

The secret Virginia account was withdrawn and redeposited monthly in other local banks by a friend of a friend of a friend of an acquaintance with a Trevane staffer or former staffer. "It can't be a coincidence," Liz reminded the team. There's a reason for everything. They all agreed that it was time to focus their investigation on Trevane, his wife, and their former law practice. The missing piece of their Greenwood puzzle was Fred Xavier. Who was he and how close was he to the top? Maybe he *was* the head. It was time for a team reunion.

***

Jasen had suggested that the team meet at the site of the former Indian chief's mansion, Malmaison. He had thought a lot about Leflore's second coded message and knew that the deceased Jake Luther was obsessed with deciphering it. He had a nagging concern that someone other than Luther was anxious to lay to rest the myth about buried gold.

Jasen thought about the Carriage House attendant back in French Camp. Phineus Blount was not who he pretended to be and had obviously given Luther a copy of the second secret note. Blount had also kept the original note in his possession, he had told Jasen. Jasen had to know if someone besides Luther or Blount had read the note. There could be other treasure hunters out there, someone with hidden agendas or names to protect.

Jasen convinced the others to join him and help him explore the Leflore property for clues. If he had successfully decoded it, someone else could too. If they were also looking for the mythical cache of gold, it could lead them to Trevane or his underlings. He wondered about the *real* reason for Trevane's visit back to Mississippi. Jasen explained Trevane's (or those who worked for him) possible urgency—bulldozers and giant earth movers were about to descend in mass on the Leflore estate. If really buried there, the gold might be buried even deeper and lost for eternity, ironically, just as Leflore wanted. It was time to test Jasen's theory.

They all convened in the open area in front of the rubble of bricks that had once been the mansion's fireplace. Jasen had made extra copies of Leflore's note and handed each member of the team a copy. Jasen told them that he had also given Willie Campbell a copy in case his memory of the property might trigger something that could aid in the search.

"You think that's a wise idea, Jasen?" asked Danny.

"I trust Willie as much as I trust each of you. He's on our side, Danny."

Marcus mused on Jasen's comments. *Trust no one*, he thought to himself, but he remained silent.

The ever skeptical Danny continued in character. "Jasen, are we on a treasure hunt or are we trying to pin something on Trevane?"

"I thought I had explained it, Danny. One can lead to the other. Two birds, one stone, so to speak. Are you okay with that?"

"I hate damn wild goose chases, that's all," Danny fired back. "Gold fever can warp the brain. Not to mention the unknown dangers of treasure hunting. Let's just say that I'm not spending my share before I get it. Or should I say, *if.*"

"Danny, my boy. You need to open your mind and relax. I know you're tired of hearing it, but, you're here for a reason."

"Damn straight. Because Marcus made me come!"

"Liz," said Jasen. "I forgot to ask you how you're feeling after the junkyard crash."

"One hundred per cent! Thanks for asking," she responded. "I owe it all to my friend here," she said, smiling broadly and locking her hands around Marcus's upper arm. He was my guardian while I was comatose. You know how dangerous hospitals can be. Marcus made sure that I got good care. I'm fine now. Hardly missed a beat."

Jade grinned and looked down at the ground as she cleared her throat.

"Great. And thank you again for what you did in DC for me and Jade. You thought of everything. We didn't exactly plan on taking a nighttime swim in the Potomac. I don't think that's what you had in mind, but it all worked out. Getting erased from society can be stressful. However, getting to drive that million-dollar Packard Town Car made up for the danger." He smiled and tried to refocus the team.

"Okay, guys. Let's get back to our reason for being here." Or maybe to our reason for just *being*, he thought to himself.

"Let's go over the note again. I think all of us agree that Leflore was referencing a buried treasure in his message, correct?"

They each nodded affirmatively.

"I think that the rumors and tales that were spun for decades around the Delta have to be at least partly based on truth. Leflore had something to hide, and I think he really thought his secrets would last for eternity. Then, again, why would he document it? Who knows?

"From my perspective, the most difficult part of the message is understanding exactly where the gold or treasure was laid to rest. Maybe Leflore intended it that way. Or maybe, it's so simple it's staring us in the face."

Marcus interrupted. "Under LeFleur's oaks is very, very vague. Oak trees live and die. Plus, how many oak trees are around here or were here back in 1865? And why did he use the spelling 'Lefleur?'"

"The spelling is interesting, but I think he's just going back to his roots. I agree. Oaks are everywhere. We can't dig around every stand of oak trees or stump of dead oak trees." He paused and looked at their faces.

"I have another theory. But, we'll have to go underground to test it."

Danny Malone took a step back. "What! Underground?"

CHAPTER FORTY-ONE

Under the Oaks

J asen, holding a flashlight in one hand and three crowbars in the other, led the way with Jade just behind him. The team carefully walked down the ten steps of the steep stone stairway leading to Colonel Greenwood Leflore's burial crypt below the family mausoleum. Jasen pushed the heavy metal door into the pitch black tomb and shined his flashlight inside. As he moved the light slowly around the chamber, a large gray-and-black rat stared momentarily at the light and then quickly scurried away into a darker corner.

Jasen turned back toward the others and said, "Watch your step, folks. Seems we have some four-legged company—rats."

"Rats!" exclaimed Danny. "I don't do rats. I'm turning around. I hate tombs, especially rat-infested tombs!"

"Don't be a wimp, Danny," said Liz. "The rats up there (pointing up the stairs) are more dangerous than these down here." She didn't realize how prophetic her words might be.

"Just shine your light at them, Danny. They're more afraid of you than you are them." Marcus chuckled in amusement.

They entered and moved toward the center of the crypt as they shined their lights around to discourage the rats from getting too close to them.

A wood-frame structure occupied the tomb's center. Jasen could see that the framed structure had a broken leg and had been partially dismantled. A long broken board lay near it on the concrete-hard dirt floor. He saw something that appeared to be blood on the board.

As they huddled near the rectangular wooden box, Jasen began.

"This is the crypt where Ariel was held captive for two days by Stefan Vosper. You can only imagine her experience in this tomb—totally dark, no food, no water, and rat infested. If it were me, I'd still be having nightmares. Ariel blew it off as 'no big deal.'

"As you can see, there is no coffin on this wooden platform. It was built to keep Leflore's coffin off of the dirt floor. I think you all know about the Choctaw grave robbers that stole Leflore's body years ago and reburied him in an unmarked grave, face down.

"When Ariel recounted her horrors of two days locked in this tomb, she told me about this wooden platform and how she managed to rip off one of the boards. She hid behind the door and used the board to coldcock a surprised Vosper, temporarily disabling him. As you know, her escape was short-lived.

"Then it dawned on me—the proverbial light bulb in the head. 'Under Lefleur's oaks.' Could he be referring to the wooden platform on which he knew his body would rest for eternity?"

Danny the naysayer was quick to jump in. "Only if that platform is made of oak. I would have guessed pine or birch, not oak."

"Ay, yes, my astute Mr. Malone. Very rational of you. However, keep in mind that Chief Leflore preferred more exquisite surroundings. His house was truly a one-of-a-kind mansion. Why not a sturdy oak platform to support him in perpetuity? Or he could have chosen French mahogany like most of his fine furniture."

"Okay, Professor All Knowing. How do we know what kind of wood this is?" asked Danny as he leaned down and picked up the broken board and teased off a small piece.

"Way ahead of you, Danny. I had one of the boards examined by a botanist over at Mississippi State yesterday when I visited Ariel. The wood is quite deteriorated, as you can see, but wood has a DNA character, same as us. This platform is made of oak."

Suddenly, the crypt was as still as Leflore locked in his coffin in his unmarked grave. No one spoke.

Marcus finally extinguished the silence. "Jasen, are you saying that we may be in the very spot where Leflore hid 200 million dollars worth of gold—blood gold?"

"That would be three and one half *billion* dollars, at today's values, Marcus. Yes, I think we may have at last found the stolen caches of gold of the land pirate Samuel 'Wolfman' Mason. Leflore apparently thought he could guard the treasure forever."

Jade leaned against Jasen's shoulder and said, "I think I may faint."

"Hold on, my love. Let's don't spend it before we count it. Marcus, you and Danny grab a crowbar. We have to take this platform apart."

They hesitated briefly, then quickly each took a crowbar from Jasen and began to rip the boards off of the rotted platform.

Jade and Liz stood behind the men and watched expectantly as the platform was rapidly disassembled. In less than five minutes the brittle boards had been removed. Jade stepped up and shined her flashlight on the ground beneath the structure. At first, it appeared to be just more of the hard packed dirt floor. Jasen dropped to his knees and leaned forward. He took his crowbar and tapped on what looked liked only dirt.

The team all heard the sound of a dull, hollow thud. Jasen dropped the crowbar and with a wiping motion quickly created a cloud of brown dirt and dust. He wiped faster and faster. Marcus and Danny fell on their knees and joined in the wiping frenzy.

Within minutes they had uncovered a wooden trap door, which would have measured at least eight feet by four feet. Jasen spied an iron ring that was recessed into the frame of the door. Fleetingly, he wondered about Leflore's message—"under LeFleur's oaks, my dirk protects the six." He had expected to find the dirk dagger. Maybe it was inside, he thought. He stood and walked to the side of the trap door with the ringed handle.

"Step back, gentlemen and ladies. It's time to see what's behind door number two."

Everyone backed up, raised their flashlights and aimed them at the secret door. Jasen leaned over, grasped the iron ring, and then slowly swung the door open.

CHAPTER FORTY-TWO
The Secret Door

They stared in perfect unison at the secret behind the door, finally revealed. They all searched for words or an answer for what to do next.

Thirty seconds of deafening silence passed slowly like several minutes. Danny was finally the first to respond.

"I didn't want to be the first one to say it, but what are we looking at and what do we do now? I don't like what I'm seeing."

Jasen scratched his chin and focused his light on their discovery.

"It appears that we've found two wooden coffins," he said. The dirk protects the six, he said to himself. Where's the dirk? And there's only two coffins?"

"That's pretty obvious, Sherlock," retorted Danny. "I'm talking about the writing on the coffins."

"We can read, Danny, thank you," said Marcus.

"Yeah, and I don't like what it says," said Danny. "'Danger! Smallpox. Do NOT Open.' I think the skull and crossbones tells me all I need to know."

Jasen tried to be more practical and use his analytical side, which on occasion had caused him more grief than relief.

"On the surface, it would appear that someone (or more than one) who died of smallpox is buried in these coffins. And someone is trying to convince anyone who may want to open these coffins that it may not be such a good idea. The apparent names on the coffins of the 'deceased' are in Choctaw. So, dead Choctaws who died of smallpox, buried deep beneath the ground, below the burial platform of a great Indian chief. Does this make any sense?"

"It does to me," said Danny. "Smallpox is a bad-ass, lethal virus that wipes out civilizations. It decimated Native Americans. The deeper you bury traces of it, the better."

"I agree with you, Danny," responded Jasen. "However, I just don't buy a great Indian chief wanting infected, dead Choctaws buried beneath him.

"Reel it back in, everyone. Why are we here? Leflore *led* us here. Where better to hide a cache of gold than in an underground tomb behind a secret door that no one knew existed except for Leflore and whoever helped him hide it? The gold is here, in these coffins. It has to be. We're here for a reason, not by accident."

Jade and Liz remained quiet as the debate continued.

Open or don't open? Is there a risk so many years after the burial of live smallpox virus contaminating all of them? Would it aerosolize into the crypt? Had all of them been vaccinated? Regardless, it was a 130-year-old strain. Would they be immune? Who would volunteer to open one of the coffins? What if they didn't look inside and the gold was really there? The debate continued for almost half an hour.

Jasen had heard enough. "Stop it, you guys! Stop it! It's time to settle this argument. I suggest that you start thinking about how you're going to spend your share of over 3 billion dollars. I'm opening the coffins. Leave if you want or stand back."

They looked at each other but no one moved.

Jasen climbed down into the grave beneath the grave and stood beside one of the coffins. He leaned down and attempted to raise the wooden lid. It wouldn't budge.

"It's nailed shut. Someone hand me a crowbar."

Marcus dropped to his knees, leaned into the grave, and passed him a crowbar.

Slowly, Jasen pried the coffin lid loose, one nail at a time. The team leaned and peered into the secret grave with anxious anticipation.

Finally, Jasen looked toward the flashlights that flooded his face.

"Okay, it's loose. Here goes nothing."

He began to raise the lid very, very slowly. He stopped half way, picked up his flashlight, and illuminated the inside of the coffin. He stared for what seemed a long, long time and said nothing.

"Come on, man!" shouted Danny. "What's in there? Is it the gold? Say something for God's sake!"

Jasen slowly raised his head and looked up at Jade.

"It's empty," he said.

"Empty? What do you mean empty?" asked Danny. "No gold? No dead Indian? Nothing?"

"I'm sorry, guys. It's an empty coffin." Jasen's long face said it all.

Jade didn't want to admit failure. "Jasen, maybe it's in the other coffin. Open it."

He climbed over the open, empty pine box and began prying the next coffin lid open. Faster and faster he worked, hoping Jade was correct. In half the time that it took to open the first coffin, he was ready to raise the second lid. He looked up again at Jade and saw her radiant smile that seemed to illuminate the dark tomb. He could read her lips. "I love you."

He opened the coffin with more haste. His stone face spoke loudly in the eerily still crypt. It was another empty coffin.

Jasen climbed up and out of the secret tomb and brushed the dust off of his hands and pants. No one wanted to speak.

"I'm sorry, guys. I really expected to find the gold. Everything said it had to be here. Maybe it *was* once but someone else got here before us. But, I don't think so. Those coffin lids had never been opened until just now. There was never any gold here."

Marcus was shaking his head. "Then, how do you explain the two empty coffins with warnings about deadly smallpox plastered all over them?"

"I don't have any explanation, Marcus. I'm mentally drained and fresh out of ideas. I don't know what to say."

They were all looking back into the empty grave when Danny broke the silence.

"I hate to be the one who said 'I told you so' but, well...I told you so."

Jasen's look could have cut him in half.

"We may have struck out, Danny, but Kate Smith hasn't sung yet…it's not over 'til it's over."

In the suspense and bitter disappointment, the team was totally focused on the grave and had not noticed that someone had been eavesdropping on their treasure hunt.

An unfamiliar voice cut through the darkness. "I think you may have that wrong, Mr. Prospero," the voice said as the crypt's metal door creaked open. Marcus turned quickly and pointed his light at the man standing in the doorway. No one recognized him. It was Fred Xavier. He pointed his semiautomatic Glocks, one in each hand, at them and grinned evilly.

"I think for all of you, yes, it *is* over. Rumor has it that your team has been tagged the 'Fabulous Five' due to your uncanny skills in survival. Congratulations. However, I could lay that rumor to rest very quickly with these Glocks—one round each between your eyes. Aaah, but that would be much too quick and painless for you five chums. Suffocation seems more of a fitting end for you.

"How ironic that you will all breathe your last whiff of fresh air in a tomb of all places, and probably all huddled together. How cozy! Too bad you won't get to sit around a campfire, roasting marshmallows, and singing kumbaya." He laughed, very pleased with his catch.

"Thanks for verifying for me that the gold isn't buried here. Personally, I never thought so, but it was a good guess. You've helped me narrow down my other choices. I'm sorry you won't be around to help me celebrate when I find the correct 'oaks.'

"If all of you would be so kind as to toss my friend here your lights and those crowbars." A second stranger stepped from behind Xavier and approached the team.

"No funny business," Xavier warned. "The ladies here will get the first shots between their eyes."

Jordan's accomplice gathered the flashlights and the three crowbars and backed toward the crypt door. He turned and started the steep climb, anticipating that his boss would follow.

Xavier backed into the doorway and said, "It was very nice meeting the real 'Fab Five.' I'll give your regards to your daughter, Mr. Prospero. Rest in peace!"

Xavier slammed the heavy door closed and locked it before any of them could reach it. The tomb was instantly drowned in total darkness.

In the stunned silence of the cold, stale crypt, Jasen said softly, "Wow! I didn't see *that* coming."

CHAPTER FORTY-THREE

Knock, Knock, Who's There?

"Okay, Mr. Treasure Hunter," said Danny, searching for Jasen. "Where the hell are you and just exactly how do you plan on getting us out of here?"

A light suddenly intruded into the darkness of the tomb. Jasen was holding a small penlight near his face.

"Right here, little man. Right here. As far as getting out, I'm working on it."

"Hey! responded Danny. "What exactly do you mean by 'little man'?"

"Cool your jets, Danny," said Jasen. "I didn't mean to touch a nerve. Let's all try to remain calm and put our heads together. We don't need to make this personal."

Danny wasn't backing down. "What's that supposed to mean? Being trapped in a damn underground tomb is about as personal as it gets!"

Jade and Liz walked over to Jasen and held on to each of his arms. Marcus walked closer until the four shared a five-foot circle on the dirt floor near the door. Danny reluctantly joined them since Jasen had the only light.

"This place is much too creepy in the dark," Jade said. "And it's actually getting chilly in here. Jasen, who *was* that guy with the guns? I didn't recognize him."

"My guess is he's Trevane's hired gun or fixer. That is, assuming Trevane is behind all of the fun, games, and adventures we've been enjoying," Jasen said facetiously. "How rude of him! He didn't even leave his calling card."

Marcus was a little concerned and like Danny didn't appreciate Jasen's levity. "Ironic, isn't it Jasen? Your last breath may be in the same tomb in which Ariel spent two days of hell. Let's see if you have as much ingenuity in getting out of here as she did."

"One thing's for certain," Liz observed. "Five of us won't last nearly as long as Ariel did in this death trap. Eventually, we're going to run out of breathable air. That creep with the Glocks cut off our life support when he closed the door. It looks as if it's airtight—no air in, no air out."

"Man, that's just great! Danny said annoyingly. "First, no gold. Now, no air. Who the hell talked us into this? Oh, yes. That would be *you!*" he said, pointing at Jasen.

Jade didn't appreciate Danny's attack on Jasen, given their dire circumstance. "Lighten up, Danny. We're all adults here. We came along willingly. I agree with Jasen. Attacking each other won't help us get out of here."

"People, people!" exclaimed Liz. "I echo that. Let's not point fingers. We need to find a way out of here. We're five reasonably intelligent people. Surely we can come up with a plan. Let's stop nipping at each other. Please, let's figure this out."

They looked at Liz, and as if they had been cued from offstage, they sat down in perfect synchrony on the cold, hard floor.

It seemed like hours had passed, when in real time it had only been one. No one had said anything, and Jasen kept turning his small penlight off for five minutes, then on for one minute.

"I suggest you save the battery in that light," Danny finally interjected sarcastically in the eerie quietness. "I'm sort of getting used to the dark."

"I think better when the light is on," responded Jasen. "But I suppose you're right. Has anyone come up with any bright, no pun intended, ideas?"

"Very funny, genius," quipped Danny. "We're all waiting on *you!*"

"No pressure, huh? Thanks a lot, Danny," said Jasen. "Marcus, any thoughts?"

"Hey, I'm a detective not a miracle worker," answered Marcus. "That's what we'll need to get out of here - a miracle. That door is probably several inches of iron. I don't suppose anyone brought along any dynamite?" He paused. "No, I didn't think so. We're at the mercy of someone on the other side of that door, and I don't think the guy with the Glocks is coming back. Who else knows that we were checking out this tomb? Jasen, didn't you say that you told Willie about our little reunion here?"

"I gave him a copy of Leflore's note and mentioned that we were going to explore Malmaison for clues. I didn't exactly tell him that we were going to be grave robbers."

"So, no one else knew that we were coming down here, right?" asked Marcus.

"I'm afraid that's true," Jasen admitted. "We're on our own unless Willie gets curious and comes over here. I didn't give him any reason to suspect that we'd run into trouble. I just don't know if he'll wonder where we are or not. I just don't know."

Danny was getting more freaked out by the minute, especially after Jasen's admission. "What kind of lame brain idiot would not tell someone that he was going treasure hunting in an underground tomb? Answer me that, Big Guy!"

Jasen stiffened. "I've about had enough of your insults, Danny. Can you just please shut the hell up?"

Marcus was more than disappointed in his partner. "Danny, you're getting on my last nerve, too. You're better than this. I'll chalk it up to your 'half-empty' personality. Back off and let's think through our options."

"Options!" exclaimed Danny. "What options? Suffocate or maybe just claw our way out of here with our fingernails? That's about all the options I can come up with."

Jade and Liz had silently listened to the men's banter which had only added to their anxiety and ever increasing sense of impending doom. Jade had trusted Jasen to come up with a plan, but any rational person would soon have to accept the certain fate that was filling the dark crypt with hopelessness. She spoke first.

"Guys. You're acting like kindergartners fighting over make believe candy. I don't know about Liz, but you're not helping my nerves. I suggest we try something else." The silence in the tomb begged for an answer. "I suggest we pray. That's another option."

"Great!" Danny snipped. "We'll pray our way through that door. Maybe we can pull a Star Trek trick and transport ourselves out of here!"

"That's enough, Danny!" exclaimed Marcus. " I agree with Jade. Let's pray for a miracle and pray that you can somehow *believe* in miracles."

Jasen tried to bring the tense energy level back down, "I think we need to limit our conversation from now on to meaningful dialogue. If we're going to be imprisoned in here for a while, we need to conserve our oxygen and minimize carbon dioxide accumulation. Every time we exhale, we're adding to the CO_2 levels. CO_2 narcosis will set in long before we run out of oxygen. Let's sit back and just try to relax, please."

"Relax? Yeah, sure," Danny whined.

"Danny!! Stop it! Liz said.

They sat quietly on the hard floor and tried to individually deal in silence with their predicament.

More hours passed as the five tried not to imagine any finality to their situation. The air grew staler, and breathing was becoming more of a conscious effort instead of a subconscious involuntary act. Jasen had briefly described the symptoms of oxygen deprivation and CO_2 narcosis.

"Asphyxia," Jasen explained, "is due to insufficient oxygen. When the oxygen level in here drops below 5%, we'll lose consciousness. But, like I said, the CO_2 will probably affect us first - fast and labored breathing, dizziness, confusion, cyanosis, pallor, and lapsing into unconsciousness. As CO_2 levels increase, you breathe faster trying to rid the body of the toxic levels. This only increases the CO_2 in our confined space, thus leading to a vicious cycle of more rapid breathing and a faster lapse into CO_2 toxicity."

"Jasen! Please stop," Jade pleaded. I don't think I can take any more of your professor side. We're getting out of here. I don't know how or when, but we *will* get out. Okay? (pause) Thank you."

More hours went by as they sat or lay down on the very hard floor without further conversation. Liz and Jade had drifted off into a fitful sleep, but the men had managed to stay awake. Jasen had saved the battery in his penlight and had turned it on only twice to check his watch. The last check showed that it was early morning - almost 6 am.

Jasen stood and walked around in the dark tomb trying to stretch his aching legs. He noticed the extra effort that it took to just stand up, much less walk. He felt slightly dizzy and asked Marcus how he felt. He and Danny said they felt dizzy, too, but were breathing okay, at least they thought so.

Jasen walked back over to the sleeping ladies and felt their arms. Both women felt cold and slightly clammy. He took off his shirt and draped it over Jade's arms. He asked Marcus to do the same for Liz. Jasen knew that he was seeing the beginning signs of oxygen deprivation and probable CO_2 toxicity. They were on the verge of a more rapid and likely fatal decline in their respiratory status. He guessed that they probably had less than two hours of breathable air. It was time to wake the ladies and acknowledge their desperate situation.

***

No one had anything to say as Jasen gave his final assessment of their waning odds. Unseen by the men, tears trickled down the faces of Jade and Liz, but there was no sobbing. Jade huddled close to Jasen, and he wrapped his arms around her. She was cold and shivering and soon drifted into a calmer sleep. Liz sat beside Marcus who put one arm around her shoulders and pulled her close to him. They both closed their eyes and fell asleep within minutes. Danny lay back on the floor and curled into a fetal position. He closed his eyes and for a moment wondered why he had never married.

Almost two more hours passed as Jasen fought the temptation to close his eyes like the others and just die in a peaceful sleep. He checked his watch one last time - 7:45 am. He gasped at the stale air and leaned down and kissed a sleeping Jade on the lips. They were cold and probably blue, too, he thought. He lay back beside her and finally closed his eyes in surrender.

***

Then, he heard it. Jasen immediately sat up and flicked his penlight back on.

"Did anyone else hear that, or am I having auditory hallucinations?" asked Jasen. No one responded. Were they dead or just asleep or unconscious? Was he dead, too? It didn't seem real.

Then, there it was again, slightly louder but still muffled by the thick, iron door.

Knock, knock, knock! Then a faint voice cried out, "Is anyone in there? Hello? Is anyone there?"

Jasen stood and charged over to the door.

He yelled back to the unknown knocker. "We're in here! We're in here! Get us out!"

The voice came back slightly louder. "The door's padlocked. Stand back. We'll try to shoot the lock off."

For a moment, Jasen thought that he was delusional from the stale air that had dried his lungs and dulled his mind. He pinched his hand and realized it was not a dream.

Within a few seconds Jasen heard an echoing, ricocheting gun shot. The huge crypt door opened into the room, and a gush of fresh air rushed in on streaks of warm morning sunlight. In the door opening stood Willie Campbell and his four sons.

CHAPTER FORTY-FOUR
The Trace and the Six

Jade decided that a relaxing drive along the serene and beautiful Natchez Trace would be a welcome relief from kidnappings, car crashes, dunks in cold rivers, and being buried alive in a 130 year-old tomb. She and Jasen had driven back to Jackson with Marcus, Liz, and Danny. They had felt safer traveling together, though Danny the skeptic reminded them that even teams can be ambushed. He told them that if Jasen had not told Willie about their exploring for clues at Malmaison, they'd still be in Leflore's crypt, never to see the light of day again.

Liz had decided to fly back to Atlanta on the Leer jet the next day. In classic Liz fashion, she decided to ask Marcus to join her for dinner that evening, just "for old times' sake" she told him. He hesitated and said he really needed to be at home with his wife.

"Just tell her it's a business dinner. We *are* business partners. Come on, Marcus. It might be a while before we see each other again, I mean, for business, of course."

Marcus looked into her pleading, brown eyes and wondered why such a beautiful, professional woman was still single at her age. Her unrelenting come-on was more than a little entertaining to Marcus on the surface. He gritted his teeth and battled his temptations.

"Let me think about it, Liz. I'll call you. Where are you staying?"

"The Embassy Suites in Ridgeland. Please, Marcus, I hate to eat alone."
She smiled, reached out, and touched his hand.

***

As Jasen drove their rental car north on the Trace from Jackson, Jade
was in awe at the understated splendor of the national treasure that was
a fine tribute to the historical role that the old buffalo trail had played
in the settlement of the Old South. The well-manicured Trace route
beside the Ross Barnett Reservoir was almost a spiritual moment, she
told Jasen.

"Yes, it's very calming compared to dodging maniac speeders on inter-
states around Atlanta. And I feel safe for a change. No one's following
us, at least I don't think so." He smiled as he glanced in the rearview
mirror.

"Jasen, do you really think the men that locked us in Leflore's crypt work
for Roger Trevane?"

"Someone important is behind all of this mystery, and Trevane is as
good a candidate as any. Somehow we have to find something that
directly relates to him or his wife, assuming she's more than his marriage partner. I'm not so sure about that. When we were in her parlor
at Wynstone, I kind of got the impression that there's some bad blood
between them. If so, she may be the weak link that opens more than
her estate gate for us."

"Did Willie mention if he saw anyone around the Malmaison property
when he came to see if we were okay?" asked Jade.

"No, he didn't see anybody or anything suspicious. Except, our cars and
no one around. We're *more than* lucky that he knew about Leflore's tomb.
Jade, I think your prayers were answered. Miracles *do* happen."

"I have a very strong feeling that we'll be seeing that pistol-packing creep who entombed us again," Jade remarked. "And what about his reference to Ariel? Do you think she's in danger?"

"I'm not sure, but Liz has an agent assigned to her for the time being. I think she'll be fine."

"I hope you're right, Jasen. And you did hear what he said about the gold? He indicated that someone else besides you thinks the gold exists. He obviously has read Leflore's secret note."

"Yes, obviously," Jasen said. "And he made the same mistake that I did. I've been kicking myself in the butt unmercifully since I opened those empty coffins. I should have guessed even before I jumped down in that gruesome grave that we'd find nothing."

"Okay, Mr. Prospero, McCoy, Givens. What exactly does *that* mean?"

"I keep reading and rereading the note. 'My dirk protects the six.' There was no dirk, number one, and number two, there were only two coffins. I should have known immediately that we were in the wrong place."

"Are you saying that there are six more coffins somewhere?"

"Yes, that's exactly what I'm saying. Then, it finally dawned on me. Marcus said it, but I sort of blew him off."

"What? What did he say?" asked Jade.

He looked at her with a satisfied smile. "Settle back in your seat, my love. We're on the road to our destiny."

***

They drove at the posted speed of 55 mph for almost an hour and a half northward on the lightly traveled Natchez Trace. They stopped and read most of the historic markers along the way and even got out and hiked short distances on the original Natchez trail. They tried to imagine the rugged life along the narrow, dirt trail that had provided many a traveler an easier, though dangerous, route to known and unknown destinations. Jasen recounted the legends of the highway brigands that terrorized the trail and cost many innocent sojourners their fortunes and their lives. The gold must have been carried over this very same route, Jasen told Jade as they stood on a section of the old road.

They took the French Camp Exit, and Jasen pulled the rental into the parking lot between the small Baptist church and the Council House Museum/Cafe. He turned off the engine and looked across the open field in front of them, then looked back at Jade.

"We're here."

"Okay, my mystery man. *Why* are we here? We've already been to French Camp. Did we miss something the first time? Please tell me what Marcus said that led you back here."

"It was so stupid of me to dismiss what he said. He asked me about the spelling in the note—why was it LeFleur, not Leflore? LeFleur was his inherited surname. Remember—his father was Louis LeFleur, the French-Canadian trader and founder of this very stand in front of us—Frenchman's Camp, now French Camp. Greenwood changed the spelling of his surname to Leflore."

"Jasen!" Jade insisted. "Where are you going with this?"

"It's this simple, Sweetie. 'Under LeFleur's oaks' means under his father's oaks, *not* Leflore's, his, oaks. Look across that field, Jade," he said pointing in front of them. "Do you see those enormous, old oak trees and large stumps all in a row? Count them."

She looked beyond the open field, and her mouth slowly gaped open. "Oh, my God. Six," she said. "There's Six."

Epilogue

CHAPTER FORTY-FIVE

Trust Your Heart

"**L**iz? This is Marcus. Is the invitation to dinner still open?"

She smiled into the phone and responded. "Why, my handsome Guy Noir. I was about to give up on you. I think I'm having heart flutters. Whew! Of course! Should I meet you?"

"I'm in the mood for Greek, imagine that! I have reservations for two at Vasilio's. Quiet, great seafood, and close to your hotel. They do a mean grilled redfish. I'll pick you up at eight."

"It's a date. See you then. Bye." Elizabeth Keys hung up the phone and looked in the mirror. "It'll be a night to remember, Mr. Bianco. You can count on that," she said as she smiled and touched up her deep crimson red lipstick.

***

"Okay, Marcus," she said. "Did you agree to dine with me just to tell me the good news or did you really want to be with me? Tell the truth, please." She reached across the table and put her hand on his.

"That's a loaded question," he answered with a broad grin. "You would have heard Jasen and Jade's news sooner or later, I suppose. But, I do enjoy dining with a beautiful woman. Of course, my wife could have joined us but she's working tonight."

"That's not funny!" Liz snapped. "Just enjoy the moment. I certainly am."

"You should have seen the look on Danny's face when I told him about the gold. Jasen claims that it was my question about the spelling of 'LeFleur' that finally led him to the treasure. The myths were true. Just that everyone else seems to think the gold is on 'Leflore' land, not 'LeFleur' land. That Jasen! Very persistent and probably the most observant person that I've ever met.

"The dirk protecting the six turned out to have a double meaning. There were three enormous, very old oak trees and three very large oak stumps all in a single row near the French Camp stand—Lefleur's oaks. Jasen found the dagger embedded in the third tree, driven into the tree with only a faded, quarter-size blue ruby gemstone on the end of the handle visible. There're six graves there, one in front of each oak or stump, all adjacent to the LeFleur family cemetery. The gravesites were marked by small, modest stones but only a single stone was engraved:

"Six Choctaws
Died of Smallpox
1832"

"It only took Jasen an hour to get the local judge to sign a court order to allow them to exhume the first grave. Someone in Washington that Jasen called must have big muscles, so to speak. Anyway, after the first coffin was opened, the judge didn't hesitate to let them proceed. All six coffins were packed full of gold and silver coins and a small amount of jewelry. They found the mother lode!

"Jasen told me it was most likely the entire cache that Sam Mason, the pirate, had hidden. Somehow, and we'll never know *how*, Greenwood

Leflore found it. He never spent a dime of it, from what Jasen estimates. In his heart, the old chief knew it was blood gold. He refused to profit at the expense of innocent people. He trusted his heart, just like Davy Crockett told him, and decided to do the right thing. Unbelievable!"

"So, Marcus, does this entire investigation that we landed smack dab in the middle of relate only to the gold or is there more?"

"Jasen nailed it at one of our team meetings. The gold is only an aside, a diversion of the mastermind of the Greenwood drug smuggling, money laundering, land grabs, and some suspicious power obsession. Whoever he is, he's not going to be happy when the gold discovery is announced. Everything still points to Roger Trevane. Our investigation has only begun. Now that Jasen found the gold, we can all get back to the primary goal—find the head of the snake and cut if off before it strikes again."

"And you and I, my dear Marcus? What about the next chapter in the exciting saga of Marcus Anthony Bianco, the private eye who's still trying to find the answers to life's most persistent questions, and Elizabeth Catherine Keys, senior FBI agent, single, lonely, and available?"

He held both of her hands in his and peered deeply into her eyes. *Share minimally. Trust no one,* he said silently to himself. *Trust no one. Except,* he thought, *your heart.*

"Well, Lizzy, I'm not sure. I guess we'll just have to turn the page."

To be continued...

Made in the USA
Charleston, SC
06 November 2014